The Woman in the Camphor Trunk

ALSO BY JENNIFER KINCHELOE

The Secret Life of Anna Blanc

THE WOMAN IN THE CAMPHOR TRUNK

An Anna Blanc Mystery

JENNIFER KINCHELOE

SEVENTH STREET BOOKS®
AN IMPRINT OF PROMETHEUS BOOKS
59 JOHN GLENN DRIVE • AMHERST, NY 14228
www.seventhstreetbooks.com

Published 2017 by Seventh Street Books®, an imprint of Prometheus Books

Cover images © Shutterstock
Cover design by Nicole Sommer-Lecht
Cover design © Prometheus Books

This is a work of fiction. Characters, organizations, products, locales, and events portrayed in this novel are either products of the author's imagination or used fictitiously.

Inquiries should be addressed to
Seventh Street Books
59 John Glenn Drive
Amherst, New York 14228
VOICE: 716–691–0133
FAX: 716–691–0137
WWW.SEVENTHSTREETBOOKS.COM

21 20 19 18 17   5 4 3 2 1

Library of Congress Cataloging-in-Publication Data

Names: Kincheloe, Jennifer, 1966- author.
Title: The woman in the camphor trunk : an Anna Blanc mystery / by Jennifer
    Kincheloe.
Description: Amherst, NY : Seventh Street Books, an imprint of Prometheus Books,
    2017.
Identifiers: LCCN 2017022702 (print) | LCCN 2017025962 (ebook) |
    ISBN 9781633883642 (ebook) | ISBN 9781633883635 (paperback)
Subjects: LCSH: Women detectives—Fiction. | Murder—Investigation—Fiction. |
    Los Angeles (Calif.)—Fiction. | BISAC: FICTION / Mystery & Detective /
    Historical. | FICTION / Mystery & Detective / Women Sleuths. | GSAFD:
    Mystery fiction.
Classification: LCC PS3611.I568 (ebook) | LCC PS3611.I568 W66 2017 (print) |
    DDC 813/.6—dc23
LC record available at https://lccn.loc.gov/2017022702

Printed in the United States of America

For Sandy, Erin, Lisa, Kristi, Marge, and Lori
because I love you so much.

CHAPTER 1

Anna Blanc was the most beautiful woman ever to barrel down Long Beach Strand with the severed head of a Chinese man. The tin pail that contained the head banged painfully against her shins as she flew. The sand churned beneath her shoes, grinding the silk from her expensive Louis heels. The wind fought against her unwieldy ostrich plume hat, bending the feathers. Regrettably, she had not dressed for a hunt that morning.

She had not planned to be hunted.

Luckily, she was young. Anna jumped over a pile of seaweed, stirring a cloud of sandflies. She unpinned her hat with one hand and let it sail, gripping the heavy pail so tightly her knuckles whitened. The pail swung and bounced erratically, frustrating her strides. It stank like old fish, rotting pork, and things so vile she could not name them. She gagged, panted, and gagged again.

In the distance, a roller coaster roared.

She heard a shout behind her and looked back. A detective in a gray suit burst from the shadows of the pier at a dead run. Though heartless and incompetent, he ran like an Olympian. He was gaining quickly.

Anna ran harder, her waist cramping, her arms aching, her skirts thrashing about her legs like sea foam. She was beginning to think she had made a mistake stealing the severed head from the scene of a crime.

But without his head, Mr. Yau would never get justice.

She veered away from the water toward the bathhouse and the crowd at the Pike, aware of heavy, hostile panting close behind her.

Music exploded from a bandstand.

A hard shove to her back launched her forward and she fell, jarring her chin on the ground and biting her tongue. She tasted hot, rusty blood. The bucket's lid popped off and the head rolled across the sand like a bowling ball. Anna crawled after it, gasping for the breath that had been knocked clean out of her.

She felt the detective's brutal hands grab her boot and tug so hard she feared her hip would separate. With a distinctly unladylike hiss, she kicked. Her boot connected with his man parts, and he dropped to the sand, howling. Anna gracefully regained her feet, scooped the head up with the bucket, replaced the lid, and bolted for the crowd.

She heard him shout, "Stop!"

People were starting to look.

"Help, help!" Anna cried, hoping the crowd would think *he* was the villain, which, in her mind, he was. She gave a final grand effort, scrambling for her freedom, pushing herself as hard as her legs would carry her, leaving the detective behind. As the great orange sun kissed the horizon, the sea of people parted for Anna. Grim, scowling men formed a protective wall behind her, confronting the monster who was causing her distress. She flew past a peanut stand, a taffy concession, a fortuneteller, and barkers guessing people's weights. She ran through popcorn smells, skirting the line for the roller coaster, and straight onto a crowded Red Car that was departing for Los Angeles.

Her pleasure trip to the beach had not turned out as she'd planned, but stumbling upon crime scenes could not be planned. It was a horrible serendipity. Anna fixed her hair. She dabbed her face with a dainty handkerchief and slowed her breathing. A gentleman with a wooden leg offered her his seat. She took it and set the bucket down. It was as heavy as her heart. The other passengers held handkerchiefs to their noses. Luckily, Anna did not look like she smelled, even when mussed. She leveled an accusatory stare at a nearby man who did.

And then she cried for Mr. Yau.

CHAPTER 2

Anna rode the Red Car back to LA, shy one expensive hat, bearing the bucket with its lid tight, the head sleeping safely inside. She disembarked at First Street and walked to the Streeter Apartments, number 502, the place where she now slept at night but was loath to call home.

Anna's apartment building catered to single ladies of good reputation; Thus, Anna had to pay extra. Though Saint Catherine, patron saint of old maids, could testify that Anna was not in fact ruined, her reputation was gray at best. She'd taken a job at the police station—something no reputable lady would do. She'd kissed the police chief's son passionately and more than once, initially to trick suspects, eventually because she liked it. She'd gone undercover in the brothels when girls were being murdered. Every scandalous bit of it had made the papers, with embellishment. While the city of Los Angeles had mainly forgiven her—she had, after all, captured a killer—her socially prominent father had not. Though he hadn't loved her nearly as well as Anna would have liked, and she might not care to admit it, she missed him desperately and felt a little lost.

Thus Anna paid high rent in a low-class brick apartment on First Street, not far from Central Station. The landlord had made a point of telling her that no men were allowed in the rooms. She assumed an exception would be made for the police chief's son, because policemen were allowed to go anywhere, provided they had a warrant. Anna would remind Joe Singer to get a warrant as soon as possible.

Anna set the bucket on the front step, her arm aching from the weight, her mind numb with shock, and rummaged in her silver mesh purse for the key. Keys were a new annoyance. At home, her father's servants had always opened the doors. Her key was gone, no doubt dropped on the beach during the chase, perhaps now resting in the gizzard of a seagull. She groaned and lugged the bucket with the head toward the landlord's office. She wasn't eager to see the man. She owed him money.

Anna hid the bucket with the head behind a bush and whispered, "Wait here, dear Mr. Yau. I won't be long."

She encountered the landlord on his knees in the yard, laying bricks into a low wall. He scraped the last bits of mortar from a plywood board and slapped it onto a brick.

She loomed over him like an Acanthus flower. "Pardon me, Mr. Cooper, but I've misplaced my key."

Mr. Cooper settled the brick and put down his trowel. "You promised me you would pay yesterday, Miss Blanc, and you didn't. I only let you move in because I thought your father was good for it."

He stood, took a shovel of white powder from a sack, dumped it onto a plywood board, and added three shovels of sand. He made a valley in the middle of the pile, splashed in water, and mixed.

Anna pointed at the sack. "Is that lime?"

He scowled. "Miss Blanc. The rent."

Anna tossed her indignant head. "My father is good for it. And I have my own money." Of course *he* wasn't and *she* didn't. But she would. She had a job as a police matron with the LAPD. Tomorrow would be her first day back after two months of leave. Unfortunately, she wouldn't be paid for another week.

Anna's eyes drifted back to the lime. She had read many a crime book and knew what lime was good for—such as abating the smell of rotting heads of friends that one might be hiding in a bucket. Deathly smells draw busybodies. But, if left too long, lime could dissolve a head entirely. She would have to use it sparingly.

"I need your rent, and I'm going to have to charge you for a new key."

Anna's attention returned to the impatient man. "I have the money, of course, I just left it . . . with a friend. I'll go get it. And besides, I have complaints of my own. I found a dead rat just rotting beneath the stove. It smells something awful. In fact, I can smell it from here." Actually, it was Mr. Yau she could smell. But she had found a little rat corpse under the stove, and it did make the whole apartment rank. She had picked it up with a newspaper and thrown it in the garden beneath the landlord's window.

The landlord sighed and reached onto his pocket for a ring hung with multiple keys. "By tonight, Miss Blanc, or you'll be out tomorrow. I don't care how many killers you've captured." He stomped back to her room, trailed by Anna, and unlocked the door.

When Anna had rented the apartment, her father sent a wagon with all of her possessions—a sign that he had washed his hands of her. Thus, Anna's apartment looked like a storage closet for very expensive things, and so it was. An abundance of white, fluffy fur rugs covered the floor. Some still had heads. A white baby grand piano and Anna's great mahogany bed covered the rugs, the bed's velvet canopy brushing the flaked plaster ceiling. These two pieces dominated the room and left little space, even for walking. Anna had to squeeze sideways, or crawl over the bed to get to the potbelly stove, which wasn't worth the space—she didn't know how to use it.

Three towers of striped hatboxes rose like penny candy sticks from the floor to the ten-foot ceiling. Beside these, four teetering towers of shoeboxes threatened to tumble at a sneeze. Rows of racks of tea gowns, day dresses, walking dresses, visiting gowns, afternoon dresses, dinner dresses, evening dresses, ball gowns, opera dresses, ice skating ensembles, tennis wear, riding habits, and more spilled from the parlor, filling the bedroom.

The landlord stared like Aladdin in the thieves' treasure cave. Anna bid him goodnight and shut the door before he could ask her for collateral. Though she had assets of sorts, she had no idea how much anything was worth or how to go about selling it. But that was the least of her worries at the moment.

She threw herself onto the great mahogany bed and pondered what to do with dear Mr. Yau. He had been her father's penultimate cook and lived in a cottage on their property. Anna liked him and his cooking. He played a sort of Chinese fiddle and gave her little cakes. He was kind to her—saintly even—when very few people were. She abhorred the idea of anyone chopping off his head. When she saw that he had been decapitated and was in the possession of an incompetent detective, she felt greatly distraught. Perhaps her judgment had been clouded by grief, but she had had to intervene.

Anna reached over to her nightstand and poured herself a whiskey from a crystal decanter. She told herself she had acted correctly. She needed the head to prove his murder. And, while her actions may have been impulsive and even illegal, once the murder was solved her superiors would agree that the ends justified the means and congratulate her. This strategy had worked for Anna before. In fact, it seemed to be the unofficial motto of the LAPD.

Anna waited until midnight and used her flashlight to find a pair of leather gloves in the landlord's shed. Collecting the pail from the bushes, she lugged it to the alley behind the apartment building where she could take her time examining the head without someone nosing in or trying to arrest her. Apartment buildings towered in front of her and behind, blocking the moon, their windows dark with night. It had been raining on and off for days. It now began to drizzle, and then pour.

She solemnly dumped the head out onto the wet concrete and shone the flashlight on his face, getting her first good look at his features. Anna let out a happy sigh.

It was not Mr. Yau.

She leapt to her feet and jumped about, clutching her hands to her breast. It didn't even look like Mr. Yau. His eyes were different. His nose was different. Anna must have simply feared it would be Mr. Yau, because he was the only man from China she had ever met.

Her friend was alive, most likely, though she doubted their paths would cross again. She could think more clearly now—like a detective.

Anna put on an appropriately solemn face and squatted again to examine the victim. Even Anna's strong stomach turned at the sight. The mouth gaped. The eyes were dark hollows. His thick, black hair was shaved several inches back from his forehead, pulled tight into what had once been a long braid, but was now cut short and unraveled. The neck ended in a stump of pink meat, with multiple cuts as if chopped two or three times with an axe. One ear had been cut clean off.

The sight and the smell made Anna feel light headed.

Though the sea had ravaged his flesh, his good white teeth and the complete absence of gray hair suggested the man had been young— much younger than Mr. Yau. Anna added words to a chorus of crickets: "Mysterious man, I will avenge you." She made a silent petition to Saint Denis, the cephalophore, who had also been decapitated and had walked six miles carrying his own head, because he would likely sympathize.

§

Anna took a bath in the communal tub, scrubbing her skin until she glowed like a beet, until the water looked milky with soap, until the scent of death came off her. She dunked her head and scrubbed her scalp. The young man whose head now rested once again in the bucket deserved a proper murder investigation. The Long Beach police were overlooking the evidence, possibly because the cop was stupid, but more probably because the man was Chinese. Either way, it was a travesty. If she turned the case over to the LAPD, they would know she'd stolen the head. And kicked a cop in his man parts. They would likely turn the head back over to the Long Beach Police Department because it was their jurisdiction.

Anna would simply have to find the killer and bring him to justice on her own—a task she'd accomplished before. This was the sunny side of murder.

Anna had a case.

§

The clock struck seven a.m., and Anna's eyes bleared from insufficient sleep. She faced her cold iron stove on which boxes of Cracker Jacks formed a wall around a pile of un-read riddles. Her supply was dwindling, as was her money. She would have to ration. Anna tore the top off a box and cast the riddle card onto the growing pile. She paced, tossing the candied popcorn and peanuts into her mouth, one piece at a time.

As a first step, she would try to determine where the dead man had originated. Most of the Chinese lived in Chinatown, but some peopled the abalone fishing village to the north. The cop had assured Anna that the corpse was an abalone diver. But abalone divers were fish themselves and unlikely to drown. From the beach, she'd seen them dive out beyond the surf and stay under for ages.

Chewing her Cracker Jacks, Anna picked her way over to her bookcase, selected volume C of the *Catholic Encyclopedia*, and perched in a chair. She opened to the entry on California, and read about ocean currents, ones that might carry heads from the site of their murder to Long Beach Strand. She referred to a map of Los Angeles County, and made calculations in her notebook—distance, time, and speed.

The head couldn't have come from the south. The currents prohibited it. Neither could he have come from the fishing village north of Santa Monica. She could tell from his state of decay that he hadn't been dead long. The water moved too slowly to deliver a body so far in a matter of days. However, the river mouth emptied onto the beach just north of where the head was found. Anna's money was on the river.

CHAPTER 3

The Los Angeles Police Department's Central Station waved its large flag near the corner of First Street and Broadway. It had a certain civic grandeur, built of heavy granite blocks, with arched windows, and multiple stories to accommodate a jail, receiving hospital, and stables in the basement. Parked out front were a police wagon hitched to white horses, half a dozen bicycles, and one shiny gas-powered police car with a gold star on the side.

Anna stood on the sidewalk wearing a mannish police matron's uniform, ghastlier even than her uniform from the convent school. She felt both honored and horrified to wear it. She carried the severed head now packed in lime and hidden in the bucket, which was covered with a red-checkered cloth in the manner of a dinner pail. It smelled less because of the lime, but it did not smell good. Like a very ripe cheese. If left behind, the scent would permeate her entire apartment building. Bringing the head into the station disguised as lunch was safer than leaving it in the bushes where a dog might find it.

While the LAPD might eventually hear that a head had been stolen miles away in the city of Long Beach, they had no reason to connect the theft with their own Assistant Matron Blanc or her lunch pail. She simply wouldn't tell them about it. Except for Joe Singer, because he was in love with her and likely would not arrest her.

A familiar, yet unwelcome face accosted her before she reached the station door. Bill Tilly was a pockmarked newspaperman with a grudge against Anna. He often skulked about the station, itching for a scoop. Her father had gotten Tilly fired from the *Los Angeles Times* for printing a story about Anna that was absolutely true. He had retaliated by writing another story about her for the *Los Angeles Herald*, which was mostly true and far more damning.

Anna hated the man.

Tilly tipped his hat. "Good morning, Miss Blanc."

Anna smiled tightly, a prisoner to her good breeding, and pretended there was chicken in her bucket. "Good morning, Mr. Tilly."

"Well I'll be. I didn't think you would speak to me."

Realizing this was an option, she said, "I'm not," and brushed past him.

He followed her like a hungry dog. "Come on, Sweetheart. Give me a chance. You know I'm sweet on you."

"You just want a story. I'm not working on any cases right now, but I assure you, you'll be the last man I call when I do."

"Let's let bygones be bygones, Miss Blanc. You and I could help each other."

"I can't imagine how you could ever be of assistance to me."

"Sometimes the best help a newspaper man can offer is his silence." He put on the kind of innocent face that made a person look guilty. "Is it true that the police chief's son visits your apartment at night unchaperoned? Because you're breaking my heart."

Anna laughed falsely. "No." And it wasn't. But she hoped it would be true soon.

He grinned. "That's what I thought. But two sweethearts are better than one."

"Good day, Mr. Tilly." She swung through the station doors.

"I love you," he called after her.

Anna filled her lungs with stale LAPD air. It smelled like cigarettes, bad coffee, and the sweat of nervous men. It smelled like her future, and she adored it. Lights dangled from the ceiling on long wires, illuminating a dust haze. The reception desk was fenced in with iron from floor to countertop. Three officers lingered, drinking the bad coffee—Smith, Clark, and . . . She forgot. They wore sharp, brass-buttoned uniforms, their hair neatly slicked back and parted on the side. Two glared at Anna. The third cop pursed his lips in a silent whistle, his eyelids lowered suggestively.

Anna's "Good morning" died on her tongue.

A man in a gray suit caught her eye and sauntered toward her, wafting lavender cologne and brilliantine. He was handsome in an oily way. He grinned broadly. His teeth gleamed white. "Assistant Matron Blanc. Welcome back. Matron Clemens was looking for you." He glanced down at the bucket and wrinkled his nose.

"Cheese." She smiled sweetly. "Would you like some, Detective Wolf?"

"No, thank you."

She bobbed a curtsy and turned her attention from Detective Wolf back to the three cops, puzzled by their hostile looks. Had she not just solved the most important crime in the history of Los Angeles?

Wolf was speaking. "How was Summerland? You were gone, what, two months? That's a long time for a young lady to be alone."

Anna turned to look at him. He licked his upper lip, and said, "You were, uh, alone weren't you?"

"Summerland was spectacular, thank you."

Anna had fled to Summerland because the story of her escapades had made the headlines, and she could get no peace. She only left Summerland because she had eaten everything in the pantry of the beach house where she was squatting and had almost no money left to buy food. Not that Anna wasn't eager to return to her work at the station. She was. It was just that killing a man had taken something out of her, and she had needed to think. But there were little hoisters, hoodlums, and moll buzzers waiting for her to reform them.

She looked past Wolf to the floor of the station. "Is Officer Singer here? I'm sure he would like to welcome me on my first day back."

Wolf hesitated. "He's coming in this morning. But I don't imagine you'll see him all that much anymore. Just after you left, he volunteered for the Chinatown Squad. He's been working that beat for two months under Captain Dixon."

Anna frowned. Why would Joe join the Chinatown Squad? Especially if it meant he wouldn't often see her.

"Matron Clemens has some mail for you."

Wolf's words barely registered. She contemplated Joe's new assignment as she clipped upstairs to the office of her superintendent, Matron Clemens. Joe loved Anna. Shouldn't he want to be with her every minute? Actually, Anna didn't want to be with him every minute, but she wanted to be with him a lot. And she certainly wouldn't have signed up to work in Chinatown, not when cops worked long days, seven days a week.

The office door stood open. Anna poked her head into a windowless room, which somewhat resembled a parlor but for an imposing oak desk and typewriter. A rag rug turned circles on the floor. A rocking chair waited for the next abandoned baby. She found Matron Clemens wearing reading spectacles, the paperwork of some delinquent child splayed out before her.

Anna admired Matron Clemens and wished to emulate her in all things, except for being plain and almost forty. Also, Anna objected to her taste in uniforms. Even so, Matron Clemens projected an air of authority, something Anna was still perfecting. But after her victory last summer, Anna could at least hold her head up high.

She did so. "Good Morning, Matron Clemens."

Matron Clemens scooted back her chair and rose, her thin lips twitching in an almost smile. "Congratulations, Assistant Matron Blanc. You managed to make the entire police force look ridiculous." She shook Anna's gloved hand.

Anna inclined her head in acknowledgement. "Thank you, Matron Clemens."

"Are you ready to return to work?"

"Police work is my everything."

"Good." Matron Clemens reached into a drawer and took out packets of letters tied with string. She handed them to Anna. "These came for you while you were gone." The older lady returned to the drawer, withdrawing three more bundles of envelopes.

Anna looked puzzled. "I don't understand."

"They are mostly from men." Matron Clemens's face remained blank. "Now, I need you to go collect a Miss Jane Godfrey and take her to Whittier State School. It's a reform school. She's wanted for shop-lifting, and she's a treat girl. She's been trading her attentions for gifts, and she's only fifteen."

Matron Clemens gathered the papers before her, stuffed them in a large envelope, and handed them to Anna. She glanced down at the smelly bucket and frowned.

Anna took the file, the bucket, and the armful of envelopes, bobbed a curtsy, and quickly headed for the door before her higher up could ask questions. She deposited the envelopes on her desk and tip-tapped down the stairs. She passed Smith, Clark, and the other one, and ignored them, focusing rather on not dropping her load. She had hoped the men would afford her more respect now that she had cracked a major case. Apparently, they still viewed her as a lying, shel-tered, ruined, decorative socialite. Which she was. But she couldn't help her upbringing or her beauty. She had made her choices for a noble reason, namely to save the day. The truth was, Anna didn't care what those baboons thought, but for a single exception.

The nameless officer called out, "Morning, Joe."

Joe Singer ambled from the back door wearing a blue wool uniform coat, looking fresh-faced and rather like the man in the Arrow Shirt Collar ads. His eyes briefly met Anna's. He stiffened and made a beeline for the kitchen.

His response hit Anna's belly like a bad kipper. She might have made a mistake telling Joe Singer that she had no intention of mar-rying him. Far more beneficial would have been to eagerly accept his proposal but insist on a long engagement. With a little finesse, she could have stretched it out ten or even twenty years. But Anna hadn't crossed her old-world father and gotten disowned just so she could be subjugated to a different man. Marriage would mean surrendering her self-determination and her property. Also, married women had babies. How could she do police work with a baby in tow? She'd sacrificed too much for her freedom—a fortune, a good reputation, a position in society, a mansion on the hill. If she married Joe, he would own her, and Anna didn't believe in slavery. She also hadn't believed Joe when he'd said he was done with her, when he'd left her alone at the beach house in Summerland. Joe Singer loved her. Truly loved her. He didn't need marriage for that. Unforgiveness was a terrible sin, even for Protestants, and she would have to remind him of it.

To fortify herself, Anna looked down at the bucket in her hand. Matters of the heart aside, she had a job to do and problems to solve, namely figuring out who had killed this man and how she would avoid being pegged for the theft of his head if anyone saw it and heard about the missing head from the Long Beach cops. She hoped that Joe would be her partner in crime, and not just because he looked like the Arrow Collar Man. As the son of the police chief, he got away with all kinds of things.

Anna toted the head into the kitchen.

The kitchen had been designed more for storing than for cooking. Shelves marched up the wall, crowded with a hundred dinner pails—provisions for the officers' long days, which sometimes stretched into nights. A table held coffee, bread, peanut butter, and preserves.

She found Joe leaning against a chair, eating a strange rice dish from a bowl, and singing in between bites: "Oh how I do love you. Say that you'll love me, love me, too . . ." He glanced up briefly and sniffed, wrinkled his nose, and then looked down at his rice dish.

She smiled at him with dazzling sunshine. "Hello."

Joe swallowed. "Welcome back, Sherlock." He glanced toward the exit. Anna shut and locked the door. She pulled aside the checkered cloth and spread it on the floor, setting the bucket on top of it like they were going to have a picnic.

Joe looked dubious. "What's that?"

Anna's eyes sparkled and her eyebrows lifted. "It's a case." She struggled to remove the lid, which she had pounded tight into place. It popped off and the face stared up, caked with lime.

Joe dropped his rice dish.

His bowl hit the floor and shattered, and a flood of words tumbled from Anna's lips. "I was in Long Beach on a pleasure trip, because I missed the ocean."

Joe gave Anna a sideways look. He was turning crocodile green. She continued more rapidly. "A woman found him washed up on the shore, just south of the river mouth. I thought I knew him, but I don't.

"The local cop said a great white shark did it and they were planning to bury him with no inquest at all. I told the cop he was wrong, but he dismissed me like I was some little fool. He didn't listen to a single word I said. Clearly, it could not have been death by shark unless the shark used a hatchet. They cut off his ear. It looks like torture to me. The cops were incompetent or they didn't care, and the man, who I didn't know after all, would never get justice. You need a body to have a crime." She took a deep breath. "So I stole it. I thought you might like to help me investigate."

Joe put a palm to his forehead. "Did you tell the cop you were a police matron?"

"Of course not. Not that he'd listen."

"Merciful Lord."

"The cop said the head was an abalone fisherman, but I disagree. There are two Chinese settlements in Los Angeles—the abalone fishing village north of Santa Monica, and, of course, Chinatown, which is, as you know, inland but near the river. Santa Monica is some forty plus miles from Long Beach along the coast. The ocean current travels less than a tenth of a yard per second or one-point-six miles per day. I looked it up."

Joe plucked up a page of newspaper from the table and wiped lime from the face of the head, looking hard at the caverns that once held eyes.

Anna sped on. "From his state of decay, he's been dead four or five days, taking into account the cold water temperature, et cetera. So let's say five days. Thus the head, if chopped in Santa Monica, would have traveled only eight miles and would not have even reached Manhattan Beach. But if you make similar calculations using the LA River from the point nearest to Chinatown—distance, speed, it's dead on target. Obviously, he came from Chinatown."

Joe peered at the face, his head cocked to the side. "That looks like Ko Chung. But his skin is kind of dissolving. It's hard to tell."

"You know him?"

"Anna, I've been working in Chinatown for two months. I know the criminals." Joe squinted at the face. "He's a highbinder. A henchman for the Hop Sing. My Lord, that was a painful death."

Anna gave a confused shake of her head.

"The Hop Sing is a tong—a Chinese gang—like a clan but without blood ties. They control vice in Chinatown. You don't cross them or you end up like this. Looks like they cut off his head slowly."

Anna dropped the lid back on the bucket, covering the ghoulish face, topping the tin with the checkered cloth. She noted Joe's furrowed brow. "Don't worry, I'll find his killer."

"He was probably killed by another assassin."

"So, we arrest them all, and—"

"Anna, men like that don't stay in jail. Nobody will testify. And even if they would, which they won't, the tongs have so many judges in their pocket, it might not ever go to trial."

"So you're suggesting I just quit? Just walk away?"

"Yes, because you're not on the Chinatown Squad, and you'd be in all kinds of trouble if anyone caught you stealing body parts."

Anna threw back her head in a cynical, wide-mouthed laugh. "Hah hah hah. I'm never going to be on any squad, no matter how good I am, and you know it. You're just like the other cops." Anna flapped her hand toward the door. "Those men out there won't even say hello to me."

"You're smarter than they are, and you made them look bad." He ruffled his hair with his fingers. "Listen Anna, we have a big, big problem, and this dead man—Ko Chung—is just one part of it. He was Hop Sing, probably killed by the Bing Kong, their biggest rival. The two are vying for dominance. Things are tense. People are scared, and they should be. The Bing Kong president's favorite singsong girls are missing. The rumor is that the Hop Sing president stole them. If Ko Chung is dead, that means somebody believed it."

"They think Ko Chung kidnapped the girls on orders from the tong?"

"That's right."

"Well, is it true? Does the Hop Sing have the girls?"

"I don't know who else would have the nerve to take them."

"So they are fighting over musicians?"

"They're singsong girls, Anna. Chinese slaves. They're used for sex."

Anna's features hardened. "Then I don't give a rap about the Bing Kong and the Hop Sing. Let them kill each other." Anna turned heel and marched toward the door.

"Where are you going?"

"To throw the head back in the river before I get caught."

CHAPTER 4

A ring encircled the moon. The roots of a giant fig tree flowed out from its trunk like oil, spilling down into the Los Angeles River. Usually, the river merely trickled, but now it flowed hard from recent rains and was chocolate brown with silt. Anna heard the rattling chirps of frogs.

Joe carried the bucket. He extended his hand to Anna, helping her navigate down the muddy bank and then along the river. Like always, he sang softly, unconsciously, and he sounded wonderful.

> My darling Lou
> Lou, how the birds are calling
> And the morning glories miss you too,
> My honey Lou, Lou how my tears are falling
> For there never was a gal like you.

Anna leaned into his hand. "I'm surprised you're not trying to stop me."

"If anyone sees you with the head, you'll get fired and possibly arrested."

"It's very gallant of you."

"And, when the Hop Sing find out this man's been murdered, they'll retaliate. Let them think he left town. We can try to defuse things—work with the tong presidents. This buys us time. No body, no crime."

"There's still a body out there."

"Harder to identify. But I promise you, Anna, I'll look into it."

"I want to look into it."

"I know." Joe squeezed her hand. The touch of his fingers comforted her, even through the leather of her glove. She expected that soon he would forgive her, finally hold all of her, and make her forget about the head. But at the edge of the bank, when she stood firmly on level ground, he let go of her hand.

Joe said, "Frogs are calling. It's going to rain again."

"I like the rain."

He looked down at the muddy ground. "Me, too."

She stopped when they reached a copse of trees where they couldn't be seen from the field above. "This place will do."

It began to sprinkle. Anna moved to the very edge of the river and scanned the vicinity to make sure they were unseen. No one was fishing. No one stood on the banks. People avoided the river when the water ran so hard and there was a risk of flash floods.

She took the pail from Joe, removed the checkered cloth and lid, and dumped the head of Ko Chung into the muddy water. It went under with a splash and then popped up again like a fishing bobber. The current caught it. They watched it being swept off toward the ocean in the moonlight. She threw the pail into the river as far and as hard as she could, along with her gloves, which were lined with sable and had been expensive. On a matron's salary, without her father's money, she could not afford to replace them. Joe bowed his head and muttered some holy words about mercy and Ko Chung's soul. Anna didn't pray, because Chinese people had gods of their own, and she didn't speak their language. Anna and Joe stood until the floating orb was no longer visible, and then they simply watched the rushing river.

She took a bar of lye soap out of her pocket, and they both knelt to scrub hands and arms to the elbow. When their skin was good and red, Anna threw the soap into the silty water, and it dropped like a stone. She slipped her arm through Joe's, and they gingerly picked their way up stream, he in his boots, she in her tarry, sandy, muddy, and very expensive heeled shoes.

When they had gone a fair distance upriver, Joe shook his head. "You're a lucky girl, Sherlock. A very lucky girl."

"Why?"

"Wolf knew you were hiding something in that bucket. If you weren't comely, you'd be out of a job."

"He didn't suspect me."

"He excused you, hoping you'd let him spoon with you in the stables."

"You don't think very highly of Detective Wolf. Aren't you friends?"

"I'm a realist, and you are an innocent."

Anna's mouth dropped open. "Innocent? Hah. I think you know what I've been through, what I've seen. I've been badly trampled by the world. Not the least of all by you."

Joe's voice rose an octave. "What did I do?"

"You knew I was back in town and you haven't called. And when I called on you, you didn't answer the door."

"Anna, it was midnight."

"So, you were home."

"Listen, you broke my heart, not the other way around. So forgive me if I'm not at your beck and call—"

"You said you loved me, and you aren't loving me."

Joe said nothing.

Anna slid closer and smiled. "So love me." She rose on tiptoes and kissed him. She knew that Joe Singer was particularly susceptible to kissing, and, though he was angry, lips could make everything right. Also, he was delicious. So Anna kissed him until he kissed her back. Her kiss was melting fiery, and burned with all the intensity of their situation, and all the passion required to overcome it—his pain, her scars, their abandonment, and a severed head floating down the river.

Anna's kiss promised everything, even intimate things she didn't fully understand. She could feel Joe's heart pounding, but his arms stayed at his sides. His lips were no longer puckering, though his pants were.

Joe took her by both arms and set her away from him, breathing like he'd just run a race.

Anna's eyes widened. This was not like Joe Singer. The only thing Joe liked better than spooning was, well, nothing.

Joe said, "You don't want my love, Anna. You just want to make love."

Anna's cheeks burned as if he'd slapped her. She crossed her arms across her breasts. "You make it sound like I'm a vampire."

Joe looked away from Anna and stared at the water's edge. He said nothing, but Anna knew what he was thinking—that she was the biggest vamp in the history of vamps. A vamp's vamp. A vamp's vamp's vamp." She felt the pressure of tears behind her eyes, but cops never cried, and so neither would she. "Well, say something."

"Anna, I'm courting someone else."

"No, you're not."

"I want a wife. You made it clear that you would never marry me. That was fifteen minutes after declaring your love, and a month after you'd run off to marry somebody else, after kissing me like a love-crazed nymph, right after telling me you couldn't associate with me."

"It wasn't like that."

"I'm not a rubber ball, Anna. If you won't marry me, what am I supposed to do? Sit at home and cry about it?"

"I have dreams—"

"I have dreams, too."

"Who are you courting, then?" It seemed silly to ask. Anna didn't know any of the girls in Joe's working-class set. She'd only been working class for two months. She exclusively knew rich society girls and prostitutes.

"I don't want to hurt you."

"Well, you're too late, so you may as well tell me." The sky began pelting her with heavy raindrops.

He hesitated. "There's a girl who works at the piano store."

Anna's insides began to swirl like turbulent water. She had seen that pretty piano girl. She had heard them sing a duet, all cozy on a piano bench.

Joe cleared his throat. "And my third cousin, Betty. Then there's

Wolf's neighbor, and . . ." He glanced up, looking pained, and stopped when he saw her expression. Anna's face was twisted. She almost couldn't breathe.

He sighed a miserable sigh. "Anna, it could have been you, but you didn't want me."

She choked back a sob.

Joe closed his eyes. "Aw Anna. Don't cry. Don't cry."

She sniffed her snuffly nose with indignation. "I'm not."

And then, Anna did what any girl would do in her situation, thrown off by a man who had once said he loved her, a man who had held her and kissed her and put his hand on her bottom, a man who wordlessly implied that she was a vampire when he himself was courting half the girls in Los Angeles.

She took a swing at Joe Singer's pretty face, slipped on the muddy bank, and went down on her backside in a particularly mucky spot. She squeaked and slid toward the water.

"Oh Lord." Joe leapt after her, bent over, and lent her his hand.

She grabbed it and, with a grunt, yanked him hard. It was a rather effective yank. Joe went hurtling down the muddy slope, slipped, and fell into the cold river. Anna gasped as he splashed, and covered her mouth with her dirty palm, leaving streaks of mud on her lips and chin. She hadn't actually meant to throw him into the water. It had turned out better than she'd planned. His wool uniform was wet to the collar, and he would surely smell like a sheep. It was but a tiny ray of sunlight in the darkest of nights.

Joe stood, rushing water to his thighs, and glared at her.

She stood clumsily and kicked the riverbank, sending mud splattering onto his angry face. "I love you!"

"If you really loved me, you'd marry me."

"Marriage is tantamount to a license to boss me. It would make me your slave. If you really loved me, you wouldn't ask."

"Just because I'm supposed to boss you, doesn't mean I would."

"You already do."

Anna lifted her skirts, and clambered up the hill, slipping and sliding, her bottom, and now her hands and knees, brown with mud. "Biscuits!" She pulled herself up by a fig tree's roots, and then spun around to face him.

Joe was climbing out of the water, soaked to the skin. He held out his dripping arms and gestured to his wet uniform. "I could arrest you for this."

"Go ahead, Officer Singer. Arrest me, handcuff me, throw me in the hoosegow. Hang me, even, because I don't care. I . . . I hope you die."

Anna gasped and put a hand to her mouth. She regretted the curse the moment it left her lips. She crossed herself in an attempt to undo it, but it was too late. Once you speak a thing, you can't take it back.

Joe let out a hollow laugh. "I reckon I will, Sherlock. We all die sometime. But I'm not gonna let you be the one who kills me."

"Fine, because I wouldn't kill you for all the tea in China. I . . . I'd rather love a Chihuahua. And I will."

Anna presented him with her muddy backside and strode off up the bank. Joe passed her in three big steps. When he reached the field, he headed in a direction away from the station.

Anna's voice cracked. "Where are you going?"

"I'm going to warn the Chihuahuas." He didn't look back.

Anna stood and watched him trudge across the field away from her. Out of the corner of her burning eye, she caught sight of a lone figure standing across the river at the edge of a grouping of trees, holding a fishing pole. He was watching Anna. She hurried up the bank, out of his sight.

§

Anna returned home muddy and trembling, her broken heart oozing with the worst kind of love—the unrequited kind. If Joe truly loved her, he wouldn't leave her for a wife. In contrast, Anna's feelings for Joe had been unwavering. That is, once she realized that she had them. True, there had been some misunderstandings before she knew that she loved Joe, and she almost married someone else because that was what she was supposed to do. Joe was mad about that, but Anna thought he had forgiven her. She should have known better. Everyone she cared about abandoned her—high society, her father, even her mother had left her, having inconsiderately died. They had broken her heart, every one of them. She had thought Joe was different. She had been wrong.

Joe wouldn't love her unless she vowed to obey him. Even if Anna did want to make such a promise, she didn't think she could keep it, and that would be a sin.

What if he commanded her to have children? How could she do police work pushing a baby carriage? She would surely be fired. Anna definitely did not want to pledge obedience to Joe Singer.

Anna stripped out of her muddy clothes, leaving them on the floor near the entryway so as not to soil the animal-skin rugs. Their taxidermied faces stared at her sympathetically. Less than three months ago, she had been a celebrated beauty, daughter of a financial magnate, buying her trousseau and contemplating life with her well-made, well-bred, well-heeled fiancé. She had liked her adoring fiancé, and she had traded him for the freedom to save brothel girls from a killer, to love Joe Singer—a common police officer—and to work as an assistant police matron earning seventy-five dollars a month. Now her father had disowned her, her friends were scandalized, and she couldn't pay her rent. It grieved Anna to be shunned, and inconvenienced her to be poor, but nothing hurt her like the knowledge that Joe Singer was courting other girls. She loved him more than anything in the world, except police work, which she loved the same. Nothing pleased her more, except trapping killers, which pleased her equally, than to be in his arms. She would give up anything, except her independence, to have him, because, for the first time, Anna was the mistress of her own destiny. She could go where she pleased, do what she pleased, and she had paid a terrible price for it. She would not relinquish that freedom, not even for the most delicious man in Los Angeles.

CHAPTER 5

The next morning, Anna arrived at work wearing spectacles that she didn't need, pinched from a man's pocket on the trolley. They looked terrible, but she didn't know it. She could barely see when she wore them; however, they obscured the puffy, pink eyes beneath the lenses. Anna didn't want Joe Singer to see that she had been crying. She planned to pretend that she hadn't thrown herself at him at the river yesterday. In fact, it had been some other girl who merely looked like Anna, and who was dying inside.

She strode to the desk clerk, a Mr. Melvin, who sat behind the long oak reception counter, fenced in with iron bars. He had bad skin and a tiny mouth, which Anna thought made him look like a turtle. She liked him very much. At her approach, he shrank into his shell.

She lowered her voice to a butterfly whisper and tried to look friendly. "Mr. Melvin, where is Officer Singer?" If she could avoid Joe, she would. He made her feel terrible, ugly, and discarded.

Mr. Melvin whispered back. "I believe he left for Chinatown. He's searching for the singsong girls."

Anna breathed out audibly. At least two things were right in the world. Joe would find the singsong girls and set them free, and she wouldn't have to see him. Squinting in the boosted glasses, Anna slunk up the stairs toward her desk. There, the stack of letters awaited her. She sat, ripped the top one open, and read.

Beloved Miss Blanc,

I read about you in the newspaper, and let me get straight to the heart of the matter. Some people call me handsome, if I may say so. I have a house with plumbing, and a good position at the box factory. I want you to be my wife. My mother will help with the chores. Please respond with a yes and make me the happiest man in Los Angeles.

    With deepest affection,

    Charlie Douglas

Anna sighed. It was a sad letter, really. She let it fall into the trash and opened the next envelope. This letter was scented with lilac.

Dear Miss Blanc,

    Roses are red

    Violets are blue

    Marry me

    For I love you . . .

It was from an old shipping magnate who had done business with her father. Anna hesitated, biting her thumbnail. Then she crumpled it and tossed it in the wastebasket. The third, fourth, and fifth letters contained additional bad poetry, declarations, and proposals. Into the basket they went. Anna threw out all the letters with male names on the return address, until they filled and overflowed her trashcan. About fifty letters remained. The first five were from jealous wives who held Anna responsible for the affections of men she had never met.

Anna threw up her hands. "There's nothing I can do about it." She scooped the rest of the letters into the pile on the floor. She noticed Detective Wolf leaning against a pillar, waiting for her to glance up. His hair was slicked back, his dark eyebrows lowered. He looked mad. Anna stood and nodded her head. "Detective."

He slipped his arm through hers. "May I speak to you in private?"

"Of course." Anna braced herself, wondering for which of her many peccadilloes she was about to be reprimanded.

Wolf steered Anna downstairs, past the rack for helmets, to the rear of the station, out the back door, and through the large gates to the basement stables. He stopped at the ladder to the hayloft. They stood alone, but for half a dozen Morgans twitching and nickering in the stalls. It smelled leathery and equestrian, like horse droppings. She sneezed from hay dust.

Wolf let go of her arm and turned to face her, smiling tightly. "My sister went to Long Beach on a pleasure trip day before yesterday. She told me the most unusual story about a sweet little vampire, dressed like a princess, who attacked a police officer to steal a Chinaman's severed head for her dinner. Apparently, the whole town is overcome with terror. Then, yesterday evening, a fisherman saw a lovely little lady throw what looked like a head into the river not far from here."

"I'm not a vamp."

"You don't need to tell me what really happened because, as amusing as it would be, it's best if I don't know. But I had to cover for you. If you assaulted a cop, you could be in serious trouble."

Anna's lips parted in surprise. "You don't believe me?"

"I believe you are an asset to the force." He grinned.

"You *did* want to kiss me in the stables."

"Honeybun, every cop on the force wants to kiss you in the stables. But last I checked, you were Joe's girl."

Anna's face flushed. "No. He doesn't want me."

Wolf pressed his lips. "Now that's a shame."

"I didn't assault that ignorant cop. He assaulted me. I simply got the better of him."

Anna heard the door creak and glanced up. Joe entered, his eyes scanning the stalls. They trained on Wolf like a double-barreled shotgun.

Anna stepped very close to Wolf and gazed up into his face. She shook his hand, holding it for far too long. "Thank you, Detective." She felt Joe's hand on her arm, pulling her away. His face was red like a tomato. Wolf's eyes shone with bemusement, guilty pleasure, and trepidation. He stepped away from Anna and raised his hands. "I didn't do it."

Anna shook Joe off. "I thought you were in Chinatown."

Joe's jaw tightened. "So you go make love to him?" He flung a finger at Wolf in a grand indictment.

"Officer Singer, you and I are not courting. I'll make love to whomever I want. It's none of your business."

Joe Singer swore and turned back to Wolf, his eyes angry slits, but his jealousy gave Anna no true satisfaction. It was all masculine bluster and pride. She knew that now. He wouldn't fight for Anna. She had finally resigned herself to the fact that Joe Singer, for all she had thought him to be, was faithless. He didn't really love her, and if he had once it had been a weak sort of love. But maybe that was the only kind of love there was in men's hearts.

She thought she had better rescue Wolf. "I tell you, it isn't his fault. And we aren't lovers, though who knows what the future will bring."

Wolf slapped his forehead. "That came out wrong, didn't it Assistant Matron Blanc?" Wolf backed away from Joe, who stood uncomfortably close and was breathing like a bull. Wolf said, "She and I were just discussing a spooky story about a beautiful vampire that assaulted a cop in Long Beach and stole a severed head."

Joe's eyes shifted from Anna to Wolf and then back again. "Oh God."

Wolf blew out a breath. "Just a rumor, but one that could get said vampire incarcerated and any officer who covered for her fired."

"So you're afraid that Captain Wells will get word of it and link that vampire with . . . with Countess Dracula?" He waved an arm in Anna's direction.

Anna said, "I'm not a vamp."

Wolf's brows descended. "Exactly that."

"You lied to cover for her? Oh boy, Wolf. You're in for it," Joe said.

Wolf wrinkled his forehead. "Lie is such a strong word."

"If you didn't know she stole the head, what in hell were you covering for?"

"Because she was up to something. It was her first day back. I didn't want Matron Clemens to fire her." Wolf grinned. "She's an asset to the force."

§

That night, Anna walked home beneath an azure umbrella. She liked the sound of rain on the fabric, and she couldn't ride a bicycle in her matron's uniform. She was jealous of men with their trousers and wondered if something couldn't be done about the immobility imposed by her skirt.

A yellow Rolls Royce convertible sailed past Anna on the street, sending up a spray of muddy water that splattered her frock. Anna hardly noticed the muck. A young man was driving—someone Anna didn't recognize—but the car she knew. Her father had given it to her for her eighteenth birthday, and it had been her favorite thing, though she'd always had to share it with a chaperone. He must have sold it. He was having money troubles. Anna followed it with her eyes until it turned down Broadway. She lifted her chin and tried to convince herself that she could live without it—that she could live without her father. She could, could she not? Anna swallowed. Hard.

She steeled herself and swished past a pharmacy soda fountain on Main Street, looking through the plate-glass window and wishing for an ice cream, which was not in her budget. Not unless she gave up whiskey, got paid, or sold something. Potted palm trees and bowls of wax fruit decorated the counter. The soda jerk filled a glass from a gleaming fountain. She saw Joe Singer sitting on a stool at the long counter next to a girl whom Anna didn't know. Beside them, behind a newspaper, she saw a gray bun, likely attached to a chaperone. The girl had golden curls and looked treacle sweet, pretty enough for a postcard. Joe was leaning toward her and smiling flirtatiously. She was leaning away, like a proper girl would, but her fluttering eyelashes told the real story.

Anna no longer wanted ice cream. She felt ill.

§

When Anna arrived home, she collected two matron's uniforms and headed straight for her seamstress's apartment. She stayed up most of the night guiding her dressmaker in the creation of the world's best, and perhaps only, custom made, semi-official, police matron bloomers.

They were necessarily sewn from her existing white wool uniform skirt and fit loosely in the thighs, tight in the calves like men's breeches but with strips of white ribbon and a ruffle at each ankle. She topped them with a skirt of the same material, which was slit in front for ease of movement and had pockets large enough to hold her new revolver. Regrettably, it required two regular uniforms to create a single new improved one.

Anna's design was worthy of Paul Poiret himself. The price had been excruciating.

§

At daylight, Anna trudged home with a headache and a twenty-dollar debt. The seamstress charged extra when customers came late and needed their clothes finished by dawn. The price had been a shock. It wasn't the first time Anna had called on her dressmaker at home in the evening. It was the first time she had had to pay the bill. Anna had given her all her money, but it wasn't enough, so the woman was holding onto the bloomers until Anna paid the balance. This defeated the point of late-night tailoring entirely. Now Anna had but one uniform. She already owed a gun shop for the new revolver she had bought on credit, her pistol having burned up in a fire. What happened to people who could not pay their bills? She feared she was going to find out. If Matron Clemens knew, she might dismiss Anna.

And how long would her Cracker Jacks and kippers last? Her toothpaste? Her scented soap?

Anna arrived home and headed straight for a jewelry box. Her father had confiscated most of her gems—pieces by Lalique, Tiffany, and Fouquet. He'd kept sentimental gifts and heirloom jewels that had belonged to her mother or had been in the family for generations. He'd taken all but three hatpins, which had been on her head, and a hair comb on loan to her best friend Clara on the night Anna was disavowed.

She selected the comb, made of tortoise shell and adorned with a golden phoenix feather crowded with opals and diamonds. One could remove the feather and wear it as a brooch. It had been a present from her grandmother, now deceased. She held it to the light, turning it, and watching it sparkle. The thought of selling it made her sick. Anna put it in her hair one last time and gazed at herself in the mirror, chin high, face red, eyes shining.

She would ask Wolf where the best pawnshops were. Cops would know. Pawnshops were the purveyors of stolen treasure.

CHAPTER 6

Anna kneeled on the floor filing envelopes containing the records of juvenile offenders. During the previous two weeks, she had trolled the city for obscene billboards that promoted salty dance shows and reported them to Captain Wells, who had them removed. She hunted the slippery, shoplifting treat girl, Jane Godfrey, albeit unsuccessfully. She encountered several young blossoms at a skating rink who disappeared into the bathrooms with clean cheeks, and then emerged wearing rouge. She lectured them, washed their faces, and sent them home. She collected two children from a brothel and escorted the offending mother to the station to pay her fine, as it was against a city ordinance to raise children in the red-light district. Anna always hated that task and had told the mother that the children were no better off with the cranky nuns at the Orphans' Asylum, and that they certainly ate better in a brothel. All of this she recorded in detail and subsequently filed the reports.

Perhaps Anna hadn't been at her best during the last two weeks, preoccupied with other things. Presently, her mind was on severed heads, jail sentences, and unpaid dress bills, so that records that should be laid to rest in the As were sometimes lost in the Bs. Once per day, she said a silent prayer to Saint Agnes, patron saint of virgins, that all the other women in LA would find Joe Singer unbearably ugly. Every second night, she washed her shirtwaist and wore it slightly damp to work the next day. Now it was she who smelled wet. She tried to overcome this by wearing extra Ambre Antique *parfum*, but the bottle wouldn't last forever.

Anna hadn't encountered Joe since their fight in the stables. Even though she could no longer love Joe because of his treachery, his absence left a hollow place in her gut, which couldn't be filled with Cracker Jacks or whiskey, though she had tried.

As Anna ruminated thus, Detective Wolf came up behind her, so close she could feel the heat of him and smell his floral cologne. He leaned over her shoulder. "Good morning, Assistant Matron Blanc. I need your help."

Anna glanced up. "I need your help, too." She blushed. "I need to find a pawnshop." Anna removed the phoenix feather comb from her purse. The diamonds and opals sparkled against the backdrop of the dingy station. Her chest ached as she put the comb in Wolf's hand.

He picked it up, turned it in his palm, and whistled. "You can't sell this in a pawnshop, honeybun."

"Why not?"

"Because no one who frequents pawnshops could afford it. It looks like something a princess would wear."

Anna took it back. "Where can I hock it?"

"Where did you buy it? Maybe they'll buy it back."

"Paris, I think. The designer is French. Lalique."

He raised both brows.

Suddenly, Anna felt self-conscious about owning such a treasure—something so precious that no one could afford to buy it from her. She colored. "It was a gift."

"Find the most expensive jeweler in town and see if they'll sell it for you on consignment."

"I suppose they'll take a cut."

"I'd guess fifty percent."

Anna nodded grimly. It was torture to contemplate. She'd been paid twice since she'd found the head. Most of the money went for back rent, and she still owed her landlord a deposit. She had a little left to buy food and whiskey, which was a priority, provided she was careful. As long as she avoided her dressmaker and her landlord, she should be all right. But she tired of wearing the same cumbersome uniform every day. She needed her bloomers. And a kettle. And a spoon. And so many things.

She extended her hand to Wolf and pressed the jewels into his palm. "Will you sell it for me? I can't bear it."

Wolf studied her face. "Sure." He slipped the phoenix feather comb into his inside coat pocket and grinned. "Don't be glum, honeybun. I've got a job for you."

Anna perked up. Wolf was a detective, and doing detective work was her life—at least she'd like it to be. She smiled the brightest smile she could muster. "Anything."

"Your eagerness pleases me greatly. I wish 'anything' was an option. But, apparently, a foul-smelling trunk's been found in an apartment building in Chinatown. We think a dead Chinaman's inside. I need you to go to Chinatown and help interview a female witness. Reportedly, she's hysterical. Normally, I'd send Matron Clemens, but she's had to leave town. Her aunt died."

Anna's face lit up. "That's wonderful news!"

Wolf grinned. "I'm glad you see the sunny side, honeybun."

"I mean . . ." Anna transformed her countenance to look deathly serious. "I am sorry about Matron Clemens's aunt. Will she be away from the station long?"

"She's going to Chicago. I'm afraid she'll be gone for a month."

"Jupiter."

With Matron Clemens out of town, Anna could do as she pleased, provided Wolf didn't watch her too closely. Anna folded her hands in her lap and, after an appropriately somber pause, burst out, "Will I be working with detectives?"

"You sure will."

Anna beamed. "I'll do it, gladly."

"You'll be working with Joe Singer."

Her smile tightened. Working with Joe would be like going to the dentist.

Joe Singer approached, his face set, his eyes fixed on Wolf. Her stomach flipped and she rose to her feet, knocking an envelope onto the floor so that its contents—the life details of some young criminal—spilled onto the hardwood.

Joe wore plain clothes, not a uniform, and didn't even have the courtesy to glare at her. He tugged at his hair. "Wolf, please. Don't send Assistant Matron Blanc. It's too dangerous. Why don't you send Detective Snow or one of the patrolmen?"

The thought of being replaced by Detective Snow horrified Anna. Detective Snow was dead up to his ear tops.

Wolf cleared his throat. "The lady witness won't talk to a patrolman."

Anna lifted her chin. "I refuse to go with Officer Singer. Send me alone. I can do it. You can put him on traffic tickets or something."

Wolf spoke in a quiet, soothing tone. "Honeybun, you aren't a detective. You aren't even a cop. We just need you to calm the woman and pry out information that she wouldn't tell a hairy ape like Joe."

"Joe's not a dick either."

Joe squeezed his eyes closed as if waiting for some impending disaster.

Wolf laid his hand on Anna's shoulder. "That's just the thing. He is. He's been promoted." Wolf turned to Joe. "Would you mind bringing me some chop suey?"

Anna said flatly, "I'm the best man-tracker you've got. I should be a dick."

Wolf grinned. "Honeybun, it would take two of you to meet the weight requirement."

Anna knew this to be true. She fell six years, eight inches, and sixty-two pounds short of the minimum requirements for being a cop in LA. But neither was she old, married, and plain—the requirements for being a police matron—and she was working out just fine. Besides, Joe wasn't twenty-five yet. He got hired because his dad was the chief.

Wolf said, "The witness refuses to come into the station because her husband, who manages the apartments, never lets her leave the building, and she's scared. I just need you to go to the apartment building on Juan Street and interview the lady with Joe nearby to help and to guide. If you do well, you can help interview females involved in other cases. And it seems you should be more amenable to whatever I ask given that I put my neck on the line for you."

Anna's face contorted in horror. He was holding the head over her head.

Joe's ears were red. Wolf put his arm around him and walked him off toward the kitchen. Anna heard him murmur, "Young Joe, you've got to separate your work from your play."

Anna couldn't hear what Joe answered back. The blood was rushing in her ears.

CHAPTER 7

Anna and Joe clopped down the stone steps together, with an order from Wolf for chop suey. Joe lugged a camera and a leather bag of tools, his weapon strapped in a holster. Anna carried a revolver, fountain pen, and monogrammed leather-bound notebook in her silver net purse. It was the swellest of all her purses. The pattern was like fish scales, which bent and glistened and flashed in the winter sun.

Joe gestured to her purse. "Is that real silver?"

"Yes, why?"

He shook his head. "You're lucky you're with a cop."

"I'd be luckier if I were with a different cop."

Joe threw back his head and laughed quietly.

Anna smoothed her skirts. "I'd rather go without you."

"You need me. I have the address."

"I bet I could find it without the address."

"I'll take that bet. What are we betting for?"

Anna tapped her lip thoughtfully. "Juicy Fruit. A year's supply."

Joe shook Anna's hand and grinned. "Juan's a long street."

"I've seen the map."

The road churned with streetcars, autos, wagons, bicycles, and reckless pedestrians that all jammed up at the corner like sticks in a beaver dam. On the sidewalk, Anna and Joe waded through the crowd toward the trolley stop. When they arrived, Anna turned to face him. "Why don't you want me to go to Chinatown? I'm a good sleuth. I've investigated in the parlor houses while a killer was slaughtering girls."

"And you almost died."

"So did you."

"Anna, Chinatown is hot right now."

"Tourists go to Chinatown."

"They don't know what I know. If violence breaks out, you don't want to get caught in the crossfire. You saw what the tong did to Ko Chung. They kill whoever they're ordered to kill, and it doesn't matter who's watching or who gets in the way."

"You're just as likely to get shot as I am."

"No, because you'll stand out like a horse in church. There are twenty Chinamen for every woman, and the ladies who are there mostly work in the cribs, so everyone will assume you're a prostitute."

"That's not new."

"The white men in Chinatown are dangerous, too. They don't like white women going anywhere near a Chinaman. They've even threatened the missionary women."

"I brought my gun."

"Most of the city's brothels are there. Every other shop is an opium den, a gambling joint, or a saloon, and they're all run by the tongs."

An engine backfired on the busy street, sounding like a gunshot. Anna flinched. "I'm not going to give up my opportunity to solve a crime because you think it's dangerous. Wolf ordered me to go, and I'm going. You might as well get used to it."

"Fine. You can interview the witness like Wolf asked you to do, and then you're going back to the station."

She speared him with a pointed look. "Are you bossing me?"

He threw his hands in the air. "Anna, I outrank you."

§

Anna and Joe boarded a Red Car. She sat on a wooden seat. He stood, grasping a canvas strap hanging from the ceiling. Neither spoke. When the trolley halted at the corner of Main and Marchessault Streets, Anna hesitated. She said again, "But tourists go to Chinatown."

"Less and less. White men come slumming because they like their gambling, and they like their women. I'm telling you, Sherlock. Even the Chinese are leaving for other Chinatowns. We don't know if, when, or how the Hop Sing are going to retaliate for the death of Ko Chung, or whether the Bing Kong are done punishing them for the missing singsong girls. They are on the brink of war. You don't want to be standing in the street when a bunch of highbinders start shooting at each other."

She took a long deep breath for courage, and stood, moving toward the door of the trolley.

§

The Plaza was a small, round, grassy park, with sidewalks that looked like the spokes of a wheel. Anna and Joe trudged across it toward a market. A hundred horses lined one half of the Plaza, hooked to wagons brimming with celery, strawberries, and other produce. There, in the muddy street, the Chinese sold vegetables to the people of Los Angeles. It was the edge of the white world, where East met West—the edge of safety.

Apart from Mr. Yau, Anna had never seen a Chinese man up close—ones with bodies anyway. They came in such variety, and it strained her propriety not to stare. There were at least a hundred of them. They favored dark pants and tunics that looked like pajamas, and broad brim hats. Some had short hair. Others shaved their foreheads and had long queues that fell to their waists or even lower. Evidently, she interested them as much as they interested her. Their brown eyes arrested her, following her among the horses, carts, and crowd without compunction. Anna averted her own gray eyes.

Joe linked his arm through hers. "Come on." Anna shook him off.
"Fine," he said.

They slipped between two wagons, Joe striding in his boots, Anna tiptoeing through droppings, which scented the air along with the earthy smells of vegetables. Chinatown lay nestled between Sonora-town, Little Italy, and Frenchtown, with slaughterhouses to the south, downtown to the West, and railroad yards to the east. All races of men shopped from the wagons because everyone had to eat.

Anna and Joe turned onto Marchessault Street, and the crowd thinned, becoming more predominantly Chinese. The buildings looked old, like a picture she had seen of LA when it was just a Wild West town. Though the January sun was shining, it had only dried the top layer of mud, so, though the crust on the street looked hard, a woman in Paul Poiret shoes could sink in up to her ankles. Anna saw no other ladies on the street to object. Apparently, Chinatown was a broken down, man's world. It sorely needed pavement and a woman's touch. Anna spared her shoes by hopping among planks and rock islands that rose above the mud, staying on the brick sidewalk wherever possible. A sudden cesspool smell assaulted Anna's nose, and her lip curled.

Joe whispered, "Chinatown doesn't belong to the Chinese, and the landlords don't keep it up. The city won't pave the streets, although I have heard they do plan to put in sewers. The rats are so bad, they've put a two-cent bounty on their scalps."

Anna nodded, thinking of her own rat-infested apartment.

Some of the buildings, despite their dilapidated state, had been freshly painted bright red, yellow, or green in preparation for the upcoming Chinese New Year celebration, which Anna's father had never allowed her to attend. Lanterns as round as the sun dangled from the eaves, and banners with Chinese writing graced the walls. The air smelled of garlic, dried fish, and incense. The people on the street, all of them men, stared at Anna like she was a goldfish in a bowl. It made her nervous.

She peered down the road but could see no end to it. "Is China-town very big?"

"Maybe fifteen streets, if you count the alleys, and a couple of thou-sand people."

"A proper town, then."

"It has everything they need, because the Chinese rarely leave."

"Like what?"

"Temples, an opera theater, a newspaper. The kids have their own school. They have their own telephone exchange. The Hop Sing have their own jail."

"I see. You're afraid I might get civilized."

Joe smiled. "Now that would be a shame."

They passed the window of the Cock of the Walk, a saloon with iron stools that spun. Sagging awnings draped across the windows. The floor was black from chewing tobacco, though spitting was against the law. Some bent rounder had his head down on the bar. Outside the beer joint, a wall of bulletins in Chinese fluttered in the breeze.

Joe took her arm and eased her around a large reddish-brown stain on the sidewalk. He whispered, "Somebody shot their star here yesterday. Got his throat slit. I guess he'd won big at a fan-tan parlor and a loser didn't like it."

Anna tensed and let him hold her arm. Not that she was afraid of ghosts. She slowed and looked back at the stain. "Did they catch the killer?"

"No. He's still at large." Joe pulled her along.

Smoke wafted from a door that opened like a maw into a dark interior. The scent was thick in her nose, floral and rich, like an odor of sanctity. He nudged her shoulder. "Smell that. That's opium. It gives you beautiful dreams, but it can turn you into a dope. Then you can't get enough. If you take too much, you'll die."

Anna held her breath.

Joe grinned. "There are opium joints for whites downtown, and there are opium joints for the Chinese, but the tongs supply everybody. It's one of the ways they make their money." He gestured to a two-story building. "This boarding house is run by the Bing Kong tong."

"It looks dingy."

"The rooms are crowded with bunks, and the men cook on stoves between the beds. The Bing Kong recruit men who are friendless and without family, help them find jobs, give them a place to stay."

"Hah. Like the Saint Vincent de Paul Society."

Joe smiled. "Sort of."

Anna wondered if she knew anything at all about the world.

"The tongs are like that. They help people with one hand and exploit them with the other. And woe to anybody who gets in their way."

Anna shook her head. "I would never."

"Smell that?" he asked. "That's hashish."

Anna nodded knowingly and resisted the urge to ask what hashish was.

He pulled Anna to a stop when they came to Juan Street. "This is as far as I'll guide you."

She examined each dingy storefront intently. "Don't worry. I'll find it."

Her eyes fell on an old woman cleaning a plate glass window under a crooked sign that read Most Lucky Laundry. The crone's hair was slicked back from her wrinkled face in a tight, gray bun. A woman, Anna knew, was a rare sight in Chinatown. As women were more civilized than men by nature, she took advantage of this one. She called out, "Hello."

Anna waved and strode over, her heart brimming with sisterly feeling, leaving Joe where he stood. After all, Anna and the woman had much in common. Ladies were a rare sight in police stations just like in Chinatown. Anna was one of two women in a force comprising two hundred and sixty-eight men. Also, this woman must be brave to live in the most dangerous beat in Los Angeles. Brave like Anna.

The woman washed the outside of the window, though the inside was clouded with condensation. It smelled as if the cleaning cloth had been soaked in vinegar. Through the steam, Anna could see a wrinkly dog and some sort of altar inside. The lady turned and gave Anna a toothless grin, replying in a heavy accent. "Hello."

Anna smiled. "I am Assistant Police Matron Anna Blanc." Anna graciously inclined her head. "There's been a murder." She smiled again. "And I'm looking for an apartment building near a chop suey restaurant owned by a man who holds his wife captive."

Behind her, she heard Joe choke on a laugh. She ignored him. The wrinkly dog growled at Anna through the glass.

"I am Ma Yi-jun." The old woman looked Anna up and down from her swirly hairpiece to her fine Paul Poiret shoes.

Anna discreetly returned the favor, assessing the woman from her plain trousers and tunic to the black cloth shoes with soles as thick as watermelon rinds. She envied her the trousers for practical if not aesthetic reasons, and they were perfectly pressed.

Ma Yi-jun nodded slowly. "Ah, yes. I know that man."

Anna sunk into a deep and courtly curtsy. "Thank you." She glanced over her shoulder and smiled smugly at Joe.

"One dollar." Ma Yi-jun stuck out a boney hand, palm up.

Anna frowned. This was a steep price for directions that Anna would gladly have given for free. A dollar fifty was all she had left after the seamstress fiasco, and she could barely make ends meet as it was. But she didn't want Joe to know that, and it was important that she win the bet. She wanted to impress him, and chewing gum for a year would be a boon. Anna reached into her silver purse for her billbook and counted out a dollar in change. She held out the coins to Ma Yi-jun. The old woman bowed her head, pocketed the money, and returned to washing the clouded windows, ignoring Anna, cooing at her dog in Chinese.

This put Anna out of sorts. She cleared her throat. "Excuse me, Madam. Could you please tell me where the apartment building is?"

The woman waved Anna off with a withered hand. "You go home, *sei gwai por.*"

Anna made a sound of objection. "You aren't going to tell me? We are sisters. We are—"

"No."

"Then, what did I pay you a dollar for?"

The old woman wiped, leaving a clean streak on the dirty glass. "Advice."

Anna turned in disgust and strode off, past Joe, face burning. Joe caught up and his smile spread. "Well done, Sherlock. But save some of your money to buy my gum."

Anna didn't answer but kept swishing down the sidewalk, past groceries, apartments, saloons, fortunetellers, and men rolling cigars in a shop. Men, men, and more men. No women, no children. Joe kept up, watching Anna as closely as she watched the street. Three blocks down, she stopped. A brick building displayed a sign that read Man

Jen Lo. Behind the window, pretty strings of paper lanterns stretched from one corner of the room to the other in a crisscross, and Chinese symbols ran along the top of the wall in a border. Palm trees flourished in ornate pots and half a dozen men in black tunics sat at tables, eating with chopsticks. It smelled delicious.

Above the establishment, on the second floor, three curtained windows lined up in a row—apartment dwellings. From an open window, she heard the faint cries of a baby. Babies, she knew, came from married women. Married woman, apartment building, chop suey. Anna pointed. "There."

Joe looked down at the address. He looked up and followed her gaze. He nodded in respect. "Well done, Sherlock."

Anna beamed. "You owe me gum."

Chapter 8

A brand new red Cadillac stood in front of Man Jen Lo's chop suey joint. The tires were brown with mud, and the paint on the sides was splattered. Anna whispered to Joe. "There's money in Chinatown."

"There are some fine businessmen in Chinatown."

"Shouldn't the rich people leave? It's not exactly Bunker Hill."

"You think the Chinese can just move to Bunker Hill?"

Anna realized how silly she sounded. Of course no one would ever welcome a Chinese man into the neighborhood, unless he was their cook and lived out back or something. "But surely they could start their own neighborhood."

"They can't own land, and no one else will rent to them."

This seemed terribly unfair to Anna.

Three white men leaned against the peeling apartment wall, ogling the elegant car. Each had the red face and unsteady bearing of a drunk. A Chinese man shuffled past them on the sidewalk carrying a toddler boy dressed in bright silks. They caught Anna's eye because she hadn't seen many children.

One of the inebriates raised a filthy hand and yanked hard on the man's braid. The man's head snapped back. His companions wheezed in merriment. The harassed man kept on walking, chin high, dignified, as if nothing had happened, but Anna could see his body tense. She narrowed her eyes. Pulling hair was rarely called for, but it was a terrible thing to humiliate a man in front of his own son.

Joe's jaw twitched, and he steered her through a green door belonging to the apartment building. "Wait here." He went back outside.

Anna peeked out the door and saw Joe flashing his shiny badge at the drunks. He growled something she couldn't hear in a low, challenging voice. Anna felt both proud of him and afraid for his safety. It was three against one. But the men merely glared at Joe, unwilling to fight a strapping young policeman.

Joe slipped through the door and joined Anna in the foyer, which smelled faintly of spoiled meat, and more powerfully of chop suey. The space was windowless and cramped for two. He shook his head, blew out a deep, disgusted breath, and gestured to a staircase. "After you."

The wood squeaked as they mounted warped steps and entered a hallway with three apartment doors. The rotten scent was more pronounced and sickly sweet, like death. The roof had leaked, staining the walls with damp in several spots along the corridor. Black mildew edged the stain marks. In contrast to the general decay, the plank floor was spick and span but for one set of muddy tracks.

Anna peered down the hallway. A girl, slightly younger than Anna, in an embroidered blue silk tunic, squatted against the wall cradling a crying baby, her silky hair twisted into a tight bun at the nape of her neck. She convulsed and made whimpering sounds. Next to her, in plain black cotton, a woman cooed her consolation. The woman had the cracked hands of one who washed clothes with lye soap. Anna deduced they were mistress and servant.

Joe stopped and gently addressed the women in Chinese. His words were halting, but confident. As Anna watched his lips form the strange sounds, her own lips parted in surprise. He had learned a thing or two on the Chinatown Squad. She was impressed. She tried not to show it.

The women turned their faces away from Joe.

Anna raised her eyebrows in a question.

He shook his head. "I didn't think they'd talk to me. They believe white men will cast a spell on them and make them do their bidding."

"They're wise to be cautious," Anna said, and squinted her eyes. "How is it that you speak Chinese?"

He shrugged. "I don't speak that much Chinese."

"It sounds like you've been studying—"

He gave her a cocky grin.

Anna asked, "Do the other members of the Chinatown Squad speak Chinese?"

"Are you kidding?"

"I think they should." Anna considered the girl. "Why do you suppose she's crying?"

"Maybe she's afraid I'll ask to see her papers and send her back to China, but I won't. Maybe she's just afraid of us. She probably doesn't leave this building except for New Year's. Or maybe she's disturbed because there's likely a dead body in one of her apartments."

"Oh." Anna addressed the woman. "There, there. We won't send you back to China."

Joe looked down the hall and smiled at a tall, broad-shouldered man who stood stoically before the door of one of the apartments. The man wore elaborate silk pajamas. His curved lips were set in a grim expression. The fingernails on his folded hands were manicured and long. His black eyes were large, his chiseled face smooth, and his hair fell to his waist in a glorious, thick, black rope.

The man wasn't just handsome. He was magnificent—like a statue. Anna wanted to stare. She whispered, "Jupiter."

Anna and Joe approached the imposing man, who Anna placed at about thirty. Joe bowed slightly from his shoulders, grinning. "*Néih hóu*, Mr. Jones."

Mr. Jones clasped Joe's hand with a warmth that suggested intimacy, but he did not smile. His words were flavored with the barest hint of an accent. "Good afternoon, Detective Singer."

Joe said, "This is Assistant Matron Blanc. She's here to interview the witnesses, and she's the smartest man on the force."

Anna flushed with pleasure.

Joe continued. "Assistant Matron Blanc, Mr. Jones is from the Chinese Consolidated Benevolent Society. Let's say he's an informal liaison between Chinatown and the LAPD—a very distinguished man. He called this in and asked for me specifically."

Anna could tell this pleased Joe. She lifted her chin, trying to mimic Matron Clemens's incontrovertible authority, and offered her hand.

Mr. Jones took it. "Good afternoon, Assistant Matron Blanc." Fatigue pulled at the handsome planes of his face, as if he hadn't slept in days. His perfect English seemed strange coming from his celestial mouth, only slightly flavored by his homeland. "This is a Chinese matter. I'd happily send you away, but I have a strong aversion to blood."

Joe nodded. "Then you haven't opened the trunk."

Mr. Jones groaned and looked up at the ceiling. "No," he said, then gestured to a wooden nameplate nailed to the door. "This says that the occupant's name is Leo Lim. The landlady confirmed it."

Chapter 9

The reek of the apartment was worse than the stench in the hall. Anna coughed, buried her face in the sleeve of her blouse, and held her breath.

The room needed a good scrubbing. Anna supposed that this was because Leo Lim was a man. She knew one thing for certain. The person who cleaned the hall so meticulously did not clean this room.

Her shoes stuck to the floor, making crackling sounds. She waved her hand before her face to swat away the buzzing flies that soared about the apartment like little vultures. Parlor furnishings, a dining table, and a kitchen stove for cooking languished, covered in a thin layer of dust. A small jade dragon sat on a table by a door—presumably the entrance to a bedroom. Across the space, she saw a trunk bound with rope. It was a Chinese trunk made of camphor wood, painted lucky red. Every old Los Angeles family had one, at least in Anna's circles.

Joe strode past her to the trunk, took out a pocketknife, and began sawing at the rope.

"So we don't really know what's in there?" Anna asked.

"We know it smells dead." The rope fell into a frayed pile on the plank floor. Joe hefted the lid and sprung back, contorting his face. "Oh God." He pulled a handkerchief from his pocket and clamped it to his nose.

The smell hit Anna like hot steam. She removed a perfumed hanky from her silver serpentine purse and pressed it to her face, though the linen didn't really help. It was all she could do not to succumb to a gagging fit. She tried to calm her senses and slowly moved closer to what she knew would be a hideous and interesting sight.

A body was folded inside the trunk like a fetus, the ghoulish face eaten away by insects, the flesh purple and oozing. The profusion of wiggling larvae gave the impression that the form was moving. It was a horror, worsened by the fact that the body wore a French satin corset with playful pink trim, lacey cotton drawers, and brown ladies' walking shoes. Anna choked on a gasp.

"That's not Leo Lim," Joe said.

"She's white." Anna strode to the table, and moved aside a porcelain tea set. She pulled the cloth off the table and used it to cover the body from décolletage to knees.

"Anna, she's dead. I don't think she cares," Joe said.

"I care."

Joe exhaled into the foul air. "I want to know where her dress is."

Anna leaned closer to the corpse and squatted. The woman's hair was a deep black tangle, cut badly, and shorter than the fashion. There were no pupils to examine on the body, no readily evident cause of death, no discernible patterns of lividity given that all of the flesh, everything left, was dark purple—almost black. Plump brown pupae, and the shells of pupae, revealed the source of the flies.

Anna said, "She's been dead at least nine days. It's takes nine days for flies to hatch. I read it in *Legal Medicine*."

"So you're the one who stole the coroner's books."

She replied absently, more absorbed in the crime scene than his well-founded accusation. "I, um . . . How dare you."

She stared down into the woman's ruined face. The dead lady's chin was tilted up as if she were listening. Anna listened in return, slowly surveying the body. She squinted in concentration, trying to think without breathing. "What do we know about you, except that you aren't Leo Lim?"

Joe said, "She's either a prostitute or a missionary."

Anna glanced up at him. "Why?"

"She's either a girl from one of the brothels, or she's come to spread the gospel. They're the only white women who go this far into Chinatown."

"She's a missionary."

Joe tilted his head. "How can you tell?"

"The shoes are this season's fashion, but the soles are worn. Obviously, she walks a lot. Prostitutes don't walk a lot. They'd get slapped with a vagrancy charge. So, she's a missionary, not a prostitute." Anna settled back on her heels." Surely you know all the missionaries in Chinatown. It's not that big, and you spend enough time here. Have any brunettes gone missing?"

"I know a few missionary girls, but no one's said anything about one going missing." Joe squeezed his eyes shut and exhaled. "This just makes things worse."

Anna stared at him. "What? You value the life of a missionary over a prostitute? At least a missionary will go to heaven." She rose brusquely, brushed off her skirt, and strode to a window to take in the less putrid air. It was unlocked and she pushed it open.

Joe followed. "You know that's not it."

Anna did. Though Presbyterian, Joe wasn't one to cast stones.

They leaned outside and breathed fresh air in gulps. The essence of death clung to the insides of Anna's nostrils. It soaked into her hair like cigarette smoke. Beneath them, on the street, people passed by as if a lady had not lost her life.

Joe's eyes caught Anna's. "If word gets out that a white lady was murdered in Chinatown, especially a missionary, the city will go crazy. All of the Chinamen are going to suffer."

Anna said, "That's preposterous."

"Anna, I know what I'm talking about. You heard about the Chinatown War? What went on in Negro Alley?"

Anna hadn't heard, so she lied. "Of course."

"Two tongs were feuding over the abduction of a woman and started shooting. A white rancher got shot. He died. Other white bystanders were wounded. Word spread that the Chinese were killing whites and five hundred angry men descended on Chinatown. Every building was ransacked. Every Chinaman in the quarter attacked and robbed. Nineteen Chinamen died. They lynched them, tortured them—chopped the fingers off some of them. The mob left bodies swinging from shop awnings, right downtown, as naked as Adam."

Anna shook her head. "I don't believe you. If that had happened, I would know about it."

He smirked. "I thought you said you did, Sherlock."

Anna kicked herself.

Joe said, "Anyway, it happened before you were born, but things aren't that different now."

"What happened to the men who committed the crimes?"

"Nothing."

Anna was silent for a moment. She gazed out the window. Across the street, she saw two children, with their long black braids and clothes like men's pajamas, pressing their faces on the plate-glass window of a grocery, no doubt leaving trails of snot that someone else would have to clean up. Anna didn't care for children, but neither did she want to see them trampled in a riot or their parents tortured and hung naked in her shopping district.

Anna tucked a loose strand of hair behind her ear. "But what if it wasn't a Chinaman? What if a white man killed this woman?"

"Maybe, but it doesn't look like it. She's in a Chinaman's apartment. Our best hope is that this woman's kin isn't vengeful and can be persuaded to keep this under wraps. If they're missionaries, they'll know the consequences. Maybe they'll want to keep the peace."

"Or maybe they won't want the world to know their wife or daughter was found unclad and eaten by maggots in the apartment of a Chinaman."

Joe whistled, long and low.

"What?"

"When Wolf assigned me this case, he assumed the victim was a Chinese man—a victim of a brawl or a run of the mill tong killing. Not a white lady. It's not what you hand a new detective to cut his teeth on."

Anna sighed. "You are so lucky."

"Lucky? It's a heck of a way to have to prove myself." Joe paced in a circle, ruffling his hair, and came to rest again in front of Anna. "We gotta handle this like a grenade. We say nothing. This stays out of the papers. The investigation goes quietly. You don't tell a soul that the victim's white. Not even Wolf. I'll get a coffin and a wagon and drive her straight to my cousin. He's a doctor. He can do the postmortem. Then, it's off to the mortuary."

"What about her family?"

Joe closed his eyes. "When we find them, I'll talk to them."

"Just tell them you found her somewhere else."

"I can't lie to her family."

"Yes, you can. If it means saving Chinatown."

Joe shook his head. "No, I'm not compromising my honor."

Anna rolled her eyes, but inside she admired him for it. His truthfulness was one of the things she liked about Joe Singer.

He continued, "Besides, they might have information we need to solve the crime."

"What about Mr. Jones. He's out there in the hall."

Joe tapped his fingers on the windowsill. "We tell him."

"What?"

"I trust him, Anna. He'll understand what's at stake."

Anna squinted. "You trust him and not Wolf?"

"If I tell Wolf, he'll take me off the case. Also, we need Mr. Jones. He's respected in Chinatown, and he's already agreed to help us with the investigation. Besides, we need a translator."

A ripple of excitement moved through Anna at the thought of working with the serious but well-made Chinese man.

Joe said, "Now let's go look in the bedroom. Maybe we'll find her dress."

Anna and Joe took deep gulps of air and strode across the sticky floor. Joe protectively held Anna back so she had to walk behind him. He opened the bedroom door, sending a stream of daylight onto a dirty Chinese carpet. Inside, the air smelled stale, but not rotten. A fishy-scented oil lamp had long since burned out. It took a moment for her eyes to adjust to the windowless space.

In the shadows, lying on a bed, was a second body, facedown. Its head was covered but for a dark braid of hair peeking from beneath a striped Mexican blanket. Next to the body, in the bed and on the pillow, was the indentation from some sleeping companion who was no longer there.

Anna put a hand on Joe's arm, her body tensing. "Jupiter."

Joe whistled. "The witness didn't say there were two bodies."

"There aren't two bodies."

"What?"

"He's not dead. He doesn't smell."

Joe sniffed the air. "You're right." He set down his camera, drew his gun, and edged closer, pushing Anna behind him. He spoke sharply. "Police. Reach for the roof."

The man didn't stir. Joe edged closer. "I said, hands up."

Heart pounding, Anna removed the pen from her purse, aimed for the sleeping man's head, and tossed it. It hit his back and bounced off.

No movement.

Joe strode over to the bed and shook him.

The man rolled over and his hair fell off.

Anna screeched.

Joe threw back the covers violently.

The body was an oblong mound of pillows and towels stuffed into pajamas, which had been topped with a neatly placed braid of raven-black hair. Anna's eyes fluttered in astonishment.

Joe rubbed his glistening forehead with the back of his hand. "Holy smoke."

Anna padded closer, leaning low to examine the braid. She recognized the silky texture of the locks. Undoubtedly, the killer had cut them from the victim, explaining the unfashionably short length of the dead girl's tresses, and the crookedness of the cut. "Well, I'm intrigued."

Joe gave her a hard look. "Don't get too intrigued."

Anna frowned. It was a cock shame being a woman.

Outside, the baby's cries grew louder and angrier.

Mr. Jones called from the hall. "Detective Singer, your witness needs to feed her baby."

§

Anna unhappily emerged from the apartment with Joe to find the manager's wife bouncing her wailing baby in her lap. Joe approached Mr. Jones, who leaned against the wall looking stony and serious. Joe moved close and lowered his voice, though no one nearby, not the whimpering mother nor her servant, likely spoke English. He was brief in the telling, skipping the more gruesome bits.

Mr. Jones listened. He closed his eyes and appeared to sink with the weight of the news. He pushed away from the wall and paced the length of the corridor, stopping to stare out a spotless window.

Anna watched him curiously. His eyes were unfocused and his hand, resting on the sill, was shaking. She whispered to Joe, "Why is he so upset about a dead white lady that he didn't know?"

Joe said, "Don't think of it in terms of one dead lady. Think in terms of a war on Chinatown."

Mr. Jones seemed to be collecting himself, his broad chest expanding with deep, slow breaths. When he returned to Anna, he was composed. "Are you ready to interview the witnesses, Assistant Matron Blanc?"

"Always. Do they speak English?"

"No. I will translate."

"She called you and not the police?"

"Her husband called me."

Anna crossed her arms, chilled in the cold, damp building. "Where is her husband?"

"I sent someone to his shop, but he was not there. The Chinese don't like the police, Matron Blanc."

Joe leaned in close. "We'll need to interview him. He's a suspect."

Mr. Jones nodded noncommittally.

The young mother still sat against the wall near her servant, cradling the mewling baby. Anna glided over and squatted beside them. Her corset restricted her diaphragm, and she had to take a moment to catch her breath. The mother looked up into Anna's face, her own pretty face splotched and puffy. She smelled like soap, warm skin, and ginger. Anna's gaze dropped to the lady's tiny feet, no more than three inches long.

Then she blatantly stared. She'd heard of foot binding but hadn't realized it would be so extreme. The girl's shoes were like doll shoes. How could a woman walk?

The servant woman had proper feet and big wondering eyes that took in everything. She was plain, but looked quick-witted.

Anna smiled. "Hello." She inclined her head. "I am Assistant Police Matron Anna Blanc, and I'm very pleased to meet you. What is your name?"

Mr. Jones translated. The girl watched Anna warily and replied in musical tones.

Mr. Jones said, "Her name is Mrs. Lo and her servant is Ah Bo." He switched between languages effortlessly.

Anna continued. "Very well, Mrs. Lo. You found the foul-smelling trunk?" Mr. Jones translated again.

The witness convulsed with sorrowful hiccups, startling the baby and making it cry louder. She said nothing.

Anna felt for the girl. Not because she'd found a rotting body in her apartment building. Anna herself would prefer a dead body to a broken heart, as long as the body wasn't hers. She felt for the lady because her husband enslaved her, confining her at his pleasure, the way Anna's father had tried to confine Anna only three short months ago. She wanted to tell the girl to revolt and run away like Anna had. But to where could a Chinese woman run? She was stuck in Chinatown.

Anna asked the mother, "When did you last see Leo Lim?"

The well-dressed girl spoke. Mr. Jones translated. "Leo Lim left the apartment ten days ago, in the morning, dragging a trunk. He loaded it into a cart."

Ah Bo shook her head and spoke. Mr. Jones translated. "Her servant said he must have come back. She saw him leave again that night carrying a bundle."

"But these ladies never leave the apartment. They saw him from the window?"

Mr. Jones nodded.

Anna's lips turned down. "Are they sure it was him?"

Mr. Jones had exchanges with the women. "They both recognized his clothing—a western-style suit and hat. He's the only one in the building that wears one."

Anna glanced between the two ladies. "Did they see or hear about any white women coming to his apartment?"

The young mother and servant eyed each other, then had an exchange with Mr. Jones. Now they both looked nervous. He said, "They don't know anything about a woman. They never saw her."

Anna smiled at the girl while speaking to Mr. Jones. "I think they're lying. White women are so conspicuous in Chinatown. How could they not see or hear about any white woman?"

Both ladies' eyes hardened in anger. The mother handed the baby to her servant, rose gracefully, and hobbled into an apartment with her nose in the air. Her servant followed, carrying the baby, eyes down at her big feet. The door shut.

Joe pursed his lips and exhaled. "I'm awed by your feminine tenderness and understanding."

Anna turned to Mr. Jones. "I thought you said they didn't speak English."

"Apparently, I was wrong."

"But don't you think it's odd that a white woman was able to walk past the restaurant, up the stairs, and down the hall without anyone noticing?"

Mr. Jones stared off down the hall. "Maybe she didn't want to be seen."

"Of course not." Anna tapped her lip. "But still . . ."

Joe glanced at the closed door, looking disappointed. "Well, if we're done here, I'm going to finish examining the crime scene." He lugged his camera back into the apartment where the corpse lay in the trunk. Anna took a gulp of fresh air and followed. Joe was already kneeling on the hardwood, considering scratches in the floorboards, preparing to take flashlight photographs with his camera. She wandered over to a table where several framed photographs rested by a candy dish full of nutmeats. Anna's lips fell open. "Jupiter."

There were five different pictures. In each, the same Chinese man posed with a different young white lady. The man had short, thick black hair, parted on the side. He wore a Western style suit of clothes and gave the overall impression of a man between worlds. Judging from the photographs, many white women sought his company, or he sought theirs. Anna selected a photograph of Leo Lim posed in front of a Chinese theater with a brown-haired girl, and squirreled it away in her skirt pocket.

She surveyed the room with intensity. A bowl sat on the floor in the corner, as if for feeding a cat. The cat herself had departed. Tea things still sat on the table—a tea towel, clay pot, two empty cups, a sugar bowl, and a dried out, crushed lemon. Anna sashayed over, the photograph in her pocket bumping her thigh when she walked. She picked up the pot, lifted the lid, and looked inside. A dark, grainy sludge coated the bottom, peppered with little islands of blue mold. She gave it a sniff. She gave it another sniff. It was like no tea she had ever known, but slightly floral and exotic beneath the mold smell. She pried a pinch of the sludge out with her fingers and dropped it onto the tea towel. Dampness spread across the cloth. Anna rolled it up and stowed it in her purse.

Joe stooped to pick a brass key up off the floor. He tried it in the door and it turned. "Leo Lim's key. He must have dropped it on his way out."

"Interesting." She bustled to the window. It was unlocked. She opened it and looked out onto a fire escape. If the killer had left footprints, they had been washed clean by the rain. Joe sauntered up behind her. "Listen, Anna. I'm going to be here a long time documenting the crime scene. Let's go down to the Cock of the Walk. Officer Clark eats lunch there. We'll tell him you interviewed a witness about the death of a Chinaman and need to be escorted home."

She pivoted and swished past Joe to the bookshelf. "I'm not done yet."

Joe stepped in front of her. He looked peeved. "Fork it over."

Anna's eyes widened in a poor imitation of innocence. "What?"

"There were five photographs of Lim, and now there are four."

"Well, I had nothing to do with it."

Joe scoffed, stuck both hands in her big skirt pockets and rummaged around, almost touching her thigh through three blessed layers of fabric. Anna bit her lip. "Masher."

He produced the framed picture. "That's it. You're out." His finger shot toward the door. "This is my case, and I won't have you disturbing the apartment before I've finished going over it."

"I haven't touched anything else." She decided not to mention the tea.

He took Anna by the arm and steered her outside. "Stay away from my crime scene."

"You're just using that as an excuse to get me out of Chinatown. Well, I don't want to go." Anna turned and went back inside.

Joe followed. "Wolf didn't authorize you to work this case." He grabbed her by the waist and pulled her backward. Anna dragged her heels. Joe pulled harder. Anna sat down. She began to crawl back toward the crime scene where she belonged. He stepped on her skirt. "I could arrest you."

"But you won't."

"And why is that?"

"I'm a good sleuth and our chance of solving this crime is even better with two of us on the case. Admit it."

"I knew once you got a taste of this case you wouldn't leave it alone. You're going back to Central Station where it's safe." He grabbed her under the arms, pulling her up and onto her backside. She scooted along on her bottom, her skirt pushing up to reveal her stockinged shins, but Anna didn't care. Why should she care? Propriety had gotten her nowhere. She simply closed her eyes tight so that she couldn't see them.

Joe sighed and let go. When she opened her eyes, he was tugging down her hem. He extended a hand to help her up. She eyed him suspiciously.

He said, "We tracked mud on that floor. If you aren't careful, you'll stain your uniform."

Anna looked at the muddy floorboards and considered. Joe knew more about laundry than she did, and she did need to wear this uniform tomorrow. She took his hand and allowed him to pull her to her feet.

"Sherlock, you make my life hell."

"My pleasure."

He pulled a pair of handcuffs out of his coat pocket and slapped one on her wrist, holding tight to the other.

Anna chuckled coldly. "You wouldn't dare."

"Mr. Jones," Joe called as he tugged her into the hall.

Mr. Jones looked curiously at Anna, and then at Joe. Joe cleared his throat. "Mr. Jones, would you consider taking her back to the station?"

Mr. Jones held out one strong wrist, which peeked from beneath a silk sleeve. "Gladly."

Anna didn't believe him.

"Consider yourself deputized." Joe handcuffed Anna to the gorgeous man and bowed. "Thank you, my friend."

Anna's mouth dropped open, and she made little sounds of incredulity—not just at the fact that Joe would handcuff her to a Chinaman, but that the Chinaman would let him.

"Goodnight, Mr. Jones." Joe gave Anna half a smile as he handed Mr. Jones the handcuff keys. "Goodnight, Sherlock."

Chapter 10

Mr. Jones threw a coat over his arm to hide the fact that he and Anna were linked together and led her down the creaky stairs to the street. He peeked cautiously out the door before exiting. Thankfully, the drunken white men were gone, or they might not have taken kindly to the sight of a white woman walking so close to a Chinese man. He must value Joe's friendship to do him such a favor, and Joe had appeared to know he would.

Mr. Jones towed a humiliated Anna to the new red Cadillac—the one Anna had seen parked in front of the restaurant. She dragged her feet but didn't forcibly resist. She knew when she'd lost a battle. She'd do better to plot her return.

He set the crank, helped her to step up and slide across the red leather seat to the passenger's side. "I suggest you cover your head so you aren't seen." He reached behind into the back seat and grabbed a blanket. He handed it to her.

"What do I care if you get beat up for abducting me?" Still, Anna knew he was right. A fight could only draw attention to the case and possibly the death of a white woman. She slipped down onto the floor-board. Her broad-brimmed hat bumped against the dash, forcing her neck into an awkward position. She threw the blanket over her head, leaving a gap from which to see. The car vibrated beneath her bottom.

Mr. Jones gripped the wheel with one large hand. The other hung down, bound to Anna, unavoidably touching hers every time he shifted. He had corded muscles in his wrists, and smooth, strong fingers. She snuck glances at his hard-looking thighs, his shoulders, and his face. His eyes had a somber, far-away look as he stared at the road. He smelled of sweet tobacco.

Anna wondered just what he did for work that he could afford such a boss machine as this Cadillac. She wanted to ask him loads of questions—why he seemed so sad, even before he knew about the dead white girl, what he knew about the Chinese massacre, why his fingernails were so long, whether he knew anything about the missionary women, and whether Chinese men ate cockroach pudding and rat roast, like the paper said. If so, was it good? But she felt such questioning would be undignified, as she had been deeply wronged by him and his complicity with Joe. Anna lifted her chin and lowered her eyelids to half-mast, but it was hard to look dignified when crouching beneath a blanket.

When they approached the edge of Chinatown, near the vegetable market, Mr. Jones reached into his pocket, retrieved the key to the handcuffs, and handed the key ring to Anna. "I've heard of you, Matron Blanc. You're the daughter of that banker, Christopher Blanc."

Anna took the key and quickly unlocked her wrist. Their hands fell apart. She stayed crouching. "You've heard of me?"

"I saw your picture in the paper when you were arrested in that brothel raid."

Anna blushed to her ears. "I was undercover."

"I understand. You will go to great lengths to solve a crime. But do not try to solve this crime."

Anna cocked her head to look at him, hat slightly askew. "Why not? Officer Singer will come around."

"Chinatown is not your world. If I had my way, the LAPD would not be involved at all. We have our own way of punishing transgressors."

"You forget, the victim is a white woman. That's my world, Mr. Jones."

"If you arrest a Chinese man and bring him to court before a white jury, guilty or not, he'll be sentenced to hang. And it won't stop there. All of Chinatown will be punished."

"I'm going to solve the crime."

His sad mouth stilled for a moment. "If I can't dissuade you, then promise me this. I want to be kept apprised of this investigation. Whatever you discover, you must tell me first, before you tell anyone."

Anna laughed in disbelief. "I'll tell Detective Singer first."

"Do I have your word on that?"

"You have my word that I'll tell Detective Singer first."

"Good. Detective Singer will tell me first. And you must tell no one else."

"What makes you think you can put conditions on me. What do I get in return?"

He spoke carefully, thoughtfully. "You think the victim is a missionary. What do you know about the missionaries?"

"I suppose they preach."

"The missionaries teach the men English. Sometimes they help them find jobs. Regardless of the denomination, they're almost all women."

"Did they teach the apartment manager's wife English?"

"Do I have your word?"

Anna nodded her head.

"Yes." He shifted the car.

She groaned with realization. "They came to her apartment to give her lessons because she can't leave the building. Her husband must not know about it. That's why they looked nervous when we asked. That's why she hid it, and that's why she lied."

"Very good, for a woman."

"You must have deduced this, too, and yet you didn't say anything."

His sad face broke into a cynical smile. "I didn't have your word."

From her crouching position, Anna could see the tall buildings that towered above First Street, and the people on the sidewalk staring at the Chinese man driving the expensive car. Mr. Jones pulled the muddy Cadillac up in front of Central Station. Anna threw off the blanket and crawled back onto the seat with as much dignity as one could have when emerging from hiding with total strangers watching from the sidewalk. Mr. Jones got out and walked around the car, opening her door. Passersby glared. Like a gentleman, he escorted her to the entrance, though wisely, he didn't try to hold her arm. He bowed to

Anna, his shiny braid swinging forward like a rope. "Good afternoon, Assistant Matron Blanc."

Remembering the insult of her captivity, Anna's face reddened again. She sniffed and snapped her head around, pushing through the door. He did not follow her. Anna flounced to her desk.

Detective Wolf accosted her, holding the hand of a sniffling child. Anna guessed his age as four, though she was no expert on children. His clothes had patches upon patches, his nose was running, and he looked like he had fleas.

Wolf grinned. "Thank God you're here. This little fellow's lost his momma." He looked down at the boy and ruffled his tousled curls. "Don't you cry, son. Assistant Matron Blanc will take good care of you."

Anna stared in fear as Wolf pressed the child's grubby hand into her palm. "What do I do with him?"

"Wipe his nose, for a start. Someone will claim him."

She opened her desk drawer and retrieved a clean handkerchief embroidered with forget-me-nots. Kneeling beside the boy, she wiped his button nose. "There, there. That's it. You're all right."

He belched.

Anna's forehead wrinkled. "Bad boy."

Wolf leaned on Anna's oak desk, which was strewn with papers. "Was it a body in the trunk?"

"Yes. A, um, yes." She wrapped her arms around the child, who had begun to cry again. She squeezed. He squirmed.

Wolf nodded once. "How did it go?"

"Fine, thank you." Anna decided not to tell him Joe had handcuffed her to Mr. Jones. Though it might get Joe in trouble, it was humiliating.

"I mean, did you interview the witnesses?"

"I did. The ladies didn't know anything."

The little boy struggled out of Anna's grip, plopped to the floor, and crawled under her desk, leaving a streak of dirt on the tile. Anna frowned intensely.

Wolf grinned. "Feed him. And I think he needs a nap." He sauntered away, whistling an unrecognizable tune.

The little boy began to wail again.

"Stay here," she commanded sternly. Anna hurried into the kitchen and searched the cluttered shelves until she found Joe's dinner pail. Hoping Joe was hungry and would miss it, she returned to her desk and knelt. When she leaned in to look at the boy, he cowered. Anna pushed the pail beneath the desk. "There, there. Have some delicious . . ." She tipped the pail just a bit to look inside. "Rice."

§

Three hours later, the child was sleeping under the desk at Anna's feet, covered with a floor-length, fur-lined cape that she kept at the station for unexpected turns in the weather. No one had come to claim him, and it had nailed her to the station.

Anna read the case file of a seventeen-year-old girl picked up that morning for public drunkenness who now sobered up in a cell. The prisoner came from a large Catholic family and was the oldest of nine. Anna looked up from the file. This girl would know about children.

Anna glanced at the clock hanging on the station wall. Ten hours had passed. Surely the girl would be sober by now.

She was about to go check when Joe arrived. He sat on Anna's desk.

Her feathered lashes lowered, and she did not look up. "Apology not accepted. Do you know the cause of death?"

Joe leaned over and took her hand, grinning. "No, but have a look at this." A chain slipped through his fist and pooled in her palm. It was a swan necklace fashioned from gold, white enamel, and a spray of tiny diamonds." Anna's breath caught.

"I found it on the floor of the bedroom in Lim's apartment and figured you knew jewelry better than I do. But even I can tell that this piece is fine. It's got an inscription. 'To Martha, love Henry.' I'm guessing that was Martha I just drove to the undertaker."

Anna's fingertips went to her mouth. She placed the necklace on her blotter and pushed it away.

Joe leaned down and bent close to look her in the eye. "What's wrong, Sherlock. I thought you liked clues."

"I know that necklace. I know who the owner is."

"You do?"

"Her name is Martha Liddle, but she's too old to be the woman in the trunk. Besides, Martha must have died years ago. She was already ancient when I knew her. She wore it all of the time, and I admired it. The necklace would have been passed down to her daughter, Mrs. Bonsor . . . who is a little old to wear frillies, late thirties at least, but I suppose one can never tell." Anna's face went blank. "She has black hair."

"Was Mrs. Bonsor—is she—a missionary?"

"It wouldn't surprise me. They converted from Catholic to Protestant and were very excited about it."

"How do you know all this?"

"They are . . . *were* old family friends. Their daughter, Elizabeth, and I were close—the best of friends." Anna ran her fingertips over the sparkling swan. "We'll have to go to the Bonsors' home." She glanced up at Joe with pain in her eyes. "I hope it's not Mrs. Bonsor. She's a lovely woman. She was always very kind to me. Elizabeth would be destroyed. We never fell out, Elizabeth and I. It was our fathers."

Anna tried to reform her face into a smile. A clue was just a clue, not a certainty, not a conclusion. She dug a fingernail into her thumb to remind herself not to be weak and turned a limp smile onto Joe. He was staring at her with his eyebrows dipping. He put a tender, comforting hand on her shoulder. Then he took it off. Then he tentatively replaced it. Anna shook it off.

§

Joe went to find the Bonsors' address in the city directory, never noticing the sleeping child curled up like a puppy under Anna's desk. That suited her perfectly. If Joe knew she was babysitting, he'd never let her go.

Anna pulled the sleeping child out from under the desk by the feet and hefted him into her arms. He felt soft and, beneath the grime, smelled sweet, like a baby. She wrapped him in one of the station's itchy wool blankets, buried her face in his neck, and rocked him. Really, she rocked herself. Elizabeth's mother might have been murdered. He whimpered. Inside, Anna did the same. However lost and upset he was feeling, he couldn't feel worse than Anna. Her stomach ached with dread.

But this was no time for sentimentality. With Matron Clemens gone, Anna had to take care of the drunk girl and the motherless child, and she had a murder to solve. It was a lot to expect from an assistant matron. She wasn't a juggler.

She carried the boy to the cell in the back of the women's ward where the seventeen-year-old girl was drying out. Her name, Anna knew from her file, was Mary Mumford.

The jail cells in the ladies ward stank a harmony of bleach and urine. They comprised iron bars, cold floors, and foul messages from previous occupants scratched into the plaster. Each cell had two steel cots made up with mattresses and scratchy wool blankets.

Mary Mumford had a cell to herself. Anna found the girl sitting up on her cot looking slightly green but relatively sober. Her homemade dress was wrinkled from sleep. She wore her tousled hair in a braid, tied with a smashed bow.

Anna smiled too wide and for far too long. "Hello, Mary."

"Hello." The girl touched her disarranged hair.

Anna quickly unlocked the cell, juggling the keys and the boy. She gently laid the sleeping child down on a steel cot.

The girl rubbed her eyes. "What—"

"Thank you." Anna hurried out of the cell and locked the door. She would find a way to make it up to her.

§

The houses in the Bonsors' neighborhood were modest. Their bright Victorian colors had whitened in the sun. No autos parked on this street—no one could afford them. Children played in the road, jumping rope or throwing balls, scattering whenever a wagon approached. Dogs sniffed about hungrily. Mothers hung out laundry on lines stretched from palm tree to palm tree.

Anna marched dully beside Joe Singer, who carried a bag containing a dead woman's walking shoes. He didn't whistle or sing like he normally would. "If it's Mrs. Bonsor, they'll recognize the shoes. I couldn't ask family to view a body that decayed."

Anna's words sounded detached, like a recitation. "Mrs. Bonsor may or may not be the victim."

"They haven't filed a missing person's report. I checked. I think her family would notice if she disappeared for ten days."

"Agreed. Possibly, she lost the necklace somewhere, but it could have been stolen, or she could have sold it. I think her husband's fortunes changed, judging from the neighborhood, and she might have needed the money." Anna mechanically brushed a lock of hair from her cheek. "The family moved, and I wasn't allowed to see Elizabeth anymore. I never knew why. I haven't seen Elizabeth in ten years."

Joe stopped in front of a tired Victorian with a lawn that needed cutting. He double-checked the address. "This is it."

Anna covered her mouth with gloved fingers. "Jupiter. This can't be right." The house looked like a shoebox compared to the grand home the Bonsors had once occupied on Bunker Hill. It seemed like a matchbox compared to the even grander estate where Anna's father still lived with its marble stairs, gilded ceilings, and ocean views. An empty milk bottle stood on the front steps.

"Come on, Anna." Joe led her up the porch stairs and rapped his knuckles on the door.

Anna tapped her foot nervously. Two full minutes passed. "They can't be far. There's a milk bottle from this morning."

The door creaked open, and Mr. Bonsor stepped into view. More than ten years and the sorrow of financial ruin had diminished him. He was slight and smelled old, like turpentine. "Well, if it isn't Anna Blanc."

"Hello." Butterflies flew in Anna's stomach. She hadn't yet faced her old society friends—not since the scandal. She had diminished in her own way: socially, financially. Her reputation was in tatters. She'd become a curiosity. Though, overall, she felt she'd gained, not everyone saw it that way.

Joe stepped forward. "Good afternoon, sir."

Mrs. Bonsor glided to her husband's side like a curious ghost. Dark hair framed her patrician face, and she clutched an embroidery hoop. Half of a cross-stitched cat stared out from the circle looking frightened.

Anna's eyes widened. Mrs. Bonsor looked old, but she most certainly lived. Anna should have felt relieved to see her. But she didn't.

Joe's face showed measured relief.

Mrs. Bonsor's smile was warm but colorless, like weak tea. "Anna, how nice to see you after all these years. We saw your picture in the paper. How interesting your life has become."

She reached out and took Anna's hand.

Anna squeezed her fingers. "This is Detective Singer. We've found your necklace and have come to return it."

"We found it in Chinatown." Joe reached into his coat pocket and retrieved the swan pendant and gold chain, holding it out. "Is it yours?"

"My daughter's." Mrs. Bonsor smiled. "Thank you, Detective."

Anna felt a faint patter of distress in her chest. The lady stood aside. "Please, come in."

Anna and Joe stepped into a cramped room made even smaller by the busy floral wallpaper. Above the fireplace, from a portrait far too large for the space, a bearded man in antiquated military attire leaned on a sword and looked down at Anna with unabashed disapproval. A brass plaque on the portrait frame read "Brigadier General Franz Bonsor." Anna had forgotten Elizabeth's ancestor was a celebrated Civil War hero.

She spoke with a nervous lilt. "It's a lovely place. Is Elizabeth here?"

Mr. Bonsor said, "She's at her aunt's in St. Louis."

His wife gave him a reproachful look. Mrs. Bonsor motioned

them to a horsehair settee. Its arms were bare where the velvet had been rubbed away. When Anna and Joe sat, the couch sighed.

After his wife had left to fetch the tea, Mr. Bonsor raised his voice almost cheerfully. "What do you want with Elizabeth now after all these years? Is your conscience bothering you? Or are you here to gloat?"

Anna smiled in confusion. "I beg your pardon?"

"It was your father who reduced us to this." His hand rose and dropped. "He's responsible for my ruin." He bared his teeth at her in a bitter smile.

He was like a wasp stinging Anna for the pleasure of it as soon as his queen left the room. But maybe Anna deserved it. Had her father played a role in Mr. Bonsor's ruin? Had he called in a loan, or refused them one? Or worse?

Joe leaned forward. "I'm very sorry for your troubles, and I'm sure Assistant Matron Blanc is as well. But we are here on official police business. We need to know, when exactly did Elizabeth leave Los Angeles?"

Mr. Bonsor stared coldly. "Why are you asking these questions?"

Joe tried again. "Sir, have you seen your daughter within the last eleven days?"

Mrs. Bonsor appeared in the doorway holding a tray laden with a teapot, cups, and cakes, her face transformed by anxiety. "No, we haven't."

The tension in Anna's belly was unbearable. She cast Joe a painful, knowing glance.

"Tell me about the last time you saw her."

Mrs. Bonsor put the tray down on a table and perched on a faded armchair. Her hands were shaking. "She was leaving for my sister's for an extended visit. I had a neighbor take her things to the station in a steamer trunk."

Elizabeth was undoubtedly dead. Anna had known it all along but hadn't wanted to accept it. Martha hadn't given the necklace to her daughter but to her granddaughter. Mrs. Bonsor didn't wear frillies. Elizabeth did. There were no gray hairs in that braid, just the rich dark tones of youth. The tension in Anna's stomach unwound into nauseous grief.

Joe shifted his eyes to her as if checking for a reaction.

Anna was a cop first, and a friend second. She wasn't actually a cop, and technically she was no longer a friend, but that wasn't her fault. Anna hardened her heart and forced herself to be fine. She even smiled. She hadn't seen Elizabeth in ten years and had no right to fall apart. Mrs. Bonsor needed her. Elizabeth needed her. She nodded her strength to Joe and made a mental note to retrieve Elizabeth's steamer trunk from La Grande Station.

Joe turned back to Mrs. Bonsor. "Please, go on. Tell us about the last time you saw Elizabeth."

"She's been working as a missionary in Chinatown. My husband doesn't approve. But she is of age. They argued, and she ran from the house." Mrs. Bonsor cast an accusatory glance at her husband. "She isn't in St. Louis, and he knows it. She never arrived at her aunt's. I assumed she had run away with . . ." She trailed off and stared out the window.

"With who, Mrs. Bonsor?"

Mrs. Bonsor's eyes focused. "That Chinaman."

"Leo Lim?"

Her eyes teared. "Was that his name? They couldn't even be married under the law."

Anna had always felt a deep sadness for lovers who weren't allowed to be married, and for unlovers who were forced to be married, and for lovers who were asked to be married and were then thrown off because they wouldn't consent so that their former lovers were now courting half the girls in Los Angeles.

Joe retrieved the dead woman's walking shoes from his canvas bag. "Can you identify these shoes?"

"No," said Mr. Bonsor.

Mrs. Bonsor smiled uncertainly. "Yes, dear. Those are most definitely Elizabeth's shoes. I bought them for her."

Joe's voice was heavy and gentle with a sympathy Anna knew was sincere. "We removed the necklace from a crime scene where a woman was murdered. She was wearing these shoes. I'm sorry."

Mrs. Bonsor cried out, though she must have seen this coming. She dropped the embroidery hoop. Anna crossed the room and knelt beside her, taking her cold hands and patting them, for Elizabeth's sake. The lady rocked, making anguished sounds.

"Where was the body found?" Mr. Bonsor's voice was too loud, and his face red. If his daughter hadn't just died, Anna would think he was angry, not grieving. But men were strange that way. Her father was always angry.

Joe said, "In a trunk in Leo Lim's apartment. She'd been dead for some days."

Anna cooed at Mrs. Bonsor. "There now."

"Do you recall what else Elizabeth was wearing when she left?" Joe asked.

The lady sagged into her chair, half speaking, half sobbing her words. "Yes, because it was obviously expensive. He probably bought it for her, but I didn't ask."

"What color was it?" Anna asked.

The lady closed her eyes as if remembering her very last glimpse of her only child. "Blue. Light blue. Was the dead girl wearing blue?"

"Yes," Anna said, cutting Joe off before he could tell the hard truth, which no mother needed to hear—Elizabeth wasn't found in a dress. She was found in her frillies.

Elizabeth's body had been stripped of its frock, and the gown had been carried off. Why?

Joe said, "You were sending Elizabeth away. Was she with child?"

Anna's breath caught. The question was indelicate. In her mind, she congratulated Joe for it.

"Not with child. Out-of-control. She did as she pleased." Mr. Bonsor was trying to exonerate himself. Anna could hear it in his tone. "She was never home. She was always in Chinatown at that mission. If you ask me, we should round up the Chinese and send them all home with their opium, their gambling, and their whores."

Then, Mr. Bonsor's face collapsed, and he took a supplicating tone. "Detective, you won't tell anyone that my daughter was found in the apartment of a Mongolian. Miss Blanc owes us that much."

Joe didn't skip a beat, though Anna knew he must be enormously relieved. "We'll be discreet."

Mrs. Bonsor spoke in sorrowful hiccups. "Elizabeth felt a burden for the Chinese. She believed they were just as good as everyone else. She taught them English. And she did evangelism plays on the streets. She often played Jesus."

"She will doubtless go to heaven," Anna said, knowing Elizabeth was not Catholic and would at the very least spend years in purgatory. Anna resolved to pray for her soul.

Joe leaned forward. "Do you have reason to believe that anyone wished your daughter ill? Someone who might have wanted to hurt her?"

"What is this? The Chinaman obviously did it." Mr. Bonsor spat when he said it.

Joe spoke in a soothing voice. "He is our primary suspect, sir, but we have to be thorough."

"Everyone loved Elizabeth." Mrs. Bonsor paused to dab her nose on a handkerchief. "I suppose some people objected to having women working in the mission, associating with the Chinese men. Many people see the men as . . ." She glanced up at Anna and halted. "You are married by now, Anna?"

Anna folded her hands to hide her naked ring finger. "Yes, of course."

"People say Chinese men have greater appetites than normal men, and none of them have wives."

Anna said, "They can't fault Elizabeth for feeding them. I would feed them, too."

Mrs. Bonsor began to wail.

§

Mr. Bonsor went to Mrs. Bonsor and held her, rocking her, muttering sweet words of comfort, and calling her darling. It was a side of him Anna had never seen. She stared, even though she felt like an intruder.

Joe asked, "Mr. Bonsor, may we see your daughter's room?"

Mr. Bonsor pointed up the stairs.

Anna and Joe mounted the steps and found two doors. She opened the first and held her breath. The room was obviously Elizabeth's, full of familiar things: a porcelain doll Elizabeth had named Brave Betty, the same lace bedspread they had always used when Anna spent the night, a collection of circus postcards featuring ladies doing tricks on horseback. It reminded Anna of her own room—remnants from the past displayed in much reduced circumstances. If Mr. Bonsor were telling the truth, Anna and Elizabeth were both economic victims of Anna's cold-hearted father.

And now Elizabeth was dead.

On the wall, a cross-stitched Bible verse read, "Charity suffereth long, and is kind; charity envieth not; charity vaunteth not itself, is not puffed up."

Anna hoped Elizabeth did not suffereth long. Elizabeth had charity. Her lower lip started to quiver.

Joe was rummaging through the dresser, the bookshelf, and the desk drawer, which were mainly empty. He produced a small black diary with gold lettering, opened the cover, and a photograph fell out. He held it so Anna could see. In the picture, Anna and Elizabeth, about age eight, were having a tea party with Brave Betty and another doll, whose name Anna couldn't remember. She had had so many. Little Anna held a rolled piece of paper up to her doll's lips like a cigar. Mrs. Morales, the Blanc's housekeeper, stood in the background, frowning alongside one of Anna's nannies. Anna had had more nannies than dolls.

Joe cocked his head. "Is this you?"

Heat rose to her cheeks. "Yes."

"You're so—"

"I know." She snatched the picture from him. Anna had been scrawny and unfortunate looking until the age of twelve, at which time she had become fortunate indeed.

"Adorable," he said.

Anna's lips parted as she marveled at this. She had been ugly, but Joe Singer never lied. "Did you find any clues?"

"Just a clue to you." He opened the book. "I don't think this will help us. The last entry is 1897."

Eighteen ninety-seven, just before their friendship had come to an abrupt end.

CHAPTER 11

Anna and Joe descended the steps of the Bonsors' faded Victorian. The weight of the parents' grief clung to them like humid air. The light was graying as the sun sank closer to the horizon.

Joe slipped his arm through Anna's. "I'm sorry your friend is dead."

"Thank you. She was a good friend." Anna couldn't help but think she herself was not. She had abandoned Elizabeth for no other reason than paternal threats of . . . what? A spanking and a night without supper? Now that she had dedicated her life to doing whatever she pleased, it seemed a waste not to have begun sooner. She had loved Elizabeth. It would have been worth a licking to see her again. Maybe two or three. Given that Anna's father only caught her in mischief about a third of the time, for three bruised bottoms, she might have seen Elizabeth nine times. To be sure, they had fought on occasion, as both girls tended to know what they wanted. But Elizabeth had always kept Anna's confidences—such as when Anna had put catnip in the nuns' tea—and never spoke ill of Anna, to her knowledge.

And couldn't it just as well have been Anna in that trunk, except for the being a missionary part. After all, Anna had run off with the wrong man.

Anna felt her head tilting toward Joe's shoulder, but was saved from the intimacy by the brim of her hat.

Joe didn't appear to notice. "Do you really think your father had a part in Mr. Bonsor's ruin?"

"I don't know. He's capable of it, and it would explain the precipitous break between our families."

Joe squeezed her arm. "You're not him, Anna."

Anna looked straight ahead, because if she looked into Joe's Arrow Collar Man eyes, she would cry. "I'm going to catch her killer. I owe them that."

"No, Sherlock. I'm going to catch the killer. You're going to keep yourself safe. Plus, don't you have prisoners to take care of?"

A woman, apron coated in flour, stepped out on a porch and rang a cowbell to call her children home for supper. Four little beasts came running.

"Only one, and she doesn't need me. You need me. We have to interview the apartment manager's wife again. She lied about not knowing Elizabeth. The missionary women have been teaching her English. Mr. Jones told me so."

"I don't like you being in Chinatown. Not now."

"It's my assignment. You don't get to choose for me."

Joe closed his eyes. "All right. Maybe her husband will be home. We need to interview him as well. I'll try to contact Mr. Jones and see if he will come to translate."

"His English is very good."

"Yep. He went to Yale."

Anna's well-groomed eyebrows met in the middle. "Yale?"

"We'll go in the morning. It's safer."

"Murder can't wait!"

"I've been invited for supper at . . ." He mumbled, "Um, someone's house. I said I'd go. I'll only stay an hour or so."

She dropped his arm.

Chapter 12

Joe escorted Anna back to the station without touching or further conversation. He made a phone call at the exchange desk and left, undoubtedly off to play beau to one of his many sweethearts. Anna had better things to do than to moon over Joe Singer. She perched at her desk, took up a fountain pen, and scrolled an account of their interview with the Bonsors in her monogrammed, leather-bound notebook. Stowing it in her drawer, she decided to see how the lost boy was getting along. Anna felt a twinge of guilt about saddling the girl prisoner with the four-year-old boy, though one could argue that the girl owed a debt to society for her crime. Still, in penance, Anna collected a box of Cracker Jacks from her desk drawer. She hesitated and then grabbed two boxes, wincing with the pain of her own generosity. Charity suffereth. She said a silent prayer to Saint Aloysius Gonzaga, patron saint of the young, that Wolf would never find out about her nursemaid scheme.

A patrolman passed her, heading for the kitchen, smelling of wool and cigarette smoke. She inclined her head in greeting. "Hello Officer Bowen."

He touched his helmet and wished her a good evening in a booming, baritone voice. Anna guessed he'd stayed in doing paperwork and now went to raid his dinner pail. Most patrolmen dined in restaurants on their beats because no one ever charged them.

Her own stomach growled. If only the cooks of the city would feed police matrons, too.

The station's tile floor shone, recently mopped by the prisoner who cleaned the building—someone in for a minor offense. The cells at the back of the station now smelled like bleach and ox-head soup. It was the supper hour. Behind bars, one of the cots distracted Anna. The sheet looked dark in the middle from the dirt of men, and mud stained on one end, as if a prisoner had gone to bed wearing boots. The dirty linens were long overdue to be changed and washed, and Matron Clemens was probably counting on Anna to handle it. But who normally washed the linens? Anna didn't know. Not Matron Clemens. She could get the girl prisoner to help make the beds, but one prisoner couldn't do all the washing on her own. Also, Wolf was bound to free the girl soon. Anna would ask Mr. Melvin what to do.

In the cells, prisoners slurped broth and chewed yesterday's bread, which Mr. Melvin bought cheap from the baker. Most of the men were white or Mexican, guilty of brawling, vagrancy, or wife beating. The police suspected one of stealing a bicycle, but Anna didn't think he'd done it. His left leg dragged, and he obviously couldn't pedal. She swished down the corridor, past the men, erect and commanding—at least she tried to be. It set off a chorus of belches, followed by wicked laughter. Anna ignored them.

She climbed the stairs to the ladies' ward and approached the girl's cell surreptitiously. She peeked in from the side. When she saw her prisoner, a ripple of tension released down her back and she smiled. The boy slept in the arms of the seventeen-year-old girl, who lay on the cot with her eyes closed. Anna watched the peaceful rise and fall of his baby breath. Her guilt subsided, and she congratulated herself. She deposited the Cracker Jacks through the bars and tiptoed away.

§

Anna flounced to the reception desk to ask Mr. Melvin if he knew what to do about the dirty linens. The wood counter glowed from being touched by hundreds of hands, despite the iron rails designed to keep the guilty at a distance. Mr. Melvin, perched on a captain's chair, typed furiously at a desk behind the counter, as if his fingers had drunk too much Coca-Cola. Anna leaned over, creasing her dress on the brass rail. "Hello."

Mr. Melvin stopped typing. "Hello," he said in a whisperish hiss, not meeting her eyes, as was his custom. His pockmarked cheeks reddened.

Anna inclined her head and whispered back. "The linens are dirty."

"The prisoners can wash them. There are tin tubs and soap in the basement behind the stables. The jailer will make them do it. You just have to remind him."

Anna sighed like a bicycle tire with its cap off. It wouldn't fall to her. She leaned close over the counter. "Thank you."

"You're welcome." Without looking up he continued. "Have you seen Joe?"

The corner of Anna's lips turned down. "No, but he's meeting me soon."

Mr. Melvin stood and slipped a sheet of paper across the glossy wood counter toward Anna. "Mr. Jones asked to meet Joe in China-town at six."

Anna swept up the note and read it. "Did Joe get this message?"

"I don't know. It came while I was out."

Anna consulted the wall clock. A quarter to six. Had Joe seen the note and deliberately gone to Chinatown without her? A distinct possibility. He had only planned to stay at supper for an hour or so. Alternately, if he hadn't seen the note, then Mr. Jones would be waiting in vain.

Anna deliberated. Though she didn't relish going to Chinatown alone, it hadn't been so awful when she'd gone with Joe. There were bloodstains on the sidewalks, sure. But there must be cops in the quarter—the Chinatown Squad. The sun would shine long enough for her to reach the crime scene in daylight. Also, Mr. Jones would be there waiting at the apartments, and he was big, strong, and full of manly vigor. Joe trusted Mr. Jones with Anna in chains, and Anna trusted Joe, for the most part. She had a good feeling about Mr. Jones. A good, hot feeling. Likely, Joe was there already, or would arrive soon and could escort her home, though he would be mad.

Mr. Melvin showed Anna a handful of papers, like bookmarks, but painted with Chinese words and symbols. "Captain Dixon confiscated these on a raid in Chinatown. They're talismans."

"They're beautiful." Anna didn't believe in charms. Except for the St. Christopher's medal she sometimes wore around her neck. And holy water.

"This one is a peach blossom talisman for luck in love." He showed Anna a yellow paper covered in elegant Chinese characters, red octagons, and a square. He pulled out several more papers, which were red with black symbols. "And these are for gambling luck. Would you like one?"

"I don't gamble." She did, actually. But playing bridge for money shouldn't count.

"In a way, cops gamble with their lives protecting the city. Especially now in Chinatown. Pick one." He extended the love charm and the gambling charm.

Anna considered. Perhaps Chinese luck worked better than Catholic luck, which was, at best, unpredictable. She was a most unfortunate girl, alone in the world, about to gamble with her life in the most dangerous quarter of Los Angeles. Joe Singer didn't love her, the Chinese didn't like her. Anna desperately needed luck.

But which one? Love luck or gambling luck?

Anna's eyes focused on the love charm. She bit her lip, and pictured Joe Singer with his beautiful Arrow Collar Man face. His only real flaw was a need to get married that bordered on pathological, and that led to his faithless pursuit of other women. But every man must have a weakness. He simply needed help in reforming. He needed to be shown that Anna loved him madly, that he could still love her madly, even without marriage, as she no longer had a chaperone. Then, he would forget about his third cousin, the piano girl, and any other unsuitable person he was caressing, and return to Anna's arms.

But . . .

Chinatown was about to explode, Anna was kicked off the crime scene, the witness wouldn't speak to her, her primary suspect had probably left town. Anna wanted Joe Singer's love, but she had a murder to solve and a Chinatown to save.

"I'll take the gambling charm, please."

Mr. Melvin handed her the pretty slip of paper. "You just burn it. That's how they work."

"It's too pretty to burn." She smiled. "Thank you."

Mr. Melvin blushed at his shoes.

§

In case Joe hadn't gotten the message from Mr. Jones, Anna hurried to his desk and left the note, scribbling on the bottom for him to meet her at the crime scene. Effects from Lim's apartment sat in a box on Joe's blotter—the empty teapot, a stack of framed photographs, the severed braid, which Anna decided she would later give to the Bonsors as a memento. She saw the picture she had tried to steal from Leo Lim's apartment. She stole it now and stowed it in her desk.

Anna took the trolley to the Plaza, which was peppered with palm trees and park benches and green from the rains. She trudged across the lawn toward Chinatown. The bells of La Placita Church chimed six. Catholics, having celebrated mass, spilled through its ancient doors and scattered like beads from a broken rosary. She crossed Los Angeles Street and was back in Chinatown. Workers pulled carts or rode in farm wagons, returning home from the vegetable fields. Anna moved conspicuously among them, picking her way along the mucky sidewalk, while the men stared their curiosity.

A cop patrolled Marchessault Street in his leather helmet and blue coat, his face set in a scowl. Officer . . . she didn't know. He swung his billy club. She tipped her hat low to cover her face and crossed to the other side of the street. She wasn't supposed to be there alone. She also avoided the white men who had come slumming, and who Joe said were such a threat. They weren't all unshaven rabble. Some wore proper evening clothes, but most appeared to have been drinking. Chinese men stood at the doors to shady-looking joints and called out in heavy accents, "American. American, come play." Periodically, she heard bells ring. Then, the men calling from the gambling dens would quiet. Anna wondered about the bells, why they rang and why they stopped.

On Juan Street the chop suey joint below the crime scene teemed with diners. A table of Chinamen stared at her through the window. Anna kept her head down and slunk through the door leading to the apartments. The entryway had been aired out and no longer smelled like death, merely like chop suey. She mounted the creaking stairs and turned down the clean, though dilapidated hallway. She expected to see Mr. Jones leaning his bulk against the wall looking sullen and striking, either standing with Joe or waiting for him. No one was there. Perhaps they were already inside.

Anna knocked at the witness's apartment. When no one answered, she called out, "Hello? Mrs. Lo?" She could see light seeping out from under the door, and a shadow crossed the peephole, but when she knocked again, no one opened. Joe and Mr. Jones were obviously not there, and she suspected that Mrs. Lo had not forgiven Anna for her earlier gaffe. Perhaps the husband would speak to Joe, if only Joe and Mr. Jones would show up.

A chair stood in the hall. Anna sat down to wait. Her stomach ached with shrinking. She regretted giving her supper to the girl prisoner and lost boy. Her eyes traced a stain down the wall, and then trained on a pair of tiny slippers set neatly by the doormat—the ones the lady had worn earlier. Anna couldn't help but pick up the peculiar things for a closer look. They were lovely, sized to fit a doll, but they smelled foul. Not the ordinary shoe smell, but like a wound. Anna dropped them. A piece of paper stuck to the bottom fluttered off, laying face up on the floor. It appeared to be a laundry ticket. Anna brightened with an idea. It would be difficult to retrieve one's clothes from a laundry if one had lost one's ticket.

She stooped to pick it up, pinching it between two fingers. Chinese characters ran up and down the sides. The top had torn off, but in the middle it read:

> *Government Licensed Laundry Man*
> *Three Cents One Piece For Big Dollars.*
> *And Turned Serge, Suit and Bry Clean.*
> *And Retape Collars.*

She knocked, much harder and longer this time. "Mrs. Lo, I have your laundry ticket." No one answered.

Anna dropped the laundry ticket. Then she picked it up again. It couldn't belong to the manager's wife. Judging from the state of her servant's hands, they did laundry in-house. Since the woman never went out into the streets, it likely belonged to a tenant. Anna doubted that the woman routinely entered the men's apartments. Judging from the state of Lim's rooms, no one cleaned regularly, or irregularly for that matter. The landlady either picked the ticket up in the hallway, or on Leo Lim's sticky floor when she came in to investigate the stench. Anna scanned the corridor, which had been scrubbed clean again since the afternoon. Anna's money was on Lim's sticky floor.

If the ticket did in fact belong to Lim, Anna could find the laundry and see if he would come back for his clothes. If Anna's fine clothes were at the laundry, she would certainly retrieve them—fugitive or no.

Anna waited another hour for Joe and Mr. Jones, knocking periodically at Mrs. Lo's door. No one was coming. She tried the door of the apartment where the body had been found. Joe had locked it. Then she trudged down the stairs into the street.

The sun was long gone, and she could see her breath. Rain clouds blocked the moon. Bawdy music played in some nearby saloon, and she heard the crash of a breaking window. She ought to call the station and have Joe come to collect her, but he would be angry and she didn't know where to find a telephone. They didn't give matrons keys to the police call boxes. She knew one thing for sure; she didn't want to linger in Chinatown after dark.

The chop suey joint glowed on the first floor of the apartment building. Inside, every table was occupied. Chopsticks pinched noodles in competent fingers. She peered through the glass. The food on the diners' plates did not look like the chop suey made by her father's cook from spaghetti noodles and tomato sauce. It looked much, much better. There were heaping plates of vegetables, chicken livers, gizzards, and tripe, all piled atop steaming noodles. Her mouth watered.

Keeping a low profile did not include eating alone in an all-male, all-Chinese establishment. On the other hand, fainting from hunger wouldn't do either. But she had given most her money to the old laundress in exchange for nothing. The man whose plate Anna coveted noticed her staring through the window and cocked his head as if she were the strange one. She quickly turned and bustled toward home.

She approached Most Lucky Laundry, where Ma Yi-jun had been washing windows. The steam was gone, and the lanterns were dark. It was the closest laundry to Leo Lim's apartment. Possibly he took his clothes there.

Anna pressed her face to the glass. Even if the lady were there, Anna didn't care to pay the laundry bill to retrieve Leo Lim's clothes. The wrinkly dog burst out of the dark, teeth bared, and charged the inside window barking viciously. Anna squealed and jumped back.

"Jupiter!" She put a hand on her chest and breathed. The dog kept barking, and Anna feared he would break through the glass.

She hurried away, planning to return in the morning with Joe and his wallet.

"*Sei gwai por!*" The words pinged with a heavy Chinese accent.

Anna turned. Ma Yi-jun had stuck her head through the door.

Anna lifted her chin and walked slowly and deliberately down the street. Ma Yi-jun scurried after her, wrapping herself in a quilted coat. She put one crooked hand on Anna's shoulder. Anna could feel the woman's delicate fingers, like bird bones. She stopped and spun around. "What? What do you want? Another dollar? Because I don't have a dollar, and I couldn't eat chop suey because of you, so don't pretend we're friends."

A drunken whoop escaped from the door of a nearby saloon. "*Sei gwai por*. Your clothes are dirty. You need laundry done."

Anna looked down at her skirt, with the marks from her scuffle with Joe on the floor. She colored. "Yes, I'm sure I do, but laundry service is not in my budget, thank you very much. And I can't walk through Chinatown naked." Anna pulled out the laundry ticket. "If you want to help me, I'd like to pick up my clothes and pay tomorrow. Honor system."

"Laundry is closed."

"So now you won't help me? Well then, good night!" Anna put the ticket in her pocket, adopted a regal bearing, and glided off.

"Watch out, *sei gwai por*," she heard Ma Yi-jun say.

When Ma Yi-jun was out of sight, Anna slunk. She wished she had more eyes and could watch all around her all at once. She was a woman alone at night in the heart of LA's vice district. Venturing out without Joe or Mr. Jones had been a mistake, though she would never admit it to Joe. At night, Chinatown oozed with threat, and the later the hour, the drunker the men who came slumming.

This deep into the quarter, most of the men were Chinese. They watched her as she passed them, saying things she didn't understand. Some had hungry eyes, like Mrs. Bonsor said, making Anna pull her cape tighter. But most simply looked curious or wary. An old-timer with a gray pigtail and no arm in one sleeve trailed along behind her, snapping sharply at anyone who dared speak to her. Did he fear her safety or for the safety of Chinatown if a white woman was harmed? After a few blocks, she glanced around and her strange guardian angel had vanished.

Chinese men called out from the lotteries, beckoning players, and girls called from brothel windows. Anna rushed along, head down, to the brewery, a large industrial building, which was closed at night and unlit. Bestial grunting sounds emanated from the side of it. She dared not look but jogged on.

Anna headed west toward the sordid playground of Alameda Street patronized by all races. Every distant shout and whoop from the barrooms seemed to be for her, every footfall her pursuer. Even the wind seemed to follow her, caressing her through her cape like a cold hand. Anna shuddered.

Anna turned a corner and stumbled to a stop. The hair on her scalp stiffened, and an icy tide rushed up her spine. She froze but for the trembling of her hands.

Illuminated by the hellish glow of red lanterns, a fistful of thugs in black hats and black tunics stood on either bank of the mucky road, the nearest not ten feet away. Highbinders—no doubt Bing Kong and Hop Sing, mad about the stolen singsong girls and the power play that the theft represented. The air crackled with menace as they postured. It seemed a mere spark would ignite their violence, and Anna would be caught in the midst of it. Not just Anna, but any drunken fool who stumbled by or who played in the adjacent joints.

Anna flattened herself against the wall, eyes so wide they watered. Hatchet men, people called them. Likely, one of them had chopped up Ko Chung, slowly, to maximize his terror and pain. They had thrown his pieces in the river. Tonight she didn't see their hatchets, but their tunics were blousy enough to hide guns.

Anna inched along the wall, back toward the brewery and the beast noises, melting into the shadows, putting distance between herself and the highbinders until she could no longer see them. Until they could not see her. She hastened between a walk and a run.

Opium smoke perfumed the lane, syrupy and floral, causing her to stop her breath again lest she become a dope. It made her feel lightheaded. Across the street, Anna saw a cigarette glow in the doorway of a darkened building. The cigarette, perhaps innocent, began moving in her direction.

Up ahead, a slobbering group of bounders crossed the road, engaged in an embrace that was five men long. They sang, "When I was a little lad or so my mammy told me. Way haul away, we'll haul away Joe. That if I didn't kiss the girls, me lips would all grow moldy." Sailors. If Anna didn't hurry, their paths would cross, and she'd be trapped between the cigarette man and a drunken game of red rover. She pivoted down a slim street, along a string of cribs with windows barred to keep the girls inside.

The cigarette man now trotted behind her. Anna quickened her steps to a lope. He slapped the wooden sidewalk faster. She was afraid to scream—afraid the highbinders would come or the drunken sailors. Her odds were better one-on-one. Anna twisted to glance behind her and assess the threat. The smoking man dropped his cigarette and lunged. His fist shot out. His punch landed hard. Anna's head snapped back. She started to fall. He grabbed her arms and drove her body against the wall. She felt dizzy and disoriented. His fingers groped for her breasts, which were mostly shielded by the armor of her corset. With his mouth so close, his spoiled-tuna-fish breath was as potent as smelling salts. Anna finally reacted, slapping him on the side of the head with her silver mesh purse. It had no weight, but surely the metal stung. Grunting, he grabbed at her purse, loosening his hold just enough for Anna to twist away and poke him in the eye with all her might. He yelled.

Anna bolted, leaving her cherished silver purse in his rotten hand. She fled unsteadily, skimming the walls where the shadows were deepest—one block, two blocks, past the cribs, gambling joints, saloons, and men, out of Chinatown, through the Plaza, not stopping until she hit the relative safety of Main Street.

She stumbled to a halt and bent over gasping, her side pinched in a stitch, her breasts burning from where the man had touched her, her head throbbing.

A rider clopped by on a Morgan horse, sending up little splats of mud. A couple stepped companionably out of a restaurant, arm in arm. A gutted seagull topped the lady's hat for decoration. It stared at Anna. Anna stared back, still dazed. The couple strolled around her, leaving her a wide berth. Possibly because she looked disreputable.

Anna straightened up. Her face ached. Her purse and money were gone. She had no trolley fare. She needed a steak for her eye. Anna let out a single sob. Holding her head with one gloved hand, she walked home.

§

It was after midnight when Anna slammed the apartment door behind her, eliciting a delayed *bang bang* on the wall from her neighbor. Her hand would not stop shaking. Her mind was racing, her body surging. She knew she wouldn't sleep that night.

Anna had taken a punch in the face. But hadn't every man in California at one time or another? In a way, shouldn't she feel initiated? She sat on her hands to hold them still. What would Joe Singer do in her position? He would swear maybe, but he certainly wouldn't cry. Anna vowed she would bear it like Joe Singer—like a cop.

Her apartment was freezing cold, but she had no coal. She looked down her front. Her uniform was filthy, and had a tear at the knee. She couldn't possibly wash it, mend it, and dry it over an empty stove, which she could not light, in time to wear it in the morning. Anna removed her shoes and stockings and padded barefoot to the kitchen, letting her toes take comfort in the soft fur rugs. She dosed herself with headache powder, swallowing the bitterness down with a dram of whiskey.

She needed her dressmaker to surrender her police bloomers, and she needed them tonight.

Across the room on a swirling art nouveau vanity, a satin pillow displayed itself like a porcupine's victim, each quill a hatpin topped with some small jewel. She climbed the summit of her giant bed, crawling across goose down on her elbows, swinging her legs onto the floor so she could reach the pins. Anna didn't know the value of her gems and hadn't planned to part with them until she'd had them appraised. She knew the emotional cost. Each was a treasure from her grandmother, mother, or father, all now lost to her through death or abandonment. Each held a memory of some semblance of love.

Now no one loved her.

She bit the edge of her thumb and selected a luminous green sapphire surrounded with seed pearls—a gift from her father upon her sixteenth birthday. As she plucked it from the pillow, it stabbed her in the heart.

Armed with the hatpin, Anna went to visit her seamstress, who lived over the shop, never mind the hour. Sleep was an impossibility. Anna knocked on the door for several minutes, and then pounded, before the dressmaker opened in her nightgown and robe. She swiped sleep from her eyes and demanded, "What is it?"

Anna, garbed disreputably and smelling of whiskey, somberly held out her hatpin. "Collateral."

CHAPTER 13

The next morning, Anna's head pounded like a tuba's oom-pa-pa. She rolled from bed, put her feet on the furry rug, and maneuvered her way past the grand piano into the corner kitchen. Her fingers were white with cold. A family of cockroaches scattered, their tiny legs skittering across the floor. Anna swatted at them madly with last Sunday's *Los Angeles Times*, but they disappeared into the walls. She squeaked in frustration.

Positioning herself by the idle stove, she consumed a tin of kippers and stuck a box of Cracker Jacks into her pocket for later. Thanks to her ill-conceived generosity, she would have to make them last all day.

She donned her new police bloomers and matching overskirt, which was slit in front, almost to the waist. She tied the ribbons that decorated the ankle of each bloomer, and wandered over to a gilt wall mirror to admire the ensemble. She froze in horror. The man's fist had left a bruise on her eye that was now a proper shiner. She looked like a wife with an angry husband. Part of her wanted the cops at the station to know she could take a punch, that she wasn't weak. But the memory was too horrific. She wanted to forget it. More importantly, her bruise screamed that Joe Singer had been right. She frantically rubbed her cheeks and eyelids with glycerin, and brushed on chalk dust to whiten her haggard face, but the marks couldn't be disguised by powder alone. She simply looked cadaverous. Anna groaned. She would have to resort to a veil, which hardly anyone wore, except for people's mothers. She would have to give her hair extra attention to make up for it. Anna found her own mother's veil in a trunk. She twisted her long locks up into a bun, and capped it with an elaborate yak hairpiece. She attached the veil to a grand hat trimmed with ribbon and artificial berries and settled it atop her coiffure.

Anna rode her personal bicycle to the station; her lace veil clung to her bruised, powdered face like a spider's web. She had two goals for the day—to return to Chinatown to persuade the witnesses to give her an interview, preferably with Joe, and to find the laundry where Lim had left his clothes—possibly Most Lucky Laundry, possibly not. While she was in Chinatown, she would also keep her eyes and ears open for the stolen singsong girls, though she wasn't sure what to look for. Joe would know. Then there was Ko Chung. Anna felt no need to find justice for the man, yet she was curious. And since she would be in Chinatown already . . .

She arrived at the station and found Wolf leaning with his elbow down on the shiny oak counter. He grinned. "Well, good morning, honeybun." He looked her up and down and wrinkled his brow. "That's an, er, interesting uniform. Has Matron Clemens seen it?"

"Yes, of course," Anna lied. "It enables me to ride my bicycle with greater freedom. I'm sure she'll have one made, too."

Wolf grinned. "And the veil?"

"It looks nice." It didn't.

Wolf nodded but seemed unconvinced. "How is that sweet little boy?"

Anna's eyes expanded to the size of bicycle wheels, her panic concealed by the veil. She'd forgotten about him. She gasped, then stammered, "Fine."

"I noticed he's not with you."

Anna nodded her head up and down, up and down, until she settled on a fabrication. "He went home."

Wolf nodded too, squinting. "Good."

"Excuse me." Anna bobbed a curtsy and marched rapidly toward the back of the station, holding her head up high as if she wasn't in a hurry. She swished through the door, around the corner, into the jail, and up the stairs.

The girl's cell was vacant but for a chamber pot, cots, and two empty boxes of Cracker Jacks.

Anna made a sound of distress. With great trepidation, she slunk out across the station, to the reception counter where Mr. Melvin typed furiously at his desk, fingers flying like a whirligig in a windstorm.

The storm stopped. His eyes rested on his Remington. He spoke softly to the keys. "The little boy was reunited with his mother last night."

Anna shifted on her feet. "The young lady offered to watch him for me, because Joe needed me to . . . Joe needed me. And she's very good with children. I meant it to be just for a little while." Anna's eyebrows formed a teepee. "You aren't going to tell Matron Clemens are you? Or Wolf? Or the Captain? They'll wipe up the floor with me."

"I would never."

"And the girl?"

"Wolf released her after the boy had gone."

Anna let out a huge breath of relief. Wolf sauntered over carrying a steaming cup of coffee, wafting his lavender cologne.

She quickly changed the subject. "Detective Wolf, has the Chinatown Squad found the missing singsong girls yet?"

"No, but they've been searching diligently for weeks."

"Good. When they do find them, I suppose they'll deliver them into my care since Matron Clemens is gone." And the girl in the cell could no longer offer her services. Actually, Anna looked forward to the task, though she had no idea what one did with singsong girls. Maybe they would send the girls to stay with her until they found a safe place for them. Maybe they would make her chop suey. Then Anna remembered her tiny apartment and frowned. It would be awfully crowded.

Wolf said, "No, I'm afraid they won't. They're going to return them to their owner."

Anna gave Wolf a confused smile. "What?"

Detective Snow lumbered up, fingering a pimple on his neck. A cluster of ugly scars marred his face like cracks in shattered glass. He snorted. "The Bing Kong president has offered a one-thousand-dollar reward to the person who returns them, and the Chinatown Squad wants the money. That's a lot of money for a couple of Chinks."

"Hah!" Anna said. Joe was on the Chinatown Squad. He did lots of stupid things, but he wouldn't trade girls for a reward. She said, "That's preposterous. Joe Singer is not a slave trader."

Wolf said, "Slave trader is such a harsh way to put it."

Anna smiled and shook her head. "But Joe hasn't been hunting the slave girls. He's not going to turn them in no matter what the others do."

Snow snorted again and lumbered off to do whatever he did for his money.

Wolf cleared his throat. "Joe's just trying to keep the peace."

"What could you possibly mean?"

The detective's brow folded like an accordion. "Honeybun, if they don't return the girls to their owner, there's going to be a tong war. Innocent people will die in the crossfire. Captain Dixon has decided the squad has to return the girls, so they may as well keep the money."

Anna frowned hard, trying to grasp the idea that her Joe, or the man who was once her Joe, could do anything so vile as deliver girls into the hands of an evil slave owner. And for money. Anna quickly decided he could not.

She tilted her chin heavenward. "I don't believe it. Where is Officer Singer? I'm going to ask him."

He grinned. "He's in the hoosegow. Would you mind bringing him his lunch?"

§

Anna walked the two blocks between Central Station and the Los Angeles County Jail. The benefits of nepotism had a flip side. The police chief was grooming his son for greater things and gave him special opportunities, but he also held Joe to a higher standard, especially when it came to the appearance of impropriety. Chief Singer had an inconvenient habit of throwing his son in jail whenever he caught Joe going to a certain parlor house to play piano, even though half the cops, all the police commissioners, and even the mayor, were regulars. Anna knew this from her time investigating undercover in the brothels, for which she had been shamed, groped, and temporarily sacked.

Anna almost understood Joe's behavior. He was as passionate about music as Anna was about trapping criminals, and when Joe played ragtime, even Baptists danced. There were two Steinway grands at Canary Cottage, while Joe's tinny wreck of a piano had no middle C. Joe said he never, ever went with the girls, and Joe Singer was truthful to a fault. Anna believed him. Even so, she fumed. He should have been with her solving the crime last night, not out making love to his sweetheart and playing piano.

The jailer escorted Anna into the concrete and iron cave where horse thieves and bank robbers served their sentences. A mesh of bars enclosed the long corridor, even the ceiling. From the smell of things, the chamber pots needed to be emptied. The chief always sent Joe here, and not to the jail at Central Station, where he might get preferential treatment.

As Anna walked the length of the corridor, the inmates greeted her with whistles, welcoming words, marriage proposals, and vile suggestions. Anna adored the jail, which was full of fascinating criminal minds, as long as she stood on the right side of the bars. She continued down the row, past the cage where she herself had once languished, and easily found Joe's cell. He looked hungover from the night before. His red eyes widened when he saw her coming in her veil and police bloomers, and he moved to the door of the cell. He looked happy to see her. "Is that you, Sherlock?"

Anna laid one hand on the iron bars, and said nothing. She had nothing to say. She set down his lunch pail.

"What? No, 'Hello, I'm sorry you're in the hoosegow?'" He had stubble on his dimpled face. He smelled like a saloon.

"You went on a bash last night instead of meeting Mr. Jones to interview the apartment manager and his wife. You should be out getting busy, but here you are rum crazed. And how am I going to get my Juicy Fruit?"

"I sent Jones a message and said I had a supper engagement and

I'd meet him later at his apartment. I looked for you at the station, but Mr. Melvin said you had gone. I went to Mr. Jones's home, but nothing doing. I looked for him in every saloon on Alameda Street."

"I'm sure."

"Canary Cottage was on the way home, but I didn't go in. I didn't get that far. Officer Clark was going in at the same time. He arrested me on the doorstep."

Anna bowed her head and rubbed her tender temple. "You knew if your father caught you you'd get thrown in the hoosegow. You jeopardized the case by going to the brothel. You could have played my piano. It's as good as the ones at Madam Lulu's Canary Cottage. Better even."

"Sherlock, I'm terrified of playing your piano. I'd never set foot in your apartment. Not unless I had a chaperone. Anyway, I needed to play." His brows drew together. "I don't like courting. I needed to blow off steam. You've got the opposite effect."

Anna lifted her chin. "You've got nothing to fear from me. I have no intention of steaming you up." Actually, she couldn't think of a single time in all of their acquaintance when they had been alone together in private and didn't end up kissing. Even the first time. Especially the third time. And the fifth time . . . Thinking about it made her feel steamy.

Joe considered her ensemble and smiled, his lips cocked to one side, making his dimples even deeper. "Sherlock, you look like a cross between a harem girl and a nun." He stuck one arm through the bars, and lifted her veil.

"No." Anna grabbed for his wrist too late.

When he saw her pale, bruised face, the rosiness left his dimpled cheeks and his sideways smile melted away. "Holy cow." He took her chin in his hand, gently moving her head from side to side and narrowing his eyes. "Who did this to you? Because I'm going to kill him."

Anna felt pleased at his distress, and considered swooning, but they had a crime to solve and a villain to catch, so she exercised restraint. "I walked into a pole."

"Sherlock, you gotta be more careful." He felt her cheek, caressing it like a very gentle, very thorough doctor. It made Anna's eyelids heavy. If she had known how he would react to her bruises, she would have gotten a black eye sooner. She would have gotten a black everything. She leaned into his hand. His brows were drawn in concentration as his fingers traveled down her cheek, to her jaw, feeling to make sure everything was right. Anna's whole body thrilled. She liked playing doctor with Joe Singer.

"Does it hurt?" he asked.

"A little. I can't believe your father threw you in jail. Isn't he concerned about the case? Chinatown's about to blow up, etcetera."

Joe dropped his hand from Anna's face. "He doesn't believe in wearing gum shoes and analyzing cigarette ash. We're putting Leo Lim's picture in the paper and sending wanted posters to every train station, harbor, post office, and police station in the state. The whole country if we have to. My pop says the rest of the investigation can wait."

"But it can't wait. What if Leo Lim is in hiding here in Los Angeles? We need to canvass Chinatown. What did your cousin say? Did he do the autopsy?"

"No apparent cause of death."

"Maybe he poisoned her tea."

"Don't go to Chinatown. It's dangerous. Things are heating up. Captain Dixon just got another death threat. The Bing Kong president is still mad about his missing singsong girls. It's just a matter of time before bullets fly . . ."

"We can't both abandon the case." Anna hitched the strap of a tooled leather purse up into the crook of her elbow and turned to leave.

"Stop. Anna. I'll go with you. We can solve it together."

"I can't wait for you to get sprung from the hoosegow. We don't have time. How long before Wolf assigns the case to another dick? Someone else might not keep it secret. You said yourself that if word gets out, Chinatown will explode." Anna began to walk away.

"Come on, Sherlock."

Anna waved her hand in the air dismissively.

"What can I do to change your mind?"

"Nothing." She flipped her veil down and stopped as she had an afterthought. She walked to the cell. "Tell me. What does '*sei gwai por*' mean?"

Joe chuckled. "Why?"

"The old lady called me '*sei gwai por*.'"

He grinned. "White devil. She must know you." Then his face became serious again. Anna was holding the rusty bars. He covered her hands with his own. "It can also mean ghost. Don't go to Chinatown."

She tugged to free her fingers. "How many suits of clothing would a Chinaman have?"

"You mean Leo Lim? I don't know. He looks like kind of a dandy in his photographs."

"How many do you have? No, that won't work. You're not a dandy. You're just the opposite. How many undergarments?"

"You're asking me about my underwear?"

"Don't be coy. This is for police purposes only."

"Six."

"Then they would last you six days."

"That depends. I don't always wear underwear. Not if it's hot."

Anna's eyes opened wide. "Taffy." She grinned and knew it was a silly grin. She put a hand over her mouth to hide it. "Then why do I have to wear so many?"

Joe blushed. "Men just don't. Why are you asking me this?"

Anna was glad that he could not read her mind, because she was trying to picture Joe Singer in his drawers. And out of them. She lassoed her wayward mind and tried to think about the crime. "Do you save up all of your underwear and then take them to the laundry, or do you make frequent trips?"

"I save up. Anna, what's your point?"

"I found a laundry ticket on Mrs. Lo's shoe. I believe it belongs to Leo Lim."

"Or it belongs to Mrs. Lo."

"No. Her servant girl washes her clothes. She couldn't have picked it up in the streets because she never goes outside. The hall was very clean. Lim's floor was sticky. Thus, she probably picked it up in Leo Lim's apartment."

"Go on."

"He's a dandy and has very nice clothes, undoubtedly custom made. If most of his clothing is at the laundry, I don't think he'd leave them behind. I wouldn't. Especially if I'm out of clean drawers. I plan to find the laundry and see if he's picked up his clothes. If he hasn't, and he's still in Chinatown, he might return for them or send someone to bring them to his hiding place. We can lie in wait and . . ."

Joe's eyes flashed. "Wait. You went back to Chinatown last night? Without me? Is that where you got the bruise?"

"No."

"Promise me you won't do that."

"I won't. Promise." Anna crossed her fingers.

Joe sighed and laid his forehead against the bars. "You make me crazy, Sherlock, but I don't know what I'd do if anything ever happened to you. I need you in the world. Do you understand?"

A warm, confused feeling flooded Anna's whole body. She said, "No." She didn't understand.

"Never mind."

She said, "What do you know about the missionaries?"

"There are eight churches active in Chinatown. They have a sort of consortium, the Chinatown Society for Christian Evangelism. It's run by a missionary lady who used to work in China. Her name is Eunice Puce. Her husband was beheaded during the Boxer Rebellion, and she's a little bit cuckoo. Mrs. Puce would know Elizabeth."

"Address, please?"

"That's where I draw the line."

"You can't stop me from hunting Elizabeth's killer, especially not with you in the hoosegow. I'll interview the missionaries, even if I have to deduce their address. I found the crime scene, didn't I?"

Joe growled.

The jailer came by with a mop and bucket and began cleaning the floor behind Anna.

She lowered her voice. "Wolf says you're hunting the singsong girls so you can give them back to their owner, and the Chinatown Squad plans to split the reward. But I didn't believe him."

The jailer hovered about them, an unwelcome third party. Anna wondered if he was spying for Joe's father, or if he simply had bad manners. She gave him a pointed, dirty look.

Joe glanced at the jailer and said cautiously, "Those are the captain's orders."

Anna gaped, bedoozled. "So it's true? You're a slave trader?"

"That's one opinion." Joe's face was reddening.

Anna let out a cry of disbelief and wondered if she knew anything at all about the world.

He groaned. "Sherlock, I'm on the Chinatown Squad. We exist to keep the peace."

"You don't have to sell those girls to keep the peace. There are plenty of other ways to prevent a tong war."

"Well, I'd like to hear them."

"You could arrest the tong presidents."

"They'd never get convicted. They have too many judges in their pocket."

"You could shoot the tong presidents."

"They'd get new presidents and send a hatchet man to kill me. When Captain Dixon shut down one of their gambling joints, they poisoned his milk. Anna, his cat died from it."

"You could rescue the girls, set them free, and let the tongs kill each other."

"That's not really preventing a tong war, is it?"

Anna made a sound of frustration. "And so you're just going to sell those poor girls?"

"Sherlock, it isn't just the tongs who get killed in a gang war. Innocent people are caught in the crossfire."

"Well, tell them to duck."

Joe threw back his head and laughed. "I'll tell Dixon you said so."

Anna hissed. "If you don't stop, you're going to go to hell."

"I'm in hell."

"You know something? I don't care. I can't believe I ever even liked you, much less loved you. In fact, I didn't. I take it all back. And you were right. I never was going to marry you. Ever."

Joe flinched at her words. "You know what, Anna? For once I believe you."

Anna took Joe's lunch pail, opened the lid to his food and spit in it. She wasn't good at spitting, and it dribbled down her chin. Joe's lunch was a rice dish.

Joe cried out, "Hey!"

She set it back on the floor just beyond his reach, spun about, and stomped out of the cellblock, through the doors of the reception area, and out onto the street. She put her fist to her mouth and uttered a single, empty sound of despair.

§

As Anna descended the stone front steps of the county jail, a slender woman in a neat blue suit ascended, her thick, wavy hair peeking from beneath a feather hat. The woman closely watched the hem of her skirt as if to avoid tripping. She carried a basket covered with a green cloth, and Anna could smell the enticing scent of fried liver. The girl raised her head as she passed, nodding to Anna, and for the first time, Anna saw her face.

It was the piano girl, one of Joe's sweethearts. Her father owned the music store. She wasn't the prettiest of Joe's girls—her nose was a bit too large—but she sang the best and played the piano almost as well as Joe. Anna herself had neglected to practice.

"Hello," said the piano girl, and smiled, brightening her brown eyes. Her smile was warm, intelligent, and awful.

"Hello." Anna couldn't muster a smile.

§

The day felt very, very cold, and there was nothing in Anna's heart to warm her. Just a tinkling of hope that she could find the singsong girls on her own and help them to escape, and that Joe Singer did not like liver. But Anna had no idea where to look. And who did not like liver?

Was Joe so cozy with the piano girl that he would send for her when his father had him arrested? Apparently so. The piano girl would understand the allure of Madam Lulu's two Steinway grands.

He had not sent for Anna.

The idea of him putting his hand on the piano girl's bottom made Anna's blood freeze. And the piano girl wasn't the only lady in Los Angeles with a bottom. Joe's hands could be on many ladies' bottoms, all at the same time. Anna's brow wrinkled. She wanted Joe's hands on her bottom.

She clutched her leather purse, which contained the laundry ticket and the picture of Leo Lim. She clutched it as if it were her life because, in a sense, it was.

She felt more determined than ever to find herself a killer. Her limbs were weak with disillusionment, and Chinatown gave her the chills. But it was daylight now, and she knew what she must do. She would go back to Most Lucky Laundry. It was the likely place for Leo Lim to have his clothing cleaned because it was only three blocks from his apartment. She would confirm Mr. Lim's patronage with the old woman by showing her Lim's picture. She'd ask if the lady had seen the missing suspect and if she would alert Anna if Lim presented himself again—even if Anna had to pay a price. She would cross that bridge when she got there. Then she would find the missionaries and interview them, and then go to the train station to try to get hold of Elizabeth's luggage. She'd have to come up with a lie to explain her absence to Wolf, as her work was piling up, and she had failed to catch Jane Godfrey, the shoplifting fifteen year-old treat girl.

CHAPTER 14

Most Lucky Laundry's windows were opaque with steam, and its sign still hung at a precarious angle. Anna parked her bike and swept through the door, causing a string of brass bells to jingle. The spic and span room was barely the size of a chicken coop. A curtain hung over a doorway that led deeper into the building. Damp heat made Anna's sleeves limp. The wrinkled crone counted out money from a cash register, which rested on a surprisingly fine, carved wooden counter. A lantern burned at the end of the counter, bolstering the light that seeped in through the mist.

Anna inclined her bruised, veiled head. "Good morning, Ma Yi-jun."

The woman said, "Good morning, *sei gwai por*. Go home."

"I am Assistant Matron Blanc," she said with emphasis. "I am very much alive. Not a ghost."

"Not yet a ghost." Ma Yi-jun pushed the cash register closed and cackled. Anna wondered if the lady were laughing at her. "I'm here to pick up my laundry. This ticket is for Most Lucky Laundry, is it not?" Anna slowly handed over the laundry ticket. "Unless my, um, servant already picked up the clothes. Have you seen my servant?" Anna produced the picture of Leo Lim, watching the crone's eyes for a telltale sign of recognition.

The old woman tilted her head and peered at Anna with a questioning brow. Then she hobbled to the brass lamp at the end of the counter, put on a pair of reading glasses, and held the ticket up to the light. Under the glow, the ticket became translucent. Anna could see a faint outline of red words on the paper—words she had not noticed before.

Ma Yi-jun's face became unnaturally flat and bland, like the face of a card sharp. Anna stretched her neck to see. "What does it say?"

The lady returned the laundry ticket to Anna. "Your errand boy already came for his clothes, but he didn't pay. Broke in after dark eight days ago."

Anna lit up. "That's grand."

Ma Yi-jun extended her hand palm up. "You pay now. One dollar."

For a moment, Anna's good breeding directed her. Her fingers hovered over the latch to her leather purse, and her mind reached for something of value that Anna could give the woman—her fountain pen? Her empty billbook? Anna stopped her hand and collected herself. If she were to be poor, she was going to act the part. "I think not." She bobbed a curtsy and sashayed out of the shop to the tinkle of bells, rather pleased with herself for resisting the woman.

She turned and examined the lock on the outside of the door. Scratch marks on the rusty metal suggested that someone had, in fact, picked the lock.

Anna had been right. Leo Lim had collected his clothes eight days ago, at least three days after the murder. He could still be hiding in town. She needed to find the missionaries. They might know something about Leo Lim and where she might sniff him out.

Anna reasoned that if she were a missionary, she wouldn't live on Alameda Street, Juan Street, or any of the seedier roads. That would be too dangerous. She'd live as far from the heart of Chinatown as possible. Thus, she began on the outskirts, peddling her bike down Los Angeles Street. She encountered the mission on the block between Arcadia and the Plaza. It lay southwest of Chinatown, on the very edge of the red-light district. There were Congregational and Presbyterian churches, the Sun Wing Wo General Store, and a tidy brick building with a sign posted high above the door that read "The Chinatown Society for Christian Evangelism." A Chinese school tinkled with the voices of children—the sons and daughters of prostitutes and wives.

Anna trudged up the stone stairs to the landing and knocked. A young white lady holding an orange kitten opened the door. She had round spectacles, pink lips, and a necktie, and looked nowhere near as courageous as she truly must be to work in Chinatown. She also looked vaguely familiar.

The girl's attention flitted from Anna's veil, to the homemade bloomers peeking from the slit in Anna's skirt, and back again. She smiled bemusedly.

Anna flipped her veil and lifted her chin. "Good morning, I am Assistant Matron Blanc. I'm here to see Mrs. Puce."

The girl's eyes widened in a look of undisguised shock. Anna imagined this reaction was due to Anna's identity and not just her pantaloons or black eye. This saintly missionary likely read the newspapers and knew of Anna's unconventional crime-fighting measures. Anna braced herself for a reprimand, but the young lady simply stood aside so that Anna could enter.

The room resembled the living room at the convent where Anna had attended school, plainly but comfortably furnished with an organ, rocking chairs, and an afghan draped over the back of a settee. An arrangement of dried seedpods sat on the mantle below a painting of Jesus. He was not hanging on a cross in his underwear—bloody and beaten—like most Jesuses Anna had seen. He looked pretty, like a girl, only with a beard. Anna crossed herself.

A middle-aged woman dressed in mourning reclined on a chaise, smiling beatifically. A plain silver tea set lay before her on the table, along with a dish of lemon and a plate of fancy shortbread cookies. She did not rise, but must have overheard the conversation at the door because she addressed Anna by name. Her words were languid, and her eyes were a dazzling amber with small pupils that made them look like sunflowers. "Welcome Assistant Matron Blanc, I am Eunice Puce."

Anna extended a hand, but the lady still did not rise. Anna let her hand drop. "Mrs. Puce, are you unwell?"

"Quite. Did you by any chance bring honey?"

"No. I'm sorry." Apparently, Mrs. Puce was not merely odd but completely cuckoo. If this was what having a husband beheaded did to a woman, Anna must avoid it at all costs—one more reason not to marry Joe Singer and put herself at risk. Anna tried to reproduce the woman's beatific smile. "Mrs. Puce, I must ask you a few questions."

Mrs. Puce closed her eyes, smiling. Anna looked to the bespectacled girl for help.

The girl cradled the orange kitten. "I'm sorry. You won't get answers from Mrs. Puce this afternoon." She lowered her voice. "I'm afraid afternoons aren't good for her."

Anna wrinkled her brow. It was barely eleven o'clock.

"I would offer you tea, but I think she's finished it." The girl sat down in a rocking chair and stared at Anna dumbly.

Manners among the lower classes weren't what they could be. Anna should try harder to be rude and fit in. So she slouched.

Another young woman appeared at the top of the staircase, the light from a window falling on her golden hair. She quickly descended the steps, as if hurrying to Anna's aid. "Perhaps I can help? Miss . . ."

For a few seconds, Anna did not speak. In fact, she had forgotten her own last name. The young woman on the stairs was the very same golden-haired girl who had made eyes at Joe Singer, and whom he had leaned toward in the soda fountain. They no doubt had met in Chinatown. A lump formed in Anna's throat, like she'd swallowed a bust enhancer. Finally, she managed, "Assistant Matron Blanc. I'm with the LAPD."

If the missionary noticed Anna's bruise, she was too mannerly to stare. Anna threw back her shoulders. The girl reached the bottom of the landing, smiling a warm and genuine smile. Her teeth had a holy glow. She was as graceful as a fluttering angel and smelled like fresh laundry, baked cookies, and clean babies. She offered her hand for Anna to shake. "I'm Miss Robins. I'm so pleased to meet you, Assistant Matron Blanc. I followed your adventures in the *Herald*."

Anna shook the proffered hand limply. All the strength had drained out of her. The pretty girl squeezed Anna's fingers like a best friend and let go. Anna wanted to wipe her hand off on her skirt. "I'm interested in your mission work."

Miss Robins gestured to a settee near the coffee table. "Please sit down. And have a cookie." She pointed to the plate of shortbread cookies, which were shaped like perfect little thistles. "I made them."

When Anna sat, Miss Robins perched beside her, knees congenially tilted toward Anna, face bright and open. "What an exciting job you must have, Assistant Matron Blanc."

Anna closed her eyes to collect herself, but images of Joe leaning toward this beautiful stranger swirled inside her head. She shoved the thoughts down. She shoved them, and shoved them, and shoved them. He was a slave trader. She took deep breaths until she didn't care. When her eyes finally flashed open, Anna was all business. Joe Singer could break her heart, stomp on her belief in the faithfulness of men, crush her hope that love could ever be true or that men could ever be good.

But she would not let him cock up her detective work.

Miss Robins waited attentively. Anna sat up straighter. "It must be very dangerous. It would be a shame if something terrible happened to you."

"The angels guard us, Matron Blanc."

"Tell me about your work."

"I teach Chinamen English—not just the language, but literature as well, for advanced students who want to learn. It's a means for understanding our culture."

"So you're well-read."

"I read, and I went to Vassar for a year. The mission provides me with an opportunity to use my head. Mrs. Puce has been teaching me Chinese, which I use every day. And the men teach me about Chinese culture. Did you know they burn paper offerings in the form of money, clothes, books, horses—anything really. They believe their ancestors can then use those objects in the afterlife. The paper objects are very beautiful. You can buy them here in Chinatown."

"That's very interesting."

"We have a school for Chinese children, but I don't teach there. We also preach the gospel. We hold services right out in the streets. Some of the men have converted."

The girl with the pink lips and glasses chimed in. "I teach the children."

Anna nodded. "How many ladies work with you?"

Miss Robins answered, "Seven, including Mrs. Puce, although we don't all live here. We were eight. One girl has left Chinatown."

"When?"

"Three months ago. Her home church pressured her to leave

because of the violence. Even some of the Chinese are leaving now with the tongs so active."

"Where are they going?"

"Who knows? Back to San Francisco to rebuild? So many people came down after the earthquake. That's one of the reasons things are so unsettled with the tongs. They've moved their headquarters here."

Mrs. Puce began to snore.

Anna scratched in her notebook. "I see. Where are the other ladies?"

"They're teaching the Chinese men at the English school on Marchessault. In Chinatown."

"How interesting." Anna held up the picture of Leo Lim posed with the brunette in front of the Chinese theater. "Do you know this man and this girl?"

The girl with the pink lips and glasses leaned forward to look at the photograph. She shifted the kitten in one arm and took the picture from Anna. "Yes. He's one of our students. Leo Lim, and that's Mary. She moved back to Chicago. We were singing in front of the theater that day." She handed the photograph back to Anna.

"When was the last time you saw him?"

"It's been weeks," Miss Robins said.

"Do either of you know where I could find him?"

Miss Robins laughed. "Honestly, Assistant Matron Blanc. We don't follow the men home. The world is scandalized by our presence here in Chinatown already. Although I can say I've been to his shop. He sells imported goods—furniture and things. He has a good head for business. He helped us balance our books."

"I have to get ready for an appointment," said the kitten girl, her curiosity about Anna apparently satisfied. She removed herself from the conversation and scampered up the stairs.

Anna turned to Miss Robins. "Which shop?"

"Canton Bazaar. Down the street."

Anna nodded. She knew the place. She walked past it every time she came to Chinatown. It was always closed. "Does he have any friends?"

"He didn't have any friends at the school. Men . . . how do I say this? The men didn't care for him."

Women, Anna knew, did. White women. They had posed with the man in half a dozen photographs, which she'd seen on his mantle. "But he was friends with the missionary ladies."

"Yes. He's a very good man. He's a convert."

This was interesting. "What did his family think about that?" Anna could only imagine what her family would say.

"I don't believe he had any. Not in America. He wasn't a member of any family association."

"Family association?"

"They're like mutual aid societies for people related somehow—by their home towns, their surnames. Los Angeles is a hostile place for the Chinese. The members look out for each other, help each other find jobs, get settled, bury their dead."

"And what if a Chinaman has no family in LA?"

"Sometimes, they join a tong. Very few make their way alone." Miss Robins' big, blue eyes looked concerned. "Assistant Matron Blanc, is Leo Lim in trouble? Is he mixed up with the tongs? The Bing Kong were pressuring him to join because, like I said, he wasn't a member of any family association and he's good with business. But he always said no. I pray for Leo Lim."

"I just want to speak with him."

"I'm relieved, because the tongs are dangerous. He's very brave to stand up to them." This idea seemed to sober her. "I wish I could help you." She lit up. "Won't you come over for dinner after church? I'm making roast beef with Yorkshire pudding, and ambrosia salad, and marshmallow cake. I'm afraid the other girls won't be there. But Detective Singer is coming. Do you know Detective Singer?"

Anna, who had been reaching for a cookie, knocked the dainty porcelain sugar bowl, which shot like a bullet clean off the table. It landed on Mrs. Puce's pillowy lap, tipped, and spilled a mountain of sugar. Mrs. Puce didn't move. She didn't seem to notice her sweetened middle.

Anna said, "Yes."

"Have you been acquainted for long?" Miss Robins asked, graciously ignoring the sugar pot, as did Anna.

"Forever." Truly Anna hadn't. She'd known Joe for less than a year, and he was still full of surprises. She had thought she knew his heart, having briefly possessed it. She knew that as a boy he had loved a girl named Eve. That his mother was dead. That he liked enchiladas. That he would run into a burning building to save a girl, if he loved her. But that he could stop loving her. Now she'd discovered that he would sell slave girls for money. She had never really known Joe Singer at all.

Miss Robins looked at Anna conspiratorially. "Tell me about him. Just between you and me."

"Well." Anna smiled falsely.

Miss Robins grinned and squeezed her shoulders up toward her ears in giddy anticipation.

Anna put a finger to her chin. "Lunacy runs in his family. They keep his mother locked away in the attic."

Miss Robins blinked. "That can't be right. His mother is dead."

"Yes. She must smell something awful."

Miss Robins was silent.

Anna said, "Thank you, I can't come for Sunday dinner. But neither can Detective Singer. I'm afraid he's in the hoosegow."

§

The Canton Bazaar faced the Plaza on the edge of Chinatown. As Anna had anticipated, the shop was shut up and locked. If he were such a good businessman, his store wouldn't flop. She looked through the window into the dark building. The bright daylight made it impossible for her to see much—just empty glass display cases and the shadows of painted letters stretching out across the floor, spelling the name of the establishment. It was as mysterious as the business-minded, lady-loving Christian, Leo Lim. She strode around to the alley at the rear of the place. An empty loading dock stood near a broad sliding door, which until recently had been locked with a chain. The cut chain now lay in a pile on the deck. She grabbed hold of the door handle and heaved it. It required all her weight to slide it on its runners. She stepped inside and let her eyes adjust to the light.

Dark, dusty rectangles marked the floor where furniture had been. The merchandise was gone, as if someone had packed it all up in a wagon and carted it away.

Anna slid the door closed and moved around to Los Angeles Street, skirt swishing against her bloomers. Surely someone in a neighboring store would have information about where Leo Lim and the contents of his shop had gone.

Vegetable sellers began congregating with their horses and carts for the market at the Plaza. Soon there would be hundreds of people and animals crowding the road. She hurried to the shop next door, which appeared to sell Chinese herbs. According to the sign in the window, the herbalist could cure everything from warts to manly weakness, like a regular doctor. A white mustachioed fellow—possibly one with manly weakness—left the shop just as Anna entered, setting a small string of bells to ringing. The scent of medicine assaulted her nostrils. Dark wooden shelves towered from the floor to the ten-foot ceiling. Bottles of mysterious brews and jars of dried who-knew-what neatly lined them. A counter with thin, built-in drawers ran the length of the room. Every sign, every label was in Chinese.

In the corner on the floor, a broad-backed man knelt, lighting incense at a small red altar decorated with gold. He was hatless, and the sides of his head were partially shaved. The rope of his braid hung enviably thick and long. Anna waited as he made his silent petition. The smoke gradually overcame the medicine smell, replacing it with jasmine. After a moment, he stood and turned around.

The man was Mr. Jones. The bones of his cheeks looked sharp and freshly shaved.

Anna flipped up her veil and gawked at him. "You're a merchant?"

He moved to the counter and stowed a silver box of matches beneath it. "I am an herbalist."

"So you know Leo Lim," she accused. "His shop is right next door. You must know him."

"I know him." His handsome face was composed, as if Anna hadn't just caught him in a lie. He collected a small clear bottle from the shelf and handed it to Anna. "For bruising."

Anna ignored his offering, feeling as baffled as she was vexed. "Why didn't you inform us?"

He met her eye. "You didn't ask."

Outside the window, Anna heard the buzzing of commerce as the vegetable market got underway. She put her hands on her hips, trying to muster some semblance of authority. "Mr. Jones, if you want me to tell you everything I know, then I expect the same from you." She inhaled deeply to see if he smelled nice today, but his scent was lost in jasmine.

He laughed skeptically. "And you are telling me everything you know?"

"Lim attended the missionaries' English classes."

"I knew that."

"He picked up his laundry eight days ago."

He raised one black eyebrow. "That's more interesting."

"The dead girl is Miss Elizabeth Bonsor, a wonderful girl. I knew her. We were friends."

Jones's voice became more subdued. "Highbinders with a wagon came and looted his store."

"There were no marks on the body, no apparent cause of death. I think Miss Bonsor might have been poisoned. There was something strange about the tea."

"Hm. The tea. Can you bring it to me?"

"It's your turn, Mr. Jones. Where can I find Leo Lim?"

"I don't know."

"Do you think he killed Miss Bonsor?"

He looked very serious, even more serious than usual. "I don't know."

Anna plucked the laundry ticket out of her purse and thrust it toward him. "All right. Explain this. Why did the lady at the laundry act so strangely when I showed it to her? It's just Leo Lim's laundry ticket."

Mr. Jones took the ticket from Anna's bare fingers, and held it up to the light. Small red characters glowed on the paper. He lowered his arm, his lips flat and grim. "It's a death threat. From the Bing Kong."

"Against Leo Lim?"

"His name is on it." He lowered his hand.

"Jupiter." Anna took the paper from his palm, careful not to touch his skin, but then touched his fingers anyway. "Leo Lim must be frightened. He would be fleeing even if he hadn't killed the girl."

She looked up and found him staring.

It was rude, but interesting. Anna stared back. His eyes were moonless black, his pupil and iris indistinguishable.

Was it so strange that Elizabeth could fall in love with a Chinese man? Yes. No. Anna started to feel warm everywhere.

He pressed the bottle into her hands. "For that eye. How did you do it?"

Anna's fingers closed around the bottle and she backed away. "I must be . . . I'm going to leave now. Good day, Mr. Jones." Anna bobbed a curtsy and fled outside into the crush of horses, the discordant sounds of a tongue foreign to her, and the market where East met West.

§

Anna was out of breath when she reached her bicycle, but not from hurrying. It was Chinatown, or maybe the assassins, or Mr. Jones with his saturnine eyes. She quickly unlocked her bike. She had to see Joe and tell him about the developments in the case. She'd confess that she stole the tea and he'd have it tested, if he ever got out of jail. She would not tell him that Mr. Jones made her feel . . . what? Strange.

Anna peddled straight for the hoosegow.

§

The jailer escorted Anna through the corridor full of gawking criminals. It didn't smell any better than before. He dragged a billy club along the bars, not caring if sometimes he clipped a finger or barely missed a protruding nose. From the cell at the end of the block, she could hear Joe's lovely tenor voice. She found him reclining on the bench in his cell, singing to the ceiling, "Just then the limb broke; holy gee! And I broke seven bones. And half-killed Maggie Jones . . ."

Joe swung his legs to the floor and in two steps stood at the bars. "Nice of you to visit." He flipped back her veil and took her chin in his hands, examining her shiner. He seemed relieved. "Your eye looks better, but the rest of you is a mess."

She twisted out of his grasp.

He was fingering a paper peach blossom amulet like the one Mr. Melvin had offered Anna. Mr. Melvin had visited. Joe had chosen the love luck charm.

He said, "Every time I see you it's like you shrank in the wash. Aren't you eating?"

Anna ignored this rude remark. She wasn't that thin. She simply didn't have a roll around her tummy when she bent over in the nude. Not anymore. She produced a box of Cracker Jacks, and began to eat them right in front of him. "Well, you could stand to skip a meal." It was true. He wasn't his lean, hard self. It was as if some motherly figure had been stuffing him. Probably, the piano girl had been bringing him picnic baskets of liver for months.

Joe's stomach growled loudly and he grinned. "I skipped dinner. I found a bug in it."

Anna pushed the Cracker Jacks at him. Then she kicked herself.

He put two fingers in the box, took out a cluster of candied popcorn, pushed his hand through the bars and popped the candy onto Anna's lips. "You need it more than I do, Sherlock."

"Hah!" She opened up. "When is your father letting you out?"

"Soon. Don't go into Chinatown. Wait for me."

He popped another popcorn cluster into Anna's mouth. She chewed.

"I don't want to wait for you. I couldn't anyway. I was thinking about Elizabeth's cause of death. She could have been smothered with a pillow, but usually it leaves the victim's eyes red. Thus, I think she was poisoned."

"Noted."

"Do you know what else I discovered? Mr. Jones knows Leo Lim. Their shops are adjacent."

Joe raised one eyebrow.

"And, Leo Lim patronized Most Lucky Laundry. I was right. He came back for his clothes. That old woman told me. Lim broke in eight days ago and stole them. Eight days ago, Leo Lim was still somewhere in Chinatown. And that laundry ticket . . . It isn't just a laundry ticket. Hold it up to the light." She placed the ticket in Joe's hand.

Joe raised both eyebrows. He held it up to catch the glow of a bare bulb hanging from the ceiling outside his cell. "Hell's bells."

Anna's lips parted in surprise. "You can read that?"

"Everybody on the squad knows these characters. It's a death threat. Leo Lim is a marked man. No wonder he ran."

"Yes, I know. Mr. Jones told me."

"The secret messages are part of the Bing Kong's terror tactics. Some people are leaving Chinatown because of it. They've gotten a death threat, or they are afraid because of the violence. And they stay gone until the tong leader who threatened them is dead."

"Everyone runs?"

"Some Chinamen join the tong. What they don't do is stay put. The fact that Leo Lim ran may have nothing to do with Elizabeth's death."

"Maybe the Bing Kong killed Elizabeth to punish Leo Lim." Anna tapped the bars.

"Maybe. I do know this. If that laundry ticket came from Most Lucky Laundry, then Most Lucky Laundry has ties with the Bing Kong. That old lady is tong."

"Taffy."

"She's tong, Anna. Stay away from her."

Anna put two fingers to her lips. "If the Bing Kong is looking for Leo Lim, they'd happily give me information that would help me find him. It would save them the trouble. Why else would the old woman give me information without getting my money first? She charged me for directions." Anna stopped pacing and gripped the bars, looking Joe in the eyes. She didn't need Joe Singer. "I'm going to ask the Bing Kong."

"That's crazy, Anna. Absolutely not. Stay away from the Bing Kong."

"I have a family debt to pay. The tongs are successful criminals, right? So they aren't stupid. They won't hurt me if they think I'm useful. And if I'm looking for Leo Lim, I imagine they'll think I'm useful." Anna spun about and paced, drumming her fingers on her hip. "The key will be to find Leo Lim without letting them know that I've found him so that the Bing Kong don't chop off his head."

Joe threw up his hands. "Sherlock, I'm gonna get out of here."

"Shall I bake you a cake with a file?"

"The cops just banned cakes in the jail. Someone smuggled in a gun." He ran a hand through his hair. "I think I can make a deal with my pop."

"What deal? I thought you didn't make deals with your father. Does he want you to hunt down some poor Mexican dissident or throw striking beet pickers into the hoosegow?"

"You don't want to know."

"Yes, I do."

"He wants me to take the mayor's daughter to an ice cream social."

Anna frowned in disgust. "Are you courting all of the girls in Los Angeles?"

"I'm working on it."

"Well, I hope she has a harelip."

"You've got to wait for me, Sherlock. It's even more important now that the people at the laundry know you're hunting Lim. They might follow you. Just wait until tomorrow morning. I don't want anything to happen to you. I couldn't bear it."

Anna's lips parted. Joe put more popcorn between them. He leaned his forehead on the bars, only inches and cold steel from her face. "Promise me, Anna. Swear on . . . Vionnet of the House of Doucet that you'll wait for me."

Her heart beat faster. Madeleine Vionnet was Anna's favorite designer. Anna could not swear on Madeleine Vionnet when she knew very well that she would break her pledge. It would be a sacrilege.

"You know I'm going to track the villain without you. I don't like you."

Joe whispered, "Sherlock. There's something I need to tell you."

"Hm?"

The jail door creaked open, and the jailer waltzed in with a bucket for emptying chamber pots. He was whistling, but not so loud that he couldn't hear.

Joe exhaled, and Anna got the impression that he wasn't going to say what he had originally intended. He rubbed his brow. "When your head is being wacked off by a highbinder, remember I . . . I will always . . ."

"What?"

Joe blew out a breath. "Anna, be careful."

§

La Grande Station cut the sky like an Arabian palace. The domes and turrets that marked the train depot promised adventure. Anna stood on the street looking up. Now that she had the freedom, and once she'd paid off her landlord, she thought she might save money for a trip. But there were so many things she wanted, even needed, and so little money to buy them. Anna turned her eyes to Bunker Hill, which rose in the distance. Somewhere on the crest, the Blanc mansion presided, with views of the city clear down to the sea. Her father might be working in his office or sitting on the patio eating his dinner. Now that Anna was gone, he had no one to ignore at the table. How her life had changed. She would never be able to afford a new dress by Madeleine Vionnet now. Her current wardrobe would become progressively worn and out of date. She would look like Mrs. Bonsor—a relic from a grand past. Or she'd be forced to wear new cheap, ugly clothes.

Now she had freedom, police work, and an important job to do. It had been worth it—barely.

Anna sashayed to the window where a man was selling tickets for the trains. She assumed her most innocent tone, her face hidden by the veil. "Good day. I am Elizabeth Bonsor, and I've come to collect my steamer trunk."

§

Anna dragged Elizabeth's steamer trunk into Matron Clemens's office so she could plunder it in secret. It contained unremarkable things—frocks, worn and homemade, and resoled Sunday boots. Each was a sadness. Anna lifted them out one by one and piled them in a heap on the rug.

Reaching the bottom, Anna found a treasure hoard—bundles of letters. She palmed one, untied the string, and opened the top envelope. It released a sandalwood scent. The salutation read, "Elizabeth, My Heart." Anna's eyes skipped to the signature at the bottom. "Your Leo."

Her heart thump thumped. There it was—confirmation that Elizabeth and Leo Lim were lovers, just like Elizabeth's mother had said. Anna plopped into the rocking chair to read the letter through. It was full of mush and sappy rhymes. There was no reference to a favorite place, friends, or any clue that could lead Anna to Lim.

Wolf stuck his head into the office. "Honeybun."

Anna jumped. She pretended to stretch and dropped the letter down her back.

"I've been looking for you. Your pretty comb still hasn't sold, but they're keeping it in the window. Lots of ladies stop to look at it. Personally, I would love to see it back on your pretty head. If you need a loan . . ." He pushed open the door. "Why do you have a steamer trunk? Are you going somewhere, and can I come?"

Anna hesitated. "Nowhere. These are . . . clothes for the poor. I collect them from . . . people."

Wolf grinned. "How charitable of you."

"Yes, I know."

Anna stuffed the large bundles of letters in her purse. It bulged like bullfrog cheeks. Then she piled the clothes haphazardly back into the trunk.

Wolf scratched his earlobe. "What have you been working on? I've hardly seen you."

Anna avoided his eyes. "I've been teaching children to be wholesome and upright and such."

"Could you be more specific?"

"There was a truant boy. I captured him and returned him to school."

"Good."

"He was devilish and tricky so it took a lot of time. And I've done filing. And other things."

"I would hate for Matron Clemens to return to an enormous pile of work because you were trying to sleuth instead of doing your job."

"If you're referring to the stiff in the stinky Chinese trunk, Joe says it's a clear-cut tong killing. He and Mr. Jones say these things take care of themselves," Anna lied.

"The Hatfields and the McCoys."

"That's right." Anna glanced at the wall clock. "It's late." She gestured to the messy heap of clothes spilling from the trunk. "I think I'll tidy up here and go home."

"Have a good night, honeybun. I'll let you know when your comb sells." With the wave of a hand, Wolf left.

As much as Anna would have liked to return home for a lukewarm bath and a tin of kippers, she didn't have the luxury. The killer's trail was growing cold, and if she didn't catch him soon, he would likely get away. There was no time to rest. Anna pushed down on the rumpled wad of clothes and forced the trunk lid shut with a thump.

She collapsed back into the chair, making it rock and squeak, rock and squeak. She fingered a doily, stretching a hole in the lace. Did she have the courage to go back to Most Lucky Laundry to face the tong alone? Anna thought about Elizabeth, who bravely saved heathen souls in Chinatown for nothing but a heavenly reward. Elizabeth had the courage. But Elizabeth was dead, and that should be a lesson to Anna.

Anna fought a little war inside herself. Yes, it was dangerous, maybe even foolish. But if Anna didn't find Elizabeth's murderer, no one would. And she had her father's debt to pay. Chinatown crawled with cops whom she could apply to in a pinch, and it was only a stone's throw to the Plaza.

If the old woman were Bing Kong, she would know where to find the Bing Kong president. Maybe the Bing Kong president had information about the whereabouts of Leo Lim, or at least where she ought to begin looking.

If she must return to Chinatown alone, the earlier she went the better. Later, when she returned home, she would read the rest of Elizabeth's love letters.

§

A mist dampened Anna's veil as she rode through muddy streets lit only by paper lanterns and the glow leaking from windows. The sewage smelled strong that night. The gun in her pocket knocked against her thigh with each turn of the pedal.

Most Lucky Laundry stood empty and dark.

"Biscuits!" She'd come all this dangerous way for no reason. Anna pushed off on her bicycle, but the back tire spread out like a pancake. She saw the broken bottle that was likely the culprit and kicked it. "Cock biscuits!"

Anna wheeled her bicycle with one hand, took her gun from her pocket and held it with the other. She wondered to herself where a tong president might pass the time, with the weight of his heinous crimes eating away at his blackened heart. Anna herself would go to confession and then drink whiskey. Or rather, the other way around. But she didn't know what a man would do.

Anna thought she'd seen a temple down a side street. She could, perhaps, ask a holy man. She encountered the red building with the grand entrance, carved wooden pillars, and a string of paper lantern moons. Two enormous deities stood guard on either side of the threshold. A stream of incense escaped through the door, perfuming the air.

She felt a strong hand on her shoulder and spun about, pointing her rod at her assailant's chest.

Mr. Jones towered above her. He ignored the gun, and reprimanded her with his tone. "What are you doing here?"

Anna lowered her gun and blew out a breath. Her pounding heartbeat slowed. "I'm looking for the Bing Kong president. He's put a mark on Leo Lim and so have I, so to speak. The tong knows things about Lim that might help me find him. I thought a priest might know where to find the tong leader." She tucked her gun back in her pocket.

"You are insane."

"I have a debt to pay. They have no reason to hurt me. I could lead them to Lim."

Mr. Jones looked thoughtful.

Anna's eyes sparked. "Jupiter. Aren't you important in Chinatown—big in the Consolidated Benevolent Society? I'll bet you could take me to the Bing Kong president."

"No."

"I'll trade information. I've spoken to Elizabeth's parents, something you could never do."

"I'll ask Officer Singer."

"He doesn't know about my progress in the investigation. We've had a falling out. I no longer tell him anything. Besides, he's in the hoosegow and won't be out anytime soon."

Mr. Jones's lips flattened. "What information?"

"Tell me where to find the president, and I'll tell you everything. Chinatown isn't very big. I'm sure you're acquainted."

"Tell me first. Something I don't already know."

"Leo Lim was Elizabeth Bonsor's lover."

"I know."

She frowned. "Why didn't you say so?"

"I don't particularly want to help you. What else?"

"She was leaving to go visit her aunt in St. Louis. She probably went to Lim's apartment to say goodbye."

Mr. Jones raised a single black eyebrow.

Anna smiled. "Ah hah. You didn't know that. Now you owe me. Where is the Bing Kong president?"

Mr. Jones said, "Matron Blanc, the Dragon Head is not to be trifled with. His people may call him 'Big Brother,' and he may help his people, but he has killed and with impunity."

"A white woman?"

"You of all people should know how to make a dead white girl disappear. You saw Joe Singer do it."

Anna paused for a beat. "Then the tongs didn't kill Elizabeth, because they would never leave a white corpse somewhere so easy to find, somewhere that would implicate the Chinese."

"Of course not."

"And yet you kept this from me."

"I told you. This is a Chinese matter."

"But we made a deal, Mr. Jones. You have to take me to the Bing Kong president. Your honor is on the line."

§

Mr. Jones led Anna toward a grocery, which appeared to be open despite the late hour. She felt glad for his company. Though he was strange and truculent, he was large and Joe trusted him. It was like having Joe by her side, only larger and with a pigtail. She almost felt safe with him, though she'd have felt safer if he hadn't warned her so vehemently, if he hadn't kept nervously clearing his throat. She snuck a peek at Mr. Jones. He caught her eye and held it. She looked away. "Joe said you went to Yale?"

"Yes. I was sponsored by missionaries."

"So you're a Christian."

"I'm not."

"Rather a shame for the missionaries."

Mr. Jones's lips curled in a hint of a smile.

By the entrance to the grocery, a man sat on a stool calling out to passersby in Chinese. He narrowed his eyes at Anna, as if straining to see her, or not believing what he saw. She smiled and nodded courteously. His face didn't change, so Anna averted her eyes.

She looked about the store. It sold rice and exotic vegetables, pots and pans. She whispered, "The Bing Kong president is here?"

Mr. Jones shook his head. He took her arm and led Anna down a flight of stairs that descended into the cool underground. They came to a steel door at the bottom of the steps and stopped. Mr. Jones rapped a rhythm on the door. The door groaned open. It was the thickest door Anna had ever seen, maybe eight or nine inches deep, like a bank vault. She whispered, "Jupiter."

The scent of stale beer overlaid with tobacco assaulted her nose. Mr. Jones ushered her through. A boy of maybe twelve, some sort of sentry, secured the door with four heavy crossbars.

Anna found herself in a vast room, among a dozen crowded tables. The dim light swirled with tobacco smoke, which rose from long bamboo pipes hanging from the mouths of a hundred Chinese men. She felt her lungs constrict and her eyes burn. She coughed. Banners with Chinese characters draped the walls. Green cloths covered the tables. Each table had one empty bowl, columnar stacks of silver half-dollars, and piles of what looked like buttons made of horn. Four or five men surrounded each table, drinking mugs of beer. They appeared to be counting the buttons in unison: "*yāt, yih, sàam, sei . . .*" A cheer rose from one of the tables. Anna guessed they were fan-tan games, which she'd seen referenced in the paper, although she didn't know the rules.

Her companion's handsome face was wrinkled with perplexity. He was speaking to the door boy, but Anna didn't understand their words. She turned back to watch the games. As the men had not yet noticed her, she took the liberty of staring at them. They were red in the face, flushed with drink or excitement. Some sat, some stood, clustered around tables. It only took a moment to deduce the rules. Each dealer grabbed an unknown number of buttons and put them in a bowl. Next, he dumped the bowl out onto the table. Then, he reduced the pile of buttons by four at a time until one, two, or three buttons remained. The men were betting on the number in the remainder—a simple game of chance—like a lotto game.

The room pulsed with masculinity and the ordinary danger Anna imagined one would find in any room full of drinking, gambling men. Losers got angry. Winners celebrated in a way that made tempers rise. But something else was going on—a kind of whispering that ran like a current through the room. Anna was excluded from the secret, and it made her feel tense. Did it portend violence? She scanned to see if she recognized any highbinders from that terrifying night she had walked alone.

To the side, an ordinary door cracked open by the hand of an unseen man. Through the gap she saw a large, ornate safe painted with an outdoor scene and the words "Safe and Lock Company."

Anna turned her eyes back to Mr. Jones, who was watching her watch the room. She smiled nervously.

There was a great, resounding crash—like a rhinoceros colliding with the thick metal door. Mr. Jones and Anna jumped away from the entrance holding their ears.

The boy shouted. All eyes turned to the door.

There was another *bang*, and another—pounding in rhythm—the hard strokes of a battering ram. The discordant clanging continued.

Dealers rolled buttons and cups up in the tablecloths and fled toward a third door, which another sentry had opened. It too was thick, like something from a fortress. They dematerialized into the darkness behind it.

Anna heard the loud crack of wood splitting, as the bolts across the front door failed. Her heart bounced to her throat. The last thing she needed was to be caught in an LAPD vice raid. She sped toward the portal where the dealers had disappeared, trusting that Mr. Jones could take care of himself. Some officer boomed, "Police!" She pressed past the door and found herself in a dark tunnel. Mr. Jones slipped through behind her, slamming and bolting the door with one, two, three bars.

He grabbed Anna by the hand and jogged down a narrow passageway, pulling her along so that she almost lost her hat. Water dripped onto the cement floor. Her heart raced and her senses sharpened. She smelled everything—the damp bricks, her own bitter sweat, and the incense that clung to his hair. He led her up a staircase and opened a door where they were met with a wall of steam. It settled damply on her skin and hair.

Heaps of clothes lay in wicker baskets along the wall, but Anna could see the merest corner of a green tablecloth from the fan-tan games buried beneath them. Three men fed sheets into a trough of hot water—the source of the steam—while long metal arms agitated more linens inside. A placid-looking man filled his mouth with water from a cup, then expertly squirted the water out in a fine spray onto a shirtwaist he was ironing.

She saw a washboard, a large wringing machine with India-rubber rollers and a mangle. Table linens and towels hung dripping on a line. Mr. Jones pushed through them, batting them out of the way, pulling Anna behind him. Soon they stood on the sidewalk.

Anna sank against the building's wall, sweating, sticky with steam, trying to catch her breath. She had a stitch in her side. Out in the night air, the dew on her skin now made her cold.

"What about the gamblers? They all stayed behind," Anna said.

Mr. Jones shrugged. "Sitting innocently at tables drinking beer."

She peered down Los Angeles Street and saw two lonely paddy wagons parked fruitlessly in the road. Detective Snow leaned with his hand on the side of one wagon, scratching his neck. Anna could easily tell the cops that the men had been gambling, and that the evidence was hidden in the laundry baskets, but she'd be alienating the Chinese and giving herself away. But there was another reason not to tell the cops. She didn't think the police really wanted to close the fan-tan games, or Captain Dixon wouldn't send Snow and his men to do it. Everyone knew Snow was as dumb as a donkey.

The cops climbed into the paddy wagons and motored off. Anna's inhalations slowed. "Why did you take me to a fan-tan parlor?"

"It's the Bing Kong president's fan-tan parlor. He should have been there. He and his number-two man. Something's wrong."

"I wanted to find him, but not at the cost of my job. You almost got me fired."

"That should be the least of your worries. I'll take you home."

Anna's shoulders sank. "All right."

No derelicts darkened the street, just a man tossing slop into the gutter. Still, Mr. Jones did not dare to slip his arm through hers, though she would have welcomed it, because it was friendly. A new brick building graced Juan Street, one Anna had noticed before. It had a balcony with a tile roof that swooped up at the ends in the Chinese style and two small palm trees on either side of the door. Light seeped from behind curtains, illuminating strips of the sidewalk.

Mr. Jones paused in front of the building. "This is the home of Wong Nim, the Bing Kong president."

"His residence? It's nice." Anna hesitated, then made her mouth form the words. "Take me inside."

"I didn't come here to take you inside, Anna Blanc, but to fulfill my promise. In fact, I forbid that you enter. I won't be responsible for you any further. If you want to meet the Bing Kong president, go with Officer Singer, in daylight, in public, at the fan-tan parlor. You won't need me. Wong Nim speaks English."

Anna stood and gazed at the building. Wong Nim was a vicious killer, responsible for countless murders. Torture even. Maybe he himself hadn't killed people, but he had ordered their deaths. Or maybe he had killed . . . But those had been his enemies, not innocent police matrons who only wanted to help. And surely he wouldn't kill a woman.

Anna glanced at Mr. Jones.

He said, "Matron Blanc, you've gone as far as you can. It's time to let it go. Forget about Elizabeth's death and leave it to me, or I'll wash my hands of you."

"I owe a debt."

"I'll give you anything you want if you leave Chinatown and never come back. Whatever you want. A pearl necklace? My Cadillac?"

Anna checked his beautiful, somber eyes. He was serious.

"Are you afraid for me or for Chinatown?"

"Both."

She considered this. A Cadillac would be nice . . . But how she missed her lovely pearls. Then she thought about Elizabeth—good, brave Elizabeth, who had neither car nor pearls—and how Anna's father had ruined her family. How she lay dead and would never have cars or pearls.

Anna steeled herself. "Hah! I can't be bought, Mr. Jones. Not when it comes to honor." To show him this was true, and before she could change her mind, she dashed to the door and knocked. She half expected Mr. Jones to pull her back, and that they would play ding-dong ditch. He didn't.

Anna trembled, but held her ground. Part of her, the weak side, hoped that no one answered. She was about to come face to face with the man likely responsible for the decapitation of Ko Chung. She said a silent prayer to Saint Dismas, patron saint of criminals, that the Bing Kong president would be in a good mood.

Joe Singer answered the door.

Despite her training, Anna's mouth hung open like a grouper.

Joe's nostrils flared. "Please tell me I'm dreaming." He looked grim. That part made sense to Anna because the air smelled like excrement.

She said, "Jupiter. You're out."

"I went to an ice cream social!" Joe looked up to heaven as if anguished. "You're in Chinatown. At night. Alone. Here."

"Not alone." Anna glanced around, but Mr. Jones had wisely slipped away. Maybe he truly had washed his hands of her.

Or maybe he was afraid.

"Um . . . I have my rod. May I come in?"

Joe surveyed the street. Anna could count three different derelicts who appeared to be watching her.

"I can't leave you outside, can I?" Joe opened the door wider.

Anna brushed past Joe into a dimly lit parlor furnished with intricately carved mahogany tables and chairs set with marble and mother of pearl. A picture of a bearded man hung above a gilded and lacquered altar. Jade ornaments and painted wall hangings decorated the space. Her eyes swept the parlor and into a dark, adjoining dining room. They alighted on the source of the smell—the foul excretions of three dead bodies slumped over at a table, in their chairs. One lay face down in a bowl of noodles. Dominoes were scattered across the table and arranged in a discrete grouping in front of an empty chair. A fourth body—a woman—lay on a chaise longue, wearing intricately embroidered silk with sleeves like butterfly wings. It was as exquisite as any gown Anna had ever seen but for the red stain that marred the fabric directly over her heart.

Anna stuttered, "We . . . we have a case."

Joe pulled Anna into his arms. She struggled free and pushed him so that he stumbled. "This is an odd time to force your attentions . . ." She trailed off.

Four living men of various builds stood at the back of the dining room, blending into the darkness. She hadn't noticed them at first, her senses occupied with the bodies. Anna guessed they were highbinders and took them in one feature at a time—scar from fighting; nose off center; a belly; a mean, piercing gaze; and a pair of giant clam hands.

A particular man stood in the center—small, yet, once she'd noticed him, his presence filled the room like smoke. He had close-clipped gray hair and the face and bearing of a pug. She'd seen unfortunate faces before—Detective Snow for instance—but this was the first truly ugly man that Anna had ever seen. His expensive western suit was poor compensation. His eyes slipped over Anna's body like rancid oil. She looked away and wondered irrationally whether his face had driven him to a life of crime.

Anna was truly at a loss. What did one do when confronted by assassins while standing over the bodies of their latest victims? Besides tremble and sweat, which she was doing already. She had to concentrate to keep her knees from buckling. If she did the wrong thing, they might kill Joe and possibly even Anna. She and Joe were, after all, witnesses. Anna turned to Joe with desperate, questioning eyes, but couldn't read him.

So she fell back on her training and proffered her most winning smile. "Detective Singer, aren't you going to introduce us?"

He laughed despairingly. "Assistant Matron Blanc, this is Tom Foo Yuen, the Hop Sing president, and his three favorite hatchet men, Lai Ying, Shi Cheng-Fung, and I don't know the fat one. He's new. Mr. Tom is a very powerful, very dangerous man. Usually, he does business from a restaurant on Apablaza Street—that one with the statues in the window. I'm not sure what he's doing here." Joe followed his pronouncement with a broken string of Chinese words. "They don't speak English. We could really use Mr. Jones right now."

Unfortunately, Anna had driven Mr. Jones away. At least he was safe. She curtsied anxiously. "But where is the Bing Kong president?"

"Wong Nim?" Joe pointed to the dead man in the noodles. "And his henchmen."

"Oh," said Anna. "And who is the woman?"

The dead woman looked plump, well-tended, pampered even. Anna hoped she'd died quickly.

"His wife, maybe? He dressed her well."

Anger flooded Anna, mixing with her fear. "She didn't deserve to die."

Joe nodded. "Tom Foo Yuen called to report the murder to the police. I just responded to the call."

"Tom Foo Yuen called the police? On himself?" she asked.

"Not on himself. He claims he found them like this. He says he came to broker peace, and speculates that Wong Nim was killed by one of his own men."

Anna swallowed. She drifted closer to the bodies. Each man had an exit wound in his back. "Wong Nim was shot by someone he lets watch him eat noodles. Someone with whom he plays dominoes. Someone he allows around his wife. His friends were caught by surprise . . ." Anna's eyes sought Joe's. "These men are innocent. Wong Nim was shot by his own man."

"Maybe someone who wants to take his place."

"Good. We'll find out who's taking his place and—"

"Anna, I won't be the detective on this case. I just got here first. I'm too new, and it's too important. Wolf will send somebody else, and it's not going to be you."

Anna crinkled her face. "Did he have to kill the woman?"

The Hop Sing president leered with his doggy eyes and said something to Joe. Anna wished again for Mr. Jones's translation.

Joe smiled and pulled Anna close again. "He wants to know if you're a prostitute."

"Tell him I'm a detective."

"That's not going to fly." Joe said something to the president, who looked disappointed. The president scanned Anna from hat to waist and back again.

"What did you say?"

"I've just made it clear that you're my favorite girl."

"You mean like a courtesan? You lied."

"He said you were very beautiful, and I said no, you're not very beautiful, and that he was much too kind."

"Hah! Is he going to steal me then?"

"He also said your feet are too big."

Anna twisted away from him. She turned on the gangster and spoke sharply, her face contorted. "Slavery is an abomination. You must set the singsong girls free."

Joe spoke through gritted teeth. "Anna, be quiet." She saw his jaw clench as he waited for the man's response.

"He doesn't even speak English," she said.

"He understands contempt."

Tom Foo Yuen's accent was as thick as glue. "This is your favorite woman? Control her, or I will put an end to her. I don't care if your father is the police chief."

Joe Singer stalked forward and pulled Anna roughly behind him.

Anna's eyes widened. She opened her mouth, but Joe silenced her. "Sherlock, be quiet." Then he proceeded to growl softly in Chinese. He sounded both threatening and conciliatory.

The president grunted and spewed out words that oozed vitriol.

Joe whispered to Anna. "Let's go." He backed out of the apartment, hand on his gun.

CHAPTER 15

When Anna and Joe stepped out into the cold night, the corner bell began to ring. They walked quickly, dodging a staggering white man, and passing the barred windows of a brothel. Joe tried to take her arm, and she shook him off.

Joe said, "Nice job, Sherlock. You can't speak to a tong president like that. If you'd made Tom Foo Yuen lose face in front of his men, you'd be dead. As it is, he's very, very angry. The only thing that saved your life is that his men don't speak English and maybe that I'm the police chief's son."

"So you think those were empty threats or full threats?"

"Definitely full threats. You should stay out of Chinatown."

"Oh." Anna felt sobered and foolish.

"I told you, Anna. But you never listen to me."

"Who do you think they will assign to the case? That poor, dead woman. She might have children." Anna thought of her own dead mother, whom she could only really remember because she had a picture, and how terrible it had been to lose her so young because the nuns at the convent school were not good mothers, as her bottom could testify.

"Wolf will probably take it on himself."

Anna tried to put the lady's lifeless face out of her mind. Wolf was a good detective, and there was nothing Anna could do to bring her back. At least the lady had been cherished in life, or so it had appeared.

When they crossed the street onto another block, the bell behind them ceased ringing, and the bell on the next corner started to chime.

Anna gazed down the street. "I understand the bells now. They're announcing you because you're a cop."

"That's right. They're sounding the alarm." Joe adjusted his derby hat. "I'm back on the investigation now, Anna, so tell me the news."

"All right. It's looking bad for Mr. Lim."

"There are other possibilities."

"She could have been killed by the tong, like Wong Nim's wife, if they were going after Leo Lim, but Mr. Jones doesn't think so. And we can't rule out a white man angry about Elizabeth's love affair with Lim. Remember the indentation next to the dummy? I thought about that. What if Elizabeth was sleeping in the bed with that dummy, someone thought it was Lim, and killed her because she was in bed with a Chinaman or out of jealousy."

"But why was she in the bed with the dummy?"

"I don't know." The wind blew on Anna's bare cheeks, making them sting. "I have Elizabeth's letters. I found them in her trunk. We can read them now if you'd like."

"All right." He slipped out of his heavy wool coat, and wrapped her in it, and dropped his hat onto her bare head. Anna stiffened. "Are you still pretending I'm your favorite girl?"

"I thought you were cold."

"I'm polar bear cold. Unhand me and let's go somewhere warm and read the letters."

He let his arm drop. "Not the station. Too many busy bodies."

"Somewhere we won't run into a cop." Anna thought about inviting Joe to her apartment but knew there were drawers drying inside on a line, and it wasn't heated. Plus, he said he would never go there, although as far as she was concerned he was as safe from her as he could be. "Your digs?" she ventured.

Joe said emphatically, "No."

"Well, we have to go somewhere private."

"Agreed. What about La Placita? Won't the sanctuary be open for prayer?"

"Not at this hour, but we can climb in the window. I've done it before." As a teen, Anna had indeed broken in to drink the communion wine, because she needed the extra holiness. Also, her father had fired the maid he suspected of tippling and began locking up his alcohol.

Joe helped Anna retrieve her bicycle and walked it for her along the bumpy plank sidewalks, through the crowd of carousers, all the way to the Plaza. The Plaza slept, dark and quiet, empty but for palm trees and star jasmine and a man snoring on a garden bench, covered with newspapers. La Placita was a small church with white plaster walls and a bell tower. It had stood at the edge of the Plaza for a hundred years. Anna had taken her first communion there.

A late trolley rattled past. It must have been nearly midnight. Anna led Joe around the side of La Placita, tiptoeing through the rosemary to where a small glass window opened into the sanctuary six feet off the ground. She picked a sprig of the herb and rolled it between her fingers, held it to her nose, felt the cooling scent. Anna unbuttoned Joe's coat. It hung almost to her ankles and would get in the way. Then she shed her own cashmere wrap, which she had worn beneath, and stuffed them through the window. Joe put his hands on her waist as if to lift her. Anna pulled away, giving him a reproachful look.

"Anna, I know you hate me, but you're not going to get through that window without my help."

Anna looked up at the window, and then at Joe's unsmiling face. Regrettably, he was right. Anna had promised herself not to let her feelings about Joe Singer stand in the way of her vocation. If she needed his body to get through the window, she would use it.

She moved in front of him and raised her arms up, not meeting his eyes. He plucked his hat off her head, replacing it on his own, and began to hum absently. She felt his hands easily lift her into the air. She grabbed the edges of the window frame with her fingertips.

The window opened with a stubborn crack, leaving Anna's fingers red and chalky with dust. She took a deep breath, and pressed down, slowly raising herself. Joe gave her bottom a helpful shove, and she swung her leg over, her skirts riding up to her knee. The places where Joe had touched her were tingling madly, and she hated him for it. She took a deep breath, rotated her frame, and gingerly swung her second leg over, lowering herself into the sanctuary.

She heard Joe's voice. "You okay, Sherlock?"

"Of course."

As agile as a cat, Joe swung through the window and landed softly beside her, still wearing his derby hat. He removed it and tossed it onto a pew. The inside of the church was dark and void. Joe plucked a candle from the upraised hand of a carved wooden angel. He took a matchbox from his pocket and set the candle ablaze. It cast deep shadows onto the plaster walls and oak pews. The light flitted across the ceiling, illuminating mandalas in turquoise, green, gold, and red. Icons with glowing gilt frames loomed over the altar. Anna had never seen the church this way, dark and beautiful. The shadows made Joe's lips appear more curved, his dimples deeper, like an angel.

They were alone again, with only God as their chaperone. The darkness and Joe's proximity made Anna feel fallen, because he was a slave trader and still she ached for him. It was only the watchful eyes of the saints, and her anger at his grave sin, that kept Anna from offering him her lips. Because the truth was, she missed Joe Singer fiercely and there was no replacing him. Anna would never love again.

She said, "Let's sit on the floor so we can spread out the letters."

"All right."

They walked up the aisle to the altar. She gracefully lowered herself onto the rug. Joe sat beside her, so that she could benefit from the light, holding his handkerchief under the candle so the drips didn't stain her skirt. On her back, she could feel the eyes of Our Lady Queen of Angels, Saint Joseph, John the Baptist, and the Magdalene. On her legs, she could feel the heat of his nearness through three inches of air and five blessed layers of fabric. She closed her eyes.

"Anna?" Joe said.

Anna's eyes popped open, her cheeks a little flushed in the candlelight. "I was thinking about . . . crime." She rustled in her bag and pulled out the bundle of envelopes, which she fumbled so that they spilled across the carpet and onto the tile like cards.

She straightened her back, assumed her most professional demeanor, and selected an envelope at random. She cleared her throat. "They must be important letters, or Elizabeth wouldn't have taken them with her." She extracted the stationery, handing it to Joe, averting her eyes. "You read? I'll hold the candle."

"All right."

Anna took the lit taper from his long fingers, accidentally dripping wax all over his pants. He winced.

Joe began to read, his voice thrumming with a rich, male sweetness.

"Dearest Mine." He cleared his throat uncomfortably. "Your silk shawl covers a garden. Orchids peek from your clothes."

Anna and Joe exchanged a glance.

"I flirt and you resist, but already we are secretly connected."

Anna bit her lip.

"Like two kinds of jade, we are right together."

Joe hesitated. Anna leaned toward him. "Go on."

He wiped little beads of sweat off his brow. "Your warm red lips melt mine. I taste your breath like a fragrant blossom, your skin, cream; your sweat, pearls. Your hair is loose and black. Oh God."

The "Oh God" part sounded very much like Joe's addition. He put down the letter and eyed Anna. "I don't know. I feel like I'm in someone else's bedroom."

"But it's from Leo Lim. You have to read it. It's part of our investigation."

Joe's eyes slipped down the page to the bottom. "It's not from Leo Lim."

Anna's shapely brows drew together. "But Leo Lim was her lover. Her mother said so, and I have a letter to prove it."

"This is from someone named Chan Mon, and it's dated three weeks ago."

"Then Elizabeth had two Chinese lovers."

Joe raised both eyebrows.

Anna scoffed. "You're shocked? You have multiple sweethearts. And it's terribly unfair. Elizabeth couldn't marry either Chinaman. It's against the law, whereas you could move to Utah and marry all of your gals at once."

"So now we have a motive for both Leo Lim and Chan Mon. Jealousy." Joe scooted his bottom away from Anna, and she felt the colder for it. Then, he stretched out on the floor, his boots nearly touching the altar, and laid his head close to her hips, so he could have the light. He put a handful of letters on his belly. "I have a headache."

Anna gazed down at his handsome, upside down face, which winced in pain. His hair looked soft and slightly flattened from his hat. He made a pained sound and pinched the bridge of his nose. Without her permission, her hand reached down and lightly stroked his temple. His face relaxed. She kept caressing him, scratching circles on his scalp. He made an *mmm* sound, shifted, and laid his head in her lap, using it as a pillow.

She cradled his head and ran her fingers through his hair, which smelled like bay rum. "I despise you," she said.

"It's probably for the best."

"I'm only petting you so your headache will go away and you can work, even though touching you appalls me."

"It's helping."

"Does the letter have an address?"

"No, and if it did I wouldn't give it to you. If you go to Chinatown, you're going with me, Anna, not alone. We're a team."

Anna didn't answer. Were they a team? Could she be a team with Joe Singer? If so, would the saints frown upon their partnership given that he was such a wretch? She gazed up at Mary's placid face, looking for a sign.

Joe picked up a second letter and cleared his throat.

My Dearest Elizabeth,

> Now on the summit of Love's topmost peak
> Kiss we and part; no further can we go:
> And better death than we from high to low
> Should dwindle or decline from strong to weak . . .

Anna said, "Hm. It doesn't sound Chinese. Does she have a white lover, as well?"

"No, this one's from Chan Mon, too."

When the meaning of the words penetrated Anna's rattled mind, she expelled a gasp. "He's proposing a lover's death pact."

"Exactly that."

"This casts even more suspicion on Chan Mon."

"Oh, I don't know. Love makes me want to kill myself."

The corners of her lips turned slightly down. "Are you in love again already?"

Joe looked up into Anna's eyes. "What do you think?"

Anna didn't know what to think, except that his Arrow Collar Man eyes were very blue. She said nothing and stroked his head as he read her more love letters, and the candle burned down, and the church became dark so that the saints couldn't see.

Chapter 16

A string of bells tinkled as Anna pushed open the door to Mr. Jones's medicine shop. She found him bespectacled and leaning on the counter, reading a book. When he noticed her, he stowed the tome under the counter and straightened up.

"Assistant Matron Blanc, where is Detective Singer?"

"That's the funny thing. I don't know. He didn't come into work this morning. The investigation can't wait, so I'm proceeding on my own." Joe's absence irritated Anna. Part of her hoped he was in jail again eating bugs.

"And what brings you to me?"

"I have information to trade. Elizabeth Bonsor had two Chinese lovers—Leo Lim and a man named Chan Mon. I think she was leaving Leo Lim for Chan Mon." Anna slapped a love letter down onto the counter, one about ducks with their necks entwined. "Read this, if you please."

Mr. Jones started on the epistle and blushed. Anna didn't blame him. It was steamy. He set it down. "I don't know a Chan Mon."

"But surely you can find him. How many people are in Chinatown? Two thousand? You could ask around. I've been to the mission. Miss Robins says he wasn't a student there."

"I can't help you."

"Can't help me or won't? I can exchange information. Last night, I found the Bing Kong president dead in his rice bowl."

"I know."

"The Hop Sing president was in his house, which is very suspicious. But the Bing Kong president may have been killed by one of his own men."

"Leave it be, Matron Blanc. The Bing Kong will avenge their president's death. They don't need your assistance."

"But what about Elizabeth? I have a family debt to pay. What about Chan Mon?"

"I can't help you."

§

Back at Central Station, Anna stood in the kitchen and held a hot enamel cup to her lips. Mr. Melvin quivered nervously at her side. She hesitated and then sipped the dark brew—the first she had ever made.

"It tastes like coffee," she said, voice full of wonder.

"I dare say you could make other things, too, if you tried." Mr. Melvin said shyly, staring at his feet.

"Thank you for teaching me, Mr. Melvin." She poured a cup and offered it to him with her best smile. He, in turn, smiled at the table.

Anna opened the door to return to her desk, and saw Joe swinging into the station. His hair shone with brilliantine. His skin glowed from being scrubbed. He wore his best suit. He had definitely not been in jail. Had he dressed up to impress her? She slipped back into the kitchen, and, hugging her belly, watched him from the slightly open kitchen door.

Wolf sauntered over to Joe. "Assistant Matron Blanc wanted to see you." Wolf registered Joe's attire and flashed his white teeth. "Look at you. You've been visiting a lady."

Joe made a shushing sound. "Miss Lory."

Wolf's grin broadened. "Have you gotten to third base yet?"

Joe answered in a quiet, irritated voice. "No."

"Because you didn't get to second."

"That's right. I didn't try. She's not that kind of a girl."

Wolf coughed. "You don't mind my asking if, uh, Miss Blanc is that kind . . ."

Joe glared at Wolf. "Anna isn't any kind of a girl."

"Of course not."

"There isn't any other girl like Anna."

"She's a special gal. So, first base with Miss Lory?"

Joe cut him off. "She's not that kind of a girl."

"There are two kinds of girls, young Joe. Those who like physical love and those who don't. If you're planning on marrying a woman and she won't kiss you, you're in for a chilly forty years."

"I haven't asked her yet."

"That's wise. But as for Miss Blanc . . ."

"What?" Joe snapped.

"Would you say she likes physical . . ."

Joe threw up his hands and turned heel toward the kitchen.

Wolf raised his voice. "If I were you, I'd—."

Joe called back. "I know what you'd do." He opened the door and collided with Anna. Her coffee spilled down the front of his suit.

Joe scooted backward. His cheeks reddened when he met her eyes. "Wolf said you wanted to see me."

By contrast, Anna looked pale. "He's mistaken. I never want to see you again."

Joe swallowed. "Did Father Depaul get you home safely?"

The priest had surprised Joe and Anna in the church and demanded to drive her home in his wagon. The priest's timing was impeccable. Their lips were getting closer and closer, and had almost touched.

Anna fiddled with the coffee pot. "He gave me a sermon about evil men. I have to say, I couldn't agree with him more."

Joe said, "I suppose it looked unseemly."

"It's all right. I told him my side of the story, and he had to listen. They have to listen when you confess. So I confessed."

"What did you confess to? We didn't do anything."

"Unforgiveness in my heart."

Joe unpacked his lunch pail and handed it to Anna. "Eat this." It was a rice dish.

Anna dumped it in the trash. "I went to see the missionaries and Mr. Jones this morning while you were out making love."

"You should have waited for me."

"Don't you want to know what I found out?"

"What?"

"Nothing. No one's heard of this Chan Mon, but Elizabeth was definitely in love with him. If she was going to run off and marry anyone, it was him."

"I'll also ask at the mission."

"You do that."

§

Anna lounged on the giant bed in her apartment writing up notes on the case of Elizabeth Bonsor—every detail, every clue. A laundry line stretched between the gilded finials at the top of her canopy bed, hung with the drab uniform and fancy French underpinnings she'd worn yesterday. Every garment was worse, not for wear, but from incompetent laundering and the injudicious use of bleach.

The bell rang. Anna opened the door as far as it could be opened with a giant bed two feet away. Joe stood outside with a cast iron frying pan, a burlap bag, and a determined look on his face. He brushed the hair out of his eyes. It was parted on the side and badly needed cutting.

Anna raised one eyebrow. "I thought you wouldn't come to my house without a chaperone. You were afraid I would eat you or something."

"You're losing weight."

Anna looked appalled, though the afternoon frock she wore hung loose in the waist. "I beg your pardon?"

"I'm thinking you don't cook. At all. I'm thinking you're living off crackers or something."

Anna threw back her head and released a high-pitched, artificial laugh. "Nonsense."

Joe squeezed past her into the apartment where he was immediately arrested by the giant canopy bed, draped in laundry. "Lord Jesus. Why is your bed in the living room?"

"It doesn't fit in the bedroom."

Joe turned in a circle, assessing the paintings, the draperies, the fluffy rugs, and the gilded antiques crammed into the small space. "It's like sweetened condensed mansion in here."

"Why, thank you. Aren't you supposed to be off with your lovers?"

"Sherlock, you're starving right in front of me. Somebody's got to look after you." He handed Anna a piece of paper. "Miss Robins doesn't know a Chan Mon, but she gave me a list of every Chinaman who comes to the mission or attends English classes. Mr. Jones and I interviewed them. Nobody knows where Leo Lim is, nobody knows Chan Mon."

Anna's shoulders slumped infinitesimally. "Biscuits."

Joe's eyes fell upon Anna's baby grand and lingered there, suddenly distracted. He said nothing.

"I would have given it to you, you know," Anna said.

"I know." Joe slipped off his boots and crawled his way across the feather tick and matelassé white coverlet, over the lavish silk pillows, past the tassels and flounces, ribbons and drapes.

He maneuvered his way into the corner that served as Anna's kitchen. A tower of Cracker Jack boxes neatly teetered on her stove next to a heaping pile of Cracker Jack riddles. "It's worse than I thought."

"I eat kippers, too."

He glanced at a little house made of kipper tins in the corner. "I see that."

Joe restacked the Cracker Jacks on a nearby vanity. He perused through the mountain of toy surprises, picked up a riddle card, and smiled. "Have you read all these?"

"No. It's not interesting to read them alone."

"Want to play a game?"

"Maybe."

"If you get this riddle, and you swear you've never heard it before, you get one wish. If you don't, I get a wish."

"So, you'll have to grant me a wish, like a genie?"

"Only if you win. If I win, you are my genie. You have a ten-second time limit." Joe dug in his suit pocket for a gold watch, which dangled from a fob.

"Oh, I'll win." She stuck out her hand.

Joe gripped it and gave it a hardy shake. He unwrapped the riddle card, read silently, and chuckled. "You ready?"

"Ready."

"What's worse than raining cats and dogs?"

Anna replied immediately. "Hailing omnibuses."

"Doesn't count. You knew that one."

"No, I didn't. But it had to be either snow, sleet, or hail. The verb 'to sleet' isn't commonly used. It could have been snow, however there is no cliché or object that immediately comes to mind, is there? You might 'snow' someone, but it implies a successful deception, which is a good thing. How could that be worse than raining cats and dogs? So it has to be hail. What does one hail? The King, but hailing the King is usually done in celebration, so it can't be worse than raining. What does one hail in which the hailing itself or the object of hailing is annoying? Hailing an omnibus." Anna sparkled like a sunbeam. "Joe, you're my genie."

"All right. What do you want?"

Anna deliberated. After reading *What a Young Woman Ought to Know*, she had endeavored to be modest and good, most of the time, so that God would be on her side. This ruled out making Joe remove his clothes or insisting that he throw off Miss Robins. She could petition on her own behalf, or, for extra points, ask for something that would benefit others. Her better nature won out.

"Join the priesthood."

"That's want you want?"

"You said I could have my wish and you never lie."

"That's a pretty big request. I'm not even Catholic."

"It's not a request. It's a command. Be happy. It could have been much worse. I could have made you kiss Detective Snow or something," Anna said. "And do note that a priest would never hunt singsong girls."

Joe rubbed his forehead. "Okay, but only if you do whatever I ask when you lose. And I mean anything."

"Of course. But I won't lose."

"Swear."

"I swear."

"This time, you pick the question."

Joe sat on the edge of her bed while Anna selected a riddle card from the pile, barely taking her eyes off him. She fumbled blindly for his pocket watch, unwrapped the card, and read. "What is it that never asks any questions, but requires so many answers?" She looked up expectantly.

Joe's brow crumpled. "Damn." He propped his elbow on his knee and rested his chin in his hands.

Anna watched him with a silly smile. "Tick. Tick. Tick."

"Oh God! I don't know. Please don't make me kiss Detective Snow."

She laughed and clapped her hands. "You're not as smart as I thought you were, but that's all right. You have many fine qualities. You have five seconds."

"Oh no!"

"Three seconds."

"Holy Mary!"

"One second!"

"Doorbell." He grinned.

Anna frowned in consternation. "You're teasing me."

"You're my genie, now, Sherlock."

Anna's heartbeat quickened, and she bit her lip. "What's your wish, then?"

"No priesthood."

Anna's mouth flattened. "I want a rematch. Best of three," she said. "And, if the riddles are going to be so easy, you ask me this time."

Joe selected a riddle card. "Why is a ship like a woman?" He checked his watch to mark the second hand.

"Because . . ." Anna's eyes raced back and forth. She threw down her hands. "A ship isn't at all like a woman. I'm not like a ship."

"Agreed. You're more like a runaway circus train. Think about other girls." His eyes sparkled. "Tick, tick, tick."

Anna frowned in fierce concentration. "She's a . . . ? Um, she's salty? She can sink?"

Joe's face split into a wide, victorious smile. "Time's up, Genie."

Anna moaned. "I can't believe it. It mustn't make any sense at all or I would have solved it. What was the answer?"

He raised one eyebrow. "Because she is often tender to a man of war."

"That's not fair. I'm not tender."

"You wanted the rematch, Sherlock."

"Oh, and what did you want?"

He considered her for a long moment, looking rather serious. "Since I can have absolutely anything I want, and because you're a genie of your word—though I'm sure I assume too much—I want to think on it for a month or two."

"You're going to hold it over my head."

"Didn't you learn anything from fairy tales, Sherlock? The characters always fail this test. I'm not gonna be one of them. I'm gonna look before I leap."

Anna studied his face and tried to ascertain just how worried she should be. He gave nothing away.

"Would you really have joined the priesthood?"

"Absolutely."

She huffed and spun around toward the stove. "Let's cook."

Joe squeezed past Anna to a blackened potbelly stove and opened up the clinker door. The ash pit was swept clean, empty, and cold.

"Just as I thought." He dumped a heap of coal from his bag into the stove and lit it. "I can only teach you the basics, because that's all I know. But my neighbor, Mrs. Macklehainey, said she'd give you lessons if you want. I recommend it. You're gonna get so skinny you'll go chase some tong hatchet man and your dress will fall off." He extracted two handfuls of eggs from the bag and looked around. Having nowhere to put them, he apparently resolved to hold them. "Can you boil water?"

There was no trace of sarcasm in his voice, and she relaxed. "Um."

Anna scanned the few neglected kitchen soldiers hanging on the ceiling rack above Joe. Her eyes rested on a pot, its bottom shiny new and gleaming like a star. She squeezed sideways toward Joe until they were face-to-face, and very close, careful not to upset the eggs in his hands. Joe's beautiful Arrow Collar Man eyes watched her warily. Anna bit her lip. "I can't help it."

"I know. It's one thing I've always loved about you."

Anna mounted a stool, stood on tiptoes, and reached above his head for the pot. She captured the pot and filled it at the sink. She began the return journey and Joe deftly backed out of her way.

Anna set the water atop the blackened stove. "Now what?"

Joe dropped the eggs into the pot. "We're gonna make sticky rice. I need another pot."

"Sticky rice?"

"Any circus train could do it, and it's what I had on hand when I lost my mind and came over here."

"You had sticky rice on hand? No one has sticky rice on hand."

Then she thought about the many enticing rice dishes he brought in his lunch pail. If he knew how to cook those dishes, why were they making hardboiled eggs?

Then Anna's eyes fluttered wide. She put her fist to her mouth and made a desperate, hollow sound. "Jupiter."

"What?" Joe said.

She negotiated her way over to the bed and began crawling across it toward the door.

"Where are you going?" Joe asked.

"Your digs."

"No, you're not." Joe dove onto the bed and grabbed Anna by the ankles, yanking her backward. Anna kicked him and he let go. She wriggled across the coverlet and raced for the door, slamming it in Joe's face. She hopped onto her bicycle, and began peddling out onto the street, fighting to keep her hem out of the gears.

She heard a rumbling sound, and Joe flew past on his motorcycle, leaving Anna riding in his dust. He disappeared into the sooty tangle of cars, carts, and trollies.

When Anna arrived on the doorstep of Joe's basement apartment, his motorcycle was leaning on its kickstand. She banged on the door until he opened.

He said, "A single lady should not be visiting the apartment of a single man unchaperoned."

"Unless she's a singsong girl."

Joe pulled her inside and locked the door.

Anna's eyes flitted around the lonely apartment, which was entirely too clean. "You're hiding them. I know you are."

Joe crossed his arms and leaned against the wall.

"You're gaining weight, because they've been cooking for you. And, they've been giving you Chinese lessons. That's why you're so good at it." She waltzed to the bedroom door and opened it. Joe's single bed sat squarely against the wall, neatly made, beside an armoire and dresser. "I know you don't make your bed."

Joe followed her into the room. "Anna, go home."

Anna opened the armoire, sliding the clothes aside with a swish. She bent over to look under the bed, lifting the quilt. Nothing.

She dropped down onto her knees and began crawling around on the floor, knocking on the clean wood planks with her knuckles, and listening for hollow spots. She came to the rag rug and lifted the edge. "You expect me to believe that you mop beneath your rug?" Anna rolled back the rug, revealing a trap door. She reached for the ring to pull it open. Joe stepped on it with his foot. Anna lifted his foot with both arms, throwing him off balance so that he stumbled backward.

"Hey!"

She lifted the trap door.

There, in a shallow crawl space, two girls huddled in silk sacques and loose trousers. Anna crowed triumphantly. "Ah hah!"

Joe sighed. He said something in Chinese.

The older of the two girls lifted herself onto her knees and rose to her minute feet, which had been broken and bound according to the old Chinese custom. She was a lily of a girl, willowy, with inky black eyes and glossy hair pulled back in a long braid. Her chin was as high and tight as Anna's, despite the fact she could be no older than seventeen. She stood over the crawl space like a sentinel, arms crossed, guarding the second girl who stayed huddled within.

Anna began to shake. "You lied to me, Joe Singer. You're not supposed to lie."

"No Anna, I didn't. I just didn't dispel your rather unflattering misconceptions. You confronted me in the jail right in front of the jailer. I couldn't tell you what was going on. If word gets out that I'm hiding the singsong girls, the girls go straight back to the tong and I'm a dead man."

Anna scrunched her face. "You could have told me later. You didn't have to let me hate you."

"Anna, I'm trying to court someone else. It was a lot easier if you hated me. Okay?"

"I knew deep down you were a good man."

Anna slapped him.

§

Anna and Joe slumped at the table. Anna's eyes were red and puffy from crying. Joe held his head in his hands, his cheek pink from where she'd struck him. The second girl, whose name was Ting Ting, had finally come out from the crawl space, and now sat in the corner, arms wrapped tightly about her legs, rocking back and forth. She was achingly young—maybe fifteen.

The older girl, whose name was Yuk-Lin, sat near her sister trying to interest her in a game of cards. She periodically eyed Anna with anger. Anna thought it was because she'd slapped Joe. No one said a word. Anna noted how gracefully the girl moved. How exquisite she was. How she had been living alone with Joe Singer in his apartment.

Anna glanced down at her cuticles. "They cook for you."

"They cook for themselves. They share it with me because I buy the food."

How long have you had them here?"

"Six weeks."

"Jupiter."

"I'll say. I'm sleeping on the floor. I can't open the windows. The grocer looks at me funny because I'm buying so much rice and toilet paper. He knows I'm a bachelor."

Anna gasped at his mention of toilet paper and covered her mouth.

Joe smiled. "For the first two days, they wouldn't talk to me. Miss Robins kept telling them I was their American brother. She brought them clothes, picture books, paper. Told me what foods to buy. She's been incredibly brave, coming here at night. She's risked her reputation and her neck."

"She's wonderful," said Anna flatly.

"Yes, she is. On day three, the girls started talking. Once she got going, Yuk-Lin wouldn't stop. I would point to things and she'd tell me the Chinese word, I'd tell her the English. It was good for me, because of the Chinatown Squad. Then she started cooking." Joe rolled his eyes. "The lady knows her way around a kitchen. She learned how to cook in China from her grandmother apparently. Ting Ting was too young, so she does the chopping. Ting Ting's kind of timid, but Yuk-Lin is down-right bossy. And smart." He grinned. "She plays a mean game of poker."

"It's unseemly."

"Nothing unseemly has happened. You know that."

Anna did know. For all his faults, Joe Singer did not take advantage of girls. She closed her eyes and nodded.

"They've been through a lot. I don't think they much care for men, but especially white men. They consider it an abomination for a Chinese woman to sleep with a white man."

"But not the other way around?"

Joe shook his head. "But they're starting to tolerate me."

"The Squad has been tearing Chinatown apart. How did you find them?"

He gave her a cocky half smile. "I figured that if I were the Hop Sing president, I wouldn't leave my favorite singsong girls alone with a bunch of highbinders. So, I asked myself, who *would* I trust." He looked Anna in the eye and squinted. "Who would you trust more than anyone in the world with a couple of young girls?"

Anna thought for a moment. Not the nuns at the convent school where Anna had spent much of her girlhood. Just thinking about them made her bottom sting. Who did Anna wish had cared for her? "That's easy," she said. "My mother."

"I knew Tom Foo Yuen was raised in San Diego and he was no little angel."

"Tom Foo Yuen?"

"The Hop Sing president. The man who threatened you. He stole the singsong girls from the Bing Kong president. I have a friend who got me his mother's address from his juvenile record. She still lives there. That's where he took the girls. They were locked in a shed. I slipped in, stole the key when the mother went to the market, and snatched them. Of course they didn't know who I was and didn't want to come—"

Anna couldn't help but feel admiration. "And you freed them all by yourself?"

"No."

There was a knock on the door. Anna and Joe leapt to their feet, and the girls slipped silently into the bedroom.

Joe went to the threshold and put his ear to the door.

A man's voice came from outside. "It's okay. It's just me."

Joe opened the door. Detective Wolf came in breathless. "I've got bad news."

Anna gaped. She wondered if she knew anything at all about the world.

Wolf looked twice when he saw Anna. "It's always good to see you, honeybun, except now." He turned on Joe. "Why did you involve her? It's not safe for her to be here."

Joe said, "She figured it out."

Wolf's brow furrowed. "Someone at the San Diego police department ratted us out. They didn't know who was asking about Tom Foo Yuen's mother, but they suspected it was someone with the LAPD. They told the Bing Kong and the Hop Sing."

Joe closed his eyes. "Oh God."

"It gets worse. A witness in San Diego saw two white men on the train with two Chinese boys the night the girls went missing. They have good descriptions and they know we got off in LA."

Anna sunk to the bench. "If they saw Joe, they'll think the Arrow Collar Man was involved."

Joe gave her a bemused smile. "You think I look like the Arrow Collar Man?"

Anna nodded solemnly. "It will be your downfall."

Joe swore and rubbed his face with both hands. "Wolf, how did you find this out?"

"Apparently all of Chinatown knows about it. Mr. Jones heard it and came by the station to let Captain Dixon know there might be some retribution."

Joe said, "There are hundreds of cops on the force. No one is going to finger us. We're not that distinctive looking."

"You're distinctive looking," Anna said to Joe.

Wolf put his hand on the doorknob. "I've got to go back to the station. The Chinatown Squad is organizing to canvass for witnesses at the train station. They're putting up posters with the girls' pictures and our descriptions. I'm going to go take them down." He slapped Joe on the shoulder, and then he was gone.

Anna said, "You can't keep these girls in your apartment. You're putting yourself in terrible danger. Why don't you give them to me?"

"Then you would be in danger. They've been here for over a month. It's just two more nights."

"And then what?"

"There's a missionary with a refuge for singsong girls in San Francisco. Yuk-Lin says they want to go there. Miss Robins has arranged for a fishing boat to take them north Monday night. We just need to lay low until then and get the girls to the port at San Pedro."

Anna couldn't wipe the hurt and disbelief from her face. "Miss Robins? Did you tell her about the murder, too?"

"Anna, she helped us free the girls. They would never have come with us without a woman along. They would never have stayed with me. Miss Robins explained what was happening in Chinese. She's very good with the language."

"She was with you on the train?"

"No. She waited and took the next train, in case we were caught." He looked out the window. "Sherlock, I think we shouldn't talk for a while. For your own protection."

Joe didn't want her help, didn't need her detective skills. He needed Miss Robins. Anna felt as if she were falling down a precipice, as if she'd lost hold of anything solid.

§

That night, it rained. Anna dreamed of ringing bells, of letters written in invisible ink, and of men so enslaved by the tong that they would shoot Anna, as if she were a marked man, even if all of Central Station were standing by watching. Anna awoke with the terrible feeling that she was going to die. Some hatchet man would kill her dead and she would never get to see Joe Singer naked. Never get to sleep a whole night in his arms. Never know the mysteries of physical love. It awoke in her an urgent need to live her life fully, now—to do those things that filled her with joy. And nothing gave her greater joy than police work and Joe Singer's lips. Anna resolved to make unrestrained love to Joe Singer, whether he was speaking to her or not. She would tell him that he made her feel alive, and that she was feeling dead without him, and would he please come to her room tonight and reanimate her, because wasn't it the duty of a police officer to save lives, and no one else would do, only him. His lips, his skin, and his Arrow Collar Man eyes. And maybe she would have to make some concessions. The idea of a ten-year engagement came to mind. But she absolutely had to have him and would even stand a small bit of bossing, and would simply counteract it with a little bossing of her own. She needed him, and would have to tell him.

CHAPTER 17

The following night was the Chinese New Year celebration. It was the year of the Monkey, and Anna was determined to go. Her father had never permitted her to attend, even in more peaceful times. But now she controlled her own destiny. Not only could she see the festivities, she could hunt for Chan Mon and Leo Lim to atone for her father's sins. The *Herald* had printed an article promoting the event, despite warnings from the LAPD to stay away, and Anna wondered if many tourists would come. She knew who *would* be there—the Chinatown Squad.

After work, Anna changed into a yellow chinoiserie frock. She darkened her lashes with walnut stain, powdered her arms and décolletage with talc until they glowed, and dabbed her lips with Princess Pat rouge, lightly so that no one could tell. She twisted her hair up around a tournure frame to make her bun look bounteous, and gazed in the mirror. She was perfect, like a calla lily waiting to be plucked.

The crowded, unpaved streets of Chinatown were still wet from last night's rain. Pyrotechnics lit the sky and fizzed in the streets, the air a blue cloud of powder smoke. The sidewalks teemed with people—men and women of every color, spilling out into the road like a tide, coating their shoes and hems with mud. Everywhere there were punk sticks burning, releasing their incense, blending with the smell of firecrackers, muck, and tobacco. A Chinese orchestra played. The doors of homes were welcoming wide, every building open to visitors, opened to be searched for Chan Mon and Leo Lim. Anna didn't know where to start.

Men stood in the thresholds of their stores offering strangers sweetmeats, nuts, cakes, and glasses of wine. Anna accepted a cake. She slipped through the crowd, her eyes large with wonder, savoring the pleasing flavor—an unfamiliar one. The rough streets had been transformed into a miracle of iridescent lights. A few proper Chinese ladies, rarely seen under normal circumstances, were out in their bright silks, their glossy hair neatly pinned up. Anna tried to catch their eyes, but their eyes were averted. Their less-respectable sisters peered out from windows, tapping on the glass of wickets. Cheeks and lips painted, hair braided with colored artificial flowers, they beckoned to the fellows passing by.

Anna heard bells ringing in the distance—a sounding of the alarm that an officer was near. The painted girls rattled their wickets, and the banging traveled like a wave down the street. Then their heads disappeared from the windows.

She surveyed the crowd looking for *her* officer and finally caught a glimpse of him floating down Marchessault Street sucking on a candy. When she caught Joe Singer's eye, his face lit up, and he began to make his way quickly through the crowd toward her.

He arrived in front of Anna grinning. "Hey, Sherlock. You shouldn't be here."

There was something in that smile that made Anna feel joyful and light. She surveyed his neat black suit and derby hat. "A person would never know you were a cop."

"I'm undercover."

"Me too." She twirled around so he could admire her chinoiserie dress. She came to a dizzy stop and found his brows furrowed in disapproval.

Anna felt perplexed. She had thought she looked beautiful. At least people's heads had turned to watch her walk by. "What?"

"Why do you insist on coming here alone?"

"I didn't. I came with friends. We got separated."

He smirked.

Anna bit her lip. "If you're so worried about me being alone, you can walk with me."

"I can't, Sherlock. I'm here to put down hooligans."

"I'll misbehave. I promise."

"I expect you will." For a moment, he looked as if he was debating, and then he slipped his arm through hers. "All right."

As soon as Joe touched her, Anna felt a charge that shot through her body, settled in her nether parts, and sizzled there. Suddenly, she wasn't thinking about Miss Robins, the piano girl, or all the other women with bottoms in Los Angeles. She could only think of this moment, and him, his arm on hers, and the ways their bodies felt, like the opposite poles of magnets.

Above them, paper lanterns hung from wires and cast colored glows on his face. Joe looked handsome green, red, blue, and yellow. He always looked handsome, and he always smelled good, like minty, manly deliciousness.

They passed the temple on Benjamin Street, where bowls of strange confections sat before happy guardian deities standing twelve feet tall. Joe took a scoop. "Hold out your hands, Sherlock." Anna did, and he filled them with candy. She wanted to kiss him thank you, but contained herself. Making a declaration was unladylike. Doing it in public was unconscionable. She put the treats in her pocket.

They passed a tobacconist handing out cigars, and Joe accepted one. He tucked it in the pocket of Anna's dress and whispered in her ear. "Do me a favor and smoke it in private. I wouldn't want to have to arrest you."

Anna took a candy and popped it in his mouth.

There was a *bang, bang, bang*, as two drunken cowboys hollering near them on the street shot their guns into the air. Anna and Joe jumped, covering their ears. Joe took her hand and they zigzagged through the crowd, away from the whooping vaqueros.

People threw firecrackers. A bright light dazzled Anna's eyes, accompanied by the blare of a horn so loud she was sure they could hear it in Venice Beach. A locomotive came rolling slowly down the street, spewing black smoke. Joe pulled Anna back onto the sidewalk, away from the tracks as people scattered. He smiled down at her with his blue Arrow Collar Man eyes, and her heart fluttered. His hands grazed her sleeves as he dropped his hands from around her shoulders.

It made her tingle everywhere. He took her arm again. "What do you want to do? I'm on until dawn."

Anna considered as she tingled. She wanted to make love. But there were homes to visit, new foods to eat, strange music to hear. Most of all, there was a villain to capture, and Joe Singer to win back. She felt light, like she should sing, because in a way, when she learned that Joe was not a slave trader, she did get him back. She tilted her head and beamed up at him. "I want to do everything."

"Then I'll show you the lilies." Smiling, he tugged her along, passing stables where horses flinched and whinnied at the pops, bangs, and drumming. He led her away from the lights and celebration. Stable after stable stood interspersed with barns where buggies and wagons awaited the next vegetable market. Anna stopped to soothe a particularly wild-eyed bay, offering him a candy. A man lay in the corner of the stall wrapped in a blanket. He squinted at her as if she were an over-bright star.

She drew in a shallow breath and squeezed Joe's arm. "That man sleeps here."

Joe said something to the man in Chinese, perhaps an apology, and the man rolled over. Joe lowered his voice. "I'll bet a hundred men sleep in the stables in Chinatown, Sherlock. Maybe more."

"I'd like to sleep outside on a warm clear night and stare at the stars."

"It's clear tonight."

Anna threw back her head and looked up at the tiny pricks of light, and the wash of the Milky Way, a river of wishing stars. "It's becoming very clear."

Joe took her hand and tugged. "Come on. You've got to see this."

Anna let him lead her past an old brick house to an open space. She held her breath. A thousand white lilies bloomed in a field, reflecting the moonlight, more beautiful than a picture postcard. They infused the air with their lily scent.

Anna breathed. "Jupiter."

"The Chinese believe it's good luck if the lilies are in bloom at New Year. It's going to be an auspicious year."

Anna's heart lifted like a bumblebee nourished by the flowers, her love for Joe buoyed by beauty. He grinned at her. Like the lilies, this was auspicious. Tonight, she would tell him that she needed him and that she might consider a very, very long engagement. She simply had to find the words.

She said, "You made a wise choice to keep me, you know. If you're undercover, you're far less suspicious if you have a girl with you. People think we're lovers, not officers of the law."

"Yeah, but I need an ugly girl. You draw too much attention." His dimples deepened.

Anna flushed with pleasure. "Hah! I'm not that beautiful." She knew that she was.

"You got those long eyelashes . . . and those honeyed lips, they're just crying out 'ooh please kiss me.'"

She scoffed. "Ooh, please kiss me?"

Joe Singer had stopped strolling and was staring at her mouth.

"Oh, please kiss me," Anna breathed.

Joe took a step away. "See what I mean. You said that twice in one minute. Your lips are very conspicuous."

Anna resolved to make them even more so. She threw her arms around his neck and drew his head down. He groaned and turned his check so that her kiss landed awkwardly against his ear. "Anna, no. I'm sorry. I was just fooling. I . . ."

Anna was no quitter. She held her lost love tight, grazing her nose and mouth against his evening stubble, his cheeks, his chin, his reluctant lips, until his protestations quieted, their lips were nuzzling, and he fell to kissing her. His kiss, though slow in coming, was like fire and burned with all the intensity of their situation, all the passion required to overcome it—his other women, her fierce independence, his pathological obsession with marriage, and a Chinaman snoring in the background.

Desire seared her, a need to touch and be touched, and somehow merge into him. She felt that there was more to do, more to know, and she wanted to know it and do it with Joe Singer.

She took Joe's hand and moved it onto her bottom where it belonged. She murmured, "Let's be in love again, because I can't stand it when we aren't. And yes, I will marry you, even though I don't want to."

Joe Singer pulled away from her, taking his hand with him. His face contorted in a look that Anna could not interpret, but it was not joy. Then he exploded, sputtering something blasphemous and kicking the stable wall.

"What?" she asked in distress.

"Anna, I can't. I'm . . . I'm already getting married."

"You're doing what?" Anna shrieked.

"Anna, I wanted a family, and you said—."

Before Joe could finish, she shoved him hard, and he fell on his biscuits in the mud. Then, she ran. She lost Joe in the stables, and hit crowded Marchessault Street, making her way through the crowd without a single, "excuse me." Pictures of Joe's women marched through her mind. The piano girl with her raven hair, songbird voice, and musical fingers. Joe's third cousin, whom Anna had never met, but whom she imagined to be as tasty-delicious as he was. Wolf's red-haired neighbor, whom Anna had only seen from behind, but whose behind was hard to miss. The mayor's elderly daughter, and poten-tially all the other unmarried girls in Los Angeles. But it was the image of Miss Robins, with her golden curls and holy, wifely nature, which stuck in Anna's mind. She was sure Joe had chosen Miss Robins. Saint Catherine, patron saint of old maids, had failed Anna, or perhaps Saint Catherine was simply better friends with the missionary. Or maybe Joe Singer loved Miss Robins more than he had ever cared for Anna.

His love charm had worked, and he was leaving Anna behind. There was only one thing Anna could do. Go back to Mr. Melvin and see if she could exchange her gambling luck charm for a love charm.

Anna stepped up onto the planks of the crowded sidewalk, weaving her way through the happy revelers, ignoring the *bang* of fireworks, the coconut drums, and the roar of voices emanating from inside. She stared up at the winter sky now swirling with a biting wind. The wishing stars of the Milky Way had closed their eyes, drifting to sleep in the lightening, wee hours of morning. A gray sun was rising, barely visible through the gloom, like a suffocated hope. Anna would never have Joe Singer because he loved another. She would never be a police detective because she was a woman.

The detritus of the New Year's celebration littered the muddy streets: sweet wrappers, cigar butts, a broken coconut drum. Red husks of the fireworks crackled underfoot. Across the road, Anna spied her father. Of course, he'd be there. He always attended the Chinese New Year's celebration. He was ambling along with a fatherly arm across the shoulder of a younger man—perhaps his new protégé or a cousin of Anna's from France. They were heading in the opposite direction. A glimmer of hope rekindled in Anna. She hurried after them calling out, "Daddy!" Mr. Blanc glanced over his shoulder and looked at her. His eyes briefly lost focus. They hardened, and he looked away as if he didn't know her. He and the younger man kept strolling. Mr. Blanc said something to his companion, and they laughed. Anna shriveled inside.

The sun brought a jubilee to Chinatown. All debts were discharged or canceled. Every Chinese man received his fresh start. Where was Anna's fresh start?

Anna had debts to pay. Perhaps it was too late to mend bridges with her father, but she could avenge Elizabeth, though the case appeared to be going nowhere. Even if she did solve the crime, what was left for her? She would be back to chasing truants, wiping rouge off the faces of young girls in dance halls, taking children from the brothels to the Orphan's Asylum, and going home to her apartment alone.

§

Anna charged straight to the station in her chinoiserie frock. Mr. Melvin was just getting in. She accosted him on the front steps. "Mr. Melvin. You know the talisman you gave me? The one for gambling luck."

He was staring at her muddy feet. "Yes, of course."

"I haven't burned it yet. May I please exchange it for the peach blossom one? For the love luck?"

He looked distressed and shifted on his feet. "I'm ... I'm sorry Assistant Matron Blanc. There are only gambling charms left. There was only one love talisman, and I've already given it away."

"Oh." Anna stepped backward, tripping on her hem. "Oh no."

§

Anna went home to sleep. She tossed and turned with frightening dreams of Miss Robins glowing in a wedding gown, and babies that looked like Joe Singer. They all held peach blossom love charms set ablaze. Late morning, she crawled out of bed still wearing last night's yellow dress. Her body was sweaty from sleep, her eyes puffy from crying. She slunk to the bathroom, filled the tub, and slipped beneath the warm water. Why did she have to choose between independence and love? Men didn't have to. They could do any job they wished, go anywhere they wished, and be their own masters even after marriage. Women had to choose, but her time to choose was over.

Joe Singer loved another, and Anna wanted to die.

Unfortunately, she was Catholic and had to wait to grow old or to be hit by a trolley or something. Even if she weren't Catholic, she couldn't die now. Not yet. She had to catch Elizabeth's killer. And she would do it alone, without Joe, because he was faithless and being around him was terrible. She would be tempted to strike him all of the time.

But Anna knew why he loved Miss Robins. Miss Robins had something that Anna lacked. Miss Robins was good.

She forced herself to think about the case. She had two suspects— Chan Mon and Leo Lim. Neither the landlady, Miss Robins, nor Mr. Jones knew Chan Mon or where Leo Lim might be. It was possible that some of the other missionary ladies knew him. She could find them and ask, and she could continue to canvass Chinatown. She didn't need Joe to solve this crime.

Anna did her best thinking in the tub, and it was a shame when, after an hour, someone began banging on the door and continued to do so every ten minutes. She finally got out, wrapped herself in a robe, and passed a scowling line of girls waiting to use the facilities.

§

Anna returned to Chinatown. The tourists were gone, and the streets were littered red with spent firecrackers. The Chinese were out and about, still dressed in their New Year's finery, going on visits, bearing gifts. She approached everyone she encountered, showing Lim's picture and asking if anyone knew his whereabouts or had knowledge of a man named Chan Mon. Very few of the men she approached spoke English, and those who did seemed afraid—possibly of the tong, possibly of Anna's desperation. They had been so generous the previous night with their open doors and treats. Today, they told her nothing. After two fruitless hours, Anna found herself at the far end of Chinatown on Concha Street. She was exhausted from a lack of sleep, and from banging her head against the wall. She dragged herself back down Apablaza, passing a tin shop, a butcher, and a tailor. She knew all of them had men on stools calling out to passersby at night, inviting them to gamble. Most shops on Apablaza were also lotteries. There were four barbers in a row, which she imagined were really something else, because who needed four barbers in a row. They must be fan-tan parlors or opium joints. The police and the tongs seemed to be engaged in a sordid dance that Anna didn't understand. There was a pretense of reform, yet these kinds of places remained. She wondered if she knew anything at all about the world.

As Anna made her way toward Alameda, she heard voices singing in Chinese to the tune of "Amazing Grace." Ahead she saw what could only be the missionary ladies—four women, unknown to Anna, hymnals in hand, standing on the street, proclaiming their god. At least she wouldn't have to walk all the way to the mission. Miss Robins was not among them, another small mercy. A few Chinese men sang with the women, and Anna imagined they were converts. Could one of them be Chan Mon? At the conclusion of the hymn, and before they could start another, Anna laid her hand on the sleeve of the closest girl. "Excuse me, I'm looking for a man named Chan Mon."

The girl left the choir and drew Anna away so that she could be heard. "I'm sorry. What do you need?"

"Do you know a Chan Mon? He's a friend of Elizabeth Bonsor, and I'm looking for him."

"I don't know any Chan Mon. Are you from Elizabeth's church?"

"No. I'm a police matron on official LAPD business."

The woman looked suitably impressed.

Anna continued. "Does Elizabeth have any man friends?"

"She's a friend to all of the men at the mission. We all are. But none of them is named Chan Mon."

"Could it be a nickname?"

She thought a moment. "It doesn't sound like one. Chan Mon is a proper Chinese name."

§

Anna returned to her desk at the station, which was stacked with things to do. Fortunately, Joe was out, probably on purpose. There were five drunk women in the cells, whom she visited—victims of Chinese New Year. Two lacked suitable winter clothes. She gave them frocks and fresh drawers from Elizabeth's trunk.

Anna stayed in the rest of the day doing paperwork. She made a plan for how she could catch up on her matron's duties, sorting tasks into things she must do, and things she could fake or lie about. She concocted cover stories that she could tell Wolf, explaining her absences— she had searched for a missing child. She had addressed a ladies' club about holding men responsible for ruining vulnerable girls. The latter, she thought, was a good idea, and she might actually do it someday.

There was nothing to do on Elizabeth's case. She had reached a dead end.

Anna went home at four o'clock, pleading a headache. She changed into a satin nightgown and ate Cracker Jacks in her big, soft bed. She drank whiskey, possibly too much. She was aroused from a fitful sleep by a knock at her door. Anna rolled out of bed, wiping drool from her cheek, and answered. Another resident stood in the hall wearing street clothes. Anna guessed it must still be early.

"Miss Blanc, there is a call for you on the tube. A missionary."

Miss Robins was calling.

Anna tasted the bitterness of bile and whiskey and scrunched up her face. Did the missionary know that Anna loved Joe? Perhaps she was calling to comfort her. Or to gloat.

"You're welcome," the girl said with irritation and huffed off.

"Thank you," Anna called. She changed into a tea gown and dragged herself corsetless into the hallway where the telephone receiver lay unhooked on a table. Anna steeled herself, summoning a false cheer. She would not betray her true feelings to Miss Robins. Ever. "Hello?"

"Matron Blanc?" The voice was unfamiliar. Anna relaxed.

"Yes."

"The clerk at the police station gave me your number. I'm calling about Elizabeth Bonsor. I heard you were interested in her man friend. Has he committed a crime?"

Anna felt a rising, tentative hope. "I don't know. I need to question him."

"I hope you don't think I'm a gossip, or a bad friend. It's just, I don't approve of her man friend."

"Of course. I understand." Actually, Anna didn't. She would never give her friend's lover up to the police, especially if he was Chinese.

"Well, his name is Leo Lim," she said.

"Do you know where I can find him?"

"No."

Anna's fragile hope dashed like a dropped teacup. "I know about Leo Lim. There is another man I'm looking for. A Chan Mon."

"Chan Mon," the girl repeated, thoughtfully.

Anna waited.

"I did see Elizabeth with a strange man one time. You can ask Miss Robins. I saw the four of them together in the street."

"Miss Bonsor, Miss Robins, Leo Lim, and this other man?"

"Yes. I don't recall his name, but they were all standing together, and I joined them. They were talking about how Miss Bonsor and Miss Robins wanted to hike to Sturtevant Falls. I said I would like to go, but we never did. And the man said he had a hunting cabin beyond the falls on the creek, but said it was too far to hike there and back in a day. It must be off the San Gabriel Trail."

"What did he look like?"

"Tall, I suppose. I don't see well, so I'm not good with faces. I would never recognize him now."

"And you think his name might have been Chan Mon?"

The girl was silent for a moment. "I don't know. Maybe not."

Anna closed her eyes and breathed out. "Thank you, Miss . . ."

"Miss Perry."

"Thank you, Miss Perry. Good night." Anna put down the phone. Her broken heart was beating faster. She tried to slow it down. The unknown man might or might not be Chan Mon, but if his cabin was on that creek, Anna would find it.

§

If Chan Mon had been a white man, Anna could have looked him up in the land registry. But Chinese men could not own land. If the unknown man was Chan Mon, he was either squatting in the mountains or renting the place. If she could find his cabin, she might be able to discover a clue as to his location, or perhaps even the man himself. The question was, did she take that step alone? Anna had never spent the night in the woods before. There were cougars and bears, wild men and bandits. There were two murder suspects on the loose—many more if Mr. Jones was wrong about the tong not killing Elizabeth. But asking Joe to accompany her alone, overnight, was out of the question. And he would try to prevent her from going anyway. She could ask Wolf to assign another officer to help, but she would be taken off the case. Also there was the risk of their secret getting out, potentially causing a riot in

Chinatown. Anna decided that this was her debt to pay, and she would solve the crime and make things right. If she perished, she perished. No one would miss her.

In the morning, she would go to Sturtevant Falls and follow the San Gabriel Trail beyond, up to the cabin. All she really needed was a gun, a map, and a proper pair of walking shoes. A tent would be nice, but she couldn't afford one. And hadn't she always wanted to sleep out under the stars? She would find the cabin and perhaps the man. She would interview him at gunpoint. If he were Chan Mon, she would take him down the mountain and let Joe figure out what to do with him. She might be physically weaker than her suspect, but she had the element of surprise on her side. She would have to catch him unaware and far away from his hunting rifle.

CHAPTER 18

The next morning, Anna padded barefoot into the cold hallway and used the phone to call the station. She feigned a coughing fit and told Mr. Melvin that she would not be into the station that day as she had influenza. She gathered four boxes of Cracker Jacks, a tin of kippers, a tin of sardines, a whiskey bottle filled with water, a silver flask filled with whiskey, a carved ivory matchbox, her toothbrush and tooth powder, soap, bullets, a sterling mirror and brush set, and a cloth for washing. She added a pair of handcuffs she had lifted from the station. Anna wrapped them all up in a thick cashmere blanket, which she planned to use for sleeping, and tied it like a present. She donned a second pair of drawers over the ones she already wore. Tomorrow morning, she would simply switch them so the clean pair was on the inside. She slipped her tired feet into bicycling boots, because they were her most sensible shoes and would protect her legs from snakebites almost to the knee. She changed into her matron ensemble for extra authority, strapped on her holster, and tossed a Frederick Worth wool coat with a mink collar over her arm. She topped everything with a feathered hat.

Anna still longed for a tent, though carrying it would be like carrying the twelve-foot brocade drapes from her father's living room, including the curtain rods. Both sets. Luckily, if the weather was foul, Anna could build a lean-to. She'd seen it in a book.

She paused before departing, set down her bag, and scratched out a will on gilded monogrammed stationery. She left everything to her best friend, Clara Breedlove, even, after some hesitation, her baby grand.

§

Anna took a Red Car heading for the foothills of the San Gabriel Mountains and Poison Oak Flats, the trailhead leading to what might be Chan Mon's cabin. She had been to the trailhead once before with Clara and Clara's husband, Theo, and they'd hiked to Sturtevant Falls. Anna still had the map. That day, it had not been forty frigid degrees outside.

The three other passengers who braved the cold morning shivered off in the town of Sierra Madre, leaving Anna alone on the Red Car with a bleary-eyed conductor with a day's growth of beard who only half-filled his uniform. At Poison Oak Flats, he stopped the trolley. She slung her blanket of supplies over one shoulder and stepped from the car. The driver drawled after her. "You're crazy going hiking alone. There are mountain lions, coyotes, rattlesnakes—"

Anna tossed her head. "Hah. They're afraid of men." At least Theo Breedlove had said so. And besides, she hardly ever heard of people getting eaten by bears and mountain lions.

"You're not a man."

Anna ignored him because he was both rude and right.

He further intruded. "It's winter, Missy. If you get caught in the rain, you could die from exposure. You won't even know it's happening. You're cold, and then suddenly you're hot. But you're still truly cold, but you don't know it. Then, you go crazy. I've seen freezing men strip off their clothes in the snow, right down to their underwear. You wouldn't want that to happen." Clearly he did. He peeled her with his eyes.

Anna squirmed. "That's taffy. I know when I'm cold. And it's not going to rain. I checked the weather forecast."

"Suit yourself."

Soon the trolley rolled off leaving Anna alone, wrapped in the warmest of wool coats with the prettiest of fur collars, and her chin lifted high. Still, thanks to the trolley driver, she felt a little naked. She exhaled a cloud of white breath.

Anna surveyed her surroundings. The grass was edged with morning frost. Flea-bitten mules slept standing up at a lonely pack station. She could rent one for riding, but the proprietor was nowhere to be seen, and Anna didn't have the money anyway. She slipped across the muddy road, sliding in her slick boots, to a wooden sign that presided over the trailhead. It announced various paths and distances in burned letters—Sturtevant Falls, two miles, the Mount Wilson Observatory, six miles, Mount Disappointment, fifteen miles, and thirty miles to Rubio Pavilion on the San Gabriel Trail. How many miles to Chan Mon's cabin? More than a day's walk. Was that ten miles? She could walk ten miles; more if she had to. In Summerland, she'd walked for hours on the beach, combing the coastline up toward Santa Barbara every single day.

Anna poked around in the brush, looking for a long stick. When she found one, she tied her bundle on the end and threw it over her shoulder. She buttoned her wool coat and embarked. The trail had seen better days and now featured tiny barrancas where rainwater had carved its way down the slope. The heels of her bicycle boots sunk into the wet earth, smeared with mud. But the wind smelled of sage, and she hoped that at the top of the hill she would be able to see the ocean. Oak trees offered shade from the glare of the silver sky, their upper branches hung with mistletoe. Every so often Anna rested, swigging water from her whiskey bottle and refilling it whenever the trail crossed a stream.

Three hour's hike up the path, Anna sat on a rock near a creek where the water cascaded down over large, mossy boulders. She thought about her father and what he would think about her marching off into danger to right his wrongs—possibly to her death. Would he feel sorry? Would he forgive her? Could she ever forgive him?

She thought not.

Anna's pink cheeks glowed, both sweaty and cold at the same time. She took out her map and spread it across her lap, which was a mistake. While she swigged from her makeshift canteen, the wind lifted the map and blew it onto the bank of the creek. Anna swore. "Biscuits!" She hopped off the rock in pursuit, but heard the clip clop of a mule coming up behind her. She abandoned the map and scrambled behind an oak tree, hiding in case the traveler was a bandit or other person of mal intent.

The traveler was Joe Singer. He wore denim waist overalls, a Stetson hat, and a red bandana. She watched him pass on a mule that he had undoubtedly commandeered from the pack station. To her dismay, he swung a leg over the beast and jumped down, bending over to fill a canteen at the creek. Anna made an involuntary sound of grief, a sort of feminine snort.

Joe's head whipped around. "Sherlock?"

Anna said nothing.

He stood and turned toward the source of the snort. "Sherlock, I know you're there. I can see your feathers."

Anna stepped out from behind the tree, feathers snagging on pine branches. "I suppose you've been to see the missionary girls and they told you about the hunting cabin. But that's no surprise, under the circumstances."

"Anna, are you crazy? You can't go up into the wilderness pursuing a criminal on your own. He could be dangerous. Not to mention the cougars and the bears."

It was true, of course, but Anna felt rather reckless with her life at the moment. And if she wasn't a sleuth, what was she? Nothing. "Please stop telling me things are dangerous. I know. I'm not stupid. I can take care of myself, and I brought a gun."

Joe sighed. "I don't suppose there is anything I can do to make you go home."

"You should go home. I was here first, and it's unseemly for you to be with me."

"Not a chance." He trudged over to where she stood, took the cashmere bundle from the end of the stick, relieving the burden on her shoulder. He rubbed the soft, thick blanket between his fingers, looking amused. "Isn't this a little fancy for the back country? What did this cost? A month's salary?"

"I don't know, but it's warm."

The mule drank from the stream. Joe left her side, walked over to the beast, and tied Anna's bundle to a saddlebag. She picked her way out of the brush, deliberately avoiding the clumps of mistletoe that hung overhead. Her map was gone, undoubtedly blown into the water and floating down stream. She lifted her chin. "Do you have a map?"

"No. The man at the pack station said I didn't need one. The trails are all signposted. Want to ride the mule?"

"I don't need any favors."

"I'm guessing you must have tried riding astride before, when your daddy wasn't looking."

"Riding like a man is child's play. It takes far more skill to ride side saddle."

"No doubt. Are you sure you don't want to ride? The man at the pack station said that hunting cabin is a good twelve miles, maybe further."

Anna blinked. It was a greater distance than she had anticipated. Still, she had no intention of riding his beast. "I'm sure."

"Suit yourself." Joe swung onto the mule in one smooth motion.

It occurred to Anna that if she were riding the mule, Joe Singer would have to walk twelve miles. This would make up for any discomfort she felt at accepting his favor. "I changed my mind."

Smiling crookedly, Joe dismounted. Anna put her foot in the stirrup, and though she didn't need help, Joe put his big hands on her small waist and lifted her. Her slit skirt bunched up around her knees, baring her police matron bloomers. He handed her the reigns. "Here you go, partner."

Anna didn't thank him.

Joe walked on ahead while Anna rocked along in the saddle. Her eyes left the stony trail and focused on Joe's backside. She cleared her throat. "Was there any trouble at Chinese New Year?"

Joe kicked a rock. "One hoodlum shoved an officer, but she got away."

"I'm sure he sorely deserved it."

"He's just trying to make a life for himself."

"I wish him luck, truly I do."

Joe turned and looked at her, brows drawn together. "You do?"

"Of course." Anna lifted her chin. "So, did you make a collar?"

"I broke up a fight. Caught a couple of white guys pilfering souvenirs from a shop. But there wasn't any shooting. Not at people anyway. And there were so many cops in Chinatown, we were competing for troublemakers."

"How disappointing."

"Wolf caught a crazy man with his pants down on Main Street."

Anna stifled a laugh. Joe turned and grinned at her.

Several miles up, the trail became steep switchbacks, and Anna was glad for the mule. Oaks gave way to pines, and the path forked. A post stood sentry, but there was no sign. Joe stopped and wiped a drip of sweat from his cheek with his bandana.

"Signposted, are they?" She pulled the mule to a halt.

Joe pointed to a charred board in a fire pit—the remnants of the sign. "That's not my fault."

She untied her cashmere blanket, found the whiskey bottle, and uncapped it, taking a swig of water. "We'll simply take one trail, and if it doesn't lead to the cabin, we'll double back. It can't be that far." She put a finger to her chin. "Except, we don't know how far it is. We won't know if we missed it, or if we just haven't gone far enough . . ."

"I have a better idea. Let's go off trail and follow the streambed. You can climb on rocks, right? If his cabin is on the creek, we are bound to run into it. No doubling back. No missing the cabin. I'll collar Chan Mon, if he's home, and we can sleep there. Our coats will be warm enough if we're inside."

"But we'll have to leave the mule."

"He'll be all right." Joe led the mule off the trail, and tied it to a tree. He took the food out of the saddlebags and put it in his pack. "If we leave food, it will attract bears."

Anna noticed he added his toothbrush. She grabbed her own toiletries from her cashmere bundle and hurried over. "If we're spending the night . . ." Handing him the comb and mirror, she accidentally let go before he'd grasped them. Joe caught the falling comb, but the mirror tumbled onto a rock, and the looking glass cracked. He frowned. "Sorry. I'm sure it was expensive. I'll get it fixed for you."

Anna stared at him wide-eyed. "You can't fix seven years' bad luck."

He smirked, placed the comb and mirror in his bag, and slung it on his back.

Joe and Anna followed the streambed up the canyon, hopping from wet rock to wet rock, avoiding the poison oak that grew near the water's edge. Joe was climbing the rocks like a human fly. Anna struggled because her bicycle boots, great for avoiding snakebites, had low heels and smooth soles, making rock climbing difficult.

The saturated air smelled of crushed, wild mint. It cooled her nose and heightened Anna's senses. Her boots were slippery on the algae-slick granite, and twice she fell in, scattering trout and water bugs, her skirt billowing out in the frigid current. Joe pulled her up with his strong, calloused hands, and she carried on, her wool coat heavy and dripping.

Anna fell in again, scraping herself on a stick, ripping her police bloomers and skinning her leg clear up to her thigh. Joe picked her up again and plunked her down on a boulder. "Give me your foot."

"Why?" Anna obliged, raising her right ankle.

Joe cradled her foot in his palm. "Because you're wearing the wrong shoes."

It was true. Her heels were slippery, and made her sink backward as she walked. She had blisters, and the wet would only make them rub worse. But she didn't know what he could do about it.

He reached one hand into his pocket for a knife, flipped open the blade, wedged it in the sole of her shoe, and popped off the heel. He began to score the sole to roughen it, and then repeated the operation on her left shoe.

"Thank you kindly for ruining my boots. These were custom made by François Pinet."

"Sherlock, they were ruined already." Joe let go of her foot, and it fell like a lead weight. She started to shiver. She consulted her wet pocket watch, which no longer ticked. Anna frowned hard. The little hand had stopped at four, and they hadn't yet found Chan Mon's cabin. The sun now hung behind the mountains, casting the canyon into shadow. The winter sun would set in two hours.

Joe looked concerned. "Let's go back to the mule. You have gotta change into dry clothes."

"I didn't bring dry clothes. I've accepted that I'm going to get influenza."

"It isn't influenza I'm worried about. People die from cold, Sherlock. You'd know that if you were raised somewhere with a winter."

"Everyone dies sometime."

He lifted his eyebrows. "Not you. I have blankets on the mule." Joe plunked down on a rock and took off his shoes. He rose, stripped off his coat, sprung his suspenders, and dropped his pants. He stood before her with nothing covering his bottom half but a pair of clingy woolen underwear. Anna put her hand over her open mouth. God had made Joe Singer well.

It gave Anna a renewed desire to live. "Jupiter." She bit her lip and said a silent prayer of thanks to Saint Agatha, patron saint of virgins, who was likely behind it.

Joe's shirt came off. He stepped out of his denim pants, standing in nothing but his tight stripped vest, drawers, and a holster. Anna's breath caught.

Joe mistook her gasp for concern. "Don't worry, Sherlock. I'll be all right. They're dry. And I still have my hat." He pitched his clothes, and they came flying at her. "Go put them on."

Anna caught them with both hands. "That's very gallant Detective Singer." She headed for the rocks to change. Rounding a boulder, she peeked back around to stare surreptitiously at Joe. He caught her looking, and she retracted her head. Blushing, Anna hid behind a fern and stripped.

While Joe wore only underwear, Anna now wore none at all. Her sopping chemise, corset, corset cover, garter belt, holster, silk stockings, and two sets of drawers lay in a heavy, dripping heap alongside her skirt, bloomers, and coat. She wrung them out and tied them into a bundle. Only her wide-brimmed feathered hat remained dry and still pinned to her head. It occurred to her that her revolver had gone swimming as well. She unholstered her wet rod and set it on a rock.

Joe's cotton shirt hung on Anna like a circus tent, touching her body only at her shoulders, her wrists, and two other places. It smelled of his sweat, which Anna didn't mind at all. His soft denim trousers dangled from a bandana tied at her waist, sliding across her bare bottom with every step. They were warm from his skin. The thought made her feel like hiding. She felt naked, and he had found another love. Donning his coat, she buttoned it to the neck before emerging from behind the rock. In one hand, she held her sopping garments out away from her body so they wouldn't wet Joe's clothes. In the other, she held her waterlogged gun.

It was now dusky dark. A pack of coyotes yipped nearby. She'd seen coyotes in the mornings, singles or pairs, hunting squirrels and cats in the neighborhood. She had heard that sometimes they attacked young children. She wondered what they would do in a pack. Anna urgently picked her way through the forest toward the sound of Joe's voice, eager for the safety that comes in numbers. His back was turned, and he was singing.

". . . Boy began to sigh, looked up at the sky, and told the moon his little tale of woe."

Anna sat down on a boulder, and called out, "I'm back." She opened the chamber of her damp gun, removed the bullets, and put the barrel in her mouth.

Joe turned. "Mother of God." He came hurtling toward Anna.

Anna blew hard, sending a spray of water out the end of the barrel. Joe grabbed her gun.

Anna made a sound of objection. "It's wet. If your gun gets wet, you blow the water out, and it works again. I thought you'd know that."

"Yeah, but I didn't think you'd know that."

"Well, I can't have it wet. I might need it." She snatched it back.

The beam from Joe's flashlight drifted down Anna's well-draped body, and she heard him swear again.

"What?" Anna looked down at her ensemble in the spotlight.

"I was just remembering the last time you borrowed my clothes. My hat got trampled, and my best suit went up in flames."

"I'll keep them safe. I promise. And, I'll wash them."

"No, thank you."

Anna's face crumpled. The faithless man she used to love did not even trust her with his laundry.

"Are you warm, now?"

"Sort of, thank you."

Joe tossed her a candy bar. "Eat." He rubbed his arms. "Let's get going."

As they followed the stream down, climbing on boulders and through bushes that must be poison oak, a mist settled in, making the night colder and the darkness more impenetrable. Above them, the tree-tops shook in an icy wind.

Joe stepped on a green, algae-ridden rock and slipped into the water, wetting one shoe. He swore. "Ding bust it."

Anna nimbly leapt to his side. "Are you all right?"

"I'm fine, but we're going to have to leave the streambed before you get wet, too. If we head in the right direction, we'll hit a trail. It won't be too far from water. We'll either hit the cabin or the fork in the trail where the mule is."

"Agreed. Right or left?"

"I don't know. Right."

They trudged into the brush, perpendicular to the streambed. Joe led, whacking at the bushes with a stick, forging a way through where there was no way. She kept the flashlight aimed at his feet, following closely in the circle of light, so close that when he stopped she bumped into him. He had goose pimples.

"Are you very chilled?" asked Anna.

"I'm all right."

She pushed her flask into Joe's hand. "Have my whiskey. It will keep you warm. Drink all of it. I don't care."

Anna put the flask in his hand, which felt Siberian cold. He swigged deeply and stuck the flask in the waistband of his skivvies. "Thanks, Sherlock."

"Drink more."

He mouthed the flask, bent his neck back, and swallowed.

When they came to the hill, he took the flashlight. "You'll need both your hands."

Anna abandoned her bundle of wet clothes because they impeded her ability to climb. She felt sorry to lose the coat with the soft mink collar, but the water had ruined it, and it would soon be out of vogue anyway. Side by side, they scrambled up a hill, pulling themselves up on branches, dislodging mud, rocks, and leaves in little landslides. Joe held the flashlight in his mouth. Finally, as the flashlight began to dim, Anna and Joe hit a long, narrow path, which snaked along the side of the hill.

Joe took a spare battery out of his pack and replaced the old one in the flashlight. "What do you think? Right or left?"

"I . . ." Anna looked up at the faintly visible mountain ridge. "Right."

The light from Joe's flashlight shimmered in the fog, illuminating only a few rocky steps ahead of them. The groomed trail represented a new kind of danger—the human kind. Inside every shadow, Anna imagined a killer. She wanted to cling to Joe, but her dignity prevented it.

Somewhere in the night, she heard a prolonged, high-pitched scream. They stopped. Anna put a hand on her gun. "Jupiter."

Joe whispered, "It's a cougar. A female."

"What do we do?"

"Keep moving."

It was frigid cold. They walked in silence. After an hour, the beam from Joe's flashlight began to tremble almost imperceptibly. After two hours, it was shaking. To Anna's relief they reached the fork in the trail not far from where they'd tied the mule. Joe dropped the light. He bent to pick it up and fell over. He mumbled something that sounded profane. Anna extended her hand, suppressing a smile. "How easily you are felled, Detective Singer."

He stood up. "I'm hot."

"That's dopey." She stretched out her hand and laid it across his brow. "You're shivering."

He grabbed the hem of his vest in both hands and tried to lift it over his head, revealing his belly and an intriguing strip of dark hair.

Fear slapped Anna in the face. "No you don't!" She pulled his undershirt back down. This was just like the conductor had said on the trolley. Joe was dopey, irrational, and hot when he was very cold. That whiskey hadn't worked at all. Would he die, then? Because of her?

Joe began to unbutton his drawers. She swatted his icy hands away from the waistband. He went back to lifting his vest.

"No, no, no," she said, wrestling with his frigid, trembling fingers.

He glowered. "I'm so hot." He yanked his body away from her.

She darted behind him, knocked out his knees, and shoved him sideways. He crumpled onto the forest floor. "Hey!"

She shouted at him. "If you don't keep warm, you'll die. You said so."

Joe rolled over on his back and began to fumble with his vest again, trying to pull it over his belly. Anna dropped to the ground and sat on him. She swatted his shaking hands away, and smoothed down his undershirt. "You need to keep your clothes on. Okay?"

Up went his shirt. Anna straddled him for better leverage and yanked his shirt down. "No," she said sharply, as if reprimanding a little dog.

Joe Singer, who was always the gentleman, now smiled like a masher. His grin was blue. "You got the right idea, Sherlock." He beat his chest and hollered. "I'm on fire."

He grabbed Anna and tried to kiss her, but she dodged it. She thought it wrong to take advantage of Joe Singer when he was cuckoo with cold and whiskey.

"Yes. We'll both be very hot once we get to camp. We'll build a fire."

"I want to get married."

"You are getting married. To a breeder."

"Sherlock, I want you. Let's make love. Right here. Right now."

"Stay there." Anna leapt up and bolted to the mule, which was still tethered to the tree. Her eyes widened. A mountain man was unbuckling one saddlebag, the other already hung from his shoulder, her cashmere bundle dangling from it. He was hairy and dirty, and he was touching her things.

She reached in her pocket for her revolver and pointed it at him. "Hey!"

He dropped her cashmere bundle and loped off into the dark forest with the saddlebag.

"Give it back!" She heard the sound of hoof beats and screamed after him, "You, you! You unconscionable hillbilly!"

Joe's spare clothes were gone. The kettle was on the ground. Her cashmere bundle lay in the mud some three feet away. She groaned. At least she had her gun and a box of dry matches, now safe in the pocket of Joe's pants. She had seen the man's pale face—English maybe, or French. He was not Chan Mon.

Joe's bedroll still hung from the mule. She quickly retrieved it— two heavy wool blankets pinned together at the side with horse safety pins. She flew back to Joe. He had pulled his undershirt halfway over his head and then quit. She could see his hairy armpits and his stubbly chin, but nothing more of his head. Anna grabbed the hem and tugged it down. "Joe, there could be Chumash Indian ladies hiding in the bushes."

His blue lips didn't answer.

Anna felt the fluttering of panic in her chest. She unrolled the blankets on top of Joe and scanned the area for shelter. There was a V-shaped gap between two boulders, and one of the rocks had a three-foot overhang. The wind couldn't reach them, and she could build a fire to warm him, and to keep away the mountain lion.

"Joe, you have to get up and walk."

"Anna, take off my clothes."

"Yes, I will. But you have to walk over to the big rock. Then, I'll take your clothes off me and put them on you."

"No. Don't put them on me. I'm too hot. Give them to the Chumash ladies. We are going to live under the rock, you and me. I'll hunt. You'll smash acorns."

"Yes, Joe. But only if you walk to the rock."

He grinned. "You bet I will."

Anna took Joe's hands and pulled him to a sitting position. She peeled off his pack, then wrapped an arm around his torso and squatted like an Olympic weight lifter. "Ready? One, two . . ."

He turned his face to hers, his breath a white cloud. "I've wanted you since the first time I saw you."

"One, two, three." She lifted, and Joe Singer rose, shaky, clumsy, and drunk with cold.

The shelter under the rock was shallow, but it had been used before. A fire pit blackened the ground by a stack of dry wood. This gave Anna pause, but she had very little choice. If the owner of the firewood returned and he was malevolent, she would simply have to shoot him.

Anna helped Joe to lie down very near the fire pit. She untied the bandana around her waist and the pants dropped to the dust. She stepped out of them. She slipped off his coat and laid it atop the covers. Anna kept only his shirt, the shirttails falling down her thighs like a nightgown, her legs bare but for her wet, knee-high boots. Very soon, she would be freezing, too. She hugged herself with one hand, and put the other on Joe's forehead. He felt like an ice cube and trembled violently. And it was all her fault. Anna draped him with the bedrolls and forced the pants over his feet, scooching them up his manly legs. She could not get the pants over his biscuits. "Lift your backside." He did not. She left his pants bunched at his thighs and wrapped the bandana around his head, tying it under his chin.

Anna went back to retrieve her bundle. She dumped her things out of the cashmere blanket and wound it around her waist. It fit snugly, like a hobble skirt. She took Joe's flashlight, which lay on the ground where he had fallen, and ventured out into the brush surrounding the cave, looking for kindling. When she had a suitable amount, she easily built a fire, having frequently played with matches as a child. The fire burned brightly within a few minutes, casting its glow on Joe Singer's shivering form.

Anna tried to recall what Kit Carson would do in such a situation. He would make coffee, certainly. And he would feed Joe.

Now Anna shivered.

She jogged back to Joe's pack and dug for coffee, sugar, and a tin of sardines. She retrieved the kettle from the ground. Emptying Joe's canteen into the kettle, she set the water to boil. Thankfully, sardines did not need to be cooked.

Anna crawled atop the two pinned blankets instead of underneath with Joe, for modesty's sake, and lay on his chest holding the tin of sardines. "Open up. Yum, yum. Sardines." She dangled a fish over his face like he was a seal who would leap for it.

"Leave me alone," he said.

Anna took his mouth in her hand and squished his lips together. "Open."

When his jaw parted to complain, she propped his teeth open with her finger and slipped in a fish. She held his mouth closed. "Chew."

"No," he garbled. The fish slipped back out. Anna tilted the tin and poured fish oil down his throat. He made a gurgling sound.

Anna unpinned her hat, lay down, and trembled atop the shivering Joe Singer, arms to arms, legs to legs, three layers between them. She tried to be warm, to think hot thoughts. "Don't die," she whispered. "I need you in the world."

"Anna, lie with me."

"Yes. I'm here." She felt the gentle rise and fall of his chest with each frosty breath. Anna was bone tired. With her cheek to his breast, she waited for the whistling of the kettle. Her breathing slowed, matching his, and before she heard the kettle singing, Anna fell asleep, her hand on the gun.

The next morning, Anna feared opening her eyes. Joe might have died. Also, he was much friendlier cold than warm. She wasn't sure what he would do if he awoke to find himself lying beneath the girl that he used to love. She guessed that the honorable, toasty Joe would not like it. Lastly, she imagined she had spoiled his kettle, as it had surely boiled dry during the night.

Anna gradually became aware that she was not lying atop the muscular body of Joe Singer anymore, but lying between two blankets on the hard ground. Anna opened her eyes and sat up, clutching the blanket around her. The sun had risen, but had not yet reached its fingers between the mountains. The fire had long since died. "Joe," she called tentatively. He did not answer.

Anna stood and dragged the wool blanket behind her, walking out from under the overhang. Above her, the sky threatened a deluge, just going to show that weather bureau was not to be trusted.

"Joe?" She surveyed the surrounding misty forest. "Joe!" She was greeted with silence, except for the sound of chipmunks and the gentle roar of the wind swaying the trees.

The pack still lay on the ground, but Joe had taken his coat and gone.

Anna's face grew hot. Doubtless, he was angry at her improprieties, even though they had saved his life. So angry he had left her behind. Some men were simply more concerned with honor than practicality. She had hoped that Joe Singer would be above honor. Because even though he was angry, she would do it again, and more, to save him. Even if it meant covering him with her body completely naked, she shouldn't have to explain herself. It made her angry, and she was glad he was gone.

The mule still loitered, tied to the tree and still wearing its saddle. At least he had left her that. Her toothbrush, tooth powder, broken mirror, and comb sat neatly on a rock. Anna took out her knife and cut a hole toward the middle of Joe's two wool blankets. She ducked her head through the hole and wore them like a poncho, repinning them on the side with the giant horse safety pins. They dragged on the ground behind her when she walked, and while trains were fashionable this one simply got in the way. She cut it off.

Anna raised her arms to the side like a massive, shapeless, wooly bird. The poncho now reached to her knees. Beneath the poncho, she wore Joe's shirt and the makeshift cashmere hobble skirt.

Anna ate a tin of kippers from the pack and brushed her teeth with tooth powder, rinsing with water from her whiskey bottle and spitting on the ground. She examined her image in the silver hand mirror, which had cracked down the middle. Even from the split reflection, she could tell her double pompadour lay flat on one side. She removed the hairpins and the rat, which gave her bun volume, and retwisted it up into a knot. The result did not inspire her. She topped the mess with her hat and pinned it in place—a feathered hat for the giant bird.

Anna considered her next step. Joe could have gone back up the stream, returned to the trailhead, or taken one of the paths up the mountain. Anna scanned the ground for evidence, starting at the mouth of the overhang. He had left tracks in the mud like a hippopotamus. She followed them to the fork where the stream and two trails came together. Other tracks marred the trail, but his footsteps led up the left fork. Anna went right so as to avoid him, pulling the mule along behind her, because she couldn't straddle the thing with the cashmere blanket wrapped tight around her waist.

Dewdrops shimmered in the chaparral. The air smelled fresh, like rain, and tiny waterfalls trickled down the hillside onto the trail. Anna would have found the hike pleasant if the way hadn't been so lonely, and if she hadn't felt so deeply ashamed, abandoned by everyone, and afraid. The thieving hillbilly might still be skulking about, and though Anna had bested him once, next time he would be prepared.

A diamondback stretched across the trail, the upper third of its body folded like a ribbon, its tale rattling. Anna went very still. The mule stomped and pulled against the lead. She backed up slowly, slowly, and then threw rocks at the thing until the snake slithered away.

Anna shed her cashmere hobble skirt, and mounted the mule, riding man-style so as to be out of the way of snakes and such. The wool poncho slid up to bare her knees. She draped the cashmere blanket over her lap for modesty's sake, though there was no one to see. She decided she should name the mule, and settled on Mule Robins, after Miss Robins, even though it was homely and a boy.

Anna followed every little path that diverged from the main trail, to see if any led to a cabin in the woods. Some meandered down to the water. Others petered out after a time, probably made by deer or coyotes. She followed each of them to their conclusion and returned back to the main trail by the way she had come, following Mule Robins's tracks.

When the sun had reached its zenith, she dismounted and ate a box of Cracker Jacks. She wondered if Joe had remembered to bring his lunch. She hoped not. She wondered what mules ate. She rummaged through the pack and found a bag of jerky, a chunk of cheese, four apples, and six peanut butter sandwiches. She ate all of it except the apples, which she saved, and three of the sandwiches, which she tried to feed to the mule.

Feeling fuller than she had in weeks, Anna remounted the mule and returned to her task, riding up the trail, exploring every side path along the way.

The shadows were growing and the forest cooling. If she didn't turn back soon, she would be caught alone in the dark. Mule Robins had eaten nothing but weeds all day. Also, she had Joe's blankets, and maybe all of his food. No matter how much she wanted to avoid him, she couldn't leave him cold and hungry. Anna decided to return to the overhang and hope he'd come back. She could find the cabin tomorrow. Maybe, if she didn't have to look at him, they could search together. She took one last trail, which ended in a crystal stream choked with giant boulders. Green lichens clung to them desperately. She would have to climb a boulder to see what lay on the other side. Considering this, she dismounted and donned her skirt, tying Mule Robins to a tree. She knelt to refill her whiskey bottle, careful to avoid the little water bugs that skated on the surface.

Anna meandered over to a boulder. It felt cold to the touch. She tentatively set her foot into a crack that ran from top to bottom. Her hands gripped the frigid surface as she wedged herself in and used her back and feet to scoot up the rock. At the top, she hauled herself out. She saw what she needed to see—a manmade pool damned with rocks. It teamed with shimmering trout over a foot long. Quietly, Anna climbed down the far surface of the boulder and landed softly on the damp ground. A mossy log stretched across the stream, half submerged in the rippling, clear water. If she removed her shoes and gripped with her toes, she thought she could cross it. She stopped to listen and heard no human sounds. Boots in hand, she deftly padded her way across the slick log, icy water lapping at her feet. At the very end, she slipped into ankle deep water and waded to the bank, holding up her blanket skirt, but it was too late. A corner was soggy and stuck to her legs. She brushed the mud from her feet with her hand, and reshod herself— always quiet, always listening.

Anna made her way to the pool where two giant trout lay cooling, strung on a string. She squatted and lifted the heavy string partly out of the water, sniffing the fish. They weren't spoiled. Someone close by still planned to eat them.

She tiptoed through the brush parallel to a stony path leading away from the water, all the while smelling the wintery odor of a fire. Soon she could see a cabin through the pines, built of river rock and logs— possibly the lair of a murderer. Anna spied a larger trail, which led off downstream. She'd seen no crossing and wondered whether both forks in the trail had led to the cabin.

A mule brayed, and the friendly sound chilled her. She stopped mid-step. This was what Anna wanted—to find Elizabeth's killer and bring him to justice. She had come to the mountain alone for just this purpose, equipped with a gun and cuffs. Yesterday, with the wound of Joe's engagement and her father's snub still fresh, Anna had felt careless with her life. She had felt hunting killers was her only purpose, and it was. But now she wondered if she wouldn't catch more killers if she let this one go. Joe still wandered somewhere in the woods, maybe nearby. Unlike Anna, he knew how to make a collar. She should swallow her pride and find him even though he had humiliated her once again by leaving her alone. Finding him was the sensible thing. Anna turned and quietly slipped down the path toward the pool of fish. She kept her gun in hand.

Something occurred to Anna. It wasn't like Joe to humiliate her wordlessly and at a distance. He usually did it in person. For the first time, she wondered if he were possibly still cuckoo, and had simply wandered off. She didn't know how long cold could rob a man of his wits. Maybe he would encounter the killer and face him crazed and vulnerable. Perhaps he had found the cabin already. Perhaps the killer had captured him. Joe might be in danger. He might need her. Anna's heart pounded. She had to think.

If Joe were still crazy, she should first check the cabin—the most dangerous place.

Anna crouched in the trees for several minutes and watched. She saw and heard neither Joe nor Chan Mon and so crept forward. The pine needles crackled softly beneath her feet. She had to circumvent a trash heap to reach the cabin wall. Most of the refuse looked old and weathered, but there was a crust of burnt rice shaped like the bottom of a pot and covered in ants, a smattering of used tealeaves, and a pile of fresh fish bones—also ant-ridden. Someone had burned dinner. Anna poked about with her long stick and counted seven fish spines. She doubted that any man could eat more than one of those large fish per day, and estimated that one man had been in the mountains at least seven days, or two had stayed three days, and so on.

Anna snuck to the outside of the hut, staying quiet, keeping low. She peeked through the weathered wooden blinds that covered the cabin's glassless windows. They let in only a little light, and Anna's eyes had to adjust to the dimness. The hut consisted of one large room with a crude table, a homemade bed covered in a gray wool blanket, and a stove. A stack of books towered on the table. She could see the front door, which stood open and allowed a rectangle of sunlight to glow on the floor. Most of the space lay within view, but a man could conceal himself if he leaned up against the wall. She listened at the window.

Anna heard a rustling behind her. She swung about, gun extended.

A lone mule—not Mule Robins—stood in the forest chewing the bark off a cedar tree. He brayed. Anna put a hand to her chest and panted.

Suddenly outside seemed more dangerous than inside. Anna moved her revolver in an arc, panning the trees. Nothing. No one. She slunk around the cabin, gun arm first, and slipped in the door. She stole to the window on the far side of the cabin and peered out between the slats. She appeared to be alone, and yet the wood-burning stove radiated heat.

Anna quickly moved backward through the cabin, keeping her face to the door and her gun arm extended, but quickly taking in her surroundings. Mud smeared the floor. There were pots and provisions. A saddle and riding tack—probably for the mule—waited on the floor in the corner. A suit of clothes lay folded on a crude wooden trunk under the far window. They looked too new and nice to be Joe's. Anna considered taking them, as they would be an improvement over her current ensemble. She picked them up, sniffed them, and dropped them immediately. They smelled like a sweaty stranger. Better to wear Joe's blankets, which smelled like the sweaty man she didn't love.

Anna leafed through the books stacked on the table. They were all written in Chinese, except for one—a book of poetry in English. A fragile hope rose in Anna. She opened the book to a marked page and read, "Now on the summit of Love's topmost peak Kiss we and part; no further can we go . . ."

It was titled "Love's Wisdom" and attributed to Alfred Austin. Chan Mon had copied the poem in his love letter to Elizabeth. Anna closed the book, her heart rising. This could be no coincidence. The hunting cabin must belong to Chan Mon, one of her two murder suspects. But where was he? More importantly, where was Joe?

Anna peeked out the window again. The sinking sun dazzled her eyes. Thirty feet off, an outhouse stood nearly black against the glare. A man ambled from the privy toward the cabin, backlit.

He drew nearer.

Before Anna could fully register her fear, a second figure—a Chinese man—sprang from the cover of the trees, as silent as death, his long braid swishing from side to side. He raised an arm above his head and Anna saw the glint of steel. Then something was spinning in the air, hurtling toward the first man like a dark pinwheel. It sunk into its mark with a terrible thud. The marked man stumbled forward onto his knees and crumpled face-first into the weeds.

Anna's wrist began to tremble uncontrollably. She couldn't peel her eyes away from the place where the man had fallen and the handle of what looked like a small axe protruding from his back.

She should flee.

Anna raced to the entrance but realized the cabin door swung in the killer's line of sight. She stumbled to a halt. He might not come to the cabin. He might not find her if she kept hidden inside. She bolted back to the window. The killer was stepping on the body and, with two hands, jerked the hatchet one way and then the other. It came loose with a crack. He wiped the blade on the fallen man's coat and gazed toward the open cabin door. His narrow shoulders rose and fell, rose and fell maniacally—fueled by adrenaline from the kill.

Anna wasn't much of a shot—not at a distance, not with the sun in her eyes. She hadn't many opportunities to practice. If she were to hit him, she would have to wait for the killer to draw dangerously near. And so he did, stalking toward the cabin, the cleaver dangling down past his knees.

Anna had miscalculated.

Her hand still trembled. She stuck the barrel of her revolver through the window shutter, steadied it on a slat, and aimed at the man. He drew nearer. She could clearly see his hardened face, not ten paces away, and hear his heavy breathing—in and out, in and out.

He seemed to notice the gun barrel sticking through the window and raised the hatchet.

Anna fired.

The shot went wide, jarring her hand with its violent recoil, sending her backward on her bottom as the axe hit the blinds and came crashing through, slicing her poncho and pinning it to the floorboards, tethering Anna.

Anna rose on one elbow and shot blindly out the window. She wrested the ax free from her poncho with both hands and scrambled to her feet, positioning herself at the side of the door, gun aimed to shoot anyone who entered.

She waited, listening, and heard silence.

Anna peeked around the door and gazed back toward the body. The killer was running off toward the woods, disappearing beyond her sight. She heard him urging a horse to move. Shadows passed through the trees, and horse hooves pounded the trail out of sight. The beats receded into silence.

Anna flew out the cabin door, shaking her wrist, saying a silent prayer to Saint Michael, patron saint of policemen, that the cleaved man was not Joe Singer. He lay facedown. Blood pooled over a slit between his shoulder blades and seeped down his coat into the weeds. His hat had tipped, covering his head. Anna quickly rolled him over. Glazed eyes stared into her face and didn't see her. She fell back onto her bottom in the mud, panting. Her head was spinning, her own lungs as breathless as the dead man's. She made an unladylike gasping sound, and tried to swallow it. The man was not Joe Singer.

Anna whispered to Saint Michael, "Thank you, thank you, thank you."

The dead man wore the beginnings of a beard, as if he'd been in the mountains for days, but his dandyish suit was completely inappropriate for a hunting trip.

He was not Chan Mon.

The man was Leo Lim.

Anna glanced nervously about. She grabbed handfuls of her cashmere blanket and twisted them into coils. She would do well to sneak away and find Joe as soon as possible—for her safety and for his. But the forest seemed as dangerous as the cabin. Anna looked down at the body bleeding out into the wild grass, staining the green stalks crimson. She used a stick to poke the bloody corpse in all the places where a weapon might be harbored. She could use an extra gun. But this had been no fair fight. The dead man was unarmed. The killer was devoid of honor. This was a paltry clue. In Anna's experience, most men were without honor in one way or another.

Anna heard twigs snapping behind her.

She swung about, raising her gun. Her eyes landed on the mule. It had wandered close enough for Anna to smell its musk. She put a hand to her damp chest.

The late afternoon sun now hid behind silver clouds, and coyotes were yipping. She would be caught on the trail after dark, and she needed to find Joe post haste. The killer was somewhere on the mountain, and Joe might still be cuckoo, needing her protection. Even if he were sane, he shouldn't be caught by surprise. Anna had to go. She slipped back into the cabin and collected the cleaver and the gray wool blanket from the bed. Leaving, she glanced over at Leo Lim's body. He lay still. She waved politely and hurried off down the path toward the creek.

CHAPTER 19

The moon rose high in the sky. Anna could see it between the tops of the pine trees. Beneath the overhang, a fire burned in the circle of stones. She saw Joe emerge from the darkness with an armful of wood. Both vexed and relieved, she watched him stoke the fire. Anna tied Mule Robins to a tree and collected the string of fish she had stolen from Chan Mon's pond. Joe straightened up, scanned the vicinity, and went back out into the night. He was heading straight for Anna, not seeing her. When he came close, she stepped out into his path. "How dare you?"

Joe Singer threw her to the ground with a fancy wrestling maneuver, making Anna wish she'd studied judo. She landed with a thud on her face in a bed of pine needles with Joe Singer's knee pinning her spine and an arm twisted behind her back. She held tightly to the string of fish.

Anna wheezed. "Uncle."

"Anna?"

"I wasn't ready."

Joe dropped down beside her. "Sherlock? God damn it. Where have you been? I've been worried out of my skin. Are you all right?" She rolled over. He took both of her hands, and pulled her into a sitting position. He squeezed her against him, apparently thought better of it, and unsqueezed her.

"I could ask you the same question," she said, barely able to speak for lack of oxygen.

"Me? I was down at the creek trying to catch you some breakfast. When I came back, you were gone. I thought Chan Mon got you. I've been looking for you all over this mountain."

Anna softened at this. While leaving Anna had been a stupid thing to do, Joe hadn't intended to abandon her. Relief warmed her. Perhaps Joe didn't think her behavior brazen. "I'm fine, but Leo Lim isn't. I saw Chan Mon kill him with a hatchet. A hatchet, Joe. Just like our severed head!" She handed him the string of giant trout. "I caught these fish."

Joe took the fish, looking puzzled. "I know. I saw the body."

"You took the right fork? That can't be. I saw your tracks. And I would have seen you."

"I went left."

"Then both trails lead to the cabin."

"Apparently so." Joe helped her to her feet. "What are you wearing?" He raised his flashlight and shined it on Anna's outfit. He shook his head. "You ruined my blankets."

Anna chose to ignore him. She had villains to catch and murders to solve, and she wasn't going to be upset by unfaithful detectives quibbling over blankets. "I think Chan Mon may have killed Ko Chung. Who else would use a hatchet?"

"A highbinder."

"Chan Mon is Bing Kong, then? And a poetry lover?" It went against Anna's idea of a poet.

"It looks like it, Sherlock. It would explain the death threat." Joe walked to Mule Robins and removed a flask from his pack. He passed it to her. "You look cold."

Anna took a swig and handed it back. "You are the one that gets cold."

Joe covered one eye with his hand. "About that . . ."

"Yes."

"You know I was crazy."

"Well, you never do make much sense." Anna tossed her head, her throat still burning from the whiskey. "I saved your life, you know."

"I could say the same thing."

"Then we're even."

Clouds covered the moon, diffusing the light, causing it to glow. Joe looked up. "I'll be relieved when we're off this mountain. We're no longer equipped for the weather."

Part of Anna wanted to stay on the mountain and for Joe to get hypothermia again, because when he was cold, he said the sweetest things. She sighed. "Let's camp somewhere else. Chan Mon may have seen our camp."

They led Mule Robins to a spot down the creek far away from the trail, where the killer would be less likely to encounter them. Anna pulled Chan Mon's quilt off Mule Robins.

Beneath her homemade poncho Anna pulled the edge of the cashmere blanket tighter around her waist and tucked it into itself. She laid the quilt on the damp earth and sat down under a tree, leaning against it, exhausted and shivering. Joe lowered himself down next to her, his back to the trunk. Anna said, "The thief got the tent."

"I'm not going to sleep anyway. You're wearing my bedroll."

Anna hugged herself beneath the poncho. "You're tired. You should try. I can keep first watch. I'm too cold to sleep."

Joe looked at her, his eyebrows drawn together in concern. "Sherlock, you're shivering."

"Yes. It must be forty degrees out."

He began to unbutton his coat, as any gentleman would.

"You can't give me your coat. We tried that last night, and you ended up going cuckoo. I need you sane if we're going to hunt the killer."

Joe looked down and blew out a long, thinking breath. He glanced up again, and they locked eyes. Anna bit her lip.

Joe extended his hand to Anna and she took it. He pulled her bulky woolen form onto his lap and let her settle between his legs, wrapping his arms around her. He cleared his throat. "I'd do the same if you were Wolf."

Anna nodded, unpinning her hat and setting it on the ground so that it didn't hit Joe in the face. She unbuckled her holster, laying her gun on the ground beside her.

A minute passed, and Joe didn't say or do anything objectionable, so Anna relaxed into him, letting her head loll against his shoulder. He smelled delicious.

He said, "We can't spoon."

"I don't want to."

"I love someone else."

"Me too."

"Damn, my hands are cold." He set his revolver down on the ground with Anna's and rubbed his fingers.

Anna unpinned a horse safety pin on each side of her poncho, took his hands, and brought them inside the blanket, settling them on her bent knees, covering them with her own. "I'd do the same if you were Wolf."

"Not if I'm within a hundred miles." He laced his fingers with hers, almost possessively.

She could feel his breath on her hair, and a pounding in his chest. She could feel his hands on her legs through the cashmere blanket, and the press of his body through four blessed layers of fabric.

Anna played with his fingers.

He said, "I love another woman."

"Me too."

"We can't spoon."

"I don't want to. I don't love you. I never did."

"Are you warm?"

"A little. It's breezy. I'm not wearing underwear."

Joe was silent for a moment. "Oh God."

There was a whistle and a thud, and bark exploded above them.

Joe dove on top of Anna as she yelped. A cleaver protruded from the bark, pinning Joe's Stetson to the tree. Joe frantically felt the ground for his gun. "Where's my rod?"

"I think I kicked it!"

Joe disentangled himself from her poncho, lifted her to her feet, and gave her back a shove. "Run! I'll be right behind you."

Anna couldn't run fast, wrapped as she was in the hobble skirt. Then the width of her strides forced her skirt to unwind, and the cashmere blanket fell to the ground. "Biscuits!" She knelt to retrieve it.

Anna ran jiggling and bare-bottomed in her long poncho, which fell past her knees, trailing her cashmere blanket in her fist. She kept running all the way to the fork in the trail.

She turned back to Joe, but he wasn't there. She whispered his name, too frightened to call aloud, and searched the forest with wide, desperate eyes. Had he been cleaved? Seeing no one, she slunk back the way she had come, looking for her almost-lover.

Anna heard a scream. This time, it wasn't a cougar, but the cry of a man. Anna tore through the forest, pushing branches aside and stumbling through patches of poison oak. "Joe!" She broke through into a meadow. There, in the moonlit clearing, the cougar crouched, her teeth on the throat of a man who thrashed blindly in a slick of gore. The cat shook her head, and the man's head bobbled like a toy. Anna could hear the grass beneath them, rustling with the struggle, but the man made no sound. Then his throat tore away and his head fell back. The cat ate.

Anna's mouth opened, but nothing came out. An owl flew silently from a tree. The cat looked up. It shifted its gaze past Anna.

She heard Joe speaking in a low, calm voice behind her. "Whatever you do, don't run. Just raise the blanket above your head. You need to make yourself look big."

Anna did, lifting the back of her poncho high above her head. She felt a breeze on her bare bottom.

"Oh Lord," he said.

Anna dropped the blanket.

"No! Lift it up," he hissed.

Anna did.

"Now slowly back away."

Anna began to walk backward, feeling blindly for every step.

The cat returned to her meal, tearing deep into the corpse.

Anna reached Joe's side. He raised his hand to hold hers and they backed away together.

When they could no longer see the cougar through the trees, they turned and sprinted.

§

They arrived back at the oak tree where they had not spooned. Mule Robins still loitered, secured to a branch. Joe leaned his forehead on his hand against the tree. Anna bent over at the waist, sucking in air, her stomach seizing. She gasped, "Why didn't you just shoot him. He's eating our suspect."

"You kicked our guns. I couldn't find them in the dark with a man throwing cleavers at me."

"Only because you leapt on top of me. I was about to grab my gun and shoot him, but I was slowed down because you were holding my hands."

"Definitely a mistake," he said, looking disgusted—with himself or with Anna she didn't know. Either way, it stung.

He found his pack leaning against the tree and retrieved the flashlight. He held it for Anna who dropped to her knees and began searching for their guns. Finding them, she handed Joe his revolver. She reached for the cleaver and Joe's ruined hat. The handle felt smooth and cold, like steel. She grasped it, yanking so that the knife dislodged from the tree and came away in her hands.

Joe untied the animal. "Anna, get on. Go down the mountain. A cougar that's just eaten isn't going to attack a girl on a mule. Still, keep your eyes open and your gun drawn." He helped her mount the beast.

Anna held the cleaver in one hand. "What about you?"

"I'll be right behind you."

"I won't go without you." Joe handed her the reins and smacked Mule Robins hard on the flank. "Yah!" Mule Robins, already skittish from the cat, bolted before Anna could object, throwing her backward in the saddle. When she regained control of the creature and steered it back to the oak tree, Joe Singer was gone. She cursed. She had hoped he knew better than to try to save a half-eaten killer.

She rode back to the path and waited.

Anna heard a gunshot.

Joe came running down the trail. "I didn't want her to eat that poor bastard."

Anna couldn't imagine why. The man had thrown a hatchet at them. "Is the cougar dead?"

"No, I just scared her off. Are you all right?"

Joe moved to Anna's side and raised his arms to lift her off the mule.

Anna wasn't about to slip into his arms, no matter how she had feared for him. She deftly dismounted on the other side, accidentally exposing her knees, and eliciting from Joe another "Oh Lord."

She lifted her chin. "Do you think the dead man is Chan Mon?"

"He was Chinese. He had a queue." Joe took the reins and brought the mule around. "We've got to go back for the bodies."

§

Anna rode Mule Robins, and Joe walked close beside her. Both held their guns. Joe shone the flashlight on the trail, lighting his steps. Night insects buzzed, and something rattled in the bushes. Anna could see her breath. She slumped in the saddle, exhausted, but afraid that if she closed her eyes, she'd fall off. She closed them anyway. Twice, she jerked awake, not having been aware that she had slept in the first place. They took the left fork and, after two hours, found the cabin and Leo Lim.

Anna wiped her cheek, leaving a streak of dirt. "Let's sleep. There's a bed in the cabin, and I'm cold and tired. It's not like the bodies will run away." She swung her leg over the beast and plopped onto the ground.

The cabin felt only marginally warmer than the wilderness outside. The fire in the stove had long since gone out. While Joe added wood and relit it, Anna unpinned her hat and let her hair down. She retied the cashmere blanket around her waist and smoothed Joe's shirttails over it. She took off her poncho and spread it out on the bed like the blanket it was, topping it with the muddy quilt. "I get the bed."

She crawled in and pulled the blankets to her chin, her bare feet like ice. Joe stripped down to his skivvies. He lifted the covers and slipped in beside Anna. "We both get the bed."

She closed her eyes and held her breath. He turned his back to her. "Goodnight, Sherlock."

She listened to his rhythmic breathing until she fell asleep.

§

Anna awoke to the braying of the mules and sat up, her long hair tumbling down her back. Joe slept beside her, looking peaceful and delicious, like an angel in his underwear, with two days' growth of beard. His head rested on his arm, as Anna had the only pillow. He lay facing her now, his lips parted, smelling of sleep. She sat up and peered through the window slats. Outside, the sky was pink. Leo Lim lay splayed on the frosty ground, having been dragged a few feet by coyotes in the night. Three mangy dogs stood around the body, vying for it.

She shook Joe gently. "Wake up, sleepy head." He opened his eyes and gave her a crooked, languid smile.

"Dogs are eating Leo Lim."

He rolled over on his back and stared at the ceiling. "That's unfortunate."

"I don't know what we're supposed to do about it."

Joe sat up and looked through the window slats. "We should have brought him inside."

"I don't share bedrooms with corpses, except for you, and only when I'm trying to solve a friend's murder and discharge a family debt." Anna swung her legs out of bed, bare feet on cold planks. She retied the cashmere blanket around her waist. It still felt as soft as clouds on her bare legs, despite all it had been through and how dirty it was.

Joe reached over and fingered the cashmere. Anna stood, and the blanket slipped from his grasp.

He sighed. "I guess I'll go save Leo Lim."

"It's too late."

Joe went outside in his underwear and coat and threw rocks at the coyotes until they scattered. A few moments later, Anna trudged out toward the outhouse wearing her poncho, once more the giant bird. The stray mule still hung about the cabin, chomping on wild grasses.

Joe loitered about, waiting for Anna to use the outhouse, in case the coyotes returned.

The privy was a horrid affair, full of fresh poop and flies—more evidence that Leo Lim had been there for several days. After using it, she burst out the door gagging.

They returned to the cabin. Joe grabbed a bucket and left. Anna added logs to the fire and looked for coffee. There was only tea.

Joe swung through the door with water and a big, cleaned trout on a string. Anna lifted her chin. "There isn't coffee, and I can't make tea."

"It's easy. I'll show you." He came to stand beside her, cheeks pink from the cold. "You put it in the pot and you add the boiling water. Then you strain it." He picked up a teapot and stared down the spout. "This one has a strainer built in."

Anna took the teapot from his hand. "How much?"

"A teaspoon per cup." He smiled at her for no reason.

Joe set about boiling rice and fried up the fish in lard. It made the cabin smell good. Anna watched in case she ever needed to do it.

Joe ate with her at the splintery table and even bowed his head when she said her prayer. The trout was flaky and flavorful. Though Anna had no appetite, she ate two servings to maintain her strength.

The tea was hot, and the tin cup burned her lips. Anna blew on the green, sugarless brew. "I think Leo Lim might be an innocent man, even if Elizabeth's body was found in his apartment. We know Chan Mon is a murderer."

"Chan Mon could have been avenging Elizabeth."

"Leo Lim too. He could have been lying in wait. He knew Chan Mon had this cabin. They used to be friends."

"Then where is his weapon?"

"I don't know. This is the trouble with love triangles," Anna said. "Either way, I resent that we have to clean up after them."

"Chan Mon will be a pretty mess if that cat came back."

Anna abandoned her dirty dish and searched the cabin for woodsman's gloves. After finding them, she emptied a large burlap sack of rice, pouring the grain onto the floor and lamenting the waste. She said, "For remains."

Joe nodded. He took the gloves and the quilt and went outside.

Anna used the opportunity to style her hair. Ten minutes later, he came back for the tack, his face grim. Anna followed him outside. He saddled the stray mule and wrestled a long, stiff bundle over the saddle—Leo Lim wrapped in the dirty quilt. It wobbled like a teeter-totter.

Anna shook her head. "That won't work."

"Grab one end."

With reluctance, Anna did. Joe grimaced and pushed hard on his legs until it took all her weight to hold Leo Lim down. The body cracked and slowly bent from the middle at a forty-five degree angle. Anna screwed up her face. "That's disgusting."

Joe looked pale, slightly green even. "We need to go, or we'll never get back by dark. Can you make it all the way to the trailhead? I guess it's twenty miles, mostly downhill."

"Of course."

"That a girl, Sherlock."

§

Joe led the funeral mule, and Anna rode Mule Robins, wending down the mountainside. She was leaden with fatigue. They stopped in the clearing where the mountain lion had killed their assailant. Joe shot his gun into the air once to spook the cougar, but the cat was nowhere to be seen. "I wouldn't look if I were you, Anna. You'll never forget it."

"I have to. In case you miss something." Anna squinted her eyes as if that would somehow take away the horror. Chan Mon was mere hair and some bone. Her mouth puckered in disgust. "There isn't much left. There's no way we can identify him."

"That and the fact that nobody's ever heard of Chan Mon."

"There's got to be something distinguishing about him. Not his clothes. Most of Chinatown has this same ensemble."

Joe's face contorted in a look of disgust as he bent to collect the remains with gloved hands, and put them in the rice sack.

Anna wandered about the area.

Joe picked up a severed foot. "What are you doing?"

"There might be a clue."

"I'm pretty sure the cat did it."

"Hah. I meant a clue to the other crimes." Anna searched the area and tiptoed across the spongy green earth near a burbling stream. She found a stiff piece of leather with blood on it, with the remnants of ties and three sheaths. One sheath still had a cleaver in it—sharp and rectangular like the one that had killed Joe's hat and Leo Lim.

Sitting in the water was a canvas pack. It contained packets of cooked sticky rice, dried fish, dried strawberries, and a canteen. Anna scooped it up, keeping it as evidence.

When Joe had gathered up all the pieces and loaded them on the mule with Leo Lim, he and Anna headed for home.

§

It was almost dark when Anna and Joe arrived at the pack station with two ripening corpses. The ominous clouds had let loose their water and sheets of rain were falling, making Anna's hat wilt and her double pompadour stick to her skull. A black horse with a star stood drearily among the mules in the pack station corral. She hadn't seen it on the way in and wondered if it had belonged to Chan Mon.

Anna waited with the bodies, pelting rocks at the occasional scavenger bird, while Joe tied Mule Robins to a tree and went to use a call box. The box hung from a tree trunk near the trailhead. She watched him open it and turn the crank on the telephone.

Joe wandered back to Anna and sat on a granite rock. They waited in companionable silence—Joe smoking a cigarette, Anna throwing rocks at any vulture that descended upon the mule. She hit a vulture square on the beak and smiled darkly. "Did you call Wolf?"

"No, the national forest is the sheriff's jurisdiction. But I did ask them to bring you some clothes."

Anna frowned. The Sheriff's Department wasn't known for cooperating with the LAPD. Likely, Anna and Joe would be excluded from the investigation. Everyone would assume that the mauled man was

Chan Mon and that he had killed Leo Lim, and so it appeared. But they wouldn't take the trouble to find out for sure—not for a Chinese man. Anna would be more thorough.

She wished she could identify Chan Mon's body with more than a cabin and a poetry book. "I think we need to review the case right away and try to figure out what all of this means. I have whiskey at home. Maybe we can trace the knives."

His lovely lips flattened into a grim line. "Sherlock, I think it needs to be somewhere public."

"You're afraid to be alone with me."

"Terrified."

"You spent the night with me last night."

"I was tired."

Anna thanked God that they had been attacked with a hatchet, that their assailant had been eaten by a mountain lion, and that Joe had insulted her, saying holding her hand was a mistake. Otherwise, tired or not, she would have succumbed to Joe's deliciousness, rolling into his arms, and other things, and it would be difficult to pretend he wasn't a temptation.

"Truly, you have nothing to fear from me. Especially when you smell the way you do."

Joe frowned, pinched his vest with two fingers, and sniffed down his collar.

Actually, Anna loved how he smelled. If it could be bottled, Anna would spend all her money on Joe Singer perfume. "We had a passing infatuation, that's all. I would never interfere with you and your charming fiancée. You know how I feel about love triangles. I wish you the best, really I do."

"I was just saying . . ."

"Besides, you're the most unattractive man I know, now that I know you. Personality is more important than physical appearance, and you don't have either. And, you're poor. Then add to that your dismal hygiene."

Joe winced. "Okay, okay, I understand."

§

Anna went back to her apartment to think and bathe alone. The bathroom welcomed her, unoccupied. She shed the ugly hand-me-down gown the sheriff had brought for her, and stepped into the tepid tub. Her feet throbbed, her skin itched, but the bath water soothed her saddle-sore bottom and the raw places on her toes and heels where blister upon blister had formed and then popped.

Her two main suspects were dead, which only made her task more difficult. She couldn't question them about themselves or each other. Maybe she should just assume one of them was guilty and give up. The possibility remained that it was a white villain who fatally punished Elizabeth for loving a Chinese man. But Anna had nobody left to ask.

CHAPTER 20

The next morning, Anna awoke with a red, runny nose and a rash on her shins from poison oak. She could hardly lift her legs to crawl over to the kitchen corner and her stack of kipper tins. The stack was lamentably short. Her police bloomers—the ones that had cost her so dearly—moldered somewhere in the woods. Despite losing three days of paid work for her trek in the mountains, her murder investigation was nowhere. Anna smeared Vick's Croup and Pneumonia Salve on her chest and donned a green velvet gown with Irish lace trim from Vionnet of the House of Doucet. She smelled regrettably of menthol. She chose an especially large hat with lots of feathers and flowers to cast shadows over her pale, splotchy face. Anna limped to the trolley stop, sneezing, and rode the tram to work.

A wanted poster hung inside the door at Central Station. It featured the faces of Yuk-Lin and Ting Ting and descriptions of the two men seen with them on the train, offering a $1,000 reward for their capture. What the poster didn't say, and what all of Central Station knew, was that the two wanted men were rumored to be LAPD cops. Worry lines creased Anna's delicate brow. She tried to smooth them, and failed.

Wolf approached, noted the poster, and, looking this way and that, quickly took it down. He grinned at Anna. "You look lovely Assistant Matron Blanc, but where is your uniform?"

Anna sneezed.

"Bless you, honeybun. About that uniform . . ."

Anna kept sneezing.

"Gesundheit!"

Anna sneezed again and planned to keep sneezing until Wolf finally went away. He did. Joe appeared at her side with a handkerchief. He extended it to her. "You should be in bed."

"I've got things to do."

"Me, too." He whispered, "Tonight's the night. Miss Robins says the fisherman won't wait another day."

Anna's mouth flattened. "You and Wolf still plan on taking the girls to San Pedro? I don't think you should."

"Anna, I don't see a way around it."

"Send Wolf alone. One man is less suspicious than two."

Joe shook his head. "He might need my help. I'm heading to the mission now to finalize the plans."

"Then I'm coming with you."

The mission was the last place Anna wanted to be. Surely Miss Robins was his fiancée. And no fiancée worth her salt would let Joe Singer take Yuk-Lin and Ting Ting to San Pedro. There was going to be a fight. As off-putting as it was, Anna needed to be there to back up Miss Robins.

§

Mrs. Puce reclined on the settee in the parlor at the mission. She had a bit of spittle in the corner of her mouth, and her sunflower eyes were shining bright, as if she had a fever.

Miss Robins glided soberly from teacup to teacup with a pot of steaming Oolong. Anna noticed for the first time that she had a tiny scar on her temple—a breach in her perfection.

"Wolf and I will take the girls. I'm not willing to risk sending anyone else." Joe dumped two heaps of sugar into his teacup and stirred.

Anna didn't touch her tea. "Both tongs are looking for the men that took their girls. So is the LAPD. They'll have eyes at the port, and they know what you look like. If the Bing Kong or the Hop Sing catch you, they'll chop off your head."

Joe wrinkled his brow. "Maybe not. I am the police chief's son."

Mrs. Puce chimed in with her lilting voice. "No, they'll chop off your head."

Anna stood. "Then, it's settled. You can't go. Am I not right, Miss Robins? I'll take the girls. Instead of dressing like boys, they can wear my clothes. I have hats and veils—"

Joe shook his head. "Unescorted in the middle of the night? Absolutely not. I can't let you."

Anna said, "True, you can't. Because you don't get to let me or not let me. I thought we were clear on that."

They were all silent for a moment. Mrs. Puce said, "Maybe we all should stay and have tea."

Miss Robins sounded vehement. "And return the girls to slavery? So that little girl can be raped every night? It's appalling. Tom Foo Yuen has beaten at least one girl to death because she defied him. And when he tires of abusing them, he'll put them in a brothel. They'll be forced to lie with ten men in an evening. I've seen it before. One day, they'll simply turn them out on the streets if the girls don't die from the pox first." She rose to her feet and came to stand by Anna's side. She slipped her arm through Anna's and lifted her chin like a brave soldier. "Matron Blanc is correct. You can't go, Joe. You'd only put yourself and the girls in danger. Anna and I will go together. We have to do what we have to do, and we'll be fine. God is on our side."

Anna grimaced.

Joe stood solidly on two manly feet. "No. I'll borrow Anna's clothes, but you're not going anywhere."

§

Yuk-Lin's and Ting Ting's colored silks lay in a pile on the floor of Joe's bedroom. Reluctantly, Anna had picked her two ugliest, cheapest gowns—which were both expensive and exquisite—and offered them to the girls as disguises. Yuk-Lin's gown fit loosely. Ting Ting swam in hers. Miss Robins cut the fabric mercilessly, while Anna moaned. Miss Robins could sew. Of course she could. The young missionary went at Ting Ting with a pincushion, tucking in the borrowed frock at the waist, making a new hem that grazed her ankles like barbed wire. "We don't have time to baste it."

Mrs. Puce sat on the bed murmuring to the girls in Chinese. Ting Ting would nod and sometimes murmur back. Yuk-Lin replied with a flood of words. She seemed manic, like she couldn't hold still. She even laughed one time.

"They must have been very bored at Joe's house," Anna said.

Miss Robins took a pin out of her mouth. "I brought them a primer. They've been practicing their reading and writing."

"Maybe they'll be teachers someday."

"Perhaps. Most of the girls are matched with Chinese Christian men. They become wives and mothers. With their consent of course."

Anna swept a lock of hair behind Ting Ting's ear. The girl flinched. Anna withdrew her hand and sighed. "What have they done to you, little mouse? And where do you belong? Not at the mission, surely."

To Anna's surprise, Mrs. Puce spoke cogently and in English. "She's from Sze Yup in Canton province. Her father sold the girls when they were eight and twelve. Wong Nim bought the pair in San Francisco for four thousand dollars."

Anna thought of her own father all but selling her to her former fiancé, Edgar Wright. "Fathers are monstrous things. A woman doesn't belong to anyone but herself. Tell her, Mrs. Puce."

Mrs. Puce said, "We all belong to God."

Anna had the blasphemous thought that if God were a woman, they wouldn't have these problems.

Anna gently rubbed lanolin over Ting Ting's face, dusting her with talc until she sneezed. Yuk-Lin dusted her own face using Joe's shaving mirror. At night, under the cover of a veil, Anna hoped they'd look white. She topped their silken buns with hats, tipping them low to cover their eyes. "There. If anything, it will be their gait that gives them away."

Joe knocked on the door. "Wolf is going to be here soon. You've got to be ready or we'll miss the boat."

"Five minutes," she called through the door.

Anna whispered, "Dear Lord. Detective Singer still thinks he's coming. We're going to have to sneak out." She assessed the casement window that opened up at sidewalk level.

Yuk-Lin moved to the window and opened it. Anna and Miss Robins exchanged a surprised look as the girl raised herself up onto a chair and climbed through. Anna said, "I think they speak more English than we thought."

Miss Robins smiled. "Joe's been teaching them."

Anna handed Yuk-Lin a basket full of Coca-Cola bottles, Cracker Jacks, and some delicious-looking sandwiches that Miss Robins had made. Yuk-Lin hauled them out and stuck her hand back through the window to help Ting Ting up. Anna and Miss Robins followed, leaving Mrs. Puce seated on the bed. Anna could hear the missionary nattering on, holding a conversation with no one. Anna raised her eyebrows thoughtfully. Mrs. Puce might be smarter than she seemed.

The girls slipped down the street to a black Ford belonging to Anna's landlord, which Anna had surreptitiously borrowed for the occasion and planned to return in the morning. Joe waited there, leaning up against the car with his arms folded across his chest. He glared at Anna.

Anna swore, "Biscuits."

"You think I don't know you?" He turned to Miss Robins. "You're risking your life. I can't let you do it."

Miss Robins lifted her noble chin. "I don't care if I die. They can harm my body, but they can't harm my soul."

Anna stomped to the auto and got in, rolling her eyes. She fiddled with the dash, got up, and set about winding the crank to turn over the engine. "You'll have to tie me up to keep me from going."

"Maybe I—"

Anna heard a *smack* and spun around in time to see Joe Singer hit the ground. He lay there unmoving. Miss Robins stood over him holding a full bottle of Coca Cola, looking rather stunned. She glanced up at Anna. "I didn't want to see him killed."

Anna rushed to Joe and knelt beside him, holding her breath. She lowered her face very close to his handsome one. Peppermint wafted rhythmically onto her lips. She blinked at Miss Robins. "You brained him."

Miss Robins bowed her head. "I'm sorry."

"No, you did well."

Yuk-Lin came forward and picked up Joe's right leg.

Each of the four ladies took a limb, Yuk-Lin and Ting Ting hobbling fiercely on their bound feet, Anna and Miss Robins straining against their corsets. They carried Joe's limp body back to his apartment. Mrs. Puce asked no questions but simply added her strength to the task. The five women lifted Joe Singer onto his bed. Anna took off his boots, and would have taken off his pants and shirt, as any good nurse would, had Miss Robins not been watching. Instead, she collected Joe's handcuffs from his belt and cuffed his arms above his head, fastened to the brass bed. She left the keys in his pants pocket, where he could not reach them, and pulled the quilt over his body, tucking it up to his chin.

Joe groaned again and moved a little. Anna straightened up. "He has a concussion. We've got to go before he wakes up, because he'll be very, very angry."

Ominous clouds darkened the sky, and the misty air clung in tiny droplets to Anna's hair. The roads were rutted from the recent storms. It was thirty miles to San Pedro, a three-hour drive on good roads. Anna didn't have good roads. She prayed a silent prayer to Saint Raphael, patron saint of safe journeys, reminding him they had to reach the port before sunrise, when the dockworkers would begin their day and the fishing boat would leave the harbor.

Yuk-Lin leaned over the side of the car and pointed her face into the wind, letting the night air toss her veil. Ting Ting sat with her arms wrapped tight around her. Anna addressed Miss Robins. "I assume you know where we're going, since you made the arrangements."

"A man's supposed to meet us at the docks. But our contact will be looking out for girls disguised as Chinese boys accompanied by two men. He's not going to find us, and I don't know what he looks like."

"We'll have to find his boat, then," Anna said.

"That's a problem. His boat will be anchored off Deadman's Island. It's named the *Juana Maria*. We'll have to walk out on the breakwater to the island, and it's going to be dark. It's far, Anna. A couple hundred yards. And if the tide is high, we could get wet. When we find the boat, somebody's going have to swim out to it."

"I can swim."

"As can I. We'll flip for it."

Anna hated to admit it, but Miss Robins was brave. No wonder Joe had trusted her.

Anna hit a pothole, and the car shook. "Joe told you about Elizabeth Bonsor?"

Miss Robins's voice became a whisper. "Yes. He did."

"Did he ask you about Elizabeth's friend, Chan Mon? I think you met him once. He was a friend of Leo Lim's. You chatted one time about hiking to Sturtevant Falls. He had a hunting cabin off the San Gabriel Trail."

Miss Robins said, "I don't know any Chan Mon."

"Have any white men threatened you because of your contact with the Chinamen?"

"We've been repeatedly threatened at the mission. And I know this sounds strange, Matron Blanc, but we've even been threatened by cops."

"The Chinatown squad?"

"Yes. Veiled threats, but threats all the same. 'Leave Chinatown or don't be surprised if something terrible happens to you.' It's not the words, so much as the tone of the warning. You understand."

"Who?"

"Detective Snow. I have a bad feeling about him, but I try not to let him frighten me."

"And Detective Singer knows?"

"Yes. I tell him everything. But we can't be run off. Missionaries die all over the world—Africa, New Guinea, China. Mr. Puce was beheaded. But the Chinamen are precious in God's sight. Someone has to show them this. Their very souls depend upon it."

Anna pondered whether Detective Snow was capable of killing a girl. He'd certainly stood by passively while prostitutes were being killed by the New High Street Suicide Faker. Anna believed he was capable. But she didn't think he'd killed Elizabeth—not alone anyway. The dummy in the bed suggested some kind of scheming. Snow wasn't smart enough for that.

§

The car motored along. Yuk-Lin tried to distract Ting Ting with fairy tales about a herd boy and a weaving maiden and the lady of the moon. Miss Robins attempted to translate. The stories and Miss Robins's silly translation errors should have delighted Anna, but her mind was on more serious things. She smiled to be polite.

After five hours, they saw the lights of San Pedro and smelled the sea air. Anna stared out over the horizon, which was blanketed in a coastal fog, illuminated by the blinking of a lighthouse. She could see the outline of a small islet. A breakwater of large, jagged rocks connected the island to a peninsula. The breakwater was at least two football fields in length and curved like a giant snake. They would have to walk along the peninsula until they reached the breakwater and then sneak across in the dark. The hike would be excruciating, since her legs still ached from her foray into the mountains, and her blisters still bled. Anna thought about Yuk-Lin and Ting Ting's tiny, bound feet and winced.

To avoid drawing attention, Anna parked the car before they reached the waterfront. When the engine sputtered and quit, she pulled out her red and black talisman, the one for gambling luck. She kissed it and handed it to Yuk-Lin. Yuk-Lin examined it and smiled at Anna. "Good."

Anna lit the talisman with an ornate silver lighter, and the paper flared. The women watched the bright flame burn down toward Yuk-Lin's pale fingers. At the last minute, she dropped it onto the ground outside the car and shook her hand.

The ladies slunk along the road that led to the harbor. The soil was sandy and covered with ice plant, which crushed beneath their feet. On every block, light shot from the windows of at least one establishment, loud with the raucous sounds of sailors deep in their cups. Saloon girls, too, giggled sharply into the smoky air, which seeped out through open doors and tasted like ash on Anna's tongue.

Anna stopped. It was imperative that she and her charges not be seen, lest they be conked on the head and shanghaied, taken captive to work on one of the many boats that sailed from Los Angeles to San Francisco, then across the Pacific to China. She had no doubt that their work would not be limited to cooking and scrubbing. Yuk-Lin and Ting Ting would be slaves again, only this time servicing a lower class of men. And Anna and Miss Robins would be servicing right alongside them.

Occasional lampposts sizzled along the road, and telephone poles stood erect like sentries. Each bore a wanted poster displaying the image of the two Chinese girls and describing the two men seen with them. It perfectly described Joe Singer and Wolf. The LAPD had recently been here. Of course they had. The harbor was under the jurisdiction of the city. Anna felt sick to her stomach. She was glad Miss Robins had knocked Joe out. Although she didn't like the lady, she admired her pragmatism. If they could get the girls onto the boat safely, Joe and Wolf would also be safe.

Anna led the girls off the main street to a foot trail that crossed a field of weeds—a shortcut down to a beach. It would be a rougher walk, and the girls would have to lean on her and Miss Robins, but there were no carousing sailors. The ladies' heels churned in the sand. Yuk-Lin and Ting Ting's faces betrayed their pain, but they did not complain. They spoke not a word, lest their language give them away. Anna wished she could have tea with them some carefree day, and that Mr. Jones could translate so that Anna might hear more of their fairytales and stories of their lives in China and in Chinatown. But would he surrender the girls to the tong? Anna didn't think so.

The foam of the waves glowed with bioluminescence, and it smelled of seaweed. The ladies followed the shadowed beach to the edge of the docks, where large cargo ships floated, their lights shining on the water. The piers and planks were deserted, except for the occasional drunken sailor, and, to Anna's dismay, a lone policeman.

Anna waited. The officer turned his back and began pacing away from them. She motioned for the ladies to move. They stole across the docks to the shelter of the nearest structure. A man's face loomed from a poster plastered on the wall. She recognized Leo Lim. It was a picture Joe had taken from his apartment on the day the body had been found. Anna stopped to read the poster. "Wanted for murder." There was no mention of trunks or missionary girls, or even of Chinatown. Lim was dead. Anna took it down lest an innocent Chinese man be arrested by mistake.

Front Street was a short street, bordered by the harbor. Mismatched commercial buildings lined one side. White awnings reflected the moon. The only lights came from four separate saloons and a few windows of the Hotel Spokane.

The port stretched farther than Anna could see. There were train tracks running past docks. Boxcars and flat cars stood ready to be loaded. Out in the ocean, a peninsula ran parallel to the shore, protecting the inner harbor from the open sea. Boats hung off the landmass like charms on a bracelet—steamships, barges, and yachts. Dozens of small sailboats anchored inside the breakwaters.

On the very end of the peninsula a line of giant boulders wound through the ocean like a chain, ending in an island—Deadman's Island. A lone fishing boat was anchored some twenty feet away from it. Miss Robins pointed. "There. It's the *Juana Maria*."

Yuk-Lin looked despairingly at the breakwater and shook her head. She surprised Anna with heavily accented English. "Nothing doing."

Despite herself, Anna smiled. It was, no doubt, a phrase Joe Singer had taught her. The significance was less amusing. There was no possibility that they could walk the length of the peninsula and breakwater to the island before dawn. The sun would soon rise and sailors would start their workdays. The girls were running out of time. Anna dragged a hand down her neck, which ached and was chafed from the poncho she'd worn on the mountain.

The lapping ocean made the boats bump gently against the dock. A wooden dinghy *thump thumped* nearby. Yuk-Lin stood over it, peering left and right, then down into the hull. She beckoned frantically to Anna. The boat was old and slightly water logged. Anna looked at Yuk-Lin intently. It might be their last chance. Come dawn, the boat might leave them, or they might be discovered. She nodded. Yuk-Lin untied the briny rope.

A large trawler floated adjacent to the dinghy. Anna scanned the deck. Half a dozen cork jackets hung from iron hooks on the outer cabin wall. It was a sign from God that she should steal them. Anna gracefully made the leap onto the deck, having taken ballet. She crept to the wall. The cork jackets felt damp and cold, and smelled like mildew, but Anna stole four anyway. She jumped back onto the dock with her bundle, landing softly.

Miss Robins stood in the front, holding onto a ring on the dock, waving frantically to Anna. The cop was strolling back in their direction. Ting Ting sat in the boat huddled against Yuk-Lin's shoulder. Anna stepped into the rocking vessel, giving each lady a cork jacket and donning her own. She took the oars and Miss Robins pushed off, just as the cop stopped, turned on his heels and paced back in the opposite direction. It was no one that Anna knew.

The dinghy rode low in the sea. A good four inches of water sloshed at the bottom of the boat, as if there were a slow leak. It wetted Anna's glamorous shoes and the hem of her velvet frock and the tiny feet of Yuk-Lin and Ting Ting. She thought the boat might easily tip, but a sliver of sun had appeared on the horizon. It was too late to search out another.

At first she rowed with attention to silence, slicing the still water quietly until they were at a sufficient distance from the tethered boats. Then Anna paddled the dinghy noisily, with all her might, keeping in rhythm so that the boat didn't turn. The *Juana Maria*, their salvation, was still fifty yards away.

Miss Robins tapped a shoulder. "Let me take an oar."

Anna scooted over on the seat. Miss Robins sat beside her, their hips touching. They began to coordinate their strokes and skimmed through the water making better time than when Anna rowed alone.

Behind them, an authoritative voice bellowed through a megaphone. "Stop in the name of the law." Anna assumed they were speaking to her and redoubled her efforts. Miss Robins kept pace. Soon she heard the splash of oars and glanced behind her. It was the cop from the docks and another man, too, in a bigger boat. They rowed separate pairs of oars in unison.

Sweat trickled down Anna's neck and between her breasts. They rowed harder but had little chance of outdistancing them as Anna's boat had only one set of oars. Miss Robins grunted beside her. The rocks of Deadman's Island glowed in the dawn. She saw the *Juana Maria* still out of reach, a little flag flying from its mast. Ting Ting cowered, covering herself with her cloak as if it could magically protect her from her pursuers. Her eyes were shut tight, and she trembled. Yuk-Lin was leaning over the helm, paddling with her hands. They would surely be returned to slavery. Anna would be canned, losing her only means of support. Her options would be severely limited. She could try to find a place as a companion to some old bat, she could take vows or teach children. Anna decided she'd rather go down with the ship.

The policeman's boat quickly ran astride the ladies' dinghy, slamming up against the wood with a thump. He flung his hands in the air in an exaggerated gesture of bewilderment. "Are you ladies crazy?"

The game was up. They were about to be screwed.

The cop straddled the two vessels, rocking Anna's boat precariously. "You are all under arrest for the theft of a dinghy."

Anna leapt to her feet and shifted to one side of the vessel, tipping the waterlogged boat. She put her foot on the very edge and leaned her full weight until water seeped over, causing the boat to overturn. Cop and girls tumbled into the sea. Anna trusted that if the girls couldn't swim, they could at least dog paddle in their cork jackets.

Anna went under and bobbed up, losing yet another hat. The cold slapped her, momentarily paralyzing her with the shock of it. Salt stung her nose. "Split up!" Anna swam for the breakwater, hoping to draw the cop away from Yuk-Lin and Ting Ting. Yuk-Lin dog-paddled for Deadman's Island, which now lay within reach. Miss Robins swam toward the peninsula, a more ambitious endeavor. The cop, who had no cork jacket, flailed in the water. The fisherman jumped in to rescue him.

Anna turned to look for Ting Ting. She barely spied her in the dark. She was splashing furiously toward the outer harbor and the open sea. Anna turned around and swam after her, keeping her eyes glued to the girl. To Anna's bewilderment, Ting Ting struggled to remove her cork jacket. It bounced to the surface with a splash. Ting Ting floundered for a moment, then sunk, hands above her head. Anna watched the tips of her fingers disappear beneath the foam. She swam to the spot, but Ting Ting was gone. Anna removed her own cork jacket and dove deep down into the water, feeling for the girl. She dove and dove until she had no breath, but Ting Ting was lost.

§

Anna sobbed as she swam, sputtering, swallowing saltwater. She reached the docks and hid beneath them, coughing convulsively. She didn't check to see if the coast was clear when she dragged herself out of the ocean like a washed-up sea creature. Part of her wanted to get caught by the cops and thrown to the tongs, but she couldn't let them win. She limped back to the car thoroughly and utterly exhausted. Passersby gaped at the soggy lady with the clinging skirts and kelp in her hair. Miss Robins, also drenched, was waiting at the Ford.

§

The winter sun was glaring down when Anna and Miss Robins set off for Joe Singer's apartment, still wet and chilled to their cores. Yuk-Lin was safe. Miss Robins had seen her climb the ladder of the *Juana Maria*. Ting Ting was lost, and there was nothing that Anna could do about it but hope that she rested in the bosom of her Chinese gods. Anna's heart felt as numb as her fingers, but her mind accused her.

Miss Robins shook beside Anna, crying quietly. Anna ignored her. Finally Miss Robins broke the silence. "It's not your fault. She took off her cork vest on purpose. She wanted to die. And at least Yuk-Lin is free."

"She's not really free, is she?" Anna said mournfully. "Now she has to be Presbyterian."

Miss Robins frowned.

The rain had stopped. The emerald hills sparkled with droplets, and the wild gray sea smashed against the shore, sending spray high into the air. Anna was mad with pain. There was nothing to distract her. She wanted to think about anything except the young girl she had lost that night. And it had been Anna's fault. Anna had tipped the boat.

§

Anna dropped Miss Robins off at the mission and drove home, parking her landlord's auto four blocks down where he wouldn't see her get out of it. The leather seats were now stained with seawater, but Anna felt certain that if he understood why she'd taken it, he wouldn't be angry at all.

She stripped and fell into bed, sleeping fitfully for but a few hours. When she awoke, she bathed, dressed in lilac taffeta, donned a feathered hat the shape of an upside-down washtub, and returned to Central Station to search for Joe Singer. The station was unusually empty. She encountered Joe sitting at his desk looking pale and rubbing his temples. No doubt he had a headache. His hair stood on end in places as if he'd been running his hands through it. When he saw her, he grabbed her by the hand and dragged her into the kitchen, closing the door behind them. "Sweet Jesus, Sherlock, I've been looking everywhere for you. I went to your apartment. I drove down to San Pedro. The boat was gone. Finally, I went to the mission. Miss Robins told me all about it."

Anna scrunched her face so that she wouldn't cry. "I'm sorry. I lost her."

"Sherlock, it's not your fault."

"But it was my fault."

"No, Anna. Ting Ting didn't want to be in this world. Not the way it is. She wanted to die."

Anna made a hiccupping sound.

"I was so worried, Anna." He cupped her face with his hands and made her look at him. "You can't do that to me again. Do you understand?"

"It was Miss Robins who clubbed you with the Coca Cola bottle."

"Anna, I thought you were done for, and I couldn't do anything to stop it. Mrs. Puce didn't uncuff me for hours."

He let go of her face, raised his manly arm, and wiped his eyes with it. Anna stared in wonder. Was he crying? He was certainly in distress. Anna stepped closer. She believed that she could comfort Joe Singer, and that comforting him would comfort her, too. She wanted to comfort him like never before. She wanted to comfort him until he was extremely comforted.

Detective Snow opened the door and took in the scene. Anna and Joe jumped apart. Snow sneered at them, poured himself a cup of coffee, and left.

Anna turned away and adjusted her hat. Comforting Joe in the station was out of the question. "Miss Robins said Snow threatened the missionaries."

"I know. I'm looking into it."

"Where is everyone?"

Joe exhaled despairingly. "I guess there were some shots fired in Chinatown this morning."

"That's unfortunate, as I need to go to Chinatown."

"No, you don't."

"I've got to see if any knife seller recognizes our dead Chinaman's weapons."

Joe looked at Anna for a long time. "I was just on my way. I've arranged to interview the manager of Lim's apartment building. He's shown up again. If Lim and Chan Mon were friends, maybe he knows something. Mr. Jones is going to meet me."

"Then we can go together. I need you to tell me where the knife stores are."

"No. You're not paid to risk your life. I am." He strode toward the door.

Anna flew to his side and fluttered next to him. "I'm going to Chinatown. You know you can't prevent it. I'm not afraid to go alone." Anna was terrified to go alone. "You'll be much safer with me along. We can watch each other's backs. Remember, I also have a rod."

Joe stopped. He clamped his eyes shut and blew out a long exasperated breath, like a kettle releasing angry steam. "All right, Anna, but only because I don't have a choice."

She followed. "Has it begun, then? The tong war over the girls?"

"Captain Dixon thinks it's just a warning, and it's been quiet this afternoon. Nobody's dead yet."

§

Few men walked the streets of Chinatown, but those who did walked with dignity, the way Joe said marked men did. Most stores and saloons looked closed. The good citizens of Chinatown weren't fools. They feared a tong war, too.

Anna and Joe encountered Mr. Jones lolling against the wall of Leo Lim's apartment building. The restaurant below stood empty, but the stairwell still smelled of chop suey, reminding Anna that she had not eaten breakfast. The trio mounted the steps to the second floor and knocked on the manager's door. A middle-aged man in black silk answered and peered at them suspiciously, never fully opening to them. He had long fingernails. Joe flashed his badge and bowed his head graciously, saying something that sounded nice in Chinese. Joe reverted to English. He fed Mr. Jones questions to translate, the apartment manager answered, and Mr. Jones reported the man's responses. Joe squinted with effort as he tried to follow the Chinese end of the conversation.

Mr. Jones cleared his throat. "He said his wife isn't home. He didn't know your Chan Mon. He had no idea who the killer might be. He said he never saw any white lady. He was quite adamant—"

"Or he doesn't trust the police." Anna herself never knew which cop to trust, except for Joe and Wolf.

"A Chinaman who doesn't trust the police? This is a rare thing." Mr. Jones smirked. "But he did offer us something."

Joe leaned back against a water stain on the wall. "He saw a strange man."

"Yes. He saw a man on Lim's fire escape," Mr. Jones said.

Anna perked up. "Really?" Her eyes widened at Joe in admiration. "You understood that."

"Small, bearded." Mr. Jones raised one eyebrow. "White."

Anna's mind began to race. She strode to the stairwell and leaned out an open window, looking toward Lim's apartment. "White. Bearded? Not a cop. Cops are clean-shaven." The winter sunlight shone dully on the wooden fire escape, which cascaded all the way to the ground. She sensed Joe leaning over her shoulder to look. He smelled clean, like Pears soap.

He stepped back. "When did he see the man? Near the time of the murder?"

"No," Mr. Jones said. "Last Thursday. At least a week after she died."

Anna pursed her lips and considered. "Who wears a beard? They are unhygienic and completely out of fashion. A mountain man, perhaps? Some reprobate come slumming? Of course the beard could be false. Then the mysterious person on the fire escape could be almost anyone. Man or woman." Anna imagined Miss Robins on the fire escape, looking devious and bearded, draped in a black cape.

"And why? Why were they on the fire escape?" Anna tapped her temple. "Take me back to the crime scene, since you kicked me out before."

§

The smell of death still lingered in the apartment, though Elizabeth's body was long gone. Elizabeth had been a kindred spirit—-adventurous and rebellious like Anna, despite their overbearing fathers. Elizabeth had chosen to brave Chinatown to save men's souls, though society frowned upon it, just like Anna chose police work. Both women had lived dangerous lives. Unlucky Elizabeth had paid for it. Would Anna's luck hold?

Anna hardened herself against the thought, and against grief for her lost friend. There was nothing she could do for Elizabeth now except catch her killer, and Anna wasn't about to back down.

She surveyed the room for anything she had missed the first time around. The furniture and all of Lim's belongings waited fruitlessly for their owner's return. Anna ran a finger along a dusty table. "The servant girl hasn't cleaned out the apartment yet."

"The manager doesn't know that Lim is dead. In his mind, Lim's just late on his rent."

From the threshold, Mr. Jones eyed the trunk tipped over and wide open across the room. It was dark with the fluids of decomposition. He looked nauseous.

Joe said, "Jones, should I meet you later at your shop?"

Mr. Jones bowed slightly from his shoulders. Then Joe bowed, so Anna bowed. Then, the well-built herbalist departed.

Anna squatted at the entrance and traced the scratches in the floor-boards with her fingers—three sets of heavy marks running across the threshold, two sets of light scratch marks. "Elizabeth had already been dead a week when the bearded man climbed the fire escape. I suppose the killer could have come back to gloat. But it's unlikely Lim or Chan Mon did it. We know Leo Lim was already living in the cabin. Besides, why wouldn't Lim use the front door? He had the key. Chan Mon was not a small man. A person could conceivably fake being larger with pillows and high-heeled shoes and all. But a person can't very well fake being smaller. It could have been a highbinder looking for Lim."

Joe sat back on his heels. "Yes, but why sneak into his apartment. The highbinders are brazen."

Anna rose and walked the distance of the scratch marks, patting her lower lip with one finger.

Joe stood. "And why the dummy in the bed?"

§

Anna and Joe returned to Central Station to find Police Chief Singer waiting at the oak reception desk. He was handsome, like his son, though he had to be in his forties, with thick gray hair and a younger man's carriage. At that moment, he looked grim. Mr. Melvin typed tremulously behind the desk.

When Joe saw his father, he froze. "What's wrong?"

Anna knew Chief Singer's frowns were not laughing matters, especially when they pertained to Joe. Her brow creased in concern, then she remembered to smooth it. She tried to appear placid, pleasant, and helpful. She wanted the chief to like her.

The chief grabbed Joe by the collar and slammed him up against the wall, causing a framed painting to tilt on its nail. "For some reason, the Hop Sing think you have the singsong girls." His eyes were bulging like overfilled balloons.

Joe swore. Anna's forehead wrinkled again.

The chief roughly let go of Joe's collar. He spoke more softly. "Guess what I found on my laundry ticket." He dropped a piece of paper into Joe's hand.

Joe held the note up to the light. Anna closed her eyes. She didn't have to look to know what she would find—the secret red writing of a death threat.

The chief barked, "That's your name written there, not mine."

"I've got to sit," said Anna. She sat down on a chair that was not there, her bottom falling toward the floor. Joe caught her under the arms and stood her back on her feet.

"You simply can't leave the station," she said. "Ever again. For the rest of your life."

"I can't live in the station, Anna." He laughed joylessly. "Who would feed my puss?"

"I'll feed your puss. It could be your genie wish."

"I'm not wasting my genie wish."

The police chief rubbed his forehead. "I'm inclined to agree with Assistant Matron Blanc. Stay in and do booking, just until I can negotiate. You can sleep upstairs in the doctor's quarters."

"I'm not staying in the station."

"You will if I say you will."

"That's where you're wrong. You do not own me." Joe turned and began sauntering toward the door.

The chief called out, "Somebody arrest Joe."

Joe bolted. Anna gave chase, followed by the lumbering Detective Snow. At the door to the station, she extended her François Pinet shoe and tripped Snow, who went down like a sack of dung. This was not because she didn't want Joe arrested. She did. It was because she didn't want a mutt like Snow to do it.

Snow shouted as Anna flew down the steps after Joe, who had already mounted a police horse. Two more cops burst from the station door. Anna hit the street and grabbed hold of Joe's boot. He tugged. Anna tugged. His boot came off in Anna's hand.

"Don't look for me, you hear me?" Joe rode away, weaving through the carts, cars, and people that crowded First Street.

The two cops swung onto their own police mounts and cantered after him.

§

The cops returned to the station without Joe Singer, having lost him in the hurly-burly of the city. Anna returned to her desk and melted onto her chair, putting her head in her trembling hands. Wolf sauntered over, his face ashen in a way that Anna had never seen it. He laid a palm on her shoulder and leaned in close. "You look in need of comfort."

Anna rubbed her face. "The man I don't love is in grave danger, and I can't think of a thing to do about it, except feed his puss. I suppose it eats horsemeat, right?"

"Right."

"Do you know where he might have gone?"

"Maybe."

"But if we follow him, we might lead the tong right to him."

"It's a predicament. Look, I'm worried, too, honeybun. Why don't you come to my place this evening for some liquid consolation? We can commiserate. Besides. I've got his key. We can go feed his puss together."

"All right."

He squeezed her shoulder. "Joe will be all right."

"Do you really believe that?"

Wolf gave her a fabricated smile. Then he met her eyes and his smile left. "No."

§

Anxiety hung heavy over Central Station. Men who were off duty came in or stayed late, waiting for news.

Anna knew that it would be futile to try to reform juveniles or caution wayward girls when her mind was clouded with thoughts of highbinders with axes trying to decapitate her former sweetheart. He might be a faithless cad, but he needed saving, even if it meant letting the children of Los Angeles fall into degradation. Anna ran through a hundred scenarios in her mind, options for keeping Joe safe. She could hide him in her apartment, but the tong thought Anna and Joe were lovers and might look for him there. She would have to smuggle him out of Los Angeles, perhaps disguised as her maid. They would have to move to the country, because the tongs had spies in every city with a Chinatown. Both plans would be frowned upon by Joe's fiancée, unless Anna invited her to come as well, which was out of the question. These two options shared another fatal flaw. Anna needed to know Joe's whereabouts, which she did not.

Anna would have to approach things from the other end. She would simply have to pay for the lost girls and Joe's safety. What had Mrs. Puce said that Wong Nim had paid for the girls? Four thousand dollars? Anna still had her furniture, clothing, and a few baubles, but had no idea how much they were worth. Wolf could help her sell them, although he'd had no luck with her peacock feather comb. Perhaps a bank would loan her the money, or an old society friend. Or she could turn to the shipping magnate who wrote bad poetry and sought her hand. But what if the Hop Sing president wasn't satisfied with the price of the girls? What if it was a matter of honor?

If Tom Foo Yuen wouldn't cancel Joe's assassination, she would simply have to shoot him.

Without excusing or explaining herself, Anna left the station.

§

The dew had settled on the hibiscus bushes and the grass outside her apartment. Anna stopped home to change into her most fetching winter ensemble. She needed every advantage to gain entrance into the restaurant where Joe said that the Hop Sing president held court—the one with statues in the window. Anna had seen it.

Though by Parisian standards Anna's gown was already a full season out of vogue, it was still a year ahead of anything ladies were wearing in Los Angeles. It was sewn from azure blue satin with white fox trim at the wrists and collar, and boasted a matching muff as large and puffy as a cloud. Perfect for hiding a gun. Compared with her semi-official LAPD Matron bloomers, it would limit her mobility, but she didn't plan to fight the man. She planned to shoot him.

§

Anna called for a hansom cab to pick her up at a yellow house three blocks down from her apartment. The owners, she had deduced, were away. The dog was no longer chained to the palm tree in the yard, and the grass needed cutting. It had been days since she'd seen empty milk bottles on the doorstep. She waited on a swing made for two, rocking nervously on the porch. When the cab arrived, she hurried down the cobbled path and asked the driver to take her to the corner of Apablaza and Juan Streets. He protested vehemently and demanded to speak with Anna's husband or father, or whoever was in charge of her, even while helping her into his rickety old hansom. He lectured her the entire way on how ladies ought not go to Apablaza Street, how Anna must be insane, how she would be mugged and worse, likely lured with opium by a Mongolian, how she should listen to him because he was a man, and how he had a mind to turn around this minute except he needed the money.

Anna had to keep up her courage and thus covered her ears. It didn't stop him from blathering on.

They arrived at the agreed upon corner and the hansom stopped. The driver helped Anna step out onto the muddy road in her finery. She held the hem of her gown up with both fists. Apablaza Street stank. There was both a trash can smell and an herbal smoke scent that Anna thought might be hashish. The street was full of men on their way to somewhere. Anna imagined that most workingmen—vegetable farmers and shopkeepers—were heading for their beds, but some must be going to visit whores or to try their luck at a fan-tan parlor. None were too shy to stare at Anna, to make her feel like the vulnerable stranger she was.

She asked the driver, "Will you wait?"

He eyed Anna suspiciously. "Pay me first, in case you don't come back."

"Of course." Anna dug around in her purse. "My stars. I've forgotten my billbook." She plucked out a pen and paper, scribbled some words, and presented the driver with an IOU.

He glared at her. "I know where you live."

Anna took pleasure in the fact that he didn't.

He drove off leaving her once more alone in Chinatown. Anna removed the gun from her leather purse and concealed it in her bounteous muff—cold steal encased in softest mink. She peered through the plate glass window of a restaurant crowded with statues made from ceramics or stone. There were Buddhas, bearded old men, gods, dragons, warriors, and birds. A stunning, life-sized woman—some kind goddess—seemed to bless Anna with her open fingers. She held flowers in her hand. It baffled Anna that Tom Foo Yuen, with his grotesque countenance and black heart, could have such a glorious treasure. But this place must be Tom Foo Yuen's lair. Anna peered past the faces, lifted arms, and tails of statues into the restaurant.

The place had ten rosewood tables and was lit with red lanterns. A fancy wooden lattice arched across the ceiling in the middle of the room. The supper hour had passed, and the restaurant appeared empty. The lanterns barely glowed, as if the wicks were burning down. Despite the fact that the lair looked closed, Anna expected that Tom Foo Yuen would do business in the evenings. Wong Nim, the Bing Kong leader, had. Weren't gambling and prostitution endeavors of the night? She would give the restaurant a closer look.

Anna tried the brass doorknob. It clicked, and the door opened with an eerie creek. She stepped over the threshold and saw no one. The stone lions and deities stood unguarded. Anna could have taken her pick of the statues and hauled them away.

This boded ill. Tom Foo Yuen was so greatly feared he didn't need someone to watch his treasures; no one would dare steal from him.

Anna wandered across the black and white tiles, the tapping of her steps sounding loud to her ears. It was all right. She planned to be discovered. She passed through an arched doorway into a kitchen where a long iron stove waited, scrubbed and dormant, for the cook to return. The air smelled strongly of garlic. There was an icebox, which Anna didn't open, and a cupboard, which she did. Lovely blue china bowls and plates formed towers next to boxes filled with bamboo chopsticks.

She heard faint music begin to play—something sweet and haunting, something strange. At the far end of the kitchen, a cotton curtain hung from a rod. One side looked frayed. Pushing deeper into the room, Anna put her hands on the fraying place and pulled the curtain aside.

It obscured a simple door.

Anna pressed her ear against it, but heard only music—slightly louder now. She hesitated, seeking her courage. She was about to come face-to-face with a ruthless killer—one she had foolishly insulted. She still had time to change her mind.

Anna deliberated. Life was cheap in Chinatown. Her life was cheap. Hadn't Mr. Jones said that the tongs could make a white woman disappear? If she didn't return tonight, no one would know where she'd gone. If she turned around immediately, she could avoid that fate.

Anna closed her eyes and pictured Joe Singer in the forest in his underwear. She found her courage.

She opened the door, which led to a staircase. It set a string of bells to clanging loudly. She cringed and descended the steps. The stairs ended in a metal door. She tried the handle, but the door was locked.

Anna rapped with her fist.

CHAPTER 21

A gun answered her knock. The barrel poked through a slim space between the frame and the steel of the slightly opened door. The music stopped. She could see part of a man holding the gun.

"I come in peace," Anna said in a squeaky voice.

The metal door swung outward revealing a man built like a boxcar—one of the highbinders from Wong Nim's death house. His hands were like giant clams. He lowered his revolver and cocked his head, squinting at her.

Anna recognized two more of Tom Foo Yuen's henchmen—the fat one and the one with a crooked nose. They were standing on high alert around a table strewn with Chinese playing cards. Anna had interrupted a game. In the corner, a lady perched on a stool, staring dumbly at Anna, no longer playing a giant harp. Her hair was shiny black and wonderfully done up with silk flowers.

Across the room, Tom Foo Yuen, his ugly face slack from shock, sat straight on the edge of a carved mahogany couch. In one hand, he held a small glass of something alcoholic. In the other, he held a smoldering cigar. Anna supposed she was the first white woman to ever visit his lair. No other woman she knew was quite that stupid.

Anna lifted her chin, "Forgive my interruption, Mr. President, but I am Assistant Matron Anna Blanc, and I've come about the singsong girls." She remembered herself and bowed.

No one bowed back. They simply stared at her.

After a moment, Tom Foo Yuen said, in his tar-thick accent, "You are a brave, strange woman, Matron Blanc."

Anna had heard that before.

He continued. "Why have you, a woman, come to speak to me? I don't buy white women, and I'm not interested in your god. I can't release the singsong girls because I don't have them."

"Your singsong girls are dead. I saw them drown with my own eyes at the port in San Pedro."

"Are you lying to me?"

"Why would I lie? You are a great man, so kind to your people," she lied. "You give the men places to live and such, like the Saint Vincent de Paul Society."

His lips curled as if he saw right through her. "I may not cross the Silver Bridge to heaven, but the gods see my good deeds. What do you care if a poor Chinese man starves in the streets? If he's alone?"

"I care that the singsong girls are dead. Their bodies will wash up and you'll know I tell the truth."

"I'm sorry, then. They were beautiful. Such small feet."

"I'll pay you for the girls if you'll rescind the order to have Joe Singer's head. How much did Wong Nim pay for them? Four thousand dollars? That sum is nothing to me," she lied again.

"Why would you do this? Is he your husband or your brother?" He curiously perused Anna's person from her hem to the crown of her feathered head. At least Anna looked the part of a wealthy woman. He appeared thoughtful, then smacked the arm of the couch as if he had just remembered something important. "You're Joe Singer's favorite whore. Such loyalty!"

"I'm his fiancée, not his whore." This wasn't true either, but Anna was tired of everyone thinking she was a whore.

"Partly correct. You are no longer Joe Singer's whore. He took my girls. I take his girl in return. Too bad there aren't two of you."

There were two, actually. Anna thought about giving up Miss Robins but decided it would extend her time in purgatory, and she imagined her stay would be long enough. She would avoid it unless absolutely necessary. She ignored her own fear and set her chin. "Don't be rude. I can pay—"

"Detective Singer will pay his own debts."

"He didn't take your girls. It was someone else." Anna thought fast. "I saw him. He was a Chinaman with blond hair and . . ." Anna wasn't good on her feet. By the disdainful look on his face, she knew she was losing.

"I don't care about the girls. I never paid for them. Joe Singer must die, or I will lose face."

Tom Foo Yuen had left her no choice. Anna lifted her giant mink muff and aimed it at the scoffing president. It was his life or Joe's, and no one would take Joe Singer out of this world. Not if she could prevent it.

Anna fired through the muff. The shot went wide and hit the arm of the highbinder who had come to stand beside his master. Tom Foo Yuen and his man screamed. The musician rushed for the door.

Anna raised her muff again and aimed. Giant clam hands clamped on her two arms from the rear and pulled them roughly behind her back. They tore a puff of fur from her expensive muff and sent the gun and accessory clattering to the floor. "Biscuits!"

Tom Foo Yuen breathed hard. His wide-set eyes protruded in anger, glassy and bright. "I have lost two hatchet men in just one month—faithful brothers who have gone missing."

Ko Chung and Chan Mon, thought Anna—the headless man and the mountain lion food. "That wasn't my fault!"

"I avenge violence against my brothers." The president reached out his hand toward Anna and said something to his men in Chinese.

Anna wondered if it would help to mention that she had been aiming at Tom Foo Yuen.

The boxcar man swept Anna forward as though she didn't weigh anything, which, thanks to her limited cooking ability, was almost true.

"Joe Singer is not here to protect you, and he won't live to avenge you." Tom Foo Yuen rose and slapped Anna hard across the cheek. "Like my little brothers, you're going to disappear."

She spun to the side and cried out. The highbinder tightened his grip on her arms, squeezing so hard she felt her skin would slide off. Her cheek stung as if a whole hive of bees had done their worst. She knew it would bruise. The president slapped her again, back-handed across her other cheek. It made her dizzy, but the hatchet man held her up. Her eyes watered so that her vision blurred. Anna tossed her woozy head. "At least my cheeks will match."

She looked about for help, but the harpist had fled into the street. Tom Foo Yuen lifted his knee and rammed Anna in the gut, throwing her up against his hatchet man. Anna wheezed. Her wind was gone and her gut burned.

The president cocked his head for a moment as if contemplating something. "Yes, you are my whore now." He nodded toward the highbinder with the clam hands. "And he will kill Joe Singer. He's a man of formidable strength."

"And you aren't a man of formidable strength?"

The president gave her a self-satisfied smirk. "So you shall see."

§

A ball of cloth clogged Anna's mouth and her head swam. Tom Foo Yuen must have knocked her out. A highbinder carried her over his shoulder like a sack of beans into the back alley and loaded her into a wagon, covering her with a blanket. She stared up at the woolen cloth that draped her nose and brushed her lashes and had the vague notion that this might be unfortunate. She felt very, very woozy. She closed her eyes. When she opened them, she no longer rode in the wagon but lay on a bed. She moved her arms and felt them slip across the sheets like a skate on ice. Satin on satin.

She saw a red trunk with ornate brass rings, a settee of latticed rosewood, a table and chairs made entirely of jade. On a table next to the bed, someone had left a tray with tea, a china plate of bread, and a honeypot. Anna felt foggy and heavy-limbed, plagued by a vague sense of panic. Her head ached.

The man with clam hands sat in a chair, blocking the only door. He appeared to be sleeping. She wondered what time it was. There were no windows that would enable her to judge by the color of the sky.

Anna felt dopey. She knew escape was imperative and the need for it urgent, or President Tom Foo Yuen would come and show her his formidable strength. She examined the room. There were two windows with shutters that had been nailed closed. The only opening out of the room appeared to be the door.

Anna searched the sparse room for a weapon and saw none except for a gun strapped to the chest of the sleeping man. His bulky arms were crossed over it, making theft impossible. Anna thought of Miss Robins and the coke bottle and Anna's recent incapacitation. There was a stone statue of a woman, which Anna thought she might lift. She lugged the goddess in her arms over to the sleeping man and, using all her strength, raised it high over her head. Sensing her presence, his eyes flashed open. Anna brought the deity down onto his head. She missed the crown of his head, grazed his brow, broke his nose, and hit squarely on his man parts. Anna winced as he crumpled to the ground, blood leaking from his nose.

She moved the chair so she could open the door. She slid back the deadbolt, but when she tried the handle the door was locked from the outside, too. Anna mouthed a silent curse, "Biscuits," and slid the deadbolt back into position. If she could not get out, at least the president could not get in.

Anna didn't believe she had killed the highbinder, though she had no desire to touch him and find out. She would need to escape before he returned to consciousness. She imagined he would not be pleased, and that his large hands could punish, and his large lungs could wake the dead. She gingerly stole his gun. Anna turned back to the room. It had high walls with ornate moldings in the European style. This was undoubtedly a grand house. If this were true, then a bedroom should have a laundry chute to the basement. Anna walked the circumference of the room, examining the walls and floor until she found what she was looking for—a small, square trap door in the floor. Only a woman or child could fit through. Anna dropped to her knees, pulled on the rope handle that opened the door, and peered down the empty space. It melted into darkness. She felt it with her hands. The inside was lined with tin. Anna wasn't certain how far down it was to the basement.

She could be on the first floor or, for all she knew, the top floor of a very tall building. Even if she were at ground level, the drop to a basement would be significant, possibly high enough to fracture a bone, even with a great pile of fluffy laundry to break her fall.

Someone knocked on the door. She heard the president's voice, "Yaen."

Anna still felt woozy from her concussion, but not so disoriented that she didn't know the meaning of the knock.

He called out again, "Yaen!"

Anna considered the chute. Spiders walked on walls, but their feet were sticky. Anna was not, dressed in satin from gown to drawers. She glanced over to the tea tray with its bread and honey. Honey was sticky. She took off everything, because satin clothes were slippery, and dumped them down the chute for extra cushioning. She could put them back on when she landed. She retrieved the honey pot and rubbed the entirety on her hands, feet, knees, and bare backside. Holding the gun, she lowered herself into the tunnel, spreading out her knees to catch herself, clutching the floor with one hand, her fingers near the trap door hinge. The door pinched her fingers. She pressed her honey-covered bottom against the wall, pushing against the tin with two feet. She let go and the trap door thumped shut.

Anna hung in complete darkness, afraid to move—a daddy long-legs spider clinging to the walls of a cave. She took deep breaths of mildewed air and sang off-key inside her head to calm her nerves, just like Joe would. "The itsy bitsy spider went down the water spout . . ."

The president started rattling the door. She forced herself to move, walking down the wall, step by step, trying to be quiet, because all eavesdroppers knew that sound carried in laundry chutes. Unfortunately, the tin creaked with each step, and the gun clanged against the metal. Gaining confidence, she let herself slowly slide, her hand, knees and bottom hot from the friction. She felt like Santa in a chimney, only naked and covered with honey.

Anna descended one floor, creeping past a second opening, a swinging door in the side of the chute.

JENNIFER KINCHELOE   247

Upstairs, the bedroom door boomed like a canon, over and over. The president must be ramming it with something, using his formidable strength. She slid faster, her skin burning, passing two more openings.

She felt a crash reverberate in the tin walls and heard wood splintering—the demise of that lovely door. Tom Foo Yuen cried out, "Yaen!" His anguish sounded real. He seemed to care for his fallen henchman.

"Cursed woman!" The president's words blew down upon her like a blast of cold fury, so chilling, so vacuous and devoid of light that she felt she could be sucked down into it, like an undertow. A square of brightness appeared above her, and the silhouette of her captor's head. Anna pushed against the wall, bracing herself.

She raised her gun, and shot up at the head.

The gun recoiled in her hand, slamming her wrist against the tin. She felt the boom in her entire body, then a drip of something sticky—Blood.

Her knees went weak and she fell—a spider washed out by the rain.

§

Anna dropped a few feet and landed in darkness, in a fluffy pile of dirty pajamas, socks, and drawers.

Male voices boomed upstairs, spewing angry words that she could not distinguish. Anna heard feet pounding down stairs, down one flight, down the next.

She heard a familiar voice calling, "Assistant Matron Blanc!" It was Wolf.

Anna shouted, "Help me! I'm naked and covered in honey!"

§

Wolf slid across the kitchen tile, heading for the basement stairs like Hermes in a footrace. "Hold tight, honeybun! Here I come!"

Joe Singer charged behind him with the lantern. Wolf was not going to see Anna in her honey, even if he had to shoot him. This was not police work. This was personal. He hurled himself at Wolf. "She's my girl!"

"Not anymore!" The men went down. The lantern rolled and extinguished, leaving the kitchen in darkness. They scrambled up, bracing themselves on each other, their eyes adjusting to the darkness, even as they hurtled toward the steps to the basement.

At the top of the stairs Joe stopped. "I'm warning you, Wolf. If you come down here, we are not friends."

"You got to play baseball with her. I should get the honey."

Joe took a blind swing at Wolf, connected, and heard him go down. Joe hit the top step and slammed the cellar door. It was pitch black. He blindly took the stairs six at a time, his hand skimming the rail. "Anna! Sweetheart! Anna! Talk to me!"

No amount of whiskey would assuage his guilt or numb his pain if anything happened to Anna. She was his songbird.

Anna called back, shrill as a gull, "Joe!"

With no light to guide him, he plowed toward her voice, crashing through wash tins and buckets of water, making the floor slick and wet. "Are you hurt?"

Her voice rippled with panic. "No."

Relief flooded Joe as he groped for her in the dark.

His face hit a clothesline, flapping with rags and wooden pins. "Ow!"

He felt the clothesline bend under Anna's hands and heard her rapid, ragged breathing. He stretched his arm out and touched a sticky finger. "Here, Anna. I'm here. Take my hand."

She made a sobbing sound. He pulled her into him and pressed her head onto his shoulder until she gasped. Anna's breasts heaved against his sweat-dampened shirt. Her words came out in hiccups. "I thought Tom Foo Yuen would kill you for sure, so I got the drop on him."

Joe made a scoffing sound. "Did it occur to you that I might kill Tom Foo Yuen? I could take Tom Foo Yuen!"

"Well . . ."

Joe tangled his hands in her loose hair, found her mouth and kissed her. She smelled like honeysuckle and a man's sweaty armpits.

Joe's hands moved from her silky hair down to her sticky body.

That was disappointingly unnaked.

Anna sobbed. "I fell into the laundry pile, and when I heard you and Wolf coming, I quickly got dressed in Tom Foo Yuen's dirty pajamas. My frock would take too long."

Wolf hit the bottom step, carrying the lantern, flooding the basement with light. He wore an official cop face, now swelling with a bruise, and searched the room with blazing eyes. "Miss Blanc!"

He saw Anna draped in Tom Foo Yuen's clothes and his face fell. He snapped his fingers. "Damn!"

CHAPTER 22

Anna paced the station floor wearing her own silk velvet bicycle bloomers and not her remaining matron's uniform, which required boiling and mending and who knew what else. Wolf had not chastised her, possibly because of her recent ordeal and bruised cheeks, which garnered sympathy, if not respect, among the men. She still trembled when she thought of Tom Foo Yuen, which was most of the time.

Joe sat with his boots up on her desk watching her, looking concerned. His cup of coffee sat neglected in front of him.

Anna picked it up and took a sip. "How did Wolf find you to tell you I'd been captured?"

"Oh, he knew where I was."

"Where?"

"His couch."

"Then, how did you find me?"

"Somebody saw you go into Tom Foo Yuen's restaurant, then you didn't come out. Not the front anyway."

"They knew me?"

"They saw a beautiful *sei gwai por* wearing fancy clothes. Who else could it be? Wolf heard and came and got me."

"Who was it?"

"A vegetable seller."

"I owe him."

"I don't know Sherlock. You took out two highbinders and the tong president all by yourself. You killed the man who was after me. You're the hero."

"That's true."

She tried not to dwell on the murderous demon or what had happened to him and his men. It would only give her nightmares. And daymares. But she couldn't help it. She constantly had to push them out of her mind—Tom Foo Yuen's angry head floating like a shadow in the opening of the laundry chute, backlit by light from the room. Silencing that head with one bullet from her gun. Wearing his smelly clothes, which, in the light, had been stained with his blood. Anna shuddered.

She had to distract herself. She decided to concentrate on solving Elizabeth's murder. She forced her mind to switch back to Joe, to the safety of the station, and to fighting a different crime. She squeezed her eyes shut and opened them.

"We still don't know who killed Elizabeth Bonsor. Was it Leo Lim in a fit of jealous rage, or Chan Mon in some perverse death pact that he was unable to follow through with?"

"Our suspects are dead."

"Correction, Chan Mon is probably dead. We never identified his body. And maybe the killer wasn't Chan Mon or Leo Lim. It could have been an angry white reprobate who doesn't approve of white women loving Chinamen, such as our own Detective Snow." Anna spun about and pointed at Joe, her eyes narrow. "But I think we have the key."

"What's that?"

"The dummy in the bed. What if the killer put Elizabeth in the bed with the dummy so that someone else would see them and think Elizabeth was sleeping with a man."

"So we're back to jealous lovers?"

Anna leaned on the desk with both palms flat. "But why ruin a dead girl? There's no point. And who was intended to see Elizabeth in bed with the pillow man? Her father? Leo Lim? Chan Mon?"

"Not Lim. It's his house. The pillow man was supposed to be him."

"Well, I doubt her father was the target. He was scandalized already. Yes, that's right. I think the killer wanted someone to think that Elizabeth was in bed with Lim."

"But why?"

Anna pressed her lips together. "Like you said. Jealousy."

"But was the killer jealous for Lim or Elizabeth?"

"Elizabeth. The target was Chan Mon—to drive him away from Elizabeth. The beneficiary is Lim. But why didn't Lim just lay in the bed?"

"How does Lim benefit if Elizabeth is dead?"

"Maybe Lim didn't kill her."

The station door banged open and Chief Singer blew in, his features frozen with anger. Mr. Jones glided beside him. Joe took his feet off the desk. The chief stopped to speak with Mr. Melvin, but Mr. Jones came toward them.

It reminded Anna that she and Joe had forgotten to find the knife shop. Mr. Jones might know whether they could identify Chan Mon by his cleavers. Whether or not Mr. Jones would assist them was another story. He had told Anna he'd have nothing to do with her, yet here he was. Mr. Jones greeted Joe and Anna with a bow of his head. Anna couldn't read his expression. His gorgeous dark eyes simply smoldered. She welcomed him with a bow and an extra-long handshake. "I'm so glad to see you. I need your help, and really we all want the same thing. Don't we?"

Mr. Jones glanced across the room at Chief Singer. "Of course. I will help your investigation in any way I can."

Anna wrinkled her brow. This was a flip-flop.

Joe clasped Mr. Jones's hand. "Hello, my friend."

Anna smiled sweetly and slid out her desk drawer. "I'm so pleased. What can you tell me about these?" She retrieved the wide leather scabbard, which contained two cleavers—the one belonging to the faceless man.

Mr. Jones removed one and turned it over in his hand, careful not to cut himself on the perilous blade. "It's a cleaver. They are used for throwing."

"Yes, we know. Who might the owner be?"

"They are weapons designed to kill, Matron Blanc. Something a hatchet man might carry." Mr. Jones examined the fancy handle with the Chinese symbols. "There is a name. Fan Gong."

"Not Chan Mon?"

"No. Fan Gong is a fearsome man. He terrorizes men without alli-ances who refuse to join the Bing Kong. He punishes the Bing Kong's enemies. He's feared in Chinatown."

"Chinatown need fear no longer," Anna said.

Mr. Jones's eyes widened slightly, then narrowed. "How did you come to possess these?"

"We found them near a body in the woods and thought the dead man was Chan Mon." Joe's eyes moved to Anna. "But it looks like we were wrong."

Anna picked up the second cleaver and traced the lovely characters with her finger—characters that spelled out the name of a killer. "Deep down, I think I knew. Why would a poet be good at hurling cleavers?" Anna shuddered. "Leo Lim never stood a chance."

Mr. Jones's eyes flickered. "Leo Lim is dead?"

"And Chan Mon is not dead." Anna smiled. "Now I have a lead again; I can hunt Chan Mon." She scratched the words in her leather bound notebook. "But, just because he's alive, doesn't mean he did it."

Joe said, "Just because he's not the mountain lion victim doesn't mean he's alive."

"True," Anna said. "But we do know one thing."

"What?"

"The motive for Leo Lim's killing. Miss Robins told me the Bing Kong were trying to get him to join their tong. They wanted him to help with the business, but Leo Lim said no." She wrote in her book. "Poor, noble Leo Lim. Unless he killed Elizabeth."

Joe said, "Dead or alive, we should find Chan Mon. I'm going to tell Captain Dixon. We'll get the Chinatown squad involved in the hunt."

"But they can't find out about Elizabeth."

"Yeah, but I can tell them Chan Mon is wanted for questioning in the murder of Leo Lim, although we know he didn't do it."

Anna had to admit it was a good idea. She simply didn't have to admit it out loud.

As Joe scooted out his chair and stood, the chief stormed in their direction. He stopped in front of his son. "Joe, you are free to leave the station."

Joe glared at his father. "I know. I'm my own man—"

The chief smiled cynically. "You're your own man when you can clean up your own messes." He gave Joe a long, hard look, turned on his heels, and stomped out of the station.

Anna frowned at Mr. Jones. "You came together. What is he talking about?"

"He convinced the new tong presidents that his son had no role in the disappearance of the singsong girls."

Anna's face lit and she clapped her hands. "That's wonderful!"

Joe sunk back down in his chair with his head in his hands. Her laughter petered out. "What?"

Joe groaned. "He paid them, Anna. I don't know if it was money or something else. The new tong presidents aren't concerned with the insult because it wasn't against them. They haven't lost face."

"But that's wonderful. All that matters is that you're safe." She patted him on the head.

Joe's eyes darkened. "No, not wonderful. I'd rather not be beholden to my father. He'll put me on Mexican dissident duty or something I'm morally opposed to. I'm not going to harass innocent Mexicans because their president pays the LAPD to do it."

Anna squeezed his shoulder. "But it's so much better than being dead." Anna smiled gratefully at Mr. Jones. "You must have helped the chief with this. You are our liaison with Chinatown."

Mr. Jones's mouth opened and closed. "I don't wish to talk about it."

Joe groaned again, louder than before, and put his head down on the desk.

Anna's mind ran wild with all the things that the chief might make Joe do. Then her thoughts wandered to all the things she might make Joe do, if she had power over him—if she still had a genie wish. Like dress for dinner, and play her piano every night. And love her.

Mr. Jones interrupted her thoughts. "Assistant Matron Blanc deserves your gratitude as well. For Tom Foo Yuen, this was personal.

Chief Singer could never have paid for his son's life if Tom Foo Yuen still lived."

§

A cold sea fog made the morning gray. Anna left work before noon, intending to nap. Also, she needed a whiskey. Bill Tilly, the newspaperman, welcomed her on the sidewalk. The mere sight of him imparted heaviness to Anna's heaviness. She couldn't force a smile. "Good day, Mr. Tilly."

"Say, darlin', I need to speak with you."

"How very unfortunate for you." She summoned her strength, flounced to her bicycle with Tilly on her tail, and strapped her notebook to the rack. He moved in front of her to block her path. She swung her leg over her bicycle and put both hands on the handlebars, squarely meeting his gaze. Then Anna peddled right for him, ringing her bell, making sure to spray him with mud as he leapt out of her way.

He called after her, "That's no way to treat your sweetheart!"

§

Anna's giant feather bed always welcomed her, regardless of the time of day. She slept a fitful sleep accompanied by her specters—the New High Street Suicide Faker, whom she had vanquished last summer, now joined by the Hop Sing president. They stood behind her—just out of sight—while in her dreams, she washed her hands.

Eve visited her—the police matron whose place she had taken, Joe's former lover, who was now in the ground. She silently glared at Anna.

But Elizabeth didn't come.

§

A horrible realization awakened Anna from her nap, causing her to sit bolt upright, sweaty with sleep. She had left her notebook strapped to the rack on her bicycle. Her dress was unacceptably rumpled, her bun smashed, but Anna didn't care. She flew out of her apartment, hatless, down the hall, and out the front door. Her bicycle leaned up against the wall.

The notebook was gone.

"Cock biscuits!"

There was only one person Anna knew who would steal a half-used notebook.

Tilly.

This was the worst possible thing. The notebook detailed the crime, including that a white woman had been found dead in the apartment of a Chinese man. It was news indeed, news Anna was sure to read in the morning paper, skewed with whatever sensational details Tilly could conjure. The whites in the city would become outraged and, if Joe Singer were right, some of the men, the worst of the city, might riot in Chinatown. They would demand blood for blood.

Anna had made a deadly mistake. The weight of it weakened her limbs. Inside her head, she kicked herself.

Anna rode her bike to the offices of the *Los Angeles Herald*, but the secretary informed her that Tilly wrote freelance from his home. Though Anna explained she was his long-lost sister—a sacrifice on her part—the woman refused to release his address.

Anna peddled home in despair, only to find Tilly sitting on the front steps of her apartment building. Her throat thickened with loathing. When she approached, he removed his hat and grinned. "Miss Blanc, would you like to make a statement, or do I have to make it for you." Tilly had a nasty habit of quoting Anna when she hadn't said anything at all.

"Mr. Tilly, write whatever you like about me. This isn't about me. This is about little children and mothers and, well, a whole lot of innocent men and a few guilty ones. You know what happened the last time a white man was killed by a Chinaman. There was a riot. Eighteen Chinamen were hanged. Not a person in Chinatown wasn't beaten or at least raped and pillaged. And they were innocent."

"Now that's a crying shame, sweetheart." Tilly paused. "Can I come in?" He waggled his eyebrows.

"How can you possibly believe your own lies about me? Do you really think I'd compromise my virtue to save Chinatown?"

"With all due respect, Miss Blanc, what virtue?"

Anna had virtue. Barely. But that was more Joe's fault.

Anna thought fast. "What if I were to tell you that Elizabeth Bonsor wasn't killed by a Chinaman. What if she were killed by a member of her own race?"

"Was she killed by a member of her own race? It's not in the notebook."

"Yes," Anna said with all the certainty of a bad liar. "I hadn't written it down yet. The killer is white."

"Well that's about as believable as a cow on the moon. Do you have any proof?"

"Since when have you required proof?"

He put his hand over his heart. "Miss Blanc, you wound me."

"Hah!"

"I'm going to make a deal with you because I think you're swell."

Anna bit her lip and waited for the worst.

"Ah, don't fret, sweetheart. It isn't bad. I'm going to have my story on the editor's desk by 5:30 p.m. tomorrow. I'm going to call on you at five, and you're going to receive me. You're going to offer me dinner and a chance to win your heart. Then, you're going to give me proof that a white man killed Elizabeth Bonsor. If you can do it, then I'll hold the story. But, if you can't produce proof, or if you talk to another newsman, I'm going to publish my story, and be sure that you, Chan Mon, and Leo Lim will feature heavily in it."

Anna's brows drew together. "What kind of proof?"

"Arrest the white man and that will be good enough for me. I'll write the story the way you call it. Or I'll write it my way."

"Give me back my notebook."

"I think not. But don't let it come between us. Will you marry me?"

"I need the notebook to crack the case."

His lips spread in a loathsome smile. "I thought you already had." He tipped his hat. "Farewell, sweetheart." The newspaperman sauntered over to a bicycle. He turned back. "I really do love you." Then he rode off into the evening.

Anna felt too ill to eat Cracker Jacks, but neither could she rest with only twenty-four hours to solve the case.

Heaven help them if the killer were Chinese.

At least the notebook made reference to the white man on Leo Lim's fire escape. But that wouldn't be enough. She needed him in custody. And who was the white man?

Anna closed her eyes and concentrated. She thought of the people of Chinatown, of childhood friends, and of Elizabeth's face smiling from the photo on her parents' mantle. She thought of the missionary women singing in the streets of Chinatown. She thought of ruthless killers, hatchet men, and dead men. Over the jumble of images, a voice rang in her head—a quavering, old white man's voice: "Don't tell anyone that my daughter was found in the apartment of a Mongolian."

§

Anna and Joe stood outside the home of the late Elizabeth Bonsor. Joe tugged the brim of his hat. "You think he killed her?"

Anna contemplated this. "He certainly seemed the angry type. I can imagine him killing his daughter in a rage if he discovered her in the apartment of her Chinese lover, except there were no marks of violence on the body. I think it might have been poison, something other than arsenic."

"Well, he didn't act too surprised when we told him she was dead. He acted angry, and embarrassed. He didn't want anyone to know about the circumstances surrounding her death. Just like we didn't want anyone to know."

Anna tapped her chin. "What if Elizabeth's father went to Leo Lim's apartment to get his daughter back from her Chinese lover? And what if, when he arrived, he found Elizabeth already dead in Lim's bed. So he came back in disguise, bringing an empty trunk in through the front door to collect his daughter's body—this would explain the light set of scratches in the wood floor leading from the door inside the apartment. Then, he placed Elizabeth's body in the trunk and voila. Now the trunk is heavy. He drags it across the floor and leaves the deep groove marks in the floorboards. But he's a small, old man. What if he over estimated his own strength and couldn't carry the trunk with his daughter's body down the stairs? He would have had to drag the trunk back into the apartment and make a different plan—the third set of groove marks. But what if someone surprised him, knocked on the door or something, so he jumped out the window and fled down the fire escape."

"And then he just gave up?"

"Maybe he thought it was too late—that the body had been discovered." Anna rang the bell. "We'll ask him."

Mrs. Bonsor answered the door. When she saw her visitors, her tired eyes lifted in expectation. "Anna. Detective Singer. You have news about my daughter's killer?" She opened the door wide.

It was as cold inside as outside. Anna wondered if they had money for coal.

Joe took off his derby hat. "Only that Leo Lim is dead, ma'am."

Mrs. Bonsor's eyes clouded over with a dark satisfaction. She smiled.

Joe said, "But, we don't know that Leo Lim was your daughter's killer. We're still investigating. Is Mr. Bonsor in?"

Her voice sounded far off. "He's taken to his bed. He isn't seeing visitors. You'll have to ask me your questions. Please. Sit down."

After declining tea, Anna perched on the worn settee near Mrs. Bonsor. Joe sat in an old chair that wobbled. Anna took Mrs. Bonsor's rough hand. "Do you own a false beard? Perhaps something Elizabeth used in the evangelism plays that the missionary ladies do in Chinatown. You said she played Jesus."

"Yes."

"And do you have a red Chinese trunk?"

Mrs. Bonsor sighed, her eyes unfocused. "We did."

"What happened to it?" Anna quietly held her breath.

"I don't know."

Joe met Anna's excited eyes. He stood. "Ma'am, we need to speak with Mr. Bonsor."

§

Anna and Joe mounted the creaking steps. Anna put her mouth to Joe's ear and whispered, "I do believe he's sickened because of his guilt."

Joe whispered back, his soft breath tickling her ear, "You think he's the killer?"

"No, because it wouldn't explain the dummy. But he is definitely our man on the stairs."

Mrs. Bonsor led Anna and Joe into a small bedroom, where Mr. Bonsor sat propped up by pillows in a double brass bed. He wore a faded dressing gown, which Anna could see above the covers, and a hot water bottle lay atop his feet. Even in the few days since Anna had last seen him, he had grown thinner. He seemed very small.

Joe asked Mrs. Bonsor to wait downstairs. She hesitated briefly, but complied.

"Good day, Mr. Bonsor," Anna said coldly.

He leaned forward and coughed a wet, wheezing cough. "I haven't had a good day in weeks."

Anna said, "Yes, because you are eaten by guilt."

Joe nudged Anna hard.

Mr. Bonsor's chapped, dry lip curled up. "I beg your pardon."

"You knew about your daughter's death before we ever came to tell you. In fact, it was you who stuffed her body in the trunk."

He looked as if he would deny it.

Anna raised her voice accusingly. "It's true, isn't it?"

Mr. Bonsor sighed. "How would you like it if your daughter was found dead in the apartment of her yellow lover? Would you want people to know?"

"I can't answer that, Mr. Bonsor. My daughter doesn't have a Chinese lover."

Joe stepped in. "Mr. Bonsor, what did you do?"

"I sent Elizabeth to her aunt's. That's it. A week later, I got a telegram that Elizabeth had never arrived." He twitched with agitation.

Anna shifted impatiently. "Go on."

"I suspected that Elizabeth had run off. Of course, my first stop was Leo Lim's apartment. The door was unlocked. I found her. She was lying in his bed." His eyes rolled tortuously. "She had started to smell."

"Next to a dummy?"

"Yes."

"Why was there a dummy in the bed?"

"I don't know why!"

Joe said, "Go on Mr. Bonsor."

"I didn't want her body to be found in the apartment of a Chinaman. So I decided to move it. I could tell the police I found her dead in Griffith Park."

His confession rubbed Anna raw inside. Mr. Bonsor cared more about his daughter's reputation than her very life. It was an all-too-familiar story for Anna. She wondered if her own father would stuff her dead body in a trunk to save the family name. She feared he would.

Joe asked, "And then what happened, Mr. Bonsor?"

"I came back with a trunk and managed to get Elizabeth into it."

"But you couldn't get it down the stairs."

His face sagged. "No. I dragged the trunk back into that Celestial's apartment and locked the door. I sat there for a while trying to make a plan. Then, there was a knock on the door."

"And you fled out the fire escape."

He made a prolonged hacking sound, then continued in a congested voice. "I assumed I'd missed my chance—that whoever knocked would find the body. But if I didn't report her missing, she couldn't be identified."

"Did your wife know?"

"Of course not. She thought Elizabeth had eloped to New York or somewhere a white girl can marry a Chinaman."

Anna took Joe's arm and steered him into the hallway. She whispered, "Do you believe him?"

"His story is too weird not to believe him."

"Everything fits. The scratch marks on the floor. The body stuffed in the trunk. The timing. This explains the man on the fire escape, but it doesn't explain the dummy in the bed, and we still don't know definitively who the murderer was. If we assume he did it and stop investigating, we run the risk of letting the true killer go free and casting undeserved shame on an innocent man." Plus Anna would no longer have a case.

"You need to go home and rest."

Anna couldn't rest, because the clock was ticking. She didn't want to confess to Joe her grave mistake. Not if there was a tiny chance she could fix it. She had done exactly what he'd told her not to do, and in the worst possible way. She had alerted the press, and not just any member of the press but the most unscrupulous, sensationalizing reporter in LA. Joe would be livid.

"You're going to be working on the case? Tirelessly? You won't rest until we have someone in custody?"

"If you'll rest, I promise I won't."

"You'll make sure the Chinatown squad is hunting Chan Mon?"

"Of course."

"You'll canvass the saloons where the white men go? Maybe a bartender or someone will know Chan Mon or Elizabeth or Leo Lim—"

"We will. I promise."

Anna knew Joe Singer always kept his promises. She breathed deeply in relief.

Joe extended his rough hand and shook Anna's soft one. "Do you need me to see you home?"

"No. Go quickly. Solve the case." She squeezed his hand and dropped it.

Joe smiled at Anna, waved his arm at her, and marched off in the direction of the station.

Anna headed for Chinatown.

Chan Mon was the key. She had to find Chan Mon.

CHAPTER 23

Anna swung through the door of Mr. Jones's medicine shop, jingling the bells, tracking in horse droppings and mud from Los Angeles Street. Her nose tingled from the sharp, herbal smells. Mr. Jones sat behind the counter reading soberly, his chiseled face intent, his sensuous mouth peaceful. He appeared to be copying something from a book to a scroll, painting elegant Chinese characters in ink with a brush. He wore a pair of pristine silk pajamas, without a single smudge. Irrationally, she wondered who did his laundry.

He didn't look up.

"Mr. Jones, I'm so glad you're here. I need your help." She was out of breath. "And you need me."

He rested the wrist of his brush hand on the edge of the counter and raised his black eyes. "I told you, Matron Blanc. It's a Chinese matter. Unless you have something to trade—"

Anna panted, "A journalist stole my notebook. He knows all about Elizabeth's murder and he's going to print all kinds of truth in the paper."

Mr. Jones's brush hand dropped into his lap, spattering ink on his pajamas.

"He gave me twenty-four hours to prove that a white man killed Elizabeth Bonsor."

Mr. Jones whispered something passionate and perhaps profane under his breath. "Did a white man kill Elizabeth Bonsor?"

"I don't know who killed Elizabeth. But help me find Chan Mon. He's the key."

He closed his book. "How so?"

"Because he was Leo Lim's friend and Elizabeth's lover. He might have killed her, and if he didn't, he likely knows who did."

Anna stopped speaking and pleaded with her eyes. "You must help me." She stepped closer—so close she could read the cover of Mr. Jones's book—the one he was translating from English into Chinese. "Jupiter."

"I beg your pardon."

"Your book."

"What about it?"

"The title. It's *Love Poems.*"

A horn honked out on the street and a donkey brayed. Anna stumbled backward, fumbling in her purse for her gun amid handkerchiefs, hatpins, bullets, and spare change. She drew her rod and pointed it at Mr. Jones with steely, detective eyes. "You're Chan Mon."

Mr. Jones returned to painting the elaborate characters on his scroll. "Chan Mon is the name my mother gave me. I don't often use it in America. That's not a crime."

"Well, if the good people of Los Angeles learn your identity, you're dead. And if you touch me, you're double dead. I'll kill you, and so will Joe Singer."

He shook his glorious head. "I don't hurt women, Matron Blanc. Especially not you. You remind me of her."

"Elizabeth? You killed her."

He laughed, but it sounded like despair. "I didn't kill Elizabeth."

"Then who did?"

"I don't know."

"But you loved her. Did she love you? Or did she love Leo Lim? Maybe you hired that hatchet man to kill them both."

His face flushed a darker shade. He enunciated, "She loved me."

"That might be hard to prove."

Chan Mon reached into the inside pocket of his shirt and pulled out a letter on cream parchment paper. He extended the letter toward Anna with both hands. She crept forward, took it, then leapt back. It was warm from his skin and wrinkled from being worn close to his heart. It smelled of lilac perfume. She unfolded it and read, gun still pointed at Chan Mon.

He simply waited.

Elizabeth had written an epistle, and in no uncertain terms declared her love for Chan Mon, her disavowal of Leo Lim, and her plans to be Chan Mon's wife. Mrs. Bonsor had been right. They were going to New York, where a Chinese man could marry a white woman. It was the bravest thing a woman could do for love, braver than anything Anna had ever done. Even in New York, Elizabeth would never be accepted with a Chinese husband.

"I am yours and only yours forever." Anna's gray eyes locked on his. He stared back with lowered lids.

Truthfully, she didn't like Chan Mon for the killer, and not just because he was handsome. Poison was premeditated, not a crime of the moment. And when men were angry, they left marks. That eliminated Leo Lim as well. She lowered the gun and let it hang at her side.

Anna concentrated, moving facts around in her head like pieces of a puzzle. Three lovers formed a triangle, but there was someone else— one more player. Her killer made a square—a love square.

It came to Anna. "You loved Elizabeth, but someone else loves you. Who loves you, Chan Mon?"

"I don't have another lover. There was only Elizabeth."

Anna placed the letter carefully in her leather purse and snapped it shut. "Come now, Chan Mon. Someone asked you to go to Leo Lim's apartment that day? A woman. Who was it?"

Chan Mon's sensuous lips parted in surprise. "How did you know?"

"I didn't," Anna said. "But now I do. And whoever it was killed your lover."

The doorbells jingled and a woman swept in, oblivious to the tension in the room. She wiped her feet neatly on the doormat. Her voice was cheerful. "Chan Mon." She paused. Her angelic eyes widened like a thief who had just been caught red-handed. "Anna?"

Chan Mon's anger bloomed like a red hibiscus, coloring his skin, filling his eyes with a deadly loathing.

"Jupiter." Anna lowered her gun. "Oh my stars."

Miss Robins ran.

Chan Mon charged after her. Anna stepped in front of him, hurling her body against his manly muscles. She wedged herself between him and the door. He would have to move her to pass. She said softly, "No, Chan Mon. This is a white matter."

§

Anna felt slightly dazed, gnawing her lip, her eyes wet from riding her bike in the wind and from something else. She had to convince Joe Singer to arrest Miss Robins, his very own fiancée. But Joe would not be easy to convince, especially since he would be blinded by love. Anna ached for him, because she knew about broken hearts. But Joe would have to face the ugly truth, and the sooner the better.

Miss Robins might fly.

Anna skidded to a stop in front of Joe's desk, where he sat studying photos of Chinese men, his eyes squinting in concentration. She opened her mouth and tried futilely to form the words. "Um . . ."

"Hi Sherlock. You should be at home."

"Um."

He stood up and smirked. "You got something to tell me?"

Drawing her brows together, she forced out a sentence. "You're not going to like it."

"Try me."

She took Joe's hand and gazed into his eyes, her eyes colored with regret. "Sit, Joseph."

Joe withdrew his hand. "Look, Anna, we can't be holding hands. I'm sorry about the kiss after the kidnapping incident. I shouldn't have done it. It's just, I had been very worried about you, and you were covered in honey—"

"Miss Robins is the killer, and she's in love with Chan Mon."

Joe laughed.

Anna grabbed his hand again. "Don't you see, poor, dear Joe? Now we have a motive for the killer. Miss Robins knew Leo Lim had left town, fleeing the tong. He had come to her for prayer or something. She posed Elizabeth in Lim's bed with the dummy to make Chan Mon think that Elizabeth was compromised. Chan Mon all but said she tried to lure him there." She squeezed his hand to comfort him.

Joe took his hand back. "You found Chan Mon?"

"Yes. In his shop in Chinatown."

He patted her on the back. "Good work, Sherlock. I'll go arrest him. What's the address?"

"You can't arrest Chan Mon."

"Anna, he's our prime suspect. I can't believe that Miss Robins killed anybody. And why set up a girl who you've just murdered? A dead girl is no rival. It's too crazy, Anna."

"I know. But she didn't mean to kill Elizabeth. She just meant to drug her, put her in bed with the dummy, and lure Chan Mon to Lim's apartment so he could see Elizabeth's ersatz infidelity. But she gave Elizabeth too much. That evening, she left disguised in one of Lim's suits, with his hat tilted low, which explains why he left his apartment twice that day."

"How did she know Lim wasn't going to be there?"

"He must have told her he was fleeing the tong. Remember? She prayed for him."

"How did she get in?"

"I don't know." Anna paced. "The key. Perhaps he gave Elizabeth a key to feed his puss. Miss Robins told Elizabeth to come tell Leo Lim goodbye or something."

"It's a big leap, Sherlock."

Anna took both his hands and met his eyes, full of pity. "You're just saying that because you're going to marry her, but I assure you, her love for you is just a ruse. She's courting you to stay close to the investigation."

Joe took back his hands. "I'm not going to marry Miss Robins."

Anna's eyes became soft and vulnerable. She looked up from beneath feathered lashes. "You're not?"

Joe's voice flared with some emotion that Anna couldn't read. "No, I'm going to marry Miss Lory. I never told you I was going to marry Miss Robins. I invited her for ice cream once, and you jumped to conclusions."

"Oh." Anna's face fell. She swayed over to a chair and sat. Joe Singer was going to marry the piano girl. At least Anna didn't have to coddle him. Her voice became flat, which was unusual when she was fighting crime. "Also, I'm sure Mrs. Puce drinks opium tea. That's why she's nearly unconscious by the afternoon and why the missionary ladies never offered me any. She drank it right in front of me. At first, I simply thought they were rude, but they were just trying to keep her secret. If Mrs. Puce has it, Miss Robins could get it. But I looked it up. Opium tea is unpredictable. It's easy to get the dose wrong. People die all the time. I collected a sample. We can test it."

"So you want me to go arrest Miss Robins? Kind, godly Miss Robins?"

"Yes."

"No."

"If you don't arrest her by five o'clock tomorrow, Tilly will publish a story in the newspaper saying that Chan Mon killed Elizabeth Bonsor."

Joe slapped his head with his hands. "Anna, what have you done?"

"What have I done? I've solved the crime!"

Anna spun about so fiercely that her bun came loose. Joe grabbed her hand and spun her back. "Anna, I can't just arrest a missionary lady. I need hard evidence."

Anna's bun hung sideways. "Then let go of me so I can find it." She wrested free. "And by the way, Mr. Jones is Chan Mon."

Joe worked his mouth like a guppy. Anna flounced out the door.

CHAPTER 24

Anna returned to Chan Mon's medicine shop at the edge of Chinatown on Los Angeles Street. He would help her if Joe wouldn't. Chan Mon was a leader. Chan Mon was smart. He would know what to do.

The shop was locked.

On the sidewalk, she accosted a man who balanced two baskets on a pole he had laid across his shoulders. They brimmed with cabbages. She said, "Where is Mr. Jones? Do you know where he's gone?"

His head, crowned with a misshapen black hat, shook as if he didn't understand, or maybe he was just afraid to speak to her. Anna groaned. Disregarding the puddles, she slapped along the street to a different man—a grandfather of a man, wizened and toothless, sitting on the box seat of a vegetable wagon. She pointed at Chan Mon's medicine shop, her face contorted into a question mark. He looked Anna up and down as if she baffled him. Then he tilted his head back and made as if he was drinking.

Anna blinked. "Saloon?"

"All Fragrance."

Anna had to concentrate to understand his accent. The man sipped again from his imaginary cup.

Anna's mouth flattened. The last thing she needed was an inebriated Chan Mon. "Thank you." She inclined her head sideways in a partial bow—half East, half West.

Anna had seen the All Fragrance Saloon as she'd wandered Chinatown. It lay sandwiched between two other saloons. If Chan Mon wasn't swilling in one, he might be debauching in another.

She pedaled swiftly, her bike making a hissing sound as it sent up spray. Chinatown felt different today. Men loitered on both sides of Alameda Street, releasing fumes of aggression. The tongs, she guessed; the Bing Kong and the Hop Sing posturing for power. This time, their numbers reached twenty-five or more. The air crackled with the promise of violence. She clutched the handlebars tighter. Joe had been right about Chinatown. It was a treacherous place. But could a war really start now, with the girls gone and the presidents dead? Clearly the tongs did not easily forgive. A terrible thought came to Anna. Did they know that she had killed their president? She ought to turn and flee, but the time had passed. She skidded into their midst, flanked on either side of the road. She peddled furiously through the center of their battle lines, her wide eyes stinging in the wind.

The highbinders showed no interest in Anna.

§

The All Fragrance Saloon smelled like spilled beer, smoke, and other fragrances Anna would never mention. Brown saliva stained the entrance on the sidewalk. They desperately needed a spittoon. She peeked inside. There were blacks there, and whites, sitting at tables, playing cards. They seemed rough and possibly drunk. They *did* show interest in Anna, eyes full of evil suggestions. She folded her arms to hide her chest. Someone belched.

She wouldn't expect to find a respectable man like Chan Mon in such a place. She turned in a circle, looking. There he sat, with his chiseled cheek down on a table, looking bent, a full glass of beer and a half empty pitcher before him.

Anna bustled over to the bar. "Chan Mon, you must not drink. You need to board up your shop, find yourself a gun, and help me."

Chan Mon groaned.

She put her palms on his shoulder and rocked him. He groaned again. Anna picked up the pitcher of beer and dumped it over his head.

He shook like a dog, spraying Anna. "Elizabeth is dead because of me. She was to be my wife, my responsibility."

"No. Elizabeth is dead because of Miss Robins." Anna spoke sharply, like an angry nun. "Get up. Elizabeth would have demanded it."

She took him by the hand and pulled him up onto his feet. She couldn't tell if he was drunk with beer or with grief. "You have to help me find hard evidence that Miss Robins killed Elizabeth."

"Miss Robins means nothing to me. She just helped me with translation. She was Elizabeth's friend not mine. She flirted with me. I never flirted back."

"I believe you."

Chan Mon stumbled against the table, and she tried to steady him, letting him lean on her. In the mirror, she saw their reflection—the epitome of East, the epitome of West.

Then Anna heard shots. She swung her head around. Two round holes appeared in the window glass. A black man in a pinstriped suit fell over sideways with a *thud*, upsetting his chair. She heard another *pop* outside.

Anna screamed. Chan Mon pushed Anna's head down, his eyes suddenly focused. "Get on the floor."

She dropped to her knees on the gritty, sticky planks. Another *pop* and the body of a Chinese man hit the front window, arms splayed out, holding a revolver. He slid out of sight, leaving a streak of blood on the glass. There were more shots and the window shattered, spraying Anna with broken glass. On the planks across the room, the blank eyes of the Negro stared accusingly at Anna. She shook uncontrollably. She had contributed to this violence by rescuing the girls, and now at least one innocent man was dead. And she hadn't even saved the girls. Ting Ting was dead, and Yuk-Lin was Presbyterian.

Anna's voice rippled. "Will the city avenge that Negro?"

"No," Chan Mon said flatly.

Pain singed her stomach. It was grief. In the street, there was a *pop* and an answering *pop*, and then a lull. Chan Mon gripped Anna's sleeve. "Come on."

They crawled across the sticky, bloody, glass-strewn floor toward the rear of the saloon and peered out the back door into the alley.

Along the narrow, muddy passage, Anna saw men in black pants and tunics scrambling from doorways, spilling in both directions. Chan Mon took her hand. Blood seeped between their palms—hers or his she didn't know. He led Anna down the alley. More shots popped in the street, and someone was wailing. Chan Mon opened a door in the wall of a tall brick building on the alley and pulled her through into a room that smelled like incense. The door trembled shut behind them, closing them into a quieter space. The ceiling rose heavenward. Five wooden giants confronted Anna, standing twelve feet tall atop a platform that made them taller still. They wore busy robes, long beards, and towering hats that exceeded even her own in grandeur. Each was a different color—black, white, yellow, red, and sea green. Smoke rose from brass censers.

Anna stared wide-eyed up at the gods and crossed herself. "So this is a temple."

He nodded. "They won't shoot in here. They won't risk angering the gods."

Sirens bleated in the streets. The cops were coming, Joe Singer no doubt among them, heading into the thick of the violence. She prayed to the five gods before her, promising to be good forever after if they would just keep Joe Singer safe. Anna looked at the angle of the sinking sun and acid began to seep into her throat. "I have to go. I need to go to the mission to get evidence. I only have until five o'clock."

Somewhere close, a gun went off. Anna dropped to the floor and huddled behind a brass urn, trembling. Chan Mon held her hand again. "Let the shooting subside. Then I will go with you."

Anna hesitated, then nodded. She couldn't find evidence if she were dead, and she would feel braver with Chan Mon by her side. Maybe Chan Mon could persuade the woman who loved him to confess, because if the city thought Chan Mon had killed Elizabeth Bonsor, he was a dead man.

Time ticked, and more shots popped in the streets. Anna huddled, sweating, though it was cold. Her opportunity to find evidence of Miss Robins's guilt was trickling away. Periodically, the doors in the front or back of the building opened and slammed shut. More Chinese were finding their way to the temple, displaced by the violence. A man entered clutching a small boy to his breast. There was blood on his shirt, his own and the child's, who couldn't have been more than seven. Chan Mon took the boy from the man's arms.

Anna's lips parted, her voice quivering with outrage. "They shot a child?"

"He was no doubt caught in the crossfire."

She wiped her dripping forehead. "I can tend him. You don't like blood."

Chan Mon laid the child on a golden bamboo mat, as cool and efficient as any doctor. It dawned on Anna that he was a doctor of the Chinese sort. She murmured, "You don't fear blood at all."

"I feared Elizabeth's blood."

The boy's red chest stilled, and Anna beheld her first dead child. She silenced an anguished cry with her fist. Her eyes welled, and she thought she couldn't bear it, couldn't bear her guilt. Then the saints buoyed her and she did. She had to. His father needed her.

The father's hand was clamped to his own arm. Crimson seeped from between his fingers. He fell to his knees beside the boy, his blood dripping out, reddening the mat. He'd been shot in the arm.

Anna spun in a circle, looking for something to stanch the blood. There was nothing but silk cushions, carved mahogany, and the gods themselves. She brazenly lifted her skirt and untied one of her petticoats, with its lace and fine pleats. It dropped to the floor. She stepped out of it and began ripping it into strips, handing them to Chan Mon. He used them to bind the wound. "I need medicine. I've got to go to my shop. Press the wound." He lifted his hands from the man's arm.

Chan Mon slipped away.

Anna pressed on the wound so hard her arm tingled. She said silent prayers to Joseph, patron saint of fathers, that the man would not die. The blood soaked her petticoat, then the cuff of her sleeve. Finally, the ferrous scent of blood overcame the incense.

Every few minutes, more men arrived, until little space remained in the temple. Most of them knelt, their hands pressed together in prayer. Some squatted beside her, perhaps offering help, perhaps holding vigil by the man, speaking to her in their mysterious language. They stank of fear. So did Anna. She scanned the many faces. Were any men highbinders? How could she tell?

An hour passed without sight of her Chinese doctor. She'd been abandoned to nurse the wounded man alone, which she did not know how to do. She had no medicine. Her arms were aching. Then Chan Mon returned carrying a long burlap sack. He pushed his way to Anna and squatted beside her. "It's bad outside." He rustled in the bag, withdrawing a long bamboo pipe, a candle, a lighter, and a black ball. Anna guessed it was opium.

He put the opium in the bowl of the pipe and held it over the flaming candle. Two of the men tried rolling the wounded man on his side so he could smoke. Anna wanted to smoke, too, because she wanted to forget the horror of their predicament, but she needed to be clear-minded.

Anna unwrapped the wound. Chan Mon washed it in clean water and applied a poultice, which he bound to the arm with silk bandages. He lifted the patient's shoulders and poured a tincture between his lips.

Anna wondered how many wounded hadn't made it to the temple, how many lay dead in the street.

CHAPTER 25

It had been twenty minutes since the last shot. Anna decided she must risk venturing outside, despite the danger. She was already late for her appointment with Tilly, and Chinatown's safety depended on it. Chan Mon's very life depended on it. Her opportunity to go to the mission to find evidence was long since lost, but she could perhaps convince the weasel to give her more time. No matter what, she had to intercept him before he submitted his article to his editor.

Chan Mon now watched over the wounded man. It would be selfish to draw him away. Anna slipped out through the front, past the two wooden giants that guarded the temple, towering like redwoods. Cops occupied the sidewalks, patrolling the streets looking grim. Joe Singer wasn't among them. Anna tried not to think of him. Flaunting propriety, armpits smeared with sweat, she jogged to All Fragrance Saloon to reclaim her bicycle, hoping Tilly would wait for her.

When she arrived home at half past the hour, she looked at her watch and swore. No Tilly.

Anna called the station from the telephone in the hall of her apartment building. Mr. Melvin gave Joe the receiver.

Anna cried out, "You're back. You're safe."

"For now. I brought in a bunch of highbinders, although I doubt they'll stay in jail for long. It's beginning, Sherlock. One Negro and four Chinamen are dead."

"Five." Anna rubbed her eyes and fell silent from shock. She had watched the black man and the boy die.

"Anna?"

"Tilly didn't wait for me."

"What do you mean?"

"I thought I would be able to stall him with, I don't know, my irre-
futable logic as to Miss Robins's guilt." Her voice cracked. "But I was
trapped by the shooting and he left."

Silence. "You were in Chinatown?"

"Yes, but I'm fine. I . . . I think the story's going out in the evening
paper. Can't we talk to the paper? Tell them that it's libel."

"Libel against Chan Mon? He's a Chinaman."

"Well, he's going to be a dead Chinaman if we can't stop the presses.
Someone will know that Mr. Jones is Chan Mon." The muscular, poetic
man would die, and it would be her fault.

§

In front of Central Station, a paddy wagon waited beside a pair of
horses, five bicycles, and one motorcycle. Joe cut his eyes to Anna. "I
can't take you on the motorcycle."

"I can't ride a horse through town with my skirts bunched up
around my waist. We'll have to take the paddy wagon."

Joe froze. "I don't have permission."

"You can ask permission later!"

While Joe fiddled behind the dash, she charged to the front of
the car, set the crank, and slipped into the passenger side. The engine
growled. The car lurched forward and into a palm tree. Joe put his forehead on the steering wheel.

"You don't care if we have permission. You can't drive an auto,"
Anna said.

"I can. A little."

Anna disembarked and ran to the driver's side. Joe got out and
Anna got in. He leapt into the passenger seat as Anna set the car rolling
backward. She eased the auto forward onto First Street and accelerated.
The speed limit was ten miles per hour. Anna drove twenty.

Joe braced himself against the door as Anna took a turn too fast.
"Mother of God. You drive like you're in a race."

"At least I haven't crashed into a tree." Anna shifted and hit the gas. She flew toward the *Los Angeles Herald* building, saying a silent prayer to the Chinese gods, because shouldn't they listen? She was, after all, trying to save Chinatown.

Anna skidded to a halt in front of the *Herald* as Joe leapt from the paddy wagon and flew up the steps. Anna scampered after him with her skirts lifted above her ankles. He threw open the door beside the loading dock and swore. "Damn it."

Anna's hopes dissolved.

The presses had already stilled. The papers were bundled and stacked near large industrial doors, smelling of hot ink, awaiting delivery. A printer stood near the doors, sleeves rolled up, hands black with newsprint.

She hadn't missed Tilly at her apartment. Tilly had never come at all. He'd written the story and submitted it for press hours ago.

Anna crossed the floor and picked up a paper. Elizabeth gazed mildly from the front page, as did her lover, the convert Leo Lim. Chan Mon's picture was represented with a framed question mark, though they used his name. Anna wondered where Tilly had gotten the pictures, and how many people knew Chan Mon's identity. She wondered, too, how Mr. Bonsor would survive this, and then realized she didn't care. Elizabeth would have been humiliated to have her love triangle splatted across the headlines so that everyone in Los Angeles knew. Anna could only hope they didn't read the papers in heaven.

But how did she stop Angelenos from seeing the papers on earth?

The newsies, faces unwashed, clothes unmended, had started to line up outside, waiting for their bundles and talking their tough-boy talk. Some sat on the sidewalk playing marbles or gambling with dice. Anna guessed nearly a hundred boys waited, plus a handful of girls, and more were coming. "Can't you order the *Herald* not to sell the papers?"

Joe said, "No, I can't order the *Herald* not to sell papers. Do you know how powerful the press is?"

"Then arrest the newsies."

"If I start arresting newsies, they're all gonna run like mad."

"As long as they run without their papers." A red, swirled aggie hit Anna's foot. She kicked it hard back in the direction from which it had come.

"Sherlock, most of these kids live on the streets. If they can't sell their papers, they don't eat. They'll come back for the papers later."

This resonated with Anna, who knew about not eating. "Okay, then. We'll win them to our cause."

Joe's forehead creased. "How?"

Anna climbed up the stone railing, not realizing her skirt had gotten hung up on her stocking showing four inches of shin. Clearing her throat, she shouted, "Your attention please. I am Police Matron Anna Blanc. Your attention!"

The newsies gabbed on in conversations of their own. Standing near her feet, Joe tugged her skirt down.

Anna looked to him for help.

He said, "Talk about the crime."

Anna brushed a loose curl from her hot cheek and called out louder this time. "A white woman was murdered. Her maggot-eaten body was found rotting in a trunk."

The newsies began quieting for the most part, and turned to stare at the beautiful, shouting woman who relayed such gore. A few young mouths hung open. No doubt they recognized Anna, having seen her picture in the paper last summer with her knees showing, brandishing a gun. She was the scandalous lady who had broken all the rules to dispatch the New High Street Suicide Faker.

For this, she commanded respect.

Joe shook his bowed head from side to side. Perhaps he didn't like her choice of words. Anna didn't care.

She called out, "The papers claim that a Chinaman did it. That's a lie. Today's headlines are lies. Lies, lies, lies. Shall I go on?"

The grimy boys stared skeptically but remained relatively quiet, marbles at rest.

Anna smiled her sweetest smile. "Good." She cleared her throat again. "Elizabeth Bonsor was killed by a white woman—another missionary. She's a vicious, vicious killer, and she roams the streets still."

Some of the smaller boys gasped. Joe sighed.

"You must tell each customer that the headlines are a lie. Shout it from the top of your lungs. 'Lies, lies. Read all about it.' Tell them the truth. If you do, I will come tomorrow and give you each a dollar and a toy surprise."

Joe whispered, "Where are you going to get that kind of money?"

"I'm bluffing," Anna whispered back.

"I'm sure they can smell it."

They were, in fact, beginning to dismiss her with their eyes. Still, they stared.

Anna bit her lip. "The toy surprise part is true."

"No." Joe shook his head definitively.

"Oh, very well." She began to shout at the boys again. "That is . . . we have patrolmen all over the city. They will be watching you. If you do not spread the word, we will arrest you. You will be held in prison for the rest of your lives, fed only wormy bread and stagnant water with spiders in it."

Joe conked himself in the head. A newsie at the front of the line scratched his greasy scalp. Anna scanned the crowd. Eyes and brows formed triangles of doubt.

Anna splayed her hands at Joe. "Help me."

Joe stepped up onto the stone railing and flashed his badge. "I'm Detective Singer with the LAPD. Spread the word. Or . . . or else."

Anna concluded loudly. "Do you understand?"

The *Herald*'s big industrial doors opened, and the boys began to file up the stairs past Anna, staring at her, top to bottom. They entered the building, buying their stacks of papers from the printer.

Once in possession, they dissolved into the streets of LA. To Anna's relief, they began calling out to passersby. "Lies, lies. Read all about it."

Anna turned to Joe. "Now what do we do? Some of the newsies might not do it, and even if they do, not everybody's going to listen to them."

Joe said, "Chinatown's flooded with cops because of the shootout. We tell Captain Dixon what's going on, and he'll mobilize the patrolmen. Meanwhile, I'll get hard evidence so we can make an arrest."

"I thought you didn't believe me about Miss Robins."

"It's a lot to swallow, Sherlock. I'm reserving judgment."

"Get Chan Mon. Maybe he'll get Miss Robins to confess. We'll say we know she didn't mean it, and that it's very understandable, even though it's not."

"Good idea, Sherlock. Stay here."

"I thought we were clear on this. You don't get to tell me what to do. I'm going back to Chinatown with you or without you."

"Anna, this tong war's not over."

Chapter 26

A bullet hole marred the door at Chan Mon's apothecary. Anna put her finger in the hole and touched the slug. Her heart pounded. "Jupiter."

Joe tried the door, but the knob wouldn't turn. He knocked, and silence answered.

Anna said, "Maybe he's still at the temple."

"First let's find Dixon. Let the cops know what's coming down the path."

Anna nodded. They rounded the corner and passed the bulletin board where notices written in Chinese fluttered in the icy wind. The place looked desolate, without a man in sight. Saloons were closed and windows were shuttered. Anna stepped around a large bloodstain that dripped from the sidewalk onto the street and soaked into the mud. It was Chinese blood. Her fault. She stopped to stare at it. There would be more of it soon.

"Come on," Joe said gently. He took her arm and pulled her along. Anna glanced back at the stain and wrapped her coat more tightly around herself.

A cop stood on the next corner looking watchful but tired, deflated after the violence. His pants were muddy at the knees, as if he'd fallen. The cop called gruffly, "Singer, get her out of here."

Anna charged to him, hat flopping, and started talking fast. "There's been a murder and you don't know about it yet—a white woman killed in Chinatown. A missionary."

The cop cut his eyes to Joe. "Just now?"

"No! It was weeks ago," Anna said.

The officer cocked his head.

Anna repinned her hat as she forged on. "We covered it up because we knew that if people found out they would storm Chinatown." Her words ran like champions. "But you have to know. A Chinaman didn't do it. And you have to stop the bad people from pillaging and burning." Anna smeared the back of her hand across her dewy forehead.

Once more, the cop looked to Joe.

Joe said, "She's probably right. She usually is."

The cop peered down the empty street, where no whites threatened Chinatown but for a blonde rat scuttling across the road. "If you say so, Joe."

"Spread the word!" said Anna. "Get the Chinatown squad ready."

"Find Captain Dixon and tell him to expect trouble from the west," Joe said.

Two *pop pops* punctured the stillness.

"If I see him. The Chinatown Squad has their hands full." The officer turned and jogged off in the direction of the shots.

Anna's eyebrows formed a teepee of concern. "We're on our own."

§

Anna's silk heels were grinding down on the rough board sidewalks as they jogged to the temple. She felt wet under the arms and could strongly smell her Ambre Antique perfume.

"Are you all right?" Joe asked.

She gulped air. "Of course."

Inside the temple, a makeshift shroud, possibly a silk tablecloth, covered the dead boy's body. The wounded man lay on his mat in an opium haze. The men who had sought refuge still knelt on silk cushions making supplications before the giant gods. Anna scuttled over, checking each man's face. None was Chan Mon.

She wilted. Joe took her arm and led her quietly outside. She hadn't eaten all day and felt shaky with exhaustion. Her stomach made an embarrassing sound.

Joe said, "Sherlock, go home, eat some Cracker Jacks, and go to bed."

"Not unless you go to bed with me."

"I think that came out wrong."

"I'm not any more tired than you are, and we have evidence to collect. Neither one of us can go home. We're not done. I want the morning papers to say we've made an arrest."

Joe's shoulders rose and fell. "All right. To the mission, then."

"To the mission." Her legs tried to keep pace with his longer ones.

He squeezed her arm. "Anna, I'm not saying I'm glad you're here. I'd rather have you anywhere else, but you are the best damn detective on the force. I mean it."

Anna wished he wouldn't talk that way. It made her weak in the knees. She said nothing.

They reached Los Angeles Street. A group of twenty or so white men loitered near La Placita Church. Anna could see them across the plaza. She looked anxiously at Joe. "Who are those men?"

"I'm going to find out." Joe moved closer, and Anna followed quietly at a distance to avoid being sent back. The men ranged in age from about fourteen to sixty-five and looked leaderless, uncertain, disorganized, angry. A well-dressed youth tapped a bench with a baseball bat. It made Anna's spine prickle.

Joe flashed his badge and exchanged words with the men that Anna couldn't hear. Ten or so persons huddled around to listen, their faces animated and skeptical. Joe waved his arms and the men began to disperse, heading back to town or down Los Angeles Street.

Joe jogged back to Anna, as serious as death.

"Who are they?" she asked.

"They say they're just passing time, but clearly they read the paper."

"Did you tell them the truth?"

"I did." Joe ran his hands through his hair. "They were more concerned that a white girl had a Chinese lover."

Shots rang out to the east, in Chinatown. Joe growled. "All hell's breaking loose."

"It's not your fault."

He stared at Anna with bitter Arrow Collar Man eyes. "Isn't it? I hid the girls."

Anna's mouth opened and closed. She felt the weight of his guilt, the weight of her own.

She heard distant shouting. A stream of black smoke billowed up into the air from some building down Los Angeles Street, barely visible against the occulting sky.

Joe's eyes widened, revealing a circle of white. He shouted, "Anna, go home!" He began running south. Anna loped after him, despite her footwear, weary state, and his admonition. Her body was floating, floating toward a crowd of white men who loitered in the street, angry faces hellishly aglow. It was the last place she should be, and yet her legs carried her forward.

The mission burned. Black smoke poured through the upper-floor windows into the first clear night LA had seen all week. In the absence of visible targets, men hurled insults at the flames. The roar of the blaze overwhelmed their voices, but Anna could guess their sentiments. They were mad about women missionaries working with Chinese men, and incensed over Elizabeth's love affairs.

Joe grabbed her hand and yanked her toward the fire. Another volley of gunfire boomed in Chinatown. He stopped, bringing Anna to a standstill, and turned to look. He glanced again toward the mission, back at Chinatown, and then at her.

He yelled, "Anna, please go home!" Then he dropped her hand and ran. Anna's legs worked furiously, bearing her toward the scene. The flames reflected in the windows of the churches across the street. The ancient proprietor of the Sun Wing Wo General Store, which flanked the mission, shuffled in and out, hauling merchandise from the vulnerable building and dumping it in the street. It promptly disappeared in the hands of looters.

Joe skidded to a stop at the back of the crowd in front of the mission. Anna overshot him, sliding past. He grabbed her arm to steady her.

She took a fistful of her frock and wrung it. "They're smoking them out. The ladies are afraid to come out."

One of the shouters noticed Anna and stared. He tapped his companion, who was armed with a switch. They began drifting toward her exuding ferocity. Joe whispered, "Act like a whore, not a missionary."

Anna hitched her skirt up to show a daring bit of shin and winked at them furiously and badly. Joe flashed his badge. "Back off. She's under arrest for vagrancy."

"She's not a missionary?"

Anna's eyelid fluttered. "Hell no."

It forestalled their attack. They were distracted by the appearance of a Chinese man in silk pajamas, who began pacing in front of the flaming building, dangerously close, his skin glistening with heat. His eyes burned as he shouted in Chinese as if he had nothing to lose and nothing to fear. He held a gun in his hand, which kept the white men back.

It was Chan Mon.

Anna kept winking, kept lifting her skirt. Pulling her along, Joe approached Chan Mon cautiously. "Jones. You planning on shooting her when she comes out? Shooting her won't make you feel better. We don't even know if she did it."

Chan Mon bellowed—not a word, but the sound of a man in anguish. He extended his gun hand to Joe. "Take it, quickly, before I change my mind."

Joe took the gun and stuck it in the waistband of his pants. "Is she inside?"

Chan Mon nodded. He caught Joe's eyes. "I didn't set the blaze."

"I didn't think you did."

Joe walked to the front door and kicked it open. He coughed, lowered his head, and called inside. "Mrs. Puce, Miss Robins. It's Detective Singer. Come out."

"No!" Anna grabbed a handful of his coat and pulled him backward. The fabric felt hot. He tried to extricate himself. She shouted, "You'll be taking the ladies out of the fire and into the frying pan. You can't fight off this mob alone. You'll get trounced, even with a gun."

"Anna, they are going to burn!" He called through the doorway again. "Come out!"

Anna snapped her head about. All the buildings on the west side of the block were attached—one continuous row. If the fire wagon didn't arrive soon, they would all be ash.

She barreled down the street, around the corner, into the alley, doubling back until she reached the mission. Five rioters waited to ambush anyone who sought escape through the back door. Two well-dressed young fellows were kicking a trashcan, spreading litter everywhere, and making crashing sounds as it crumpled. They had smashed the lamps up and down the row. Their companions were drunkenly chanting, "Death to Chink lovers." In contrast to the wealthy men, they looked rough and low class. Hate had brought them together.

Anna shouted, "Good evening. I'm a prostitute." She flashed her shins like they were her badge. "Please help me. They are attacking missionary women in the front yard. Pulling their hair and such. Hurry. Hurry."

The men hooted despicably and charged down the alley to partake of the imaginary bloodshed.

As soon as their backs were turned, Anna banged on the door. "It's me, Matron Blanc. There are no men back here, but it won't last. Come out while you can."

She heard a bolt slide and Mrs. Puce opened the door, arms loaded with photographs, and stumbled into the back yard wheezing. Her face was red against her gray hair. Miss Robins followed, all aglow, carrying a framed picture and a wad of clothing. She dissolved into a coughing fit.

Anna whispered, "Is everyone out? The girl with the spectacles?"

"Gone home." Miss Robins bent at the waist to spit. It gave Anna fleeting satisfaction.

"Then run toward downtown as fast as you can. Go to my apartment." She pressed a key into Miss Robins's hand.

Anna wanted to flee, too, but she had to go back for Joe, as he had unfortunate heroic tendencies. It would be a horror to save Miss Robins and lose Joe. As Anna rounded the corner onto the street, she came face-to-face with the trashcan kickers. Anna's voice was two octaves higher than usual. "Biscuits." She spun about and ran back through the alley. She could hear their drunken feet pounding behind her. They had longer legs and better shoes, but she had sobriety on her side and wasn't screaming. At the end of the block, she looked back. One fop had tripped. One had folded over.

§

The mission burned, igniting the school and the Sun Wing Wo General Store. Joe and Chan Mon were gone. The fire brigade, with their team of white horses, unrolled their hoses and sprayed while the rioters chanted.

There was nothing left for Anna to do. She limped back toward the plaza, streaked with soot, smelling like fire. She wanted out of Chinatown. She heard her name being called and jogged toward the sound. She found Joe and Chan Mon searching the sidewalks, calling her.

Joe blinked at the sight of her. He ran and clutched her to him. "Damn you, Sherlock." He stepped back like she was a hot stove. "We can't be embracing."

Chan Mon said flatly, "Miss Robins is dead. No one got out of the mission."

"Actually, she's at my apartment."

§

Anna drove the paddy wagon back to her house, with Chan Mon deadly silent in the back. Joe perched on the edge of the passenger seat, his knee working up and down with adrenaline. The frigid night air stung Anna's nostrils. Her cheeks felt too sunburned to touch. She led the men to her rundown apartment building, in through the hall, and knocked on her own door, having surrendered the key to the missionaries. Miss Robins answered. She had washed her face, fixed her hair, and changed, presumably into the dress she'd rescued from the mission, which was gorgeous and blue. She looked angelic, though she smelled like hell. Mrs. Puce had taken no such measures, and was sleeping on Anna's bed, atop the white matelassé coverlet. She looked smoked. Anna wondered if you could get soot out of white coverlets. She would ask Joe.

Miss Robins stepped outside and closed the door with a quiet click, presumably to avoid waking Mrs. Puce. Then she saw Chan Mon. She screamed and flew to Joe like a startled bird, moving behind him, using his body as a shield.

Joe glanced at Chan Mon, who was staring open-mouthed. "Don't worry, Miss Robins," Joe said. "He's not going to hurt you. I won't let him."

Like a striking snake that's been cornered, Miss Robins reached into Joe's waistband, where her hand did not belong, and grabbed Chan Mon's gun. Joe caught her wrist, holding her hand down in an awkward position behind his back. As he turned around, she dropped to her knees and put the muzzle in her mouth.

The noise smacked Anna's ears like a rock, leaving them ringing. Miss Robins lay dead in the hallway of Anna's apartment building, blood spattering her stunning blue gown.

Chapter 27

I was midnight before the coroner removed Miss Robins's body and Anna could finally retire, though she had to share the bed with Mrs. Puce. Anna bathed in the communal tub, which was always frigid after six, and changed into a negligee trimmed with lace. She drew back the matelassé coverlet, which was now smudged with gray, and lay down beside the quietly sobbing missionary. She slept like she was dead.

In the morning, she left the woman sleeping and stepped into the hallway dressed in black. Someone had scrubbed the tile outside her door clean of blood during the wee hours. She wondered if Joe had done it.

She rode her bike to the station. Joe was in conference with Captain Wells, and she could see them through the glass of the captain's office window. The door opened, and Joe came out. He strode past Anna with the barest nod of acknowledgement. His eyes were pained.

Anna followed him. "It's Chinatown, isn't it? Everyone is dead."

"Anna, not now."

Anna blinked. She'd been insulted by Joe Singer on many occasions, but she'd never been dismissed. "Joe." She reached out and took his hand. "Thank you."

He gave her a potent look that she couldn't read and took his hand back. It left her mightily confused. Was he angry with her? She said, "For cleaning the hall outside my apartment. Thanks."

He sauntered to the reception area where a young woman waited with a basket full of bread, cookies, and other good things.

It was the piano girl. She stared dazedly at Anna, like a bird that had flown into glass. Joe took the girl's gloved hand and kissed it. He led her outside into the sunlight. The girl cast Anna a backward glance, her brows knit in confusion. Anna stared back, because she couldn't help it, because she'd lost her mind and manners. She was stricken.

§

Later, Anna sat at her desk typing nonsense in a mad flurry. Anna couldn't type, but the feel of the pounding of the keys almost soothed her, and it made her look busy on a day in which she could not focus. Her mind raced with images: The dead child; Ting Ting disappearing under the water; Miss Robins pulling the trigger, and her blood on the tile; Joe Singer kissing his fiancée's gloved hand. Anna pushed the carriage return. The typewriter made a grinding sound and pinged. She typed some more.

Joe appeared and coughed. "Uh. Good morning."

Anna looked up from her papers, but her eyes rose no higher than his collar. "I upset your fiancée with my familiarity. I regret—."

"Never mind," he said. "She'll forgive me eventually. But things are different now. I'm going to be a married man, Anna." He hesitated. "I mean, Assistant Matron Blanc."

Anna nodded. "Yes, Detective."

"You were right about the murder. We have evidence that Miss Robins was the killer. That dress she was wearing—Chan Mon identified it as one he bought Elizabeth as a gift."

"The missing dress," Anna said vaguely.

"Yes. And that tea you took from the crime scene—it was opium, like you said."

"I suppose she'd rather take her life than face the gallows." Her smooth brow furrowed. "And how is Chinatown?"

"Six more dead. All suspected highbinders. Chan Mon is trying to broker a truce with the new tong presidents."

Anna nodded as the news sank in and settled in the silt of her remorse. She wanted to ask him if he felt guilty too. If he thought they had done wrong by rescuing the slave girls, especially since they weren't truly rescued at all, but she said nothing.

Joe knocked once on her desk with a false levity. "That's it. That's all I've got. So, see you later . . . Assistant Matron Blanc." He smiled and Anna held her breath.

"Oh." Joe produced her beloved, stolen silver net purse from behind his back. He set it on her desk. "I confiscated it from a pawnshop."

"Thanks."

"Open it," he said.

Anna did. It was full of Juicy Fruit. When Anna glanced up he was walking away.

CHAPTER 28

Anna stood at attention in Matron Clemens's office, wishing she had washed her uniform. To compensate, she wore her ugliest dress, which, regrettably, looked quite nice, albeit slightly too big. She could summon no cheer at her superintendent's return, though Anna loved the plain, stern woman. Recent events had left Anna devoid of all joy. She had nightmares. None of the officers seemed at all impressed with her accomplishments. They credited Joe with solving the murder, refused to believe that Anna had dispatched Tom Foo Yuen, and gave her either hot looks or the cold shoulder. Joe credited Anna, but he was never around.

The piles had grown on Matron Clemens's desk during her absence, mostly due to Anna's negligence. Anna bobbed a somber curtsy. "Welcome back."

The lady nodded in stoic acknowledgement. She glanced at the heaps of files on her ink blotter.

Anna said, "The children have been very naughty, and I've mostly been out—"

"You never found Jane Godfrey."

"Jane who?"

"The fifteen-year-old thief? The treat girl?"

"Yes. She moved to Alaska. She's the Eskimos' problem now." Jane might have for all Anna knew.

Matron Clemens stood, scraped up the files, and plopped them in Anna's thin arms. "You're dismissed. Get to work."

"Thank you, ma'am." Anna walked quickly toward the door. She would catch up on her duties, even if it meant working night and day. She would keep Matron Clemmons proud.

"Oh, Assistant Matron Blanc."

Anna turned. "Yes?"

The older woman's eyes were fixed on a document before her, and she marked it with a pen, never looking up. "To walk a mile is a trial, to walk a yard is hard, but inch by inch, it's a cinch."

"Yes ma'am."

§

Anna's upper lip, which she tried to keep so stiff, quivered. She took a velvet cape from the station's coat rack and slunk toward the door. She wrapped up in it and hugged herself, whispering under her breath, "To walk a mile is a trial, to walk a yard is hard, but inch by inch, it's a cinch. Inch by inch by inch . . ."

She opened the station door and it creaked closed behind her. She didn't want to be in the station when Joe might appear, and she had work to do. The municipal band played on Friday afternoons in a bandstand at Hollenbeck Park. If not monitored by the authorities, some people would dance too close. A matron was duty-bound to prevent it. Anna used to be in favor of love and hated to tap sweethearts on the shoulder, flashing her matron's badge, forcing them to separate. So instead, she usually fed the geese. But not today. Today she wanted to warn them all.

She took the trolley to Boyle Heights and walked to Hollenbeck Park, the very place where she and Joe had first kissed last summer. She had responded by kneeing him in the groin. In retrospect, it had been the exact right thing to do.

The park spread out for acres, covered in lawns, lovely ponds, tall jutting pampas grass, the twisted roots of a giant fig tree. There were hedges, bushes, and trellises—places for trysts. The music had started and people were waltzing. She peered into the crowd. Couples whirled in circles. No one danced too closely, but Anna glared at couples anyway. Then she hated herself for being heartless, and for having too much heart, and for everything she'd ever done or said. She left the lovers to their own precarious fates and wandered down to the geese.

Anna sat on a bench facing the pond and whispered to herself, "Inch by inch, it's a cinch. Inch by inch by inch . . ." The geese came waddling up in large numbers, quacking, but she had no bread. Anna tried to shoo them, but they quacked forward, nibbling the fancy ribbons on her skirt. Anna stood and bustled away, stepping on at least one webbed foot. They followed her. She broke into a run, heading for the pampas grass, away from the water, the music, and the people, chanting in rhythm with her footfalls, "Inch by inch—"

"Anna!"

She heard footsteps behind her. The geese were gone, so she stopped abruptly. A man collided with her backside. "Sorry."

Anna swung about. Joe Singer looked agitated and serious. He ran his hands through his hair, which still needed cutting. Her stomach sank, and she hugged herself. "You're angry because I'm not doing my job. But I am. I saw lovers nearby, and I'm going to stop them."

He laid his hands on her shoulders, looked her sternly in the eyes, and commanded her. "Magic Genie."

Anna's lips trembled. He was going to do it. He was going to use his genie wish. He would command her to go away and leave him alone so that he could go off and marry the Piano Girl. He would tell her not to interfere, maybe even to move to China or somewhere far away so he never had to see her again. He'd come all the way to Hollenbeck Park to tell her.

All the strength left her. She felt insubstantial, like the barest wisp of smoke from an extinguished fire. Her words came out like a sob, "No. Don't ask me. I can't."

She started to sway. Joe pulled her behind a trellis. "You give me whatever I ask. You can't say no. You're a genie of your word."

"No, I'm not. Don't make me!" Anna looked at her feet and made little hiccupping sounds. Red splotches spread across her face and chest, and her eyes ached from holding back the tears.

Joe hiccupped, too, one big, stifled gulp. Surprised, Anna glanced up. His cheeks were turning crimson, and his eyes looked like blown glass. His voice, normally so smooth, sounded low and choked, "You're right. I can't make you do anything. What kind of man would I be if I even tried? But if I can't, then I'm getting out of town."

Anna shook her head "No! You can't leave me."

"Anna, listen. I never know what you're gonna do. You say you love me, but you won't be my wife. All the other girls in LA—they're on their best behavior around a man, acting modest, playing it coy. But not you. You're on your worst behavior, all of the time."

"I'm sorry!"

"I walk around aching 'cause I want you so bad. I think about you constantly. Don't you see? I can't love anybody else with you around. I could never marry anybody else because I'd always be thinking you might change your mind. And I'm never gonna get over you if I don't go away. So if you don't want to hook up with me, I'm leaving."

"You were going to command me to marry you? I thought you were going to send me to China or something and marry that Piano Girl."

"She and I are quits. I can't marry her, Anna. I love you. That's why I have to go."

"No! I'll change my mind. I promise."

"When."

"Soon. Very soon."

"Anna, that's not good enough."

"There. I just changed it. My mind's changed. But it has to be a very, very long—"

Joe kissed her.

AUTHOR'S NOTE

While this book is entirely fictional, it was inspired by historical events. The storyline of the two stolen girls, the reward money offered by their tong "owner" for their return, and the Los Angeles Police Department's efforts to find the girls in order to return them to the tong president to collect the reward and avert a tong war, was taken from a single 1908 newspaper article in the *Los Angeles Herald*. ("Tong president" is the term used by whites in Los Angeles. The Chinese called their tong leaders "Dragon Head" or "Dai Gor," which means "big brother.")

A second historical event also inspired the novel. In 1909, a nineteen-year-old missionary woman, Elizabeth Sigel, was murdered in New York City's Chinatown and found in a trunk in the apartment of her Chinese lover, Leon Ling. Her lover fled. The police never solved the crime. She really was entangled with two Chinese lovers. She really was the daughter of a famous Civil War general, Franz Sigel. There was a national backlash against the Chinese. Although white New York residents didn't storm Chinatown in 1909, the Chinatown Massacre that Joe Singer refers to in the novel did occur in Los Angeles in 1871, as he described it.

There are other things in the book that I lifted right out of history and fictionalized—the tunnels under Chinatown, the bells rigged to announce cops, the death threats written in red ink on laundry tickets, the number and locations of opium dens and lotteries, what fan-tan parlors were like and how they were raided. Donaldina Cameron, a Presbyterian missionary in San Francisco, really did steal Chinese slave girls away from the tongs. The Cracker Jacks riddles actually came by way of Cracker Jacks boxes from the turn of the twentieth-century.

During the years following the 1906 earthquake in San Francisco, many Chinese Americans relocated to Los Angeles, which became a new headquarters for some tongs. Violence was on the rise, tourism was down, and the tongs were vying for power. Hatchet men or high-binders did assassinate people. Some residents left Chinatown because of the violence. There was a large police presence in LA's Chinatown at the end of the first decade of the 1900s. According to the *Los Angeles Herald*, half the men of Central Station were assigned there. It was the center of vice in LA, and the most dangerous beat in the city.

Most of the historical documents I found relating to LA's Chinatown in the early 1900s are written from a white perspective and therefore reflect a Caucasian rather than Asian perspective. This is regrettable. The Chinese language newspaper published in Los Angeles during the period was edited by a Christian Chinese American man, and to my knowledge hasn't been translated into English.

The character of Anna Blanc bears some resemblance to Fanny Bixby, one of California's richest young women, who became a "special constable" in Long Beach in 1908. She carried handcuffs and a gun. However, this resemblance is purely coincidental. I learned about Fanny Bixby after I wrote *The Secret Life of Anna Blanc*. My novel was actually inspired by Alice Stebbins Wells, who in 1910 became the first woman police officer in Los Angeles. She was nothing like Anna Blanc.

Lastly, the unattributed poem in this novel is also inspired by history. It is a combination of words and ideas taken from a dozen English translations of Chinese poems that would have been read in Anna's day, taken apart, shaken up, mixed together with my own words, to produce a single, short poem.

Acknowledgments

As with my first novel, *The Secret Life of Anna Blanc*, this book feels very much like a team effort. I'd like to thank my husband for his unfailing support, and my children for understanding my need to write. They all made sacrifices. Many thanks to Zoe King, Josephine Hayes, and Neil Blair at the Blair Partnership. I couldn't ask for better agents. I'd like to thank everyone at Seventh Street Books (SSB) for being so good at what they do—Dan Mayer, Sheila Stewart, Jill Maxick, Cheryl Quimba, Nicole Sommer-Lecht, and my fellow SSB authors for their support and advice.

I'd like to thank Paul Foley for teaching me how to tell a story. My gratitude goes out to Matthew Boroson for his comradery and advice while we both wrote books set in California Chinatowns around the turn of the twentieth century, his set in San Francisco, mine in LA. Thanks to Stephen Kuo and Jimmy Lui for advising me on Chinatown culture and language. I feel enormously grateful for my beta readers Stephanie Manuzak, Susan Spann, Thea Pilarczyk, Cassi Clark Ward-Hunt, Eric Stebbins, Joe Weber, Heather Bell, Jamie Gordon, David Weaver, Jonathan Owen, Susan Ludes, and of course, Elizabeth Bonsor.

Thanks to the many others who gave feedback on sections of this book—the Denver Writer's Workshop, Linda Joffe Hull, Melisa Ford, Mark Stevens, Christine Goff, Suzanne Proulx, Suzanne Blanchard, Christine Jorgensen, Jeanette Baust, Laurie Sanderson-Walcott, and Mike McClanahan.

Thanks to my mother, sisters, cousins, and in-laws (especially you, George) for cheering me on.

Most of all, I want to thank my readers for taking a chance on a relatively new author. If you liked this book, please spread the word. Tell a friend. Post on Facebook. Write a review. It's the number-one way readers find new authors.

ABOUT THE AUTHOR

Jennifer Kincheloe is the author of *The Secret Life of Anna Blanc*, winner of the Colorado Gold Award for mystery and the Mystery and Mayhem Award for historical mystery. The novel was also a finalist for the Macavity Sue Feder Historical Mystery award, Left Coast Crime "Lefty" Award, and Colorado Authors' League Award for genre fiction. Formerly, Dr. Kincheloe was the principal of a health consulting firm and a member of the research faculty for the UCLA Center for Health Policy Research. She currently does research on the jails in Denver, Colorado.